Joe is an ex-estate agency owner from Bristol, with a love of Roman history. Being from an Italian background he is a very cosmopolitan person and has spent his life exploring the world in addition to building his career. Some achievements he is proud of include hitchhiking through South Africa in the early nineties and visiting places such as Soweto and the poorer townships around Cape Town to meet the locals. Joe has a love of literature and music. His diverse life has included living in the Canary Islands, Spain and Sweden, had his own music venue in Bristol and was in a rock band called Aquarius in the 1990s.

To Paride Masiello, whose inspiration and love of history spurred me to begin this novel.

Joseph J Pitarella

THE HOUNDS OF DIANA

The Romulus and Remus Trilogy – Part One

AUSTIN MACAULEY PUBLISHERS™

LONDON • CAMBRIDGE • NEW YORK • SHARJAH

A CIP catalogue record for this title is available from the British Library.

ISBN 9781788233477 (Paperback)
ISBN 9781788233484 (Hardback)
ISBN 9781788233491 (E-Book)
www.austinmacauley.com

First Published (2018)
Austin Macauley Publishers Ltd™
25 Canada Square
Canary Wharf
London
E14 5LQ

Acknowledgements

Thanks to my writing group, Guy Coldwell, Adrian Estement and Peter who have been my sounding board. To the authors who inspired me to take the chance and give my writing my all. Last, but not least, to T Keating who has been my rock.

Preface

Following the great siege of Troy, in approximately 1200 BC, a group of refugees led by Prince Aeneas wandered the lands surrounding the Aegean and Mediterranean seas. The people had been broken and betrayed by the adultery of the Trojan prince, Paris, and Helen, the wife of a Greek king. Brought to ruin by a war they never wanted, the survivors were driven from country to country by unwelcoming rulers, forcing them to endure a long and gruelling journey. Finally, after many years of searching, they found a new home on the shores of the Italian peninsular.

This bountiful land was already inhabited by tribes who collectively called themselves the Latinii. Emissaries were sent out to their chiefs and leaders by Prince Aeneas. He offered them gifts of friendship, and knowledge of new ideas that would make the Latinii stronger. The Trojans were cautiously welcomed and, over time, alliances were formed.

Prince Aeneas, who was a charismatic man, soon convinced the tribes to unite with the Trojan refugees and form a nation. He suggested he should become king while the remaining noble families from Troy should inter-marry with the existing tribal leaders' families. As a gesture of faith, the prince offered the Trojan daughters to the Latinii sons, guaranteeing the future of both races. The tribes agreed and the Kingdom of Latium was born.

A great temple was built, in honour of the god Apollo, over-looking Lake Nemi, which was a sacred site for the Latinii. Within the temple walls two great pyres were kept ablaze night and day to guide people to the new kingdom. Rumours of the rich lands found their way back to the ruined city of Troy and over the following years more people arrived. Cities were built, law imposed and a civilisation re-established.

Yet, there were many nobles from Troy who lacked faith in their new king. They had learnt a harsh lesson from the fall of Troy; they knew how a foolish king could bring about so much death and destruction. In order to protect their new nation, some of these nobles formed a secret sect. They named themselves after the goddess of the hunt, Diana, and vowed to pursue any that acted against the country, or any of their group. They called themselves The Hounds of Diana.

Over the following centuries The Hounds of Diana watched the affairs of the kingdom and intervened when they felt it necessary. Using their web of spies and assassins, known as the Dormienti – the sleepers – they steered the kingdom to prosperity by building alliances and eliminating threats or problems.

The penalty for betraying The Hounds of Diana was death, without exception. Those that went against the organisation were doomed to failure as the Hounds had the eyes and ears of their spies everywhere. Once the Dormienti were tasked with a target, they would not return until it was eliminated. Fear of these assassins kept the members honest and loyal.

However, after five hundred years of success, The Hounds of Diana had become comfortable and complacent, and they failed to notice the traitor amongst them.

Chapter One

Alba Longa, the Kingdom of Latium, Italy 788 BC

The unforgiving heat of the mid-afternoon sun had all but emptied the paved streets of the city of Alba Longa. Most of the residents were inside their cooler stone buildings, eating and sleeping whilst waiting for the more forgiving hours of evening. As the Latin people rested, the silence above the quiet city was penetrated by the cries of an eagle, soaring over Mount Albanus.

Inside the palace courtyard the whitewashed walls reflected bright sunlight as Prince Numitor held his sword defensively, circling his larger opponent. The twenty year old prince eyed the tall, powerfully built man before him, nervously; paying close attention as his adversary swung the long blade left then right, as he slowly advanced. The athletic younger prince retreated cautiously as he tried to anticipate the bearded assailant. Hearing the cry of the eagle above, Prince Numitor resisted the urge to glance up, and instead concentrated his blue eyes on the man, who was smiling menacingly at him.

Suddenly, with a grunt of effort, the swordsman sprang forward with a cascade of powerful strikes, forcing Numitor to back up as he deflected the iron blade. The attacker's long reach made it difficult for the prince to retaliate as he skipped backwards, narrowly avoiding marble benches and a tall statue of Neptune that looked down on the duellers with staring eyes.

Using the sleeve of his tunic, the prince wiped away a line of sweat under his hairline and, holding his sword with both hands, he sprang forward and advanced on the man with a flurry of strikes, each one of which was skilfully blocked.

The counter-attack came quickly and the prince was forced to parry the heavy blows that were being rained on him by the sunburned man. Trying a different tact, Numitor swiped at the man's long legs in a futile attempt to trip him. His blade merely struck the hard ground, causing the prince to stifle a yell as needles of pain ricocheted through his fingers and wrists.

For a moment Prince Numitor had no idea where his adversary was, but a glint of sunlight reflecting off a blade gave him barely enough time to avoid a strike; the swish of the long sword sent a breeze over his hair. He instinctively raised his weapon but felt a hammer-like blow to his midriff. He hit the ground with a thud as his breath left him and watched helplessly as the victorious swordsman stood over him like an executioner, the blade held ready to finish him.

'You call that a defence?' mocked the man, the words said with a deep, relaxed timbre.

Numitor struggled for air but summoned his strength. 'I am not finished yet,' he replied with a tremor in his voice as he jumped up and locked eyes with the grinning man.

'We will see now, boy.'

A prickle of anger flitted across Numitor's square features, but he had no time to dwell on it as the iron weapon came slicing down through the air once again. He dodged to the side as the blow found the spot where his head had been a moment earlier. A look of surprise briefly veiled his opponent's dark eyes as the prince gave a smile of his own, his weapon ready. 'Too slow,' his barely broken voice mocked.

They separated and circled each other again, glancing around, sucking in lungfuls of the hot afternoon air, waiting for the other to move. Numitor charged forward, stabbing his weapon toward his opponent. Repeating the action, he forced the man to back up against the white courtyard wall. Seeing the opportunity to finish the battle, Numitor lunged again, but this time he hit stone, the blade leaving a scar on the wall as the other man disappeared from his vision.

Numitor listened intently and was rewarded by a light scraping sound coming from behind him. In a fluid movement the prince pivoted around, his sword positioned to defend the potential strike. He tensed his forearms, expecting to feel the tremor of the blow and, yet again, his opponent was not where he should have been. He grunted his frustration as the sound of the blade whooshed from his right, causing him to duck and bring his own blade up to protect his head.

Hearing the man chuckle, the annoyed prince lunged sideways towards the sound, hoping to catch his attacker by surprise. Underestimating his reach, Numitor's momentum betrayed him as he tumbled forward. The blade struck air and was answered with the cold, sharp feeling of iron on the back of his neck.

'Ha,' declared the attacker, 'that is the second time I should have taken your head today, your highness. This was too easy.'

Numitor, who was now on his knees, scratched his fingers vigorously through his thick chestnut hair. 'I apologise, Brascus. My concentration is absent today; there is so much on my mind.'

Brascus shook his head as he sheathed his sword and offered the prince an arm up. With a little disappointment coming through his low voice he replied, 'Even so, if I were an enemy today, you would not have a mind left to consider. You should not let your problems cloud your judgement when in battle, Numitor.'

'It is difficult when my birth-right is at stake, Brascus,' came the frustrated response. 'How am I to concentrate when my own brother is trying to take what is rightfully mine. How would you react to such a situation?' He accepted a clean rag from a servant that had appeared from inside the palace and wiped his face. Shaking his head, the prince placed himself down onto a bench as a heavy feeling of despair came over him. As he sat there he looked down to his right hand where the ring his father had given him on his fifteenth birthday, shone on his middle finger. The golden band was cast into the image of an eagle, the wings wrapping around his finger. Not for the first time, he admired the engraving of the feathers and wondered at the skill it must have taken to make it so detailed. It was his ascension ring, his right as a first born son. Although he wore it with pride, he had learnt that it came with a burden. He twirled the ring around his finger before looking up to Brascus. 'For years I have followed my father's instructions, never setting a foot wrong, complying with his every wish, and now he means to condemn me for one mistake.'

Although he sympathised with the prince, Brascus did not agree with Numitor. That one mistake had cost the lives of many Latin warriors and would have been avoided if the young prince had not been so arrogant in his confidence; *He lacks experience*, he mused, recalling the day in question. Brascus believed it was a battle that should have been easily won, but Numitor had underestimated the Phoenicians.

Whilst the prince had met the main force on the coast, he had failed to anticipate the three thousand enemy that had landed elsewhere and flanked the prince in a surprise attack. He then suffered the humiliation of being rescued by a force of reserve warriors led by his eighteen year old brother, Prince Amulius; a fact that had since been used against him by Amulius – who was well known to covet his brother's future appointment to the throne.

Their father, King Proca, had heard the story from his victorious younger son, along with Amulius' challenge to be taken seriously as the possible future monarch, given Numitor's apparent incompetence. Swayed by the argument but not willing to make such a decision, the aging king set a challenge to the two young men.

Conflicts with neighbouring Samnium and Etruria were ongoing problems, so the king decided to task each prince with tackling one of the nations, either by making peace, or subduing by force. Numitor was to deal with the Etruscans, and Amulius with the Samnites. Each Prince was given a small army of two thousand men to do with as they pleased. The first prince to return with a resolution would gain the throne once King Proca passed. The wise king was testing both his sons' ability to rule, and Brascus hoped the right man would win.

After a moment of thought the mentor responded. 'Your mistake gave your brother the opening he has been waiting for, your highness. He has put your father in an impossible situation. But he should fail in the long run – his lust for blood will be his undoing.'

'In the name of the gods, I pray you are correct, Brascus, or this kingdom is doomed.' Numitor stood up and made his way over to a table at the edge of the courtyard where a jug and two goblets had been laid out, and beckoned his mentor to join him, 'Come, let us drink some wine and discuss our plans. If I am to prove my worth to my father, then we must decide how to deal with the Etruscans and reach a resolution before my brother slaughters all the Samnite tribes in his own bid for the throne.'

'You are assuming Amulius will wage war on Samnium. He may well surprise us all and become a diplomat.' Brascus knew that the young prince's famous temper left little room for negotiation, but nothing was to be discounted when it came to Amulius.

Numitor raised his eyebrows as he gave Brascus a quizzical glance. 'You are jesting with me Brascus. Maybe you should skip the wine,' he said humorously.

'And maybe you should not underestimate your brother again, your highness. That is what got you into this mess in the first place.'

The statement was acknowledged with a shrug. 'My brother is crafty. Hiding his cavalry behind the dunes was shrewd, and I have to admit, if not for that, we would have been penned in.' Numitor scratched behind his ear as he thoughtfully concluded. 'It is almost as if he foresaw my error when he came to our rescue. If only I had not been so sure that the Phoenicians had landed all their men on that forsaken beach. It is a mistake I will never make again.' He bowed his head in shame for a moment before declaring, 'But not all is lost. Amulius is not a diplomat. He will try and win this competition with force.'

Brascus reached over and grabbed the prince's shoulder affectionately, 'Well, let us not worry about your brother, your highness, and instead decide how we are going to approach your part of this test. How are you going to make peace with Etruria?'

'Well, I have an idea,' Numitor replied as he met Brascus' eyes, 'but I am going to need your help.'

You need all the help you can get, young prince, mused the mentor as he took a large mouthful of wine, savouring the dry, smoky flavour. Through the courtyard gates he gazed over the city of Alba Longa which sprawled at the foot of the mountain, below the palace, ending at the calm lake beyond. He worried for the young prince going up against his younger, more ruthless brother.

Amulius' hunger for power was something that had been apparent even when they were young children – the number of runaway slaves from the palace had attested to that. In contrast, Numitor's compassion and pleasing looks had won him the love of all who knew him. He guessed that Numitor's popularity was the reason for his brother's bitterness. He couldn't prove it, but he was sure the older prince had been set-up by his brother to fail at the doomed battle with the Phoenicians, and he wondered just how far Amulius would go to gain the throne.

Chapter Two

The Samnite chieftain, Sabus, felt the bonds tighten around his wrists, his ribs aching from being punched and kicked by his captors as they tied him to a wooden post. The tribal camp, spread around the valley floor, was overrun with Latin warriors. They had appeared suddenly at sunrise and surprised his people as they prepared for a new day. Everyone had been dragged out of the goat-hide tents and ushered to the centre of their camp. Across the valley scores of goats grazed the sparse landscape, their brays and calls echoing around the steep rises to the north of the encampment. The noise added to the frightened wails coming from some of the chieftain's three hundred-or-so subjects, who now huddled in one large group. Surrounding them were hundreds of battle-scarred men wearing the red symbol of the crossed burning swords of Mars. He knew what that symbol represented. It was the symbol of the Latin tyrant, Prince Amulius.

Sabus had never seen the prince but had heard of him from travellers who came from Latium to trade or make their way to the east coast. The tales of the prince's victory over the Phoenicians, and the slaughter that followed, was well known to all the Samnite tribes. The tribes were always in petty conflict with their Latin neighbours, though none had ever faced the tyrant in battle. With that thought, Sabus looked around anxiously to see if the notorious leader was amongst them. The guards had taken orders from an older, grizzled looking warrior – *he's probably a veteran*, thought Sabus dismissively, as he caught the senior man's glance.

'What are you staring at, goat man?' growled the bald warrior.

The fearless leader didn't reply and held the man's gaze for a few moments before looking away and searching out his wife, Nola. He spotted her petite form standing next to the main hearth at the centre of the tent village. Their three-year-old son, Lohran, was clinging tightly to his mother's skirt. *One so young should not have to experience this*, Sabus sighed, blaming himself for not protecting his son. His people shuffled nervously as

16

the warriors around them chanted in unison, as if they had won a great battle rather than just ambushed a camp tending to its everyday life. He sent a silent prayer of thanks to the goddess that, so far, no-one had been killed, but a feeling in his gut told him it would not remain so.

The warriors suddenly silenced and formed to attention. A feeling of anticipation swept through the Latin invaders as some of them stepped aside. A black stallion advanced into view. Sabus's pulse quickened as a shadow of fear grew inside him. The silhouette of the rider, black against the background of morning sky, cantered into the camp. The cloaked prince, who sat straight in his saddle, looked down on the warriors around him. Sabus was surprised at the sight of the young man whose long strands of black hair fluttered against his face in the breeze, some clinging to his light goatee, as he stared down at the tribal leader with deep-set blue eyes that burned with malice.

The prince was much younger than Sabus had ever imagined and yet he had the intense look of someone who had killed before: the murderous reputation of his captor left the tribal leader more than anxious for his own safety, and that of his people. He studied the boy prince: Amulius was suited in black leather armour, the red emblem prominent on his breastplate; knee-high black boots finished the outfit – he was dressed for battle. Sabus felt the spasm of an involuntary shiver as the younger man addressed him in the common language.

'You lead these peasants?' asked the prince, casually.

Angered by the insult, Sabus fought to keep his composure as he saw the expectant look on the prince's smug face. He replied proudly, 'I am the tribal master, Sabus of the Pentri. What do you want with us?'

Amulius shook his head in a disappointed manner as a fist connected with Sabus's cheek, knocking his head backwards into the post. As broken visions swam before the chieftain's eyes, he heard an anguished scream from his wife and a frightened murmur rise from the tribe's people.

The prince glanced at Nola and broke into a smile. 'General Pinarii, cut out the tongue of the next peasant that murmurs,' he ordered. The general, a short, stocky man, wore a brown moulded leather breastplate and a red crest on his egg-shaped helmet. Scratching his bulbous nose, he dipped his head in acknowledgement and snapped his fingers at one of the standing warriors, who drew his sword, a smile of broken teeth on his hardened face.

'Leave them alone,' growled Sabus. 'They have done nothing wrong. We are peaceful herders.'

A nod from Amulius and again Sabus felt the slam of a fist as his legs failed him, only the tight bounds holding him up. With a dull ache in his head and his mouth numb, Sabus slowly regained his senses and fought to support his own weight. With pink drool spilling down his chin, he looked up defiantly as the prince addressed him again.

'You will be silent until I say you can speak, Sabus of the Pentri, do you understand me?' Amulius didn't wait and continued. 'Good, now that I have your full attention I will explain the reason for my visit to your encampment.' The young prince gestured casually towards the tents. With an air of authority, he continued, 'I want you to take a message to your tribes. Tell them Latium requires that they surrender themselves to me or else they will face annihilation.'

'They will not listen to me,' laughed Sabus. 'I am not part of the war council – our tribe is too small for consideration.'

'Oh, they will listen,' retorted Amulius, 'if the message is strong enough.' He gestured to the crowd. 'General, get his family.' Pinarii nodded, and four more warriors immediately walked into the terrified crowd and easily singled out Sabus's wife and son as Nola's earlier pleas had been noticed by all. The general looked appreciatively at Nola as the party came back through the frightened prisoners.

Sabus noticed the look and felt his stomach lurch as panic surfaced. He struggled against the burning ropes binding his arms. 'Leave them alone. They have not hurt anyone,' he screamed at the prince, the anger rising as he strained. Nola was crying and holding Lohran close as the warriors manhandled them to the front. Sabus tried to calm himself, to try and reason with the prince. 'You don't need to hurt them. I'll do what you ask, just leave my people alone.'

Amulius clicked his heels urging his steed forward, the rising sun behind covering Sabus in shadow. 'If you want your wife and son to live, then you will not only deliver my message,' Amulius paused and made eye contact with Sabus and, with a serious tone, continued, 'you will convince them to meet me here in ten days' time, unarmed and ready to surrender. If not, they will all suffer the same fate as this tribe.'

'What do you mean by that?' cried Sabus. 'There is no reason to do anything. I will deliver the message. You have my word.'

'And you have my word that your wife and child will live, if you succeed,' replied the prince, 'but I need to convince you of the penalty for failure. You need to understand what life will be like for your tribes if they refuse me.' He turned back to Captain Pinarii. 'Kill ten men and round up the women.'

Sabus's shouts of protest were drowned in a sea of screams as he helplessly watched the bloodthirsty warriors tear into his people and drag ten men out into the open. The struggling captives were thrown onto the ground and held down as the warriors began to hack at their necks with gladius and axe. Meanwhile, the other warriors' voices were raised in unison as they urged their comrades on. Sabus felt the bile rising in his gut as men he had known all his life were slaughtered with no more regard than livestock. He stared at the prince with hatred as the tyrant watched with fascination as his warriors held up the dismembered heads and impaled them on spears, while screams of horror came from the victims' families and friends.

When all ten men were dead, more warriors stepped forward with swords drawn and rounded up the women, young and old alike. Their shocked and distressed screams pierced Sabus's heart as he watched helplessly. Amulius then raised his hand to signal for silence and again addressed Sabus.

'You have ten days to bring the tribes here. If not...' Amulius let it hang for a few moments before continuing, 'well, let us say that I have many ways to make their lives uncomfortable.' He gestured to Nola and Lohran. 'For the present they will become my guests, just until you return of course,' he added. 'It would be a great shame if you did not.'

'If you hurt them, I will kill you,' Sabus growled at the prince.

'You are in no position to make threats,' Amulius replied. 'At the end of the tenth day, if you have not returned, I will execute every man, woman and child here. In the mean time I have promised some of my men a little entertainment.'

With another nod the women were dragged towards the tents, their protests drowned by cheers as the warriors urged their comrades into frenzy. The children and remaining tribesmen were forced to listen, as lust-hungry warriors began raping their mothers, daughters and sisters. Sabus looked away in disgust as screams and begging cries filled his ears.

Without a second glance Amulius turned his horse and ambled back up the path, followed by Captain Pinarii, who frowned with apparent disappointment at leaving so soon. Sabus began to struggle against his bonds again as a retinue of warriors grabbed Nola and Lohran and carried the terrified mother and child out of the camp.

Chapter Three

Numitor urged his horse along a steep, narrow trail toward the temporary Etruscan camp where the talks were to be held. The prince's red cloak billowed in the breeze as he thought about how pleased he was, by the ease with which the meeting had been arranged. Brascus, who owned a small taverna in the city and had many contacts in the wine trade, had helped; it still surprised Numitor that with all the conflict and skirmishes between Latium and Etruria, wine from both countries seemed to miss the action and find its way to tables on either side. This was information that Numitor hoped would help win him the competition against Amulius.

Over the last few weeks the prince had been busy sending out messengers across the River Tiber with invitations to the various Etruscan kings, princes and nobles. As a gesture of good will, Numitor suggested that the meeting take place at the crossing closest to the Seven Sisters marshes, on the Latium side of the river. The collection of hills north of Alba Longa was close to the natural border between the two nations and, for Numitor, easy to get to. Barges could ferry the Etruscans over from their side.

Eventually, Brascus' contacts reached an agreement to use the hill overlooking the small island just downriver from the crossing. The Old Sister, as the hill was known to the Latins, was topped with a large meadow which afforded a good view of the wide river and surrounding marshes. At the lower slopes small trees and bushes clung to rocks, encircling the hill in a way that gave one the impression of a bald head when seen from a distance. The Etruscans were being cautious and had chosen the meeting-point well.

Now, with the threat of rain in the sky, Numitor prepared himself mentally for the meeting. He hoped to convince the Etruscans that good relations with Latium would create more wealth for all of them. However, the collection of ever-changing kingdoms and dukedoms that was known as Etruria was difficult to deal with. *Like a monster with many heads,* he recalled his father commenting on the subject. He hoped the monster had the sense to recognise a proposition that would benefit all.

Accompanying the prince, dressed in his usual leather leggings and armless tunic, was Brascus; four tough guards followed behind. As they approached they could see that the camp had been set up with three large, square tents – one each for the representatives of the two countries, and a larger one to host the actual meeting. Horses and grooms loitered around the meadow, whilst Etruscan guards kept a look-out, close to the tents; they turned their heads toward the approaching prince, who kept his horse steady as he headed across the grass toward the larger, central tent. A young man, who seemed to carry his wealth in gold chains around his neck, exited the hide structure and watched the prince's approach. Apart from the chains, the darker skinned Etruscan wore an impressive cloak that sparkled in the dull light. The black material had been embroidered in colourful threads, depicting birds and animals of all description, their eyes set with twinkling stones. Numitor was beginning to wonder if talk of wealth and riches would be enough to sway these people.

'That is Prince Castur, from the Tarkna royal family, your highness,' whispered Brascus, leaning over slightly towards Numitor. 'He is heir to his father's throne – and the father has been dying for the past three years,' he chuckled quietly. 'You may find him a little highly strung, as are all the northern Etruscans, but he is still very much under his father's control.'

'As are we all,' smiled Numitor, nodding to the waiting Etruscan heir. He sympathised with the young man, understanding all too well what it felt like to wait for a kingdom.

After dismounting and handing the reins to one of his guards, Numitor and Brascus were led into the dim interior of the main tent. The floor had been laid with woven straw mats and most of the space was occupied by a variety of flamboyantly dressed men and women, all of whom were either sitting cross-legged on the floor or on small carved stools.

Numitor instantly noted the differences between the Latins and the Etruscans as he looked around at the visitors. Their darker skin and high cheekbones gave them an exotic appearance, and blue or green eyes seemed to be abundant. The clothes they wore were also strange to the prince. The men seemed to favour short wraps and boot-like sandals that wrapped around their calves and shins. The women wore elaborate hair pieces of thin golden chains, like shining spider-webs fixed across their heads.

A group of older men sat on large wooden thrones near the centre of the big tent. Their authority was evident from the heavy golden crowns they wore along with skilfully engraved leather tunics set with bronze rosettes and buckles. Some also had golden torcs around their necks, whilst others had painted their faces in lines and circles. Numitor began to see that the various factions seemed to favour different customs, and he began to understand his father's statement about the many headed monster.

Various lamps sent shadows flitting across the tent's interior. The prince wondered at the effort it must have taken to bring all the furniture and floor coverings, but then he recalled the large encampment that he had spotted earlier in the distance, on the opposite side of the river. He had dismissed the sight as a wandering camp, but now realised the Etruscans had brought far more with them than grooms and a few guards. For a moment he wondered if his decision to come so poorly accompanied had been wise, but he instantly put aside his doubts – this was an errand of faith and he had to trust his instincts.

Aware that all eyes were now firmly set on him, Numitor unconsciously rolled his eagle ring around his finger and began to speak. 'I trust you are all comfortable to be addressed in Latin?' His voice betrayed his nervousness as he addressed the older nobles. He examined the faces around him and felt his confidence grow as accepting nods of approval urged him to continue. 'Good, then let me introduce myself. I am Prince Numitor, son of King Proca, heir to the throne of Latium.' Numitor paused for a moment before continuing. 'With me today is Brascus,' he gestured to his mentor, 'he represents one of our noble families, the Julii. His taverna in Alba Longa stocks some of your best wine and his trading links made this meeting possible.' A few curious eyes darted towards Brascus but Numitor quickly resumed his speech. 'May I start by showing my gratitude for your attendance at this gathering?' He nodded to Brascus, who stepped forward carrying a small carved box.

Numitor removed the lid to reveal a collection of gold articles inlaid with green olivine crystals and dark obsidian stones. Bracelets and heavy rings were arranged next to medallions and pendants that hung on thick chains. 'These gifts,' continued the prince as he began to go from person to person, offering the box so that they could each choose an item, 'are only found in Latium and are mined from Mount Albanus, above the sacred lake Nemi. Legends say the olivine crystals are the hardened tears of Venus and that wearing the stone will bring good health. The dark obsidian stones change colour in water – they will protect you from Hades while you sleep.'

He paused as a large woman took her time in choosing. Lines of red dots were painted under her eyes, while her long locks of platted hair were woven with red cloth into a sculpture that stood high over her head; the prince eyed it nervously as she leant forward to dip her hand in the box. When Numitor felt his cheeks ache from his forced smile, the woman finally settled on a ring set with a large olivine solitaire on a band of gold inlaid with obsidian shards. 'Good choice,' he uttered almost triumphantly as he came around to the next dignitary.

Most of the Etruscans seemed to receive the gifts well, with nods of approval as they examined the fine workmanship and elegance of these obviously valuable items. When the whispering had died down, Numitor raised his hand.

'I have come to you this day, not with aggression but with the hand of friendship.' The dignitaries looked on with passive expressions. Optimistic that he would break them down, Numitor continued. 'Our nations have had many…' he paused to find the best term, 'unpleasant encounters, let's call them. Some we have won and some you have. Yet, we have all lost. We lose men, land, resources and most of all, we lose time.'

He looked around the tent, making eye contact with a few of the visitors, but still saw no signs of enthusiasm. Numitor pressed on. 'Of course, every time we have these unpleasant encounters, we are denied your fine wine.' A murmur of approval rose from some of the Etruscans and, urged on by the reaction, he announced, 'I believe that we would all benefit more from trade than conflict. You have great goods to trade – your wine and cloth. I have seen the quality of the goods produced by your people.' The headpiece came into view and he ignored a smouldering look from the choosy woman. He glanced around as he approached the end of his speech. 'These goods are favoured by our citizens and, in return, we can offer iron ore, obsidian and many other things. We would both profit, we would have peace and, most importantly, we would become great allies.'

A few nods from the gathering gave Numitor a glimmer of hope as he came to his central proposition. 'Today I would ask all of you here to agree free trade routes between some of our cities. I seek a guarantee of safety for all who come to trade.'

For a moment all were quiet, but then a powerful-looking man lent forward in his throne. He wore a long green robe and had a thick crown sat upon his shaven head. 'Does your good favour extend to the return of my father's land at Fidanea? Your own father's foraging is not easily forgotten.'

'I cannot answer for my father, Sire… for I believe I am addressing the new King of Veii, King Corros,' replied Numitor as he respectfully lowered his head to the ruler. He had heard his father telling the story of the border dispute along the banks of the Tiber, many years ago. Both sides had lost men but Latium had won that encounter. 'I believe he only took back what once belonged to us, Sire.' Numitor tried to sound fair but quickly moved on.

'However, we are not here today for this. We all have to forget what went on before and look to tomorrow. Bitterness will get us nowhere.' King Corros conceded the point with a slight nod but Numitor could detect a smile behind the king's serious gaze.

'Some things cannot be forgiven, not for trade or goods,' came another raised voice, this time to Numitor's right, 'and will not be forgotten by trading wine that is too good for Latin tongues.'

Numitor turned to find the face of his insulter as murmurs of approval again emanated from the dignitaries. He met with an angry-looking man of similar age to himself. The dark rings around his cold eyes told Numitor this was a troubled man. 'Whom am I addressing?' he asked politely.

'Someone who has lost much to your kingdom,' came the reply. 'Someone who has lost kin and friend in the name of Latin advancement.'

'I understand you may have—' started Numitor, but was halted mid-sentence.

'You understand nothing,' shouted the man. 'You try to bribe us with your gifts with one hand, whilst the other takes our birth-rights and kills our loved ones.'

More murmurs of agreement stabbed at Numitor as the atmosphere became tense. Brascus, who until now had been standing behind the prince looking fairly relaxed, straightened as his gaze became alert and he eyed up the rowdy Etruscans. Numitor scratched his sparse beard as he gave his mentor a warning look to stay calm. He prepared to talk again when a noise from outside drew his attention.

The tent flap flew open and a guard stumbled in. 'We are being attacked, it's a tra—' He fell forward choking as an arrow pierced his throat from behind, sending a spray of pink misty blood onto the closest Etruscan. More arrows followed the guard, one piercing a dignitary in the chest.

Everybody scrambled at once in a cacophony of shouts and calls of alarm. Most made for the flap, some producing previously unseen weapons from clothing and under rugs. In all the commotion Numitor quickly looked to Brascus for support, but his stomach lurched as he saw his comrade surrounded by a group of men, one of them holding a blade to his throat. The prince cursed himself for coming unarmed. His eyes skimmed the chaotic scene for a weapon, but a sudden sharp pressure under his chin stayed him. The cold-eyed Etruscan was holding the blade. 'You're going nowhere,' he growled. 'You're going to pay for this deception, Latin.'

Numitor feared for his life, his mind reeling with unanswered questions, as the gravity of his situation became instantly apparent. Surrounded by angry enemies, he waited for the sensation of iron penetrating his flesh, expecting to be slaughtered as Brascus was cajoled to stand next to him. However, instead of being attacked, the two Latins were quickly herded out of the tent into a bloody scene outside – the meadow had been transformed from its previous tranquillity.

Groups of warriors wearing Numitor's eagle emblem were attacking the Etruscan guards and grooms. The prince was shocked as he watched men who appeared to be his own, killing his former guests. There seemed to be more Etruscans on the meadow than when he had arrived and they were putting up a good fight. The bodies of Latin warriors strewn around the area were a testament to the Etruscan's quick reactions. He tried to reason with his captors: 'I did not order this. This is not my doing. I swear to the gods, this was not me.'

As he began to think that nothing more would surprise him, a large group of Etruscan horsemen appeared at the edge of the meadow. Their pointed helmets were distinctive of the elite riders, whose reputation as fierce warriors was known throughout Latium. It occurred to him that the Etruscans had been prepared for an attack. Yet it did not explain why they had been attacked in the first place. Then the answer struck him, just a moment before the hilt of an Etruscan sword rendered him unconscious.

Chapter Four

Opening his eyes to complete darkness, Numitor took a moment to clear his confused mind as he tried to figure out where he was. As he moved, pain shot down his shoulders and arms and he came to realise his hands had been bound behind his back. Upon trying to move his legs, he also found his feet in the same predicament. He felt a throbbing at the back of his head and experienced a moment of confusion and panic as memories came rushing back of the disastrous meeting with the Etruscans, and the carnage that followed it. Guessing he had been taken captive, he tried to sit up but felt something holding him in place.

'You're awake then?' The sound of Brascus' deep voice echoed around the space.

Numitor's heart skipped a beat at the sudden question. 'Yes,' he replied weakly, 'although my head feels like I was hit by a hammer. What happened?'

'Falconussi hit you on the head,' came the matter-of-fact reply. Brascus sounded more alert than Numitor felt. 'He was the man who got angry during the meeting. They must have hit me next as I do not remember anything else until I came around a short while ago.'

'I wonder where they have taken us. Surely Commander Agrillis would have missed us by now?' Numitor said, hiding his fear from his voice.

'You would have thought so,' Brascus replied. His own voice was tainted with worry. 'Come, let us try and sit up. It's as dark as Hades in here and I need to get my bearings.'

It took a good few moments to jostle and fidget before the two men found a way to slowly jerk into a sitting position. The floor beneath them seemed to bounce with their movements, giving Numitor the impression they were inside a box. *My father is going to skin me for this – if he gets the chance,* he worried to himself, wondering how he was going to get out of this mess. He could feel Brascus pulling at the knots that bound them and realised his hands were numb from where the cord had been cutting into his wrists. When he couldn't stand the silence any longer, he whispered, 'What is going to happen to us, Brascus?'

Without warning, the space around them started to shake, and nearby a horse nickered as the box started to move. Numitor guessed they were in some kind of cart and began to realise the extent of the danger they faced. Although he had been in battle, he had always been surrounded by his father's best warriors, but now with only Brascus beside him, his chances of surviving this encounter seemed impossibly low. 'Where do you think they are taking us?' he asked as he tried to figure out how they were going to escape.

'Back to Falconussi's fort, I expect,' Brascus answered with venom. 'I wondered if he would present a problem. He is not well liked amongst the Etruscan chiefs, and I relied on that fact to keep him in place. He will probably try and ransom us for his old territory, I expect.'

'He will die then. Father will not stand for this. Do you think he planned this, or did he just take advantage during the attack?'

'That's just it, Sire. Falconussi and his men reacted very quickly when the attack started. Almost as if they knew it was going to happen.' Brascus paused for a moment, before he spoke with bitterness in his tone. 'It is possible that this predicament we find ourselves in was not an accident.'

Numitor sighed and listened to the crunching cartwheels as they rolled over the ground. He let his mind wander back to the attack.

They were my men attacking the Etruscans – at least, it looked like my men. But I never ordered anything like this. Agrillis was in sight of the Old Sister hill, so surely he would have missed all those warriors if they had been ours. 'There is only one explanation for this mess,' he voiced aloud.

'Amulius,' said Brascus. 'He is the only person who would gain by your failure, and he would have also had access to your warriors' tunics.'

'I suspected my brother the moment I saw the attack.' Numitor's tone changed as he continued. 'He always plays dirty, and I should have been more cautious. Leaving Agrillis with all our men by the barge crossing was stupid. I should know better,' he berated himself. 'You were right to arrive at the meeting as you did, Sire. Without the attack, things may have had a chance. They were listening to you – do not blame yourself.'

Feeling his hands numbing from the tightly bound rope, Numitor wriggled his fingers a little to get the circulation going. 'Whether I blame myself or not, we may both die because of my stupidity. And if we do not, then I may have lost the kingdom to my scheming fox of a brother. Plus my father is never going to trust me again.' He hung his head as the full weight of his worries threatened to smother him.

'You should have some faith, Numitor, all is not yet lost. Now, I can't undo this knot. Do you have anything sharp that could cut through the rope?'

'No, nothing.'

'That is unfortunate,' Brascus sighed. 'If it makes you feel any better, Sire, I also should have foreseen these circumstances, but to know that Amulius would stoop so low was beyond me. You are brothers, yet he would see you in the hands of an enemy. That is a cold heart.'

Numitor let the words sink in as he rocked unevenly to the rhythm of the cart. *I will teach my brother a lesson, if I get out of this,* he thought angrily. Where he had previously put his brother's behaviour down to competitiveness, now it felt different, as if loaded with malice and hate. He absorbed his pain, trying to reconcile what he thought he knew about his younger sibling with the ugly truth. Amulius was a danger to him, and he would have to be careful in the future. *If I even have a future,* he worried again.

With no way to cut themselves loose of the ropes, the prince and Brascus sat in silence, swaying to the movement of the cart. The ride was bumpy and uncomfortable, making it impossible to sleep – something which Numitor desired. His headache had not abated and now, with his worry over his situation, it was making him feel dizzy and sick. He bore his discomfort quietly, remembering what his father had taught him: *do not show weakness when courage is needed.* It was a saying he had heard many times but had never understood its meaning until now. His life was in danger and he was angry with himself for being so naïve.

A while later the cart stopped with a lurch. Numitor held his breath nervously as he listened for any signs of life. After a few moments he heard the sound of metal scraping and the creak of a hinge as a breeze blew in. The space became a few shades lighter as the enclosure was opened to the night. Someone jumped in and spoke in a raised whisper. 'Keep quiet and follow me. I'm here to help.'

For a moment Numitor didn't move, not sure if he had heard correctly, but his excitement rose as he felt the cold edge of a blade cut at his bindings. He turned his head and caught the dark outline of the man, who was wearing a long hooded cloak. As the rope fell away from his wrists, Numitor moved his arms quickly and immediately regretted it as pain burned into his muscles. He rubbed his arms to encourage the blood to flow as he slowly followed Brascus and the stranger out into the dead of night. The sky was featureless as he unsteadily stepped out and waited a moment to gain his balance and allow his eyes to adjust. He rubbed his aching hands and noted with a small sigh of relief that his eagle ring was still on his finger. He touched it to his mouth in a silent act of thanks before glancing around the area. The cart, which he could now see was a slave transporter, had stopped next to a rock escarpment, but he could see little else ahead other than some tall bare trees.

Feeling relief as he looked back towards his temporary prison, Numitor was surprised to spot the figure of a man sitting very still, holding the leather reins of the cart's horse. It took a few heartbeats for the prince to understand that the driver was dead. Numitor looked to his rescuer, who was now walking away from the scene. With a mind full of questions he caught up with the stranger, whose face was covered with a tight black cloth, revealing only the glint of intense eyes. 'Who are you?' demanded Numitor. 'How did you know to come for us?'

'There's no time for questions,' replied the man in a gritty voice. 'We have to get going before someone comes back looking for their cart. Follow me.' With that, he hurried off at a good pace.

'Come, Sire, keep up,' Brascus harried the prince as he passed.

They skirted around the outcrop and across a stretch of open ground before coming to another set of large boulders. This time the hooded man headed straight toward the middle of the rocks and led them through a gap, along a pathway that felt hard underfoot.

In a short while Numitor could feel the ground rising below him as his strides became shorter and the path started to climb. He had no idea of his surroundings other than that there was a rock face to his left, which he used to steady himself as the path got steeper. He walked in silence but for his laboured breaths and began to wonder who his rescuer might be and how the cart had come to be alone. *Maybe the riders have gone on ahead,* he guessed, *or perhaps they've stopped off to camp for the night and the cart was supposed to be catching up;* it seemed like the most obvious explanation. Relief at having regained his freedom mixed with fear of recapture, spurred Numitor along. He upped his pace and caught up with the stranger who continued to lead the way. 'How did you know we were there?' the prince asked again.

The man replied without bothering to turn. 'I watched them take you both, Sire. The Etruscans avoided the barge crossing and took you downriver, past the island. They had their own barges waiting there.'

The prince waited for further explanation but none came as they started to descend. Brascus, who had not spoken until now, posed a question. 'So, where are we now?'

'Half a day's ride up the River Tiber, Dius. They have been hugging the north bank. I guess they would have eventually turned west further up and headed for Velzna.'

'Velzna?' enquired Numitor.

'Falconussi is from Velzna,' explained Brascus.

'And how did you come to be witnessing our capture?' enquired Numitor, turning back to the stranger. 'How do you know so much about our captors?' He was determined to find out the identity of this mysterious man.

'Please do not ask. I cannot answer.'

'Of course you can,' asserted the young prince. 'If you work for the king, then you can answer to me.'

No reply came. Numitor felt the ground underfoot become softer, and into view appeared the dark outline of a large tree, beneath which were two horses tethered to a low branch.

'This is where we must part, Sire,' announced the man, coming to a stop beside a patchy brown and white mare. Pointing to the other horse, he said, 'Take the stallion across the meadow behind me, and you will find the river. Head upstream until you reach a ford. You will find another horse there. Cross over and head south.'

'And you?' asked the prince, suddenly feeling anxious as Brascus walked over to the larger horse and released the reins from the branch.

'I have to take care of Falconussi, Sire,' replied the stranger. 'He cannot go unpunished for his actions or others will devise similar plots against you.'

Numitor was extremely intrigued by this man and stood his ground as he addressed the stranger again. 'So, you do work for my father then?'

'No, Sire, I do not.' The reply was firm. 'There are greater powers in these lands than kings and princes. You must never tell anybody about me, Sire. Be thankful you have been rescued, but forget about me.' The tone sounded almost like a warning. The man then climbed onto the horse, nodded to the two Latins and, with a kick of his heels, galloped into the night, leaving Numitor and Brascus alone with the stallion.

'What did he mean by that?' asked the puzzled prince, turning to Brascus. '"Greater powers than kings and princes". Was he threatening us? And what was that he called you? "Dius?" I have never heard that word before.'

'Did he?' replied Brascus, sounding confused. 'I didn't hear that. You must have misheard, Sire.'

Numitor was sure he hadn't. His thoughts remained on the hooded man. 'I wonder who he works for, if not my father.'

'I am not bothered who he works for, Sire. I am just glad he was there,' Brascus commented. 'Who knows what that sick bastard Falconussi had planned for us? Especially me. I am not worth anything. Come, let us get out of here before they start looking for us,' he added. He climbed up on to the stallion and offered an arm to Numitor.

'I suppose you are correct,' conceded the prince. 'We have been fortunate today.' He accepted the lift up and relaxed slightly as they began to move. 'Now I just have to face my father and explain what happened.'

Brascus leaned his head back as if not wishing to talk too loudly. 'None of this is your fault, Sire. I am sure your brother had a part in this. We just have to prove it.'

'That will never happen, Brascus. My brother is too clever to leave witnesses. There will be no way to prove this. I expect I have lost my kingdom.'

'Well, you may still have a chance, Sire. We do not know how Amulius' endeavours are developing. Maybe he has also failed.'

'Then how will my father choose? A fight to the death? Running a race?' Numitor's sarcasm did little to hide the real worry in his voice. 'I have very little chance of making things right with the Etruscans now. I can only hope that my father sees that I am the better choice to rule, despite my failures.'

Not for the first time that day, Numitor felt powerless to control his own destiny. Whether it was duty, obedience or other forces that directed his path, he was once again at the mercy of others. For a moment he wished the cloaked man had simply left him in the cart.

Chapter Five

Watching the mist hover above the ridge further up the mountain, Amulius led a thousand lumbering warriors along a trail towards the tribal pastures of the Samnite herders. As a precaution he had arranged for another thousand warriors to flank the northern ridge of the valley, protecting the only other way in, even though he did not expect any trouble. *Fear of my name alone will be enough to subdue these peasant tribes,* he assured himself.

Amulius had made certain that rumours of his fierce reputation were widely known, encouraging traders and merchants – who curried favour – to pass on his stories of battle and triumph during their travels. It had cost him – he was generous to those who served him, yet he parted with each gold coin in contempt. Amulius didn't see why he had to pay to gain loyalty. *One day, it will all come back to me,* he smiled to himself, as the trail ahead began to steepen.

Pulling on the reins, the prince brought the horse to a stop and waited for General Pinarii to catch up, addressing him as he arrived. 'Get a few scouts up there,' he pointed to the ridge. 'I want to make sure there are no surprises waiting for us.'

'I'll see to it now, Sire,' replied the red-faced man. After a pause he added, 'Although I wouldn't worry about it, Sire. I've had both entrances to the valley watched since last we were here. Only the leader and a handful of men have come back – that was yesterday evening.'

'Just do it,' Amulius hissed impatiently before turning his mount back up the trail.

A few moments later, two mounted warriors left the ranks and galloped up the slope, overtaking Amulius. They were followed by Pinarii, who brought his horse level with the prince. 'I shouldn't think we will be up there for very long, Sire,' he commented casually. 'Just long enough to collect Sabus and the other leaders and bring them back to your father to pledge their loyalty.'

Amulius stayed silent. He had very little time for the general, who had been put in place by his father. The prince was not impressed with the king's choice. Pinarii smelled of wine most mornings and, even though Amulius liked to drink, he knew how the stuff dulled the senses and left the drinker open to mistakes.

'Should I get the woman and kid upfront, as soon as we arrive, Sire? Or will you return them before we go?' Pinarii asked, using a different tactic to engage the prince.

'What are you talking about, General?' came the snappy retort. 'Why would we return them today? Have you no sense man?'

'But I thought you said—'

'Said what?' interrupted the prince. 'I do not believe I gave you any indication that I would be returning them today,' he remarked bluntly. Kicking in his heels he pushed his mount forward and left the gawping general behind.

By the time the two warriors returned, Amulius had reached the top of the trail. The mist he'd seen earlier had cleared slightly, revealing a pale circle of the sun through a thin cloud covering in the east.

'All the camp has gone, Sire. Only one tent remains and no sign of people or goats,' reported one of the men.

Amulius hid his surprise as he absorbed the news. *How can the Samnites leave the valley, with hundreds of noisy goats, without the lookouts knowing?* He was at a loss to understand it and turned to the arriving general.

'Can you explain this, General?' the prince enquired.

When the warrior repeated his statement, Pinarii blanched. 'I – I – don't know. Are you sure about this?' he asked the messenger, accusingly.

'Yes, sir,' replied the second warrior, backing up his comrade, 'just one tent and no signs of anybody else.' To make his point he turned to Prince Amulius. 'Almost deserted, Sire.'

'Yes, yes, I get it,' snapped the arrogant prince. 'Well then, let us see what Sabus has to say.' He turned to the general, who fidgeted nervously in his saddle. Narrowing his eyes, he addressed the man. 'Are you sure the peasant is there, Pinarii?'

'Positive, Sire,' came the certain reply. 'My best men were on the job and they assured me that Sabus and five other men went up towards the camp. They reported that only Sabus left, ten days ago, shortly after the last of our warriors finished up -if you know what I mean, Sire.' A smile started to tug at the general's lips with the last statement, but he quickly abandoned it under the cold, serious gaze of his prince. 'And then he returned with these five new men,' he added hastily, 'who I assumed were some of the other tribe leaders, but there were no signs of any other people leaving, Sire. We would have seen and heard them.'

'Well, if your men have been watching the camp, would they not have noticed all those tents and goats disappearing into thin air?' Amulius voiced with quiet anger.

The general looked confused for a moment, as his previously ashen face became bright with the heat of humiliation. A look of resignation appeared in his round features as he confessed. 'Well, they weren't exactly watching the camp, Sire. I set watchers on the north pass to the valley and one over this route,' he pointed back down the trail. 'No-one could have got in or out without us knowing.'

'And what of the eastern slopes?' suggested the prince. 'Could they not have escaped that way?'

'It's very steep, Sire. There are some woods at the bottom, but further up its sheer cliffs to the top. You would have to be a goat to get up—' He stopped abruptly, more colour rising to his cheeks. 'The goats maybe, Sire, but the people? With all their belongings? There must be some other explanation. Maybe they are hiding in those woods.'

'Do not be a fool,' snapped Amulius. 'They are long gone by now, and you know it.' The prince pointed an accusing finger at the general. 'You have been deceived by a bunch of goatherds, General.' Smiling, the prince continued, 'I can see why my father favours you so much.'

Pinarii scowled at the prince for a moment before silently looking away. He noticed a few of his captains sniggering at the implication. They stopped abruptly when he gave them a warning glance.

'It changes nothing,' commented Amulius. 'I only need the tribe leaders to win this competition. Let us not waste any more time.' He spurred the stallion and continued on to the moor that topped the western approach to the pastures. As they began to cross the bare, sodden ground, Amulius studied the steep eastern slopes of the valley ahead. He imagined the tribes-people would have gained plenty of experience climbing similar slopes in search of their goats, and he blamed the general for the oversight. He still had the woman and child as hostages but would have felt better if he'd had a few more people to punish should the Samnite peasants fail to show. He felt his mood brighten as he thought about the humiliation of Pinarii. *When I am king, I will demote him to latrine duty,* he planned with a smile.

When they reached the gentle slope that led down to the valley floor, Amulius was annoyed by the sight of just one tent. He had imagined a larger audience and felt as if a little of his glory had been taken. Studying the high cliffs on the opposite slope, he could barely make out the winding trail that led out of the valley. He wondered how hard it would be to take that trail at night, with goats and children. *They won't get away from me, for long,* he assured himself as he steered the stallion down to the green valley and eventually stopped a few hundred strides from the lone goat-hide tent. He guessed the tent could hold twenty or so people. Pinarii positioned himself beside the prince whilst the warriors fanned out behind. Amulius felt slight discomfort as he looked around at his thousand warriors, all facing one tent with possibly six people inside. Putting aside his thoughts, he straightened in his saddle.

'Sabus of the Pentri, come out and greet your new leader,' he called.

Sabus appeared from a large flap, followed by five men. 'Where are my wife and child?' he shouted.

Amulius didn't answer and instead rode forward until he had covered half the distance, Pinarii trailing close behind. 'They are safe and they are here, as I said they would be. Now tell me, who are your companions?'

'They are the leaders of the five closest tribes,' answered Sabus. 'You did not give me much time,' he added sarcastically.

The prince studied the other men. They all carried themselves with pride and confidence, although he would not have judged them leaders by their attire. 'Well, the six of you will have to do,' Amulius muttered angrily. It annoyed him that so few of the tribal leaders had come, and yet he was running out of time and needed to proceed. 'All I need now is for you to return with me to Alba Longa and swear fealty to my father, and our business will be done,' he explained.

'My wife and son first,' ordered Sabus. 'We will not go anywhere with you unless they are safe with my people.'

Looking around the valley, the prince considered the Samnite's words. Finally he shrugged. 'You really are not in a position to make demands, Sabus of the Pentri,' he said. 'However, there is no harm in showing you a gesture of my good faith – after all, we are all going to be countrymen together.' He smiled before turning to Pinarii, who signalled to the waiting entourage.

A few moments later the two hostages were led through the parting warriors. Nola held herself proudly as she led her son through the silent men. Amulius waited impatiently as they walked past him and into the arms of Sabus, who hugged his wife and child ferociously before whispering something to Nola. She promptly took her son and started walking – not toward the tent, but to the tree-line behind.

'Where is she going?' asked Amulius, pointing to the woman, who had picked up her son and upped her pace towards the large conifers.

'Out of your dirty clutches,' replied one of Sabus's comrades. The man was only slightly older than Amulius but had the weathered features of someone who had faced many hardships in his young life.

'You will pay for that remark, boy,' scowled the prince.

'And how will you make that happen?' asked an older man with a goat-skin wrapped around his wide shoulders. He held the prince's gaze. 'You are out-numbered and surrounded.'

'I fear you are mistaken,' laughed the prince. He pointed back towards the Latin line. 'Are you blind? Do you not see the warriors behind me? Do not play games – I am not in the most patient of moods,' he said threateningly.

'Do you hear that, comrades?' asked Sabus to the men surrounding him. 'The good prince has moods.'

The five men laughed in unison. Then a ripple of laughter emanated from the surrounding valley, instantly alerting Amulius and the Latin warriors, who looked around nervously for the source of the ghostly sounds.

'I suggest you turn around and leave now, your highness. These highlands can be very unhealthy for those who are not accustomed to our wetter climate.' The challenge in the words was evident as Sabus's voice took on an aggressive tone.

'Or what?' retorted the prince, although his voice betrayed the uneasy feeling that was forming in his gut. A moment after asking the question, Amulius began to regret it.

Suddenly, the ground across the valley began to ripple and move. Rectangular carpets of green turf seemed to rise from the earth, whereupon hundreds of Samnite warriors emerged from pits in the valley floor, their bows pulled back with lethal bronze-tipped arrows aimed at the Latin warriors.

Amulius backed up his horse in surprise as suddenly he and Pinarii were surrounded by hundreds of mud covered, semi-naked men. The sight sent a murmur of fear through the men behind the prince. As he looked around in obvious panic, he noticed hoards more Samnites coming out from the tree-line. The spectacle drew the eyes of his warriors, a hum of confusion infesting their ranks as they shuffled nervously. Within moments the whole area was lined with thousands of enemy warriors. Many held spears aloft, challenging the Latins with shouts and taunts. As the noise became louder, Pinarii began to retreat back to the safety of his warriors, leaving Amulius alone between the two sides. Murmurs of fear spread through the Latin ranks as some men began to edge backwards, looking for escape. The rest nervously clung to their weapons as they faced certain death by the force of the far larger Samnite army.

'You have two choices, Prince,' shouted the younger Samnite leader over the din. 'You can turn tail and run for your life, or you can die here. We do not want your kind here. Neither do we want war with Latium, and for this reason alone, we are letting you live. We know your father would have to answer his son's death with war – if not, you would have been slaughtered already.'

Amulius didn't answer but inwardly heaved a huge sigh of relief, having expected a more brutal outcome. *This is all Pinarii's fault,* he seethed silently. *How could he have let this happen?* He could not understand how so many men had remained hidden so well, but more so, he could not fathom how so many had come to the valley, undetected. He guessed the whole Samnite nation must have slipped in via the steep cliffs. *Under the watchful eyes of Pinarii's men. He will pay for his oversight,* Amulius promised himself. He felt a judder of fear as he judged that his men were outnumbered by at least four to one and were penned in on all sides. They would be slaughtered if conflict ensued.

As if reading his thoughts, Sabus then added, 'Before you leave, your highness, you will offer ten of your men for me to sacrifice, as you so casually sacrificed mine.'

Amulius fought to keep his calm as he resisted the urge to charge forward and take the Samnite's head. He knew he was beaten. He had no choice but to comply or risk dying. His instinct for survival overtook his pride and so he turned to Pinarii. 'Give them what they want,' he growled. *And count yourself lucky you are not to be among them* – he kept the thought to himself as he glared at the general.

Pinarii nodded and turned his horse back towards his men. He looked around at the faces of his warriors, wondering how he would choose ten to die. His own impulse was to gallop away in retreat, but he controlled the urge as he looked at his men; he wanted nothing more than to get out of the situation with his head intact. Ever since the king had assigned him to Amulius, the general had suspected that the young prince's arrogance would get them into a mess. Now, he realised that the mess would be dropped firmly at his feet. He had truly underestimated the guile of the Samnites, and would pay for it dearly. He tried to put the thought out of his mind as he struggled to come to a decision.

The first man who came under his eye was a section leader, responsible for eighty men. With the chance to place the burden of choice on someone else, he headed toward the man. 'Section-leader Dursus, choose your ten worst men and have them brought forward,' he said to the sunburned middle-aged warrior, whose rough skin shone with white scars that covered his arms and bare brown shoulders. The brown leather tunic he wore was marked with the symbol of two swords side by side, denoting his rank. Dursus gave a subdued nod and turned to his warriors, making his decisions quickly.

The ten men were soon jostled forward by their comrades, out into the open, behind Amulius. They looked around nervously, the panic evident in their darting eyes as they moved as one in a tight group, heading for the six tribal leaders. When they were far enough forward, a group of Samnite warriors rushed at them with long spears and surrounded the frightened men. Cries of protest were heard from the condemned men as the Samnites cruelly harried them over to the waiting leaders. With a little encouragement from the sharp, bronze points of the enemy's spears, the men were forced to kneel, facing their prince. Some of them, to Amulius' disgust, were begging for mercy, whilst others merely stared ahead, either in shock or in acceptance of their fate.

'We repay blood with blood,' announced Sabus to the prince. 'With this act we are avenged, and today you can leave with your life. But if we ever see you on our lands again, we will call on all the tribes to help. These men here today,' he gestured around the valley, 'are only a small number of our warriors. We can call on many more and bring you a war you will never finish.'

Amulius stayed silent, his angry plans for revenge on the Samnites dominating his thoughts. He believed they had shown weakness in their actions against him, and his fear of them lessened. He watched with disinterest as his men were held by the enemy warriors. Sabus came to stand behind one of the men with a long knife and cut the warrior's throat. The Latin man was kicked down to the ground to bleed out in choked gasps. One by one, Sabus moved from person to person, quickly cutting their throats, his gaze fixed on the prince the whole time. Amulius returned it without expression.

Silence returned to the valley as the men's lives drained away, and, when the last man had stilled, Sabus and the five chiefs turned and began to walk towards the tree line, leaving behind the warm bodies and the prince. The valley floor came to life again as the Samnite warriors silently followed their leaders, and soon they all disappeared into the trees. Amulius turned his stallion and led his warriors back to Alba Longa in defeat and humiliation.

Chapter Six

It was daybreak by the time Prince Numitor and Brascus arrived at the palace. There were more guards than usual as they headed for the stable area and Numitor could feel the heightened sense of alert amongst them. When they had dismounted, one of the guards immediately ran up to the pair. 'Your father is in the throne room, Sire. I've sent someone to tell him you are here – and safe,' he added.

Numitor nodded his thanks as he became aware that all eyes were on him. Even the guards on the high battlements that loomed over the palace had stopped and were looking down in his direction. *What must they be thinking of me?* The shame at having been captured seemed to encase him and he avoided their looks. Leaving Brascus behind, Numitor briskly walked away, towards the large stone stairway that led into the whitewashed main building. Making his way through the narrow corridors he rehearsed what he would say to his father. He would not mention his mysterious rescuer, having discussed it with Brascus during the ride; between them they had concocted a somewhat different account involving a discarded knife and a lucky steal of a horse. The rest of the tale would leave his father in no doubt as to where the failure lay.

Rounding a corner, Numitor walked through an ornate doorway carved with the insignias of all the noble families, into a high-ceilinged vestibule. The area was usually deserted but was now busy with chatter as nobles and uniformed men awaited the king's orders. Numitor guessed they were all there because of him. He hid his embarrassment with a purposeful look, pulling his shoulders back in grim determination. He was making for the large oak doors that separated him from his father, when he spotted Amulius standing on the other side of the vestibule, deep in conversation with someone unseen.

All pretence of calm left the tired prince as his senses were overcome with frustration and anger at his conniving brother. 'You traitor,' shouted

Numitor in righteous outrage. He made for his brother, fists clenched and eyes firmly set on his blood rival.

The surprised onlookers parted as the prince rushed through the now silent crowd. Amulius looked around as his enraged brother descended upon him. 'What is your problem?' he asked sarcastically as he turned to meet Numitor.

An angry fist shot out and connected with Amulius' beakish nose. It crunched under the blow and blood exploded around his nostrils. 'You set me up, Amulius,' Numitor bellowed in anger. He punched his brother in the gut, but Amulius was prepared and took the blow, returning with one of his own, catching Numitor in the face. The prince stumbled back as his brother lunged at him. Numitor shot his fist out again, this time finding Amulius' left cheek, leaving a cut where his eagle ring made contact.

Amulius reacted by grabbing his brother in a headlock before they both fell to the floor and began trading frenzied blows, brawling under the eyes of Alba Longa's gentry.

The vestibule echoed with shouts and jeers as nobles and guards alike joined in a chorus of encouragement. The doors to the throne room sprang open and four guards rushed out, followed by King Proca, his sword in hand. 'What in the name of the gods is this?' he shouted over the din.

The onlookers immediately became silent, but the princes were too deep in their rage to hear the king's arrival. Numitor was now on top of his brother. Proca crossed over and grabbed Numitor by the scruff and pulled him away, his son's legs flailing in anger. Brascus arrived at the scene at the same time and grabbed Amulius as the younger prince was trying to get at Numitor.

'Inside,' the king beckoned to Brascus. Both the princes were half-dragged into the room beyond the oak doors and dumped before the throne. King Proca ordered the guards out, and the doors were closed before he came to stand in front of his sons.

'I shall not ask again,' stated Proca, his heavy brow lined with annoyance as his gaze fell onto each prince individually. 'Amulius?'

Nursing his nose and sounding muffled, the prince shrugged his shoulders. 'I have no idea father. He just attacked me whilst I—'

'Liar,' hissed Numitor, and to his father he added, 'He is a traitor. He set us up.'

Amulius feigned a laugh as he wiped away a bead of blood oozing from where Numitor's ring had cut him. 'He is obviously sun-stroked, Father. He is talking nonsense.'

'Quiet,' Proca barked, instantly halting the younger prince. He turned back to Numitor. 'I take it you are talking about your ill-fated talks with the Etruscans?'

Numitor swallowed hard and nodded. 'Yes, Father, but it's not my fault. The talks were going well and then we were attacked by—'

'Yes, yes I know what happened,' snapped the king, 'you were foolish and left yourself open to failure.'

'But that is not fair, Father. My plan was working – they were listening to me, then they witnessed our own people attacking them, but I didn't order it. He did.' His scowl barely showed through his bruised face.

Amulius opened his mouth to speak but snapped it shut as the king gave him a warning look. Proca then turned to Brascus, who was standing quietly behind the younger prince. 'Tell me what happened, Brascus – and I do not want any interruptions,' he warned his sons.

After hearing the tale, the king turned to Numitor. 'It seems that you were lucky to get out of this mess with your skin intact, my son. If, as you believe, your brother did organise these unfortunate events, then you were played and you lost. You made grave errors of a kind that a king cannot afford to make, and you underestimated your rival.'

Numitor nodded with shame. He agreed with his father's assessment and felt foolish for his oversights. He guessed the lesson had been learnt too late to win him the throne. He avoided eye contact with his father and sighed in disappointment.

King Proca glanced across to Amulius. The younger prince wore a smirk, his bloodied nose crooked and red, the broken bone confirmed by the darkening patches under his eyes. 'You have shown a lack of judgement with your trickery, Amulius, and yes, I have confirmed that you organised this little heist.' The prince's eyes widened at the king's revelation. 'I worry for your state of mind, Amulius. Whatever your reasons for committing such an act, you have forgotten what is important.' The prince attempted a reply but the king stayed him with a sharp look. 'By placing your brother's honour in doubt, you also place your whole nation's honour in doubt. You must learn the value of family and honour if you want to rule a kingdom. Your actions were stupid and irresponsible,' Proca growled. 'Your brother could have been killed, and now I have a major situation on my doorstep with countless Etruscan leaders.'

Proca continued to address Amulius. 'We lost twenty-one men on that hill. Twenty-one loyal Latin men now knock on the gates of the underworld. That is twenty-one families who are now without a man to watch over them, twenty-one fathers missed, twenty-one warriors absent when you most need them.'

Amulius bowed his head as another drop of blood fell from the gash on his cheek whilst he concentrated on the patterns of the ancient mosaic that covered the throne-room floor. The pictures, showing various extracts from the voyages of Aeneas, were a welcome distraction from his father's angry gaze.

The king continued. 'And as if that were not enough, you waste another ten men on your useless endeavours with the Samnites. What in the name of Zeus was the reasoning for your actions?'

Amulius looked up. 'The mere mention of our country should be enough to make those peasants cower. If you had not been so soft on them—'

'You have no idea what you are talking about, Amulius,' the king growled. 'We will always have neighbours, there will always be conflict, but a king must know when to act and when to talk. You...' he pointed accusingly at his younger son, 'do not have to conquer every one you meet, or you will come to be viewed with suspicion instead of honour. It is honour that makes a king a king.'

'There is no honour in being weak,' snapped Amulius. 'Only the bowed back of a coward. You taught us that,' he finished accusingly.

An angry frown flitted across the king's forehead as he grunted, 'And does a brave man slaughter men for fun, Amulius? Does he send warriors to rape the wives and daughters of his neighbours? Does a brave man return home with his pitiful little tail between his legs, like a broken puppy?' The king taunted his son.

'He had women raped?' asked Numitor in disbelief. He had not heard about any of these events and was curious to know more. 'What happened, Amulius, did your scheming go awry?'

'It has nothing to do with you,' hissed the younger prince.

'What is the matter, Amulius? Do you not want to share your news with your older brother? Why not tell him, show him how a real king behaves.' Amulius stayed silent so Proca continued. 'No, well then, let me tell him.' He turned to Numitor. 'Your brave brother here decided to make peace with the local Samnites by attacking a tribe, killing ten of their men and having the tribe's women raped.'

Numitor could only listen in stunned silence as his father explained the humiliating outcome of his brother's actions. When Proca spoke of the sacrificed Latin warriors, the older prince shook his head, saddened that more men had died because of his brother. At the end he turned to Amulius. 'I am ashamed to call you kin. You will never be king.'

42

'We will see.' Amulius spat out the words with venom.

'Neither of you are fit to be a king,' sighed Proca as he stepped back and sat on the marble throne.

'But surely I have won, Father?' cried Numitor. 'My failure was because of him.' He pointed at his brother.

'You failed to see the danger, Son. You were too trusting and too naive. Now I have to clear up a mess that you both contributed to. I seem to have one son who is too trusting, and one who is too thirsty for blood. If I could take the better of you both and put it into one man, then a king of kings would rule this land.' Proca shook his head in bewilderment.

Numitor slowly got up and, with his head bowed in shame, he addressed the king with an angry tone. 'Well, if you are finished, Father, I would like to clean up and get some food – my journey back was hard and long.'

'You can go when I am finished,' was the harsh reply. 'You can get off your knees also, Amulius, and face your father like a man.'

The younger prince got up quickly and waited with his hands behind his back.

'I believe,' continued the king, 'that the only way to teach you both a lesson is to force you to work together. As I have no other heirs to consider, I have decided that you will have to rule together, with a council of peers to help steer you. Neither of you will act without the other's consent. If you disagree on a subject, then the council I have chosen will vote on it.' Proca shook his head in disgust. 'A Greek democracy! Who would have thought we would come to this.'

Both princes objected simultaneously in a roost of pleas and argument. The king let them continue for a moment before silencing them with a look. 'One day you will learn to appreciate each other's qualities and learn to co-operate. In the meantime, until I am no longer of this world, neither of you may act without my permission.'

Proca got up and walked toward the oak doors, giving Brascus a parting nod, and left his two sons standing before the throne. They were speechless as their father's proclamation began to sink in.

Chapter Seven

The carpenter waited until the sun had set over the city of Alba Longa before putting down his tools, grabbing his bag, and bidding his master a good evening. Nodding to a few of his colleagues, he left the workshop and headed into the steady throng of city life. He made his way along the stone pathways, towards the tall, defensive walls and took in the sight of the battlements that crowned the two gate towers. The long walls curved away in opposite directions. Since first seeing the great walls of Alba Longa as a child, he had always thought they looked like the wings of an eagle protecting its nest.

Avoiding people in his path, the carpenter manoeuvred around barrows heaped with the produce from the fertile mountain valleys. Orange pumpkins were piled high alongside strands of wild purple carrots and clumps of white onions. Stacked beside the small stalls were large vats of fermented fish, filling the air with a pungent scent that overpowered the senses. He passed old ladies sorting crates of dried figs and apples, whilst the sight of creamy round cheeses wrapped in fennel leaves caused his stomach to grumble.

Stopping at one of the better presented barrows, he took a few moments to choose an apple from the neatly arranged lines of green and red fruit, turning a few over to expose any bruises. When he was satisfied with his choice, he flicked a small bronze coin to a scrawny boy who clung to the side of the wooden cart as if it might escape him, and then continued on his journey.

He crunched on the apple as he walked, and casually avoided the steady flow of people, keeping his head down and taking a few precautionary turns into smaller alleyways. Climbing up some steps, he came to the main street which led to the city's entrance.

The warm day had kept people out later, talking in doorways or bartering goods with traders. He dodged some children who blindly carried armfuls of chopped wood that had been collected outside the city walls. Others balanced urns of water from the communal wells. The carpenter enjoyed the bustle, and the crowds were always welcome; he could blend in and become nobody for a while.

Once through the large city gates, he followed the pathway downhill towards the lakeshore, where the last of the fishing boats were coming in to unload their hauls. Groups of sweating men pulled on ropes, dragging in nets of wriggling fish, whilst others sorted them into sizes and types. He watched them for a while, taking in the scent of fresh fish and loam that permeated from the muddy beach. When he had seen enough, he turned his back on the fishermen and followed the path beside the water, eventually leaving the trail and darting into the woods that grew along the edge of Lake Albano.

The thick canopy hid the day's remaining light, making it hard to navigate through the trees. Squawks and chatter came down from the branches as birds argued over perches, the noise competing with the evening's first cricket calls. The darkness brought a change to the lakeside as the sanctuary of daylight surrendered to the perils of night. Only he and his kind – harbingers of death – prowled the shadows. Somehow, it felt safer to him.

The uneven ground began to rise steeply as he made his way along the overgrown trail, but it soon levelled out and then descended back down towards the lake. He stopped and listened intently for any signs of movement from beyond the bushes. When he was sure that he was alone, he took a cloak from his bag and put it on, lifting the hood before making his way down to the water's edge. As he got closer, he could see the silhouette of a similarly cloaked man waiting in a boat: one of the thirteen Dius' that collectively called themselves *The Hounds of Diana*.

The carpenter thought back to when he had been recruited. He had been a warrior for the Latin army when he found himself inducted into a world of clandestine assassins and spies. They called themselves *Dormienti* – those that slept – and they served a master more powerful than the king. Ancient techniques, handed down over centuries, formed part of his training, making him an expert in silent deception and stealthy executions. He had excelled in his new role and, after many years of service, was now trusted with the most important of missions. As a result, the carpenter had met many of these powerful Dius'. He was one of the few who had seen some of their faces, but he had been able to learn very little about these secretive and powerful Hounds, other than that they seemed to control the kingdom. The best he could surmise was that each Dius represented a noble family and that, through centuries of systematic planning, they were able to rule the country without anyone knowing.

As a Dormienti assassin, he was sworn to serve The Hounds of Diana until death and carry out their wishes. In return, he was highly rewarded for his services. He gained insight, riches and protection. Loyalty was the only requisite, and none of the Dormienti had ever betrayed their masters – the honour of serving the Hounds was too great and the penalty for betrayal too high.

Without any greeting, the carpenter climbed into the boat and grabbed the oars. Sitting with his back to the man, he rowed out towards the middle of the lake, stopping only when they were far enough from the shore not to be overheard. He then pulled in the oars and waited.

'The Hounds need your services,' stated the deep voice behind the carpenter.

'I am honoured to serve, Dius,' he replied before waiting respectfully for the man to continue.

'This command comes directly from the Prima.' The Dius shifted in his seat as he drew his cloak tighter against the strong breeze coming off the lake. 'You are required to arrange a death that will appear to be an accident. Make it public – a fall from a horse would do it, or perhaps drowning?'

Hearing mention of the Prima had raised the carpenter's interest. The grand leader of the Hounds held more power than the king himself, and this was the first time that the carpenter had been asked to undertake a task directly for the mysterious leader.

'This is a very delicate situation,' continued the Dius, 'and needs to be undertaken with care.'

'May I ask who the target is, Dius?' enquired the carpenter, his interest piqued.

'General Pinarii.'

'Amulius' general?' He hid his surprise, though it intrigued him.

'Same one,' sighed the Dius. 'Won't be much of a loss, I can assure you.'

The carpenter sat silently and watched the moving points of torchlight coming from the other side of the lake as he thought about the request. To kill anyone and make it look like an accident was never easy. Killing a general in the Latium army who was also from a noble family could have dire consequences; the Pinarii family were powerful people. 'As you wish, Dius,' the carpenter finally answered, 'but his high status will mean taking a few extra precautions. I will require a little more time than usual, if that is possible.'

'Before the next full moon would be preferable,' replied the Dius, firmly.

The carpenter did a quick calculation – it gave him twenty-three days to plan and execute the task. 'I will either have the job done or I should be close to finishing it in fourteen days, Dius.'

'We have faith in your abilities.' The statement hinted at the degree of importance placed on the task.

'If it pleases the Dius, can you inform me of his crime?' asked the carpenter. 'The information may assist in my planning.'

'I doubt it will,' the Hound replied, shifting again and gently rocking the boat. 'Suffice to say, he is to inherit a position within the Hounds of Diana, and yet he does not understand our rules very well – the rules regarding anonymity, in particular. They exist to keep us all safe. Pinarii has condemned himself by speaking of us.'

'Who did he speak to?' the carpenter asked. 'Do you need me to track them down?' It was his duty to help preserve the secret of the Hounds, and he was ready to pursue anyone who was deemed to be a threat.

'Unfortunately for Pinarii, he spoke to the wrong person, someone loyal to us. This is why his execution must be done in the manner I have described. It must not look suspicious, but it still needs to send a message that our kind will understand.'

Another thought came to the carpenter. 'As I recall, the rules state that a Dius has to die in the boiling sulphur pools. Is that not the punishment for betrayal?'

'No, *Hades Fire* is only used on members who have taken the oath. Pinarii is not yet part of the gathering, so the rules are different. He is, however, a member of a noble family. It cannot look like murder, or we will have a severe problem on our hands.'

'I understand, Dius. It will look like an accident,' promised the carpenter, picking up the oars.

'Diana be with you,' finished the Dius.

'I am honoured to serve, Dius,' replied the carpenter as he rowed to shore. He wondered who would replace Pinarii. A new Dius from the Pinarii family would be chosen by the Mother Vesta, the head priestess of the Vestal Virgins. The other Dius would never know the identity. It was forbidden for a Hound to reveal his name or face to another member. The rule had served them well.

The carpenter reflected on the way the Hounds organised themselves, marvelling that they even went to the extent of using the revered head priestess to choose their members from the large extended families of the noble classes. As he pulled on the oars he let his thoughts wander until the boat had arrived at the lakeside. He then climbed out promptly, leaving the

Dius in the boat. Without another word, the carpenter melted into the trees and disappeared amongst the shadows.

***

A few weeks later, the carpenter was hiding on the wide branch of a tree, a black cloth covering his face as he waited for General Pinarii to ride by. The task of planning the job had proved to be trickier that he had first imagined. It had not been easy to establish his target's routines, but in the end a fortunate piece of news had reached the assassin: Pinarii had a mistress.

Now, with the sun about to rise behind Mount Albanus, the carpenter watched the path, anticipating that the man would be passing by shortly as he returned from his lover's home. The carpenter knew Pinarii would be heading back to the army camp, situated south of Alba Longa, after a night spent with his mistress. *Probably told the wife he was staying at the camp,* thought the carpenter, smiling at the likely deception.

As the eastern sky turned a delicate shade of pink, the image of the mountain mirrored on the calm water, the peaceful vista seemed to belie the act about to take place. The carpenter eventually spotted Pinarii riding down the ridge at a lazy canter, his head rolling slightly with the movements. *Obviously feeling the effects of the powder,* reflected the assassin; he hoped that the sedative he had added to the couples' wine would be enough to subdue the general without rendering him unconscious. The tall plants he had used worked slowly, and the carpenter had taken care while trying to administer just the right amount. He was now pleased to see that his estimations had been correct: the general looked decidedly drunk, and the carpenter felt his excitement rise as the task approached its pinnacle.

When the unsuspecting man came within striking distance, the carpenter grabbed a tree branch firmly and swung himself forward, feet first. The force of the collision launched Pinarii from his horse, which reared up with a scream. The dazed man hit the ground, hard, breaking ribs as a stifled wail of agony left his lungs.

The carpenter landed in a crouch next to the fallen general and slapped the horse's rump, promptly sending the frightened animal down the path at a gallop. Without hesitation he then pounced on the injured general. Wrapping his arm around Pinarii's neck, he used his free hand to take a firm hold of the target's chin and wrench it up, diagonally. The general's neck broke with a crunch and his head rolled to the side, his surprised eyes staring into death's vale.

The carpenter stayed in position for a few moments, holding the twitching body and watching a patch of wetness spread across the victim's leggings. He turned his face to avoid the pungent stench and lowered the corpse to the ground. Glancing around, he sent a silent prayer to Diana that all had gone well. The secluded location was perfect for the ambush, but he knew from previous jobs that there was always the chance of someone coming along at the wrong moment. Taking hold of Pinarii's limp arms, he dragged the body to the path. Arranging it into an appropriate position, he twisted the head around to look like a fall had broken the man's neck. He removed all signs of his own presence, including the drag marks on the path, until he was satisfied that every detail was perfect. By the time someone discovered the stiff body and the unattended horse, there would be little doubt as to how the general had died.

Looking down at his work, the carpenter committed the sight to memory, pleased with the results. He took pride in his tasks, preferring to kill in the same way he worked with wood; taking his time, using his tools skilfully and ending up with a masterpiece. This time it had been different though, not quite so satisfying. He shrugged off the thought before retrieving his bag from the tree.

The emerging sun had turned the sky from pink to light blue as he made his way back to the city. He loved the feel of a fresh morning – the peace and tranquillity before the citizens awoke filled him with cheer. Feeling in a celebratory mood, he decided to go to the workshop early, stopping for some warm fresh bread along the way. Until his next summons, he would blend into the world around him again and 'sleep'. Only when the call came from the Hounds of Diana, or death desired it, would he awaken and once again become Dormienti.

Chapter Eight

Fifteen Years Later

Coaxing his horse through the dangerous terrain of the mountain forest, Prince Numitor watched the trail intently as it weaved through the carpet of half-buried tree roots that threatened his mount with every step. Behind him, his entourage of nobles, advisors and a multitude of Latin warriors carefully followed through the overgrown vegetation. Riding ahead of the prince were his personal guards, sweating under their bronze breastplates and getting little mercy from the tight-fitting black tunics that separated the metal from their skin. Each wore a matching conical helmet and carried a round, red shield decorated with a golden eagle in flight.

Numitor had not wanted to take so many warriors on what was supposed to have been a mission of peace and trade, but the council had insisted, pointing out how disastrously the last such meeting had ended. Numitor was sure their paranoia was fuelled by the ramblings of his younger brother. As it had turned out, the journey to and from Etruria had passed without any major incidents, despite the whole trip taking longer because of the large entourage. However, they were now only one day from Alba Longa and everyone was in good humour as they looked forward to reuniting with family and friends after a ten-day absence.

The prince had been visiting King Corros in the Etruscan city of Veii. He had been impressed by the city's large buildings and wide streets that presented such a contrast to the tighter thoroughfares of Alba Longa. However, he had been surprised to see that a large portion of the population lived in modest wooden huts while only a part of the city and its walls were built of stone; in contrast, Alba Longa was constructed solely from the rock provided by Mount Albanus.

Numitor's encounter with the king had gone better than expected, and the visitors had been treated well by the Etruscans. Numitor had been a little surprised, having anticipated a cooler reception, considering the events of fifteen years earlier when he had last met Corros. Both countries had had very little contact since Amulius' treachery, and while Numitor's father, King Proca, had done his best to make amends with all the Etruscan kings and leaders, Numitor had remained unsure how he would be received. The friendliness of the Etruscans had therefore come as a relief.

Looking down he noticed his golden ascension ring digging into his thick finger. He recalled how it had fit loosely in his younger days and the fine detail of the eagle, wrapped around his finger, was a little duller than it had been back then. Numitor sighed as he realised how much had changed since those events.

He stroked his full beard, which had the first vestiges of grey showing at the edges, as he remembered the younger man he had been; full of life and confidence, unaware of the dangers and pitfalls that would befall him. His hair had grown longer, skirting his broad shoulders, and the lines around his eyes betrayed his cheerful demeanour. He had married at twenty-two and his daughter, Princess Rhea, had been born a year later. Rhea was affectionately known as Lillia, and she meant the world to Numitor, but he required a male heir in order to continue the family line. He had, therefore, been overjoyed when he had discovered he was to become a father for the second time. Then tragedy had struck his young family: his wife had died during the birth of their second child, a boy. The infant survived only a few moments before joining his mother in the afterlife. In one night Numitor had lost both his wife and his son.

Putting aside the pangs of pain and emptiness he still suffered from his loss, Numitor turned his thoughts to his father, King Proca. The king had now been dead for two years following a long illness. Having never changed his mind over his decision regarding the sharing of power, the old king had doomed Numitor and Amulius into joint kingship upon his death.

Since then, under the restraints imposed by the King's council set up by their father, the two princes had clashed on every issue. Numitor had been keen to commence talks with their Etruscan neighbours in the hope of forwarding his ideas on safe trade between the two nations. However, getting the idea through the King's council had in itself been a trial, with his brother's constant objections forcing a vote on every count. Eventually, Amulius' resistance had been overruled by a slight majority, and envoys were dispatched to arrange the talks. Only King Corros had responded.

Smiling to himself, Numitor thought about Corros. During their meetings both men had discussed their desires and requirements to make an agreement work. Over the following days Numitor had grown fond of the clever and witty king. He had been impressed by the presence of the man, who, even at his advancing age, still resembled a warrior in his prime. Numitor had been drawn to the charismatic king and had left the meeting feeling sure that an accord between the two nations could be reached.

Before leaving, King Corros had given Numitor a gift that intrigued the prince. A chest filled with clay tablets and scrolls, some dating back hundreds of years, would not normally be considered of great value, yet the king had assured Numitor that there was information inside that was pertinent to Latium and would be fascinating to anyone interested in its history.

Ever since Numitor had been rescued by the mysterious hooded stranger following the disastrous first meeting with the Etruscans, he had been filled with a desire to know more about this secretive man, and who he worked for. Over the years, the prince had examined many historical notes and documents, snatching information from gossip and stories, to try and discover whatever he could. He had covered his true purpose by feigning an interest in Latium's five hundred years of history, and most were pleased to indulge his curiosity by providing any written accounts or stories. His pursuit of ancient stories had become well known and had consequently reached the ears of the Etruscan leader.

The prince had been informed by King Corros that the chest had been pillaged many years earlier from a Latin estate and, as it had appeared to have no valuables within, had lain untouched ever since. Numitor had examined it immediately and discovered some of the tablets were hundreds of years old. He was looking forward to returning to Alba Longa and examining the contents in more depth.

The path through the forest levelled as Numitor pulled on the reins, waiting for the procession to catch up. Feeling the heat rising off the forest floor, he wetted a rag from his water-skin and wiped it over his hair and around the back of his sunburnt neck. As he waited he saw the slim figure of the captain of the Royal Guard, Miron, riding forward. He stopped beside the older general, Agrillis, who nodded and spurred his horse towards the waiting prince.

'The supply cart is stuck up the hill, Sire.' The stocky general pointed up into the trees. 'Some of the lads are trying to free it, but it could take a while. I suggest we stop here and rest up whilst they sort it out.' He removed his helmet and wiped away the sweat that had collected on his forehead.

Numitor thought for a moment before responding. 'We are not far from that small village where we stopped on the way up to the meeting. They were very accommodating, and they have a well. Maybe we should stop there again and water the horses, General. And the rest can follow when they are done.'

Agrillis wasn't convinced as he rubbed his greying, cropped hair. 'If it pleases you, Sire; but would it not be better if we pushed on to Gabii and rest there?'

The prince considered it. 'You are correct, General. There is no need for us to stop at the village for long, just enough time to let the horses drink, then we can push on.' He gestured to the long line of men. 'We hardly need this lot now that we're so far into our territory – they can catch up.'

'I am sure you are right, Sire,' replied the grizzled soldier. 'At least we won't have to listen to any more stories about leaf spirits and imps. Such nonsense these forest people believe.'

The prince batted away an annoying fly that seemed to find fascination with his beard. After a moment of thought he addressed Agrillis again. 'Come to think about it, General, we have gods that reside in water, such as Neptune. So why not a spirit in a leaf?'

'Neptune is a god, Sire. It is different,' Agrillis answered with certainty.

Numitor shook his head and smiled at the general's serious expression. 'I will lead the nobles and half the guards to the village. Meet us there.'

With a dip of his head, the general rode back to the others while Numitor continued along the trail. The way ahead was now far easier on the horses as the prince found a worn path through the thinning trees. He looked forward to stretching his legs at the settlement. Rounding a copse of damson bushes, he then brought his ride to an abrupt halt as a sight of carnage suddenly met his eyes.

Where there had been a collection of round wooden huts only six days earlier, there were now just charred ruins and motionless bodies. Numitor hurriedly dismounted, shocked at the scene but anxious to check if anyone was still alive. He called to the nobles as they arrived and ordered them to check the village, sending one back to collect Agrillis.

The first victim he approached was an older woman who had been shot in the chest by an arrow, the broken shaft poking out from beneath her. Numitor turned her over and felt a pang of sorrow as her lifeless eyes stared back at him. He reached down and gently pushed her eyelids shut and sent a silent prayer to the gods before moving on to the next body. A rotten smell floated in the air along with the faint odour of smoke that hung around the ruins. Some of the villagers had perished in flames, and the prince's stomach turned as he saw their blackened remains poking through the ashes. By the time General Agrillis arrived, the body count had reached over forty, only a few of which were women. It didn't take the general long to realise what had happened after looking around and examining one of the arrows.

'Samnites,' stated Agrillis as he walked up to the prince. 'And there were a lot of them, judging by the horse tracks. I think they came from the east – there are broken plants and branches through there,' he pointed to an opening at the edge of the clearing. 'We are going to have to be careful, Sire. We are vulnerable here.'

Numitor gave some thought to the situation and came to a decision. 'I think the others should go on to the city, while we take Miron and the guards to make sure that these… these Samnites have gone.' His anger was barely controlled as he looked to the forest's edge.

'Not sure if that is a good idea, Sire,' said the general, looking serious. 'We are just fifty-odd, and a few hands. There must have been double that in Samnites from what I have seen.'

'And what if they attack another village, General?' Numitor didn't wait for an answer and continued. 'We will do as I say. They have captured Latin women who need to be freed, and we must make certain that they are not going to attack any more of my people.'

Agrillis accepted the prince's statements, though his creased forehead barely hid his doubt. 'I will send a few of the lads ahead then, Sire. Best to be careful.'

'Good. Tell the rest of your men to help with these bodies, and send these others onto Alba Longa,' he said, pointing to the nobles who had all dismounted. 'We will build a pyre in the centre of the village and give these poor souls a decent send-off. It is the least we can do for them,' he murmured, as he walked away.

***

Leaving the burning bodies behind, they journeyed through the forest at a much faster pace, with Numitor leading the retinue in pursuit of the attackers. The trail was easy to follow through the trees but became less so when they left cover into open meadows. Agrillis dismounted a few times to inspect the ground, and very soon they were heading up a hill in the dwindling light. As they reached the top, the two riders that had been sent ahead returned with worried looks in their eyes.

'Report,' demanded the general as he dismounted.

'There's a camp on the other side of the next hill, sir. Must be at least two hundred strong, all riders.'

'Did you see any prisoners?' interjected Numitor, who stayed in his saddle.

The guard slowly shook his head. 'Sorry, your highness, we didn't see any, but we could hear them.' He paused with a look of pity. 'I think the Samnites are using them for entertainment, Sire.'

Numitor felt his anger rising again as he considered the plight of the women, his first impulse to go and rescue them. He turned to Agrillis, who was watching him intently, but before he could say anything, the general spoke.

'Sire, there is no way we can act, with so few of us. Two hundred against fifty-three are not good odds. We need to go back for some reinforcements if we are going to wipe that lot out.' He turned back to the guard. 'How settled is the camp – did it look like they were going to leave anytime soon?'

The young rider thought about it for a moment, wrinkling his forehead beneath his bronze helmet, before replying. 'It looks like they've been there for a while, sir. There was a lot of mess. I reckon they're using the place as a base whilst they're out raiding, sir.'

'Your Highness, they will be here when we get back,' announced Agrillis. 'Let us get some help, and then we can pummel them into Hades.'

'And abandon all those Latin women, General? If one of them was your daughter, you would think differently, I am sure.' Numitor felt a strong tug at his heart as his own daughter, Lillia, came to mind. He took a moment to control the powerfully violent urge he felt at even the slightest thought of someone hurting her.

Agrillis stayed silent while Numitor questioned the two guards about the camp. Finally the prince turned back to the general. 'It seems you are correct not to attack yet, General. Accept my apology for my outburst. I do, however, want to see this camp before it becomes too dark.'

* * *

Prince Numitor, Captain Miron, and two of his best men watched the activity in the Samnite camp intensely from their vantage point on the brow of a hill. The observers were barely concealed by the bushes they lay beneath. The former meadow was dotted with small goat-hide tents and debris; the ground, uneven and broken where the horses had churned it up during the recent rains.

The prince surmised immediately that it was not a permanent camp, just by the lack of women and children, save for those that had been herded into a pen at the centre of the haphazard temporary dwellings. There were far more Latin women huddled into the enclosure than he had expected, indicating that other settlements must also have been raided. He presumed the females were probably headed for the slave markets, if they made it that far.

'It is a big camp, Sire,' whispered the captain, 'but easily overrun, if we can take them by surprise.'

'Yes, it is,' agreed the prince. 'However, the prisoners are not easily reached. We will have to go in quickly, but it should not be a problem.' He smiled for the first time since seeing the burnt village. 'Have you noticed they have no look-outs posted? Such confidence will go in our favour, provided Agrillis arrives before morning with reinforcements.'

'Do you think he will be that quick, Sire?' asked Miron, his hazel eyes expressing doubt.

'You have not witnessed the general riding when he is in a hurry,' chuckled the prince. 'Even a falcon would have trouble keeping up. So long as nothing delays him, he should be here by sunrise.'

Miron considered the assertions for a moment before replying. 'I will pray that Hermes gives him the speed to return before daybreak, Sire. If we can attack whilst the Samnites are sleeping, we will have a better chance of rescuing the women before they are killed.'

'And we will make a few of our own slaves at the same time,' replied Numitor as he shifted his weight and started to draw away from the hide-out. 'I will instruct the men to take as many Samnites alive as they can. It will show the other tribes what happens to those who dare to raid our villages.'

Numitor thought about the raiders as he walked back down the hill to collect the horses. His anger at the Samnites lessened as he remembered back to the time when the two countries had lived without tension between them, and he reflected on the reason that peace had ended. His brother's ill-conceived actions in trying to win the competition set by their father had gone on to have further consequences. Since that time, there had been various reports of trouble between the two nations, and the reports were now becoming more frequent. The prince realised that something would have to be done. He would call a meeting of the King's council when he returned.

After mounting the horses, the small group headed back to the cover of the forest, to await the return of the general.

Chapter Nine

General Agrillis waited as the last of his men found their positions. His horse pranced impatiently as if it sensed the anticipation of the riders as they prepared to attack the sleeping camp. The general had returned from Alba Longa with eighty more men from the Royal Guard, which was as many as he could muster in the time he'd had. They had raced through the Latium countryside during the night and had made it back to Numitor with time to spare. After meeting with the prince and the other fifty guards, it was decided that the force would be split into two groups. Each would attack the camp from opposite ends. Numitor had already taken his men and would now be waiting for Agrillis to commence the attack before acting. The prince had insisted that he and a few of his riders would make for the goat pens where the prisoners were being kept, to protect them against any Samnite retribution. The rest were to deal with the two hundred sleeping warriors. They would not be sleeping for long once the attack started, reflected Agrillis; surprise would quickly turn to anger.

Leading his men forward, General Agrillis carefully guided his mount up the hill. Further up, look-outs gave the all-clear to the advancing guards. Once over the brow they would descend partway down the slope and get as close as they could to the camp without alerting the Samnites, then they would charge. His confidence in the plan increased as he reached the top of the hill and saw mist clinging to the slopes below him. The Samnite camp was barely visible. The sky in the east had begun to redden with the first glimpse of a new day as he led his men into the morning haze.

* * *

Armed with resin torches and heavy swords, Numitor's riders watched the camp from the cover of trees, ready to move at the first sign of Agrillis' attack. The torches were in the process of being lit; the resin that had been infused into the cloth at the end of the sticks spluttered as it caught fire. The prince, who had changed into a battle tunic and thick leather leggings, allowed his horse to graze a little as he waited for the sound of the war horn. He went over the plan in his mind and gauged that the odds of rescuing all the women alive were good. The report from his look-outs was that the Samnites had consumed many amphorae of wine the previous night, and Numitor suspected that they would now have trouble rousing themselves. His concentration on the raiders' camp was broken as Captain Miron approached.

'Maybe I should go with you to help with the women, Sire. The pen will be guarded and you may encounter difficulty.'

Numitor shook his head. 'No, Captain, you need to lead your men. The Royal Guard are probably all a bit out of practice and may have grown soft in their service.' He smiled as Miron's face took on a look of disbelief. Before the captain could retaliate, the prince continued, realising his poor attempt to hide his worries behind humour had failed to raise a smile from the serious captain. 'I jest Miron, they are fine men, but we will keep to the plan. If your riders do their job well, then I will be perfectly safe. Do not concern yourself.'

'As you wish, Sire.' Miron nodded obediently and became silent.

The blast of a war horn sounded in the distance, signalling the start of Agrillis' attack. Numitor raised his flaming torch and shouted, 'Remember, they will be concentrating on the general's men. Get as close as you can, quietly – and then rain the fire of the underworld on them!' Raising his eagle ring to his lips, Numitor said a silent prayer to Mars, before he kicked his heels and led the riders forward.

The thunder of hooves was softened by the damp ground as Numitor's warriors charged. As they approached at full gallop, the western end of the camp presented itself as a vista of flames and chaos shrouded in mist. Elsewhere, half-naked men ran around, frantically searching for weapons as others stumbled from their tents. The prince raised his torch as he came to the edge of the camp and then hurled it at a tent. The resinous projectile hit true, splattering burning droplets of the sticky substance over the taught hides of the shelter. In moments, the sky ahead was lit by points of streaking flame as the other riders launched their own torches.

Latin war cries combined with the panicked shouts of the defenders as Numitor hacked down the first Samnite he came upon, nearly decapitating the man. He kicked away the still-standing body before continuing onward. A glance around revealed that more tents had caught fire as his men began to hunt down the confused Samnites. Swiping and slashing at the enemy, the riders were spreading around the camp, trampling those who got in the way and dispatching any who offered resistance. With three of his guards following, Numitor quickly headed for the pens, steering his horse around the array of rubbish and goods that littered the camp.

Suddenly, a warrior ran at the prince from the left, a clear scream of anger coming from the enraged Samnite. Numitor barely had time to raise his blade before the attacker jumped at him and collided with the prince's leg. Clinging tightly, the warrior attempted to pull Numitor from his horse, but then became still as one of Numitor's men skewered the Samnite through the neck. The prince signalled his thanks to the vigilant guard and continued on to the pens. He dismounted on arriving at the enclosure, and, upon hearing the frightened cries of the women, he then jumped over the roughly assembled log fence to release them.

The frightened prisoners were huddled together. Before Numitor even had a chance to act, several of the captives were forcibly thrown to the ground, revealing five Samnite warriors hiding amongst them. Instantly finding himself outnumbered, the prince looked back for help, but all three of his guards were battling with raiders. Numitor prepared to defend himself to the best of his abilities as the first of the previously concealed warriors, who was clad only in leggings, rushed at him with a roar, his bronze sword aimed at the prince's face.

Rising to the challenge, Numitor sidestepped the attack and quickly spun around to follow through, slashing at the back of his opponent's neck. As the warrior fell, two of his comrades rushed forward, attacking in unison. The prince parried the first blade, pushing it into the path of the other sword, which had been threatening his right side. With a practised ease he brought the hilt of his weapon up into the larynx of the nearest man, sending him choking to the ground. The other warrior regained his balance and made to hammer his own blade down upon Numitor's head, but expecting the move, the prince skipped aside and drove his weapon through the perplexed Samnite's back.

The remaining two warriors, who were still standing before the women, hurried to face the prince. Numitor was shocked at the size of one of them. Huge muscular arms and a thick neck protruded from a massive torso; the scars across his face and chest confirmed the man's survival in many battles. The Samnite carried a large iron axe, and the prince knew he would have to make a priority of avoiding the big warrior's blows. Numitor decided to attack the smaller Samnite with a series of strikes, pushing the warrior into the space between himself and his larger opponent. The small warrior looked back to encourage his comrade forward and, making use of the brief distraction, Numitor plunged his sword into the man's throat.

The big man didn't wait for his choking friend to die before roughly shoving him aside to swing a punch at Numitor's chin, sending the prince sprawling to the ground. The Samnite laughed and lifted his axe. 'Latin scum,' he roared, the words barely recognisable in his thick Samnium accent. The axe came down just as Numitor had regained his wits and rolled out of the way, the thick blade missing him by a hand's width. He sprang up and held his sword ready to defend himself against the heavy axe. As the weapon came down again, the prince's blade struck the axe's thick handle, and Numitor staggered backwards as the force of the collision sent jolting pains through his arms. The prince dodged a second swipe aimed at his legs and retaliated immediately.

Numitor rushed forward and swiped at the warrior's throat, but his sword was deflected with such force that it flew out of the prince's hand and landed out of his reach. Before he could react, a large foot collided with the prince's stomach, sending him to his knees, winded. The Samnite ambled forward with his weapon poised to swing at Numitor's head. 'Now die, Latin pig,' he growled, raising the axe for the final blow.

Numitor's eyes widened and he lifted his arms in defence, realising he was about to be killed – but the axe didn't come. Instead, the hulking Samnite warrior stood still, a look of painful shock in his eyes as a bloodied blade appeared from his stomach, and then he dropped to his knees, dead. Behind him, a small, middle-aged woman stood equally shocked, her hands held out in front of her and her mouth agape as she began to tremble.

With a huge sigh of relief, Numitor stood up and quickly grabbed his weapon before glancing around the camp. The fighting seemed to have calmed with only a few pockets of resistance remaining, and a smile came to the prince as he realised that he and his men had succeeded in overcoming the Samnites. One of his guards lay dead, while the other two were nursing wounds and surrounded by several dead raiders. He looked back to the woman that had saved him. She was now being comforted by some of the other women. The prince walked up to her. 'You saved my life,' he stated. 'You have my thanks and my gratitude.'

'Well, I couldn't let that bastard hurt one of our men,' she replied curtly.

Numitor laughed, 'Or one of your princes, for that matter.'

The woman hesitated and studied Numitor closely. 'You're a prince, are you, sir?' she asked nervously. 'You don't look much like one, sir. If you don't mind me saying,' she added quickly.

The prince looked down at the tunic and nodded his head in amusement. 'No, I do not,' he agreed. 'What is your name?'

'Nima,' she replied.

'Well, I am honoured to meet you Nima,' smiled the prince. 'You are addressing Prince Numitor, joint ruler of Latium, and I am forever in your debt.' He bowed to the woman.

Nima expressed her surprise with a gasp as the prince walked away to join his men.

Chapter Ten

Brascus watched the masked men enter the huge volcanic cavern, each one emerging from a different passageway. Their footfalls echoed softly around the sacred space as the men appeared from the walls of the black sparkling dome which glistened with the obsidian imbedded within it. As they took their seats around a stone altar, Brascus avoided looking at the others. They were all identically robed in black. Their identities were hidden beneath hoods and colourful masks painted in red and gold to resemble demons from the underworld. The black garments were embroidered in gold and silver, depicting the goddess Diana aiming her arrow at a golden buck.

Around the cavern, the dark stalactites that draped the walls shed droplets of water onto the smooth rock surface with small splashes. It made Brascus a little nervous to be so deep underground in the labyrinth of volcanic tubes that tunnelled beneath the mountain. By his reckoning, Lake Nemi was above his head and he wagered that was where the droplets of water came from. He comforted himself with the knowledge that the cavern had been used for over five hundred years now and had never yet flooded. As he gazed from behind his mask, he traced the rivulets of water as they meandered down to a dark pool at one end of the cavern. A candle flickered next to the pool, sending dancing shadows over the still water.

His attention was diverted as the last of the twelve masked men took their seats and all eyes turned towards a passageway next to the small pool. From the passage appeared a column of girls, also masked. They walked to the circle of men, and each stood before one of them.

'I serve you, Dius,' the girls said in unison, and then turned their backs on the men to face the altar. Brascus admired the oval white masks, carved to resemble the goddess Vesta, which hid the girls' features so well. Like her counterparts, the girl before him wore a white wrap that hid very little of her lithe pale body. He had become accustomed to seeing these acolytes from the Vestal Virgins, whose purpose at the meeting was to provide protection and secrecy. The girls were the voices that would speak for the men.

The quiet whispers of breathing were broken as a small bell rang out, its high pitched jingle reaching every part of the cavern. The young women knelt down and began singing softly, the words of the song from a language forgotten by most: the language of ancient Troy that was only ever uttered in secret. The tones and rhythm of the song rose as the echoes of the girls' voices reverberated around the cavern.

From the same passageway by which the acolytes had just entered, appeared another masked and robed man. This one was wearing a pair of golden antlers that seemed to grow out of his oversized mask. This was the group's leader, the Prima, and Brascus watched as he made his way to his position in the cavern. He was followed by another girl, the rhythmic singing controlling the pace of their steps. Carrying a small silver bowl, the grand leader stopped next to the altar and placed it on top. The singing stopped and the young women resumed their standing positions in front of the seated Dius.

Producing a blade, the Prima pricked his thumb and squeezed a drop or two of the resulting blood into the bowl. The girl, who now stood to the Prima's left, stepped forward and began to talk. "I honour you, brave Diana, with my blood. I offer you my hounds to bring about your order. They shall follow your arrow and hunt the unworthy, and bring your justice upon them."

In turn, Brascus and the other eleven men walked to the altar, each adding a drop of their own blood to the bowl, whilst the oath was recited by their acolytes. "I honour you, brave Diana, with my blood. I vow to protect your secrets, to follow your arrows and to hunt your prey. I promise to seek out the unworthy and bring your justice upon them."

Once all members had taken the oath, the Prima stepped forward. He held a small wooden container which, when opened, revealed a yellow powder. Pouring some of the powder onto the blood, the leader stirred the mixture to form a thick, ochre paste. A torch was passed to the Prima and he carefully lowered the flame into the bowl. The mixture sizzled as the sulphur caught with a clear blue flame and sent up a cloud of brown smoke which rose up and soon disappeared in the darkness of the domed ceiling. The rotten smell stayed, however, as the Prima's woman spoke again. 'The oath has been made,' she announced. 'The Hounds of Diana are gathered.'

The first Dius to rise leant towards the masked girl before him and whispered in her ear. She then turned to the Prima and spoke. "I have some interesting news regarding Prince Amulius. He has been busy with his warriors along the Samnium border, raiding for slaves." She waited whilst the Dius imparted more information, before continuing. "We understand he has been pushing slaves through market, using the accounts of associates to hide the transactions from Prince Numitor."

The Dius settled back into his seat to give another member a chance to speak. Instead, the Prima rose to address the matter just raised. "Amulius seems intent on increasing his personal wealth," said his acolyte. "This is not the first report I have heard about his recent escapades. A few traders have reported a rise in Samnite goods available for sale. Further investigation has revealed that the goods are coming from within Amulius' training camp near Gabii. It would seem that he has stationed himself there in order to keep his activities from his brother's knowledge."

The next Dius to stand had similar reports to offer. Brascus listened intently as a discussion arose regarding the reasons that lay behind Amulius' actions, offering his own thoughts at one point. It was finally agreed that the Hounds of Diana would try to uncover the prince's intentions by placing a spy close to him. One of the Dius announced that he had the perfect person for the task and, with an exaggerated nod from the Prima, the action was agreed.

The leader stood again. "The Prince should not be underestimated. Who knows what his plans are? I believe his ambitions lie in conquering his own kingdom. With the control of so much personal wealth, he may actually succeed." The Prima whispered more to the girl. "Then our problems will be greater," she stated, "as Numitor is not strong enough to resist his brother alone, and we would be left with a fraternal war. We need peace in our country if we are to prosper, and Amulius seems eager for conquest."

"I agree, Amulius is ambitious," another Dius voiced via his acolyte. "He is also cunning. To try and overthrow his brother would be madness, especially if we do not desire it. However, we must beware that he does not end up controlling the country by manipulating Numitor."

After a few more voices had given their opinions, the Prima ended the subject. "We are agreed that Prince Amulius is to be watched closely, both here and in the fields of battle. In the meantime, we will guide Numitor in our own unique way," spoke the Prima's acolyte. Nods of understanding and agreement rippled through the gathering.

During the rest of the meeting, the Hounds of Diana discussed a variety of issues, including a minor land dispute that threatened to erupt into a bigger problem if not dealt with soon, and the actions of a noble who was embarrassing one of families. By the time they reached the final subject, Brascus had begun to feel stiff from sitting still too long. He listened patiently as the Prima's acolyte listed the latest additions to the Dormienti and their various abilities. The Dormienti were a resource to which every Dius had access, and Brascus had been grateful for their talents on more than one occasion.

"Our last discussion concerns matters of judgement," announced the girl on behalf of the Prima. "Geradius Conillius was one of our spies in Lavinium. As you know, he used knowledge that he was supposed to have passed on to his Dius for his own personal gain, stealing a large sum. In doing so he has given his target much cause for suspicion, and put the Dius in a difficult position."

Waiting for the Prima to whisper more, the acolyte briefly nodded her head before continuing. "It has taken some time to track him down. He fell into the hands of the Dormienti just a few days ago. Tonight we must decide his fate."

A few seats down from Brascus, one of the Hounds rose and leant towards his speaker. "There is only one just punishment for betrayal – Death," said the girl, her voice lacking impact.

The Prima responded through his acolyte, "His crime does not warrant death. He has not spoken of us, but merely failed to report his findings to us while stealing from his target. I suggest a thief's punishment."

"Losing a hand is not enough," voiced another acolyte. "If he cannot be trusted to fulfil his obligations then he cannot be trusted to keep his silence. I suggest tongue and hand be removed."

For a moment nobody moved, then Brascus himself stood and whispered to the girl before him. "I agree with the Dius. He may become bitter with the loss of a hand, and bitter men do scornful things. Loss of hand and tongue would better fit his crime."

"I consent," replied the Prima's acolyte. "It shall be thus. I shall order the Dormienti to carry out the sentence immediately. He will have to replaced, but I shall leave this to the Dius concerned. The matter is now closed."

The proceedings ended after a final prayer to Diana. Then the Prima produced a cloth bag and passed it to the closest Dius, who dropped a pebble into it. The pebbles were numbered and soon the entire group had each deposited one. The bag was returned to the Prima, who gave it a shake and began to remove pebbles individually to indicate the order in which the Dius' were to leave. The first stone out of the bag had XI painted on it; a Dius stood up and walked to the altar before bowing and retrieving the pebble. He left the chamber through one of the many passageways. After waiting a few moments, the next in line repeated the process, and so it continued until only the Vestal Virgin acolytes and the Prima remained.

Brascus pulled up the hood of his riding cloak as he emerged into the cool night air; his ceremonial robe and mask were now neatly hidden in the dark passageways. He slid down the slope, avoiding the rocks and boulders strewn around the steep rise, and headed for the pathway that circled Lake Nemi. The light from the half-moon offered little visibility in the darkness as he spied the silhouette of the Temple of Diana, its three columns dimly lit by the faint moonlight. Beside it, The House of Vesta was shrouded in tree-lined shadows and all but hidden from view.

As he walked through the small woods further down the slope, Brascus considered his position within the gathering. It impressed him how powerful they all were, and it gave him a thrill to know how much he gained from his association with the sect. His only hope was that he could use his power to guide the prince, wisely.

Chapter Eleven

Lillia stood on the large terrace of the royal villa and watched the last rays of sunlight skip over the calm surface of Lake Albano. As the red sun set behind the distant hills, darkness coloured the water and twilight slowly subdued the day into night. She gazed, with wonder, over the great walls and towers, down to the foot of Mount Albanus, which marked out the city below her. A cool breeze came down from the mountain and Lillia wrapped her shawl more tightly around the top of her pale blue dress as she watched points of torchlight coming to life one by one. Shivering slightly, she thought about going back into the villa, but the scene held her and she still had prayers to offer.

Allowing her gaze to wander from the city, Lillia looked across to the smaller Lake Nemi. Only the southern end was visible, the high cliffs around it obscuring most of the water. Hiding in the shadows of the cliffs, she knew, was the sacred Temple of Diana. The bowl of the lake resembled a half-filled cup of dark wine, with very little shoreline except for one plateau of ground to the north. Her thoughts turned to the House of Vesta, which her father had told her about. Lillia had been intrigued by what she had learned of the Vestal Virgins – the beautiful, forbidden women who lived within. She had never seen one, nor had she seen their house, so she could only imagine their mysterious ways. When she had asked what exactly a "forbidden" woman was, a year earlier, her father had answered firmly: "You are only twelve years old, Lillia. When you are a little older, I will tell you."

Staring at the temple of Apollo on the opposite side of the lake, Lillia recalled her father telling her how it had been built hundreds of years earlier by the second king of Latium. The dark building seemed to grow out of the rock, making her think that perhaps the gods themselves had sculpted it. The steady streams of smoke that normally rose up from its pyres were a beacon to locals and travellers alike, although her father had explained that the fires were originally intended as a guide to any lost refugees from Troy, and because of this, they were always kept burning. The smoke was now hidden from Lillia by the hues of evening but the glow from the two pyres cast a misty halo above the temple like a golden crown.

She was disturbed from her thoughts by the sound of someone approaching from the villa's atrium. She turned to see her father's personal assistant, Lucius, coming towards her. He was a nervous young man, who seemed always to be fussing over his robes or losing things, but Lillia liked him. On more than one occasion, she and her friend Sylvanna had hidden his stylus just to see the assistant work himself into a frenzy trying to retrace his steps. Her father had eventually found out about the mischief and made the two girls apologise. Thankfully, Lucius had immediately seen the funny side of the prank, saving Lillia and Sylvanna from any further consequences.

'Princess Rhea, I have news of your father's return,' he announced as he came to a stop before Lillia.

'Please don't call me that, Lucius. You know you can call me Lillia – everyone else does.' Lillia had asked the young man to call her by her preferred name many times before, but he seemed to ignore the request.

Looking a little abashed and with colour rising to his cheeks, Lucius nodded. 'I am sorry Princess Rh… Lillia. It's just… well, it's just…' He thought for a few moments before finishing the sentence, 'It's just that it doesn't feel right for me to call you by your private name. That is just for your family and friends to use.'

'But you are family, Lucius,' was the princess' surprised reply. 'Father said that the Pinarii family were distant cousins of the Silvii's, so you can call me Lillia.'

Lucius hesitated before nodding his head vigorously. 'Well, if you put it like that, then… fine, I will try to call you Lillia from now on, Princess Rhe… Lillia, sorry.'

Lillia giggled at the uncomfortable man. 'What were you saying about father?'

'Father? Oh, yes, sorry,' he stammered. 'I… No… I mean… he, he will be arriving this afternoon,' Lucius finally spurted out.

'But it is evening already. Where is he?'

A guilty look spread over Lucius's pointed face. 'I have been… a little busy, sorry Princess R… Lillia,' he shook his head. 'It's just that… well, I was given the message by one of the guards, but I also received orders from Prince Numitor – your father,' he followed quickly, 'to arrange a meeting with Brascus about some slaves he wants to sell. It has taken me all afternoon to track Brascus down.'

Slaves? thought Lillia. 'Father was going to meet King Corros; what has that got to do with slaves?'

'I'm not sure really, Princess. That is the message I was given.' With a slight hesitation he continued. 'Oh, and to tell you that your father wishes to see you when he returns. He has a surprise for you.'

Numitor had been gone for twelve days, and Lillia's excitement grew as she thought of being reunited with him, her curiosity about the surprise only fleeting. She missed her father dearly, having not been separated from him for this long since her mother and baby brother had died during childbirth, three years earlier. She felt a sharp pang of sorrow as an image of her mother crossed her thoughts, but it passed without taking her smile. 'When is he arriving, Lucius? I must get ready, and go to the culina and tell cook to prepare some food – Father is sure to be hungry.'

'I believe he is down at the palace now, Princess,' answered Lucius, nervously scratching his head. 'Something about convening the King's Council. He will be here shortly, I'm sure,' he assured the young girl.

* * *

A short while later, Lillia was waiting at the wide steps of the villa, watching the large wooden gates for her father's arrival. The stone pathway beyond the entrance led steeply down the mountain, winding its way through the woods before it forked, one branch leading to the Palace while the other continued further downhill into the city. Lillia watched out for the torchlight that would herald her father's arrival and was soon rewarded as the first Royal Guard rode into view. Expecting her father to be following, she was surprised when she saw instead a donkey pulling a loaded cart, a woman sitting next to the driver. Then, upon seeing her father appear behind, Lillia jumped up and ran towards the open gates to meet him as he rode up the final stretch of pathway.

Even before reaching the gate, Numitor jumped from his horse on seeing Lillia running towards him and scooped her up into a tight hug.

'Lillia, my little princess,' the prince whispered, his face buried in her long brown hair. 'I have missed you so much, my daughter.'

Lillia was crying. 'I missed you too, Father,' she blurted through her tears of joy. 'It has been so quiet without you. No one bothers with the villa when you are not here.'

Numitor put his daughter down and wiped the tears from her cheeks before giving her a kiss. Holding hands, they led the horse into the villa

69

compound. 'I hear from Paridé that you spent a good few days with his daughter, so it could not have been that quiet,' jested the prince.

'Yes I did, Father, but it was quiet the rest of the time.'

'I have also heard that you went to the lake cabin on three occasions, and made numerous trips to the market. You could not have been that bored.'

'Even when I was busy, Father, I missed you,' she answered in sincerity, then quickly changed the subject. 'Who is that woman, Father?' she asked, pointing to the cart that had now stopped before the villa steps.

'That is your surprise, Lillia. She is your new handmaiden.'

'But I have maids, Father.'

'Yes, Lillia, you do, but those maids do general tasks. Nima is going to be your personal maid, someone you should learn to trust, who can help you with things – girl things – like your mother would have done.'

'Oh,' the confused princess replied. 'Like a mother... but I don't want another mother.'

Numitor stopped and faced his daughter, who had instantly developed a determined look on her thirteen-year-old face. 'Not a mother, Lillia, a handmaiden. There are certain things that men do not concern themselves with, things that are the business of women only. I cannot guide you in these things, as I do not know how, but Nima will be able to help you when you need it.'

Hearing the words, Lillia nodded her agreement. 'I hope she is nice then, Father.'

'She is lovely, Lillia. The poor woman has lost her husband and has no-one to look after her. She was very kind to me recently, and I wanted to make sure that she has a good home and plenty to eat, so I gave her a job.'

Lillia's face softened as she heard the tale, and she quickly hugged her father. 'You are so kind, Father. I'll try to like her, I promise.'

'I am glad, Lillia. Why don't you go and introduce yourself, and show Nima where her room will be. I think she should be close to you, so she can have the smaller room, next to yours.'

'The crib room?'

'It has not been called that in a long while, Lillia. Let us call it Nima's room from now on.' The prince's voice barely hid the sadness in the statement.

Lillia's features softened and she nodded her head in quiet agreement. Numitor grabbed her for another hug before sending his daughter across the yard to meet the woman, who now waited next to the cart.

Numitor watched Lillia walk away and felt a moment of pride to see how mature she was becoming. The death of her mother had hit her hard, and the prince knew that Lillia prayed to the gods every evening to watch over her and the little brother whom the princess had never known. Numitor hoped his idea of providing Lillia with a handmaiden would fill some of the gaps left by his departed wife, but even if the plan proved to be unsuccessful, he intended to keep Nima around. Her bravery had impressed him immensely, and when he had learned of her husband's passing, he had felt obliged to help the woman who had saved him from an almost certain death.

The prince's thoughts turned to the gift he had received from the Etruscan king. He ordered two of the guards to have the chest brought to his quarters. Lucius was waiting patiently outside the atrium to speak with the prince and quickly ran to Numitor when summoned.

'Lucius,' Numitor greeted the young man. 'All has been well, I hope.'

'Oh yes, Sire,' he beamed, 'all – all has been good. I have one or two discrepancies with the wine stocks, and we have lost a sheep to wolves, but otherwise, everything is fine.'

'My brother obviously has not been around then,' joked Numitor.

'No, Sire, he hasn't,' Lucius' reply was humourless as he continued. 'I haven't seen him since you left, but then, I haven't been to the palace much.'

'No Lucius, I jest – Amulius is at his training camp.'

Lucius thought for a moment. 'Oh yes, I remember, Sire. Sorry, I have been a little pre-occupied lately.'

Numitor glanced at his assistant, a frown of annoyance creasing his forehead. 'We have important things ahead, Lucius. You need to be on form if you are going to be any good to me.'

Lucius bowed his head slightly in acknowledgement and waited for the prince to continue.

'Good. Now that I have your attention, let me tell you about the events of the previous two days, and then I shall explain how we are going to deal with the situation.'

***

The following, evening the Palace courtyard was dark and empty as Lucius made his way over to the large gates that sat between the two watchtowers. The guards let him out and bid him a good night as the assistant headed for a path that skirted the slopes above Alba Longa. Ignoring the flickering spots of torchlight dotted around the sleeping city, he thought about the meeting that he was now on his way to attend; it troubled him deeply.

He headed uphill for a long while toward the royal villa, before leaving the path and following a thin trail into the dark woods. Peering through the thick trees, he cautiously wound his way around the slopes of Mount Albanus, looking over his shoulder and fearing the darkness.

It wasn't long before Lucius then left the trail and began to make his way downhill, the slippery leaves underfoot causing him to slide and stumble as he picked his way through the foliage. Ahead of him he could see the shadow of an almost impenetrable wall of bushes and bramble. When he arrived, he slipped through a hidden gap and made his way into a small clearing. Waiting there in the company of a masked acolyte of the Vestal Virgins, was the frightening figure of the Dius.

Lucius suppressed a shiver at the demonic mask that hid the man's identity – at least, he presumed it was a man. He'd had nightmares over the years dominated by that fearsome painted image. Lowering his eyes as he came to a stop, Lucius saw the gold embroidery on the Dius' dark robes glittering in the moonbeams that shone through the high canopy. The nervous assistant had often felt like the stag represented in the stitching: hunted and in mortal danger.

"What news have you to offer me, Lucius?"

The girl's soft tones helped to sooth his nerves as Lucius looked up at her feminine mask and tried to see her eyes behind it. Having rehearsed what he would say, he was able to ignore the claustrophobic feeling that the clearing evoked, and he spoke to the girl without stumbling over his words. 'Prince Numitor has returned from Etruria and attacked a Samnite raiding camp.' He paused when the robed Dius leant forward to whisper to the girl.

"Yes, I know all about that, and the forthcoming council meeting," said the girl on behalf of the Dius. "It is the chest that I am interested in."

Lucius shook his head in confusion. 'Chest? What chest?'

After taking further instruction, the girl replied. "Prince Numitor was given a chest by King Corros. I need to know its contents."

'Oh, um… Well, I – I'm afraid haven't seen this chest.'

"Then you must locate it and then discover why Numitor has it. We know that it contains documents, but we need to know what they are, and why they were in the hands of a foreign ruler." The girl waited while the Dius communicated more to her. "When you find the chest, you are to get me a sample of the documents from within. In the meantime, you must be observant, and tell me if the prince does anything out of character or unusual."

The girl stopped talking and for a moment the only sounds were the shrill cricket calls that seemed to intrude into the darkness from all directions.

Lucius felt a burning in the pit of his stomach as he fretted over the tasks that now faced him. The idea of skulking around Numitor's chambers in search of a chest worried him immensely. *I never wanted this for myself,* he thought, frustrated at the misfortune of having been born a Pinarii. His obligation to the Dius brought with it dangers that he did not feel equipped to deal with. Becoming acutely uncomfortable under the gaze of the masked couple before him, he suddenly remembered something else.

'The prince brought home a new handmaiden for Princess Lillia... um, Rhea, sorry. She was one of the women the prince rescued. Single-handed I hear.' The pride was evident in Lucius' voice. 'I suppose you could say that was unusual.'

'But not important to us. If you do not have anything more to report, then we are finished and you may go. Summon me when you have located what I require.'

The acolyte said no more, and without further hesitation Lucius quickly walked away, eager to get out of these trees that held so many secrets. He hastily made his way back along the trail and only slowed when he had reached the stone pathway, feeling a little safer as he drew lungfuls of the cool mountain air to calm his nerves. Then the Dius' instructions came back to mind, and Lucius felt his stomach growl and the burning sensation return.

Chapter Twelve

By the time he had a chance to begin searching through the chest he'd received from King Corros, Numitor was tired and longed to close his eyes, but curiosity urged him to stay awake long enough to learn a little about its contents. The prince had been on a long term quest in pursuit of information regarding his hooded rescuer and the man's employers. During his research, he had been able to piece together enough to suspect that the man may have worked for a secret branch of the cult of Diana. At first the clues had come from tales and stories, but as Numitor had researched further, he began to notice patterns: payments, acquisitions, murders and disappearances. Slowly, the prince had drawn to the conclusion that the hooded man's claim was true – there really were powers beyond kings. He became certain that these shadowy people somehow managed to operate in plain sight, and he had to control an impulse to look over his shoulder many times whenever the feeling of being watched came upon him. Numitor had learnt from the lesson of his younger days and was now accustomed to experiencing a little paranoia, especially since the demise of his father.

He pushed back the heavy lid of the plain chest and spent a moment looking at its contents without disturbing anything. The inside had been divided into compartments – one containing scrolls, another for tablets, and the third bearing folded sheets of vellum. The vellum sheets would be of particular interest to the prince because they were usually only used by the very rich, the process of making the calf-skin parchment being too costly for most.

He pulled out one of the clay tablets and examined the writing upon it. It was an account of grain harvests and subsequent sales. The next one listed someone's holdings and livestock. *Quite a wealthy man*, mused the prince whilst glancing at the totals. He became a little disappointed when he found that nearly all the other tablets contained more of the same. One tablet, however, did puzzle him. It was an account of payments, various sums paid to someone who was not named. Nor was any reason given for the payments even though the sums involved were very high. Numitor put the tablet aside for further consideration later on, and turned to the scrolls.

The first scroll he opened caught his attention immediately. It seemed to be some kind of record of a ritual, or perhaps instructions for performing one. The scroll was covered with small illustrations, the colourful scenes appearing to show the various stages of a sacrifice. With no writing on the document, the prince could not identify who had commissioned it, but then a symbol at the top of the page caught his attention. Although he recognised it, at first he could not work out what it was, then it hit him. It was a set of antlers – Numitor had seen the symbol before on a hunting map. From what he remembered, it was meant to represent good hunting grounds.

The next few scrolls continued the same theme of rituals, some of them sending shivers down Numitor's spine as he deciphered each act. He began to wonder if any of these gruesome ceremonies still took place; he hoped not. Putting down the last scroll, he picked up the first of the vellum sheets. The page creaked a little as he gently prized it open. It felt stiff and old, and he saw that there were two lines of writing on it, but not in Latin. At first he thought it was Greek – the letters were similar – but suddenly he realised the text was Trojan.

Numitor had learned to read the old Trojan stories when he was younger, written by the first settlers in Latium, but had rarely come across the language since. It took him a while to begin to decipher the words, the memories of their meaning coming back to him slowly. Some of the writing had faded in places but after some difficulty he managed to translate the first line. It read: *The vengeance of Diana requires the dogs.* Numitor scratched his head, mystified by the statement, although the reference to the goddess Diana had aroused his interest and he carefully read the next line aloud.

"'Assemble… the… gathering,'" he enunciated each word as he translated it in his mind, "'and wake… the sleep.'" The prince shook his head. 'No, that's not it,' he scolded himself, "'wake the sleeping.'" He read it again. "'Assemble the gathering and wake the sleeping.'" It meant nothing to Numitor but he was intrigued, nevertheless. He picked up the next sheet, which revealed more writing. It looked like a letter, this time in Latin, and it was addressed to *the Dius of the Manilii.*

The prince recognised the name Manilii. They were one of the noble families who occupied territory in the north-east of Latium. He looked at the name again, something bothering him about it, and he searched his mind for the reason. Then he saw it: the word *Dius.* He had heard it before. He remembered it was the name that the mysterious stranger had called Brascus, on the night of the rescue.

* * *

Densara Potitii shifted his heavy frame in his seat and rubbed the side of his balding head as the men of the King's Council entered the large chamber next to the throne room. As usual, the portly merchant had arrived at Latium's royal palace a little early, preferring to be seated at the round table before the arrival of the others. His chubby bearded face hid his irritation at some of the councillors who were making idle gossip while standing next to the statues of long-dead kings that lined the cold walls. The posturing of these men, all of whom seemed to have a need to brag about something, never failed to annoy Densara. He didn't share the need to boast of his achievements – he was the most successful merchant in Latium and, in his opinion, he had nothing more to prove. His desire for wealth had not dwindled in all his years of trading, but power was no longer a goal, for he had long since acquired power in abundance. He now preferred to listen for opportunities, and he learnt much from a few well-placed questions while the speakers learnt very little in return.

However, he did enjoy being amongst these powerful council members, dressed in their colourful togas and skilfully embroidered robes, with their mock friendships and implied associations. He often gained insights just by interpreting their body language and gestures – a wrinkled nose, a raised eyebrow. It never ceased to amaze him how easy to read people really were.

Densara had learnt much from the mistakes made by others, and he believed it was the secret to his great success. He remembered the lesson his father had told him at nine years old, when he had first joined the family business. *Watch, listen, and learn to lose your tongue.* He hadn't comprehended it at first, but he had followed the instructions to the letter. It had been the best advice ever given to him.

Looking back, it had been the only advice on offer at the time, and the irony wasn't wasted on the merchant. His father had almost lost the family fortune due to a loose tongue and eyes misted by wine. Fortunately, Densara had opened other avenues of trade, and succeeded in rescuing the business. More fortunate was the sudden death of his father shortly after the incident; the merchant felt little sorrow for the deceased man.

As he waited in the cool chamber, Densara studied the council members, who had all seated themselves at the table now. There were twenty-one men on the King's Council, including the two princes. To his left was the civil judge, Arbitrator Fabii, his face stern, glowing red as he wheezed with every breath. Beside Fabii sat the high priest, and further around the table was the tiny figure of the chief Augur, the latter looking dishevelled and dirty. Densara wrinkled his nose, thinking of the unpleasant odour that constantly followed the little man. Casting an eye around the table, the merchant tipped his head to one of his competitors – the horse breeder, Ugo Curiatii – who returned the gesture without changing the expression on his long face before continuing his conversation with the councillor from Lavinium, the first city to be built in Latium. Other representatives from the towns of Cora, Ostus, Gabii, filled some of the other seats. Most of them were of little interest to Densara, who was very cautious in choosing his associates.

As he waited for the princes to arrive, he looked back at the line of statues that commemorated fourteen generations of kings. His gaze fell on to the worn image of Aeneas, the first King of Latium, who had escaped the carnage of Troy as a young prince. The tale of how the invading Greeks, led by King Agamemnon and Achilles, had deceived the inhabitants of Troy, was one of Densara's favourite stories. The Trojan horse was a lesson to all: *appearances are sometimes deceptive,* he mused as his eyes scanned the seated councillors.

Prince Numitor entered the large room followed by Lucius, who was having difficulty keeping a stack of scrolls and slates in his overloaded arms. Densara was confounded by the man's need to carry so much, but he had to admit that the assistant offered much more than note taking. Although he was a clumsy and dim-witted man, Lucius was unusually gifted with numbers and Densara knew that he kept Prince Numitor's treasury balanced and well accounted for.

The seats around the council table were almost full as Numitor took his place and his brother strode into the cold room with an equally cool manner. The younger prince scowled at Numitor as he pulled his fingers through his long black hair; the white crescent shaped scar on his left cheek, illuminated against his tanned skinned. The large athletic figure of General Tyco followed, alongside his older counterpart, General Agrillis.

'What is this nonsense that demands me to ride for nearly a day to get here, brother?' asked Prince Amulius across table. 'I hear you attacked a Samnite camp, and yet I am the one labelled as a war monger,' he laughed sarcastically.

'Sit down, Amulius, and let me explain why we are here,' said Numitor.

Amulius walked to his seat and dumped himself down, lifting a foot onto the table top. When the two generals had taken their places between the princes, Lucius stood and announced, 'The King's Council is now in session. Will the first speaker stand?'

Numitor rose and recounted the events of the previous days that had resulted in the rescuing of the Latin women. The councillors listened with an occasional comment or exclamation, and General Agrillis added his own account of the events at the end.

'I have always said we should wipe out that menace,' announced Amulius when the general had sat down. 'If father had listened to me, we would have dealt with this problem years ago.'

'I believe it was you that started this mess years ago, Amulius, and now, as per usual, someone is going to have to clear it up.' Numitor's tone sounded tired and frustrated.

'And you are the man to do it, are you, brother?' challenged Amulius as he removed his foot from the table and sat up in his seat. He leant forward in an exaggerated posture of intrigue and smiled at Numitor. 'Come, tell us all how you are going to make peace with the Samnite tribes.'

'They will never make peace,' came a shrill voice from across the table. The bent figure of the Chief Augur began to rise slowly from his seat beside Numitor, his long staff aiding the old man to stand. With his head barely over the table-top and his long thin beard touching it, he continued to speak. 'I have seen it in the sky. Three crows flying east into a blood-red sky. They summon Mars to war.' The cryptic announcement caused a flurry of whispered comments that echoed around the chamber as the Augur sat down again.

The next man to stand was Ugo Curiatii, who bore an unfortunate resemblance to the horses he traded. He straightened his ochre tunic and cleared his throat before speaking. 'It will be difficult to bring war to the tribes. They are spread over a large area, and those mountains are treacherous. Horses are of little use when you get to the higher ground.'

'You are just worried about your profits,' remarked Amulius to the wiry man who was responsible for supplying most of the horses to the Latin army. 'By foot or hoof, we need to get up there and put an end to these raids. And this time, the Samnites will not be getting any gifts.' The snide comment elicited a few smirks from some of the other councillors, causing Numitor to look down at the table uncomfortably.

'Those bastards need to be dealt with, that's for sure,' interjected General Agrillis, placing his hands on the table top as he rose. 'We now know of fourteen settlements that have been attacked along the Samnium border. They are making entertainment and slaves of our women, and killing good working men. This has to stop,' he shouted, shaking one or two of the quieter councillors out of their reveries.

'I agree with the general,' stated the deep voice of Arbitrator Fabii, an old friend of Agrillis. 'We cannot let this behaviour go unpunished or we will be seen as weak.'

'At last I hear you talking sense, Arbitrator,' replied Amulius, who had even less time for the judge than he had for Agrillis. 'We need to bring war to these peasants before they become a threat.'

'For once, I find that I agree with my brother,' sighed Numitor as he looked at Amulius. His brother's face changed to one of surprise at the statement but Numitor ignored it and continued. 'I suggest we combine my warriors with my brother's and go into Samnium without delay. It should not take long to teach the Samnites a lesson that they will never forget.'

Nobody moved or spoke as the statement sank in. Eventually Amulius addressed his brother. 'Who do you suggest lead this army, brother – you?'

Numitor shook his head and answered with a little resignation in his voice. 'No Amulius, we both know that you are better suited for the task. However, I only agree to this on two conditions.'

'And what, I pray, are they?' Amulius resumed his sarcastic tone as he drummed his fingers on the table.

'General Agrillis will be second in command, and any spoils will go directly to the treasury to pay for this war.'

Amulius stopped the annoying drumming and studied his brother for a moment before nodding his agreement. Not wanting to reveal his joy at the decision, he kept a stern façade as he answered. 'That seems reasonable, brother. I agree.'

'But we haven't voted on it.' The objection came from the slender man who sat next to Densara. Fidgeting in his white robe, High Priest Cluillii, who had listened quietly until that moment, stood up to continue, but promptly sat down again as Numitor interjected.

'My brother and I have both agreed on this course of action, Your Grace – for the first time since my father passed, I hasten to add. Therefore, it would be understandable if you have forgotten the rules set down by King Proca. The council only vote if Amulius and I disagree.'

Nods from some of the other councillors reinforced the statement, and the high priest signalled his understanding with a slight bow of his head to the princes.

The news pleased Densara. War meant profits for him. He would supply mule-carts, wine and grain to the Latin army, and in return there would be slaves and goods at reasonable prices. He remained seated as the other councillors began to leave and allowed his mind to wander back over the meeting. He wondered what Numitor had experienced to make him so agreeable to a war. Allowing his warriors to come under Amulius' command was unexpected and not a wise move on the part of the older prince. There was surely an opportunity to be found in this surprising turn of events, and Densara was eager to make the most of it.

Chapter Thirteen

Densara was about to leave the council chamber when Brascus walked in and headed directly for the merchant. Numitor's former mentor, who was managing to make a casual outfit of leather leggings and loose shirt look smart, excused himself as he made his way past the other councillors. *He seems eager to see me,* thought Densara as he watched the tall, sun-tanned man approach.

Drawing up his barrelled chest, Densara rose to meet the well-built entrepreneur and, without giving the man a chance to speak, he put on his biggest smile and greeted him. 'Brascus, shouldn't you be in Numidia, hunting for stock?' he said with a serious look in his eye. Then, with a smile he added, 'I understand you had to give back all the gold for the last lot of slaves you sold.'

'I never return gold, Densara,' came the hearty reply. 'If they can stand at market, it is a fair trade.'

'Well, you certainly seem to have a steady supply of standing slaves,' responded Densara, allowing a little admiration to appear in his voice. 'In only a few years you have managed to build yourself a good business, and I hear you have even bought a fleet of ships.'

Brascus scratched his greying beard and laughed. 'I would hardly call three coast-huggers a fleet. I only use them as transport to and from Neopolis – the slavers there do a good trade with the Phoenicians in Sicilia.'

'Trade that has been pirated from our Numidian friends, I've no doubt,' chuckled Densara.

'And anyone else who gets in their way!' Brascus exclaimed. 'They are fierce fighters, those Phoenicians. I faced them once with Numitor and would not want to repeat that experience.'

'Yes, as I remember, you used to mentor and advise his royal highness.' Densara omitted any references to the outcome of that particularly ill-fated battle, led by Numitor. 'What has happened since to bring about such a change in your career?' asked the merchant. 'Did the lure of the slave trade whet your appetite?'

Brascus laughed. 'I suppose it did. After all, it is a profitable business, and I do trade in other goods as well – just on a smaller scale, like yourself. My years with Numitor were interesting enough, but when Proca travelled to the underworld and the princes succeeded, my obligation was complete and I found myself with much time on my hands.'

'The Julii family have always been close to the Silvii's, have they not, Brascus?' commented Densara, referring to the man's tight family association with the royal dynasty. 'Sometime, you will have to tell me how that came about. I am sure it must be an interesting story.' Densara smiled at the cheerful man, knowing that Brascus would never tell him. Besides, the merchant already knew the tale of how, centuries earlier, a dispute between the two families had ended abruptly when a mysterious intervention had forced them to settle their disagreement.

'My family history is not my strong point,' laughed Brascus, 'but if you would like to learn more then you must join me at my taverna tonight as my guest. I will have a boar on spit and a jug of Tarquinii wine to share.' Leaning forward he added, 'And we can take the opportunity to discuss some ideas I have.'

Intrigued by the offer, Densara took a moment to think about it. 'I believe I am free,' he answered casually. 'Of course, the promise of Tarquinii wine would force me to change my plans, regardless of what they might be,' he joked. The wine was famous for its smooth flavour and a rarity throughout Latium. The merchant had only ever tasted it on the odd occasion during visits to Etruria in the past. 'I would be honoured, Brascus.'

'Then it is settled, I will see you tonight. I am at Taverna Dionysus, do you know it?'

'Lakeside, I believe,' replied Densara, not wanting to use the derogatory term of *low-town* for the poorer district where the taverna was located. 'Around mid-evening?'

Brascus smiled. 'That will be perfect.'

* * *

Later that evening, Densara strolled into the city on foot after leaving his horse at the stables. Built outside the city wall near the large gates, the stables were convenient and all were encouraged to pay the small fee to use them. Many of the city's inhabitants had horses, and prior to the building of the stables, the overpowering smell of old horse urine during the summer would burn the eyes and steal the breath. Piles of dung trodden into the pathways had made the uneven streets treacherous in the rain. After one noble too many had fallen into the mess, King Proca had commissioned the stables and ordered that the animals be kept outside the city walls overnight. Consequently, the streets had become less crowded and travel through the sectors was quicker. Densara was enjoying his walk, and the cool night air was helping to clear his thoughts.

The Taverna Dionysus was in the fishing district, close to the quay that serviced the lake's fishing boats; he guessed that many of the taverna's clientele would be fishermen and associated workers, so he was expecting the place to be rough and dirty. Not being one for excessive drinking and whores, Densara rarely entered tavernas unless there was profit to be made.

The small streets of the fishing district hummed with activity as Densara walked past the tall wooden buildings that flanked the eastern shore of Lake Albano. Eventually he found the doorway he was looking for and spent a moment admiring the painting of the grape-adorned Dionysus above the taverna's otherwise unremarkable door. He imagined that the god of wine probably hung over hundreds of tavernas from there to Greece. *People are so predictable,* he chuckled to himself.

Upon entering the building, Densara was surprised to find himself in a clean, well-decorated room furnished with large cushions and thick, colourful rugs. The walls were painted with vibrant and explicit scenes of couples performing acts of love. The merchant admired the art, smiling at the depictions. Candlelight flickered in shallow bowls, adding to the ambience. *Overall, an unexpectedly endearing establishment,* he decided. A few patrons looked up as he removed his cloak, but they quickly got back to their drinks and their girls as he glanced their way. The merchant sniffed a little as a pleasant odour of cooking filtered through from somewhere.

'Densara.' Brascus appeared from a doorway opposite the entrance. He was dressed casually in a long brown robe and sandals. Scrutiny of the garment revealed embroidery around its neck and cuffs: the merchant was beginning to see his rival's fondness for quality, evident even in the immediate surroundings. The brightly coloured drapes that adorned the walls were not to his taste, nor were the bronze statues of Eros and Aphrodite, but nevertheless, they were expensive furnishings.

'I am so glad you made it, Densara. I was beginning to think you had lost your way,' laughed the big man.

'I nearly did,' replied the portly merchant, shaking his head at the confession. 'It's been a while since I was last in this part of the city.' He glanced around at one or two familiar faces who were busy enjoying the attention of some especially pretty whores. 'Maybe I should come more often,' he said, grinning at one of the passing workers. The girl, who was wearing a revealing ochre dress, returned the smile.

'Any time you are in the area, my door is open.'

Not for the first time that day, Densara wondered what the man wanted. *I am being pounded like leather, made supple for later use.* He recognised the signs and decided that he would humour the taverna's owner. 'Your kindness is appreciated, Brascus. Hopefully I can repay it someday.'

'Think nothing of it, my friend. Come, let us eat.'

He followed Brascus through the door, the mouth-watering smells of roasted meats and fish making his stomach rumble. They had entered a much plainer room in the middle of which was a short, rectangular table filled with a spread of food. Brascus motioned Densara to settle himself upon one of the cushions scattered around the table and then clapped his hands before lowering himself onto a large one opposite the merchant. Two slaves walked in carrying jugs of wine, which they poured into goblets at the table.

'Are we dining alone?' asked Densara, surprised.

'In this instance, I have to say yes, I am afraid,' replied Brascus with sincerity. 'What I wish to discuss is not for the ears of my wife and daughters. If you would care to meet them, then you must join me later at the family home.'

'So, you don't live here, then?' enquired Densara, intrigued.

'We lived above the taverna until recently,' Brascus answered casually, handing a goblet of wine to the merchant. 'But with the girls getting older, we needed more space. I have now converted the upper level here into small rooms,' he said. 'The income from the extra whores pays for the house that we've moved into.'

Densara admired his host's thinking – it seemed the man had good sense when it came to exploiting an opening. The merchant sniffed his wine, its woody aroma instantly recognisable. Eager to taste the dark red Tarquinii, he held up his goblet. 'I have to toast your business sense, my friend. I can see why you are becoming so rich,' he laughed. Taking a sip, Densara savoured the smoky taste as memories of days long gone came flooding back. 'Exceptional,' he said, before taking another mouthful.

'Well, do not get too used to it,' laughed Brascus. 'There is a very limited supply these days. Hopefully, that should now change with the Etruscan trade agreement. I believe Prince Numitor is having some success there, but even so, there are no guarantees.'

'These things tend to sort themselves out in time,' Densara assured him. 'People need to build confidences and bridges again. Our previous conflicts have left both nations nervous.'

'Bridges are certainly needed,' replied Brascus, popping an olive into his mouth. 'The Etruscans burnt all the old ones down, denying us an easy route to their fantastic wine.' He smiled at his joke and spat the olive stone over his shoulder onto the floor.

The two men ate for a while, making light conversation. After his second piece of boar and at least a dozen crayfish tails, Densara casually asked, 'So tell me Brascus, what has got you so excited?'

Brascus finished chewing some peppered snails and swallowed quickly before replying. 'I have been talking with Prince Numitor recently. His wish to subdue the Samnites has provided me with an opportunity that will be extremely profitable, but I cannot handle it alone. I need your help.'

Densara considered the request. Much of his success had been acquired through the careful grooming of his associates, but in this instance he would have to rely on his instincts. Nevertheless, before he could commit to anything, he needed to hear more. 'I'm listening,' he said, urging the man to continue.

Putting down the plate of snails, Brascus sat back as he addressed the merchant. 'I understand that you tend to handle the sale of any slaves that Prince Amulius might happen to provide.'

Densara nodded. It was not a secret.

'Well,' continued Brascus, 'I have found buyers who wish to take as many slaves as I can supply. If you and I were to work together, we could both garnish a fortune, but only if we have enough slaves to sell, and somewhere large enough to hold them all before they're transported.'

Densara understood Brascus' concern for finding sufficient space for the holding of slaves. The merchant owned the largest compound in Latium and was able to hold hundreds of slaves at once. He guessed that Brascus would have only limited space so early on in his slaving career. 'How many are we talking about? Lots of traders have holding pens, so why would you need my help?'

'Normally I would handle this alone. However, I have people in Neopolis that are willing to pay double the usual price for any slaves I can provide – and they need thousands.'

'Whatever for?' exclaimed the merchant, his voice rising in surprise.

'It is because of the recent fall of Egypt to the Kushites of southern Nubia. They plan to rebuild their new country to its former glory,' Brascus replied, dryly. 'Unfortunately the invasion was so bloody that it left the country short of labour.' He shook his head in pity as he finished by saying, 'I hear they will even offer two Egyptian women in exchange for a male slave, if he can work.'

The merchant had been listening quietly, sipping his wine. He had already heard about the Egyptian war and its subsequent outcome. The Kingdom of Kush was bathed in riches, from the tales he had heard, but the new ruler of Egypt had begun to spend his new country's gold in abundance. It was a route to disaster for the ancient people, but Densara could see that the situation also represented a wealth of potential opportunities.

'So, we would be talking about my holding pens, and your boats,' he mused, nodding his head. 'I can see the sense of it, and if your contacts in Neopolis are really paying as much as you say, then I would be foolish to resist such an offer. However, I will need a little time to consider the matter as I still have obligations to our friends, the Gaganii.' He was referring to the noble family who owned the city's slave market.

Brascus smiled. 'I understand. I have also been considering the Gaganii. They have been fair in their dealings with me, so I was going to suggest that we supply the local market first and then ship out the unsold rather than keeping them until the next market – at least, until the supply begins to dwindle, as I'm sure it will before long. Such good fortune as this will not last.'

'It never does,' Densara shook his head. 'We must bake bread whilst the oven is hot.'

'Then, we have an agreement?' Brascus held his fist to his heart and waited for Densara to mimic the action, thus sealing the agreement.

Densara took a little time to consider the proposition before coming to a decision. He could see there was plenty of gold to be made, but of more importance would be the gaining of another trading partner who might prove to have additional uses. With a nod of his head, he smiled at Brascus. 'I think we can work together, and I am sure we will both profit greatly.'

Brascus lifted his goblet in a toast. 'Well then, if you have eaten enough, it is time for some entertainment!' He clapped his hands twice and whispered something to a servant who promptly left the room. A few moments later the servant returned, followed by five of the most beautiful women Densara had ever seen. They were all dressed in black wraps that contrasted strongly with their pale skin and golden hair. He had only ever seen a few light-haired women before, so to see five at once was highly unusual. As he looked at them, his gaze settled on one woman in particular. She was petite and her eyes were different colours: one brown and one green. His heart raced as he caught her look, the reaction taking him by surprise. Mesmerised by her beauty, he fought to look away but her eyes drew him back.

Brascus laughed at the merchant. 'Do not worry, my friend – Louisa has that effect on everyone. She is my second most profitable worker.'

'Only second?' Densara was almost offended for the girl.

Brascus nodded and beckoned one of the other girls to come forward. 'This is Helena.'

The whore, although pretty, did little for Densara. He watched with mild interest as Brascus patted her bottom, eliciting a giggle from the flirtatious girl. 'This one loves her work so much that even the ugliest customers leave here feeling special. She is a favourite of many of my patrons.' He winked at Densara. 'With girls like these, I can gain favour in the most influential of places.'

Densara laughed. 'You are full of surprises today, Brascus. I should have had an evening like this with you a long time ago. I haven't enjoyed myself so much in ages.'

'You are welcome, my friend. I can ask one of these lovelies to stay, if you wish?'

'Tempting,' the merchant replied, 'but I am already enjoying myself too much for further distractions. Let's talk more. I think I am going to enjoy doing business with you.' He glanced at Louisa again and turned back to his wine.

* * *

Puffing with exertion as he walked up the narrow streets back to the stables, Densara thought about the proposal. *Brascus has positioned himself well for a prosperous future.* It was much as Densara had done a few years earlier. *One thing is certain; I underestimated his intelligence and his potential.* He had grown fonder of the man as the evening had progressed. Densara decided he would keep a close eye on the trader from now on.

He guessed Amulius would be agreeable to the idea of earning more gold. *The prince is always obliging when it comes to making profit.* However, Densara was all too aware of the problems that could be caused by conducting business for both princes at once. *I will have to manoeuvre very carefully with this particular partnership,* he decided, *otherwise I could lose much more than gold.*

Chapter Fourteen

Numitor watched his daughter from the shadows of the atrium as she rose from her prayers. She prayed to honour her mother, and the prince knew that the ritual had now become an important part of her life, so he never disturbed her. Most evenings at sunset, Lillia would find a private spot, turn herself to face towards Lake Nemi and pray. Although he found her commitment admirable, Numitor also felt the whole thing was a little disturbing. *A girl of her age – almost a woman – needs more than gods and prayers.*

Lillia gave him much cause to be proud. For one so young, she had dealt very well with the death of her mother and her stillborn brother. *I wonder if the gods to whom she prays to so frequently have helped.* Considering the vibrant girl she had now grown into, he thought that maybe they had. She had a strong character, like her mother. She was fair, honest, and by far the most beautiful girl in all of Alba Longa. The prince tried to concede that it was just a father's pride talking, but he knew her beauty seemed to stun people when they first saw her. *They know not to stare for too long;* He thought, recalling a few instances when she had received too much attention for his liking.

When he was sure that Lillia had finished her prayers, Numitor made his way across the wide terrace. His daughter barely moved as he approached, and he wondered if she had been crying. However, Lillia gave such a start as he placed his hand on her shoulder that he concluded she had probably been daydreaming.

'Good evening, Lillia,' he said, smiling.

She let out a squeal and huffed. 'Father, you shouldn't creep up on me like that, you frightened me. I nearly joined Hades.'

Numitor laughed, then added playfully, 'And I could have been a Sabine kidnapper, ready to take you into a life of slavery.'

With a serious tone, Lillia retorted, 'They would not dare take a Princess of Latium.'

Numitor looked down onto the courtyard where the last of the day's chores were being completed by a handful of the villa's servants. Partly to himself, he whispered, 'We must always be vigilant, my love. One can never tell what dangers may be awaiting.'

'Are you troubled, Father?' Lillia asked, concern on her young face.

He looked up and studied his daughter for a few moments. She could have been destroyed by all she had lost, but instead she was now growing into a fine young woman: tall and graceful, just like her mother had been. She had the same long, dark curls that teased the side of her face as she moved, and she bore the Grecian look of her family's ancestors. Since the days of Troy, the kings of Latium had tried to keep the bloodline clean, choosing their spouses from the original twelve noble families whenever possible. Lillia's grandmother had been an exception: she came from a Sabine tribe. Lillia had thus acquired a unique look, her blue eyes and high cheekbones giving her an exotic appearance. Numitor felt a twinge of sadness as he acknowledged that she would eventually leave him. The time to choose her a husband was drawing near. *Perhaps no one will be able to afford the dowry I set*, he mused wishfully, but he knew in his heart that he would have his child for only two or three more years, and then she would no longer be his little girl.

'Father?' The princess put her hand on his arm. 'You were staring.'

He smiled. 'Just pensive, my dear. There is much to think about these days.'

'Are you worried about the Samnites?' she asked. 'I'm sure Uncle Amulius will conquer them.'

Lillia was perceptive – he was indeed worried. He knew all too well the ambition of Amulius. Numitor understood that it would never be enough for his brother to share the responsibilities of ruling. Yet, these were not worries that he was prepared to share with his daughter. She seemed so grown up, but nevertheless, politics was not an arena for women or children. 'You always see things with such innocence, Lillia. You need to remember that there are some matters you cannot hope to understand yet.' Then, with a slight smile, he added, 'You should not concern yourself with Amulius and the Samnites. You have far more important things to think about.' He raised an eyebrow, teasing her. 'Such as the feast I wish to throw in honour of King Corros of Etruria.'

Lillia's expression changed instantly, her eyes now wide with excitement. 'When are we having it?' Numitor opened his mouth to answer but Lillia was not finished. 'Are we having it at the palace? We must have dancers; one of those Grecian fire-eaters; I have to invite Sylvanna and have a new dress made...,' she paused and looked up at him expectantly.

Numitor chuckled as his daughter once again became the child. 'Yes to everything, Lillia, and more, if I can arrange it all in time.' With a serious expression, he added, 'Of course, I will be relying on your help with the organising of everything, if we are to be ready in twenty days.'

'Twenty days!' she shrieked. 'That's too soon, Father – there is so much to do.' She started to count something out on her fingers. Frowning, she said, 'No, we won't have enough time to prepare.'

'Do not worry, my dear,' Numitor replied, placing his hands on her shoulders to stop her from pacing. 'I already have most of it in hand. It will be a feast to remember, and you will be the best-dressed girl there. I have already arranged for someone to visit you in the morning with a selection of the finest of fabrics from which you are to choose your outfit.'

'Oh thank you, Father,' Lillia cried, throwing her arms around his neck in a tight embrace. 'I must go and tell Nima to make me the finest dress in Latium. I will make you so proud.' She gave him a kiss on the cheek and ran into the villa, the slaps of her sandals echoing on the marble tiles.

* * *

The next few weeks were the busiest Lillia could remember. Although she had a flotilla of servants at her beck and call, she preferred to involve herself in the preparations for the feast. She liaised with Lucius, letting him note all the costs and arrange payments. She also made numerous trips back and forth between the palace, the city and the villa. After the fourth such trip on a single day, the journey started to drag her down. Going downhill was fine, but the trek back up became exhausting. She made use of the servants to find and fetch supplies for the banquet, although she would arrange and barter for the goods herself. There was fresh meat to be organised. Most of it would come from the palace stock, so Lillia sent the head cook, Giovannus, to talk to the shepherds and pig herders in person. Meanwhile, beef would be coming from the lowlands, and hunters had been dispatched to capture deer, boars, badgers, birds, and hare from the surrounding countryside.

Whilst she busied herself with the cooks to source vegetables and fruit from the palace stores, she sent runners to the fish merchants who were instructed to provide sturgeon and shellfish. The sturgeon were sourced from villages further west in the lowlands. The shellfish came from the town of Ostus, which was set on the edge of a natural harbour, and was famed for its mussels, clams and urchins. However, it was a two-day journey by cart, and in hot weather it was hard to keep the jars of brine cool enough to prevent the shellfish from cooking.

To make matters rather more difficult for Lillia, Numitor had invited a further one hundred guests. Suddenly she was required to source more food and organise more accommodation. To add to her frustrations, she had also needed to make an extra trip into Alba Longa to speak with the main wine merchant, Faro Tulii, and arrange the purchase of another twenty amphorae of his best wine. Subsequently, only fifteen amphorae were delivered to the palace, resulting in Lillia having to make a second trip to see the large man. His excuse was that his supplies were running low, owing to fewer grapes having been produced the previous summer. At this point, Lillia had become annoyed and reminded him that her father may decide to appoint a more forthcoming wine merchant at any time. Faro had been rendered speechless. Lillia worried that she may have pushed him too far, but he had immediately backed down and promised delivery for later that day.

That afternoon, a further seven amphorae of wine arrived. A message from Faro explained that the additional two amphorae were a personal gift and an exceptionally special vintage, fit for a king. When Lillia told Numitor what had transpired, he had laughed aloud. 'You know how to use your wits. Those extra two are a rare wine that comes from Neopolis.' He chuckled. 'It is the best wine you will find this side of Greece. It came from his personal stock.' The prince shook his head in wonder. 'An army would have been troubled to relieve him of even one amphora. Yet, my daughter has managed two,' he stated with pride.

Lillia glowed under the praise.

Some of the princess' time had been devoted to the making of her dress. Nima had promised Lillia the best outfit she would ever own, so the princess had taken to stopping by in between errands, offering a measurement or choosing a pattern for a section of embroidery. On one of her trips into the city, she visited the forge to collect some gold wire that had been requested by Nima. When Lillia had asked her why it was needed, Nima replied, "Because if I used bronze wire, it would not be a dress fit for a princess." That was all Lillia had been able to get out of her. The princess knew she would not get an answer even if she demanded one, so she had let the matter drop, trusting that Nima would not let her down.

One decision that Lillia did have to make, however, was the choosing of a design for the main embroidery that would decorate the front of her dress. Her first thought was that it should feature her favourite animal, a deer, but then she thought that perhaps a swan would look good. After changing her mind three times, she decided in the end to opt for an eagle to honour her father, knowing that it would please him.

* * *

It was only a few days until the feast, and Lillia was worn out. She felt in urgent need of a break. She had woken early that morning, just as the first rays of sunshine were warming the villa's high turrets. After breakfast, she had gone down to the cellars and put some food into a basket before bidding Nima farewell.

Lillia was allowed to visit her closest friend, Sylvanna, in the nearby village of Vilini without having to be accompanied by guards. Her father had granted her this freedom some time ago. Her only requirement was to inform the villa guards before leaving. Having spoken to the guards, Lillia now made her way down the winding pathway that offered the most direct route to the city, though the descent was steep. She had decided that she would take the longer route to Sylvanna's village, so she branched off from the path about halfway down and walked through trees for a short while, before coming out into the meadow beyond. The village of Vilini was to the south-west of the lake. There was another path that would have taken her there, but she would have encountered too many people along the way. Her chosen route was further to walk, but at least it was peaceful.

Lillia loved the meadows and the quiet that they offered. At the villa and the palace there was always someone around, and she would find herself longing for some time alone with her thoughts. This route to Vilini would give her that. It would take her half the morning to get there, by which time she would be hot enough to welcome the cool waters of Lake Albano for a lazy swim with her friend.

For the first time in days Lillia felt calm. The warmth of the morning sun felt good on her bare arms as a slight breeze tugged at her hair. Winding her way along the trail, she surprised an occasional bird and watched rabbits dart into the bushes. Her only other company were the bees that buzzed around the trees.

Leaving the trail, Lillia started making her way across the sloping meadow. Looking up, she saw a young shepherd further up the slope who seemed to be staring at her. He had broad shoulders and a thick mass of black, curly hair. He smiled at Lillia, and she felt the heat coming to her face as she shyly looked down and stepped up her pace, stealing a quick glance back at the handsome stranger.

I have never seen him before, she thought to herself. *I wonder if Sylvanna knows who he is*. Lillia had never really taken an interest in boys until recently, but her friend had become obsessed with one particular lad, Jason, whom she had met at a feast. For the first time the princess began to understand the attraction, given the way that the shepherd had just caused her to feel. As her embarrassment rose again, she tried to put the thoughts out of her mind.

Over the meadows, the sun rose higher in the sky and Lillia started to feel beads of perspiration forming on her side and back with the rising heat of the morning. When she came to the end of the trail, she made her way down towards the lightly wooded area to the south of the lake.

Beginning to feel thirsty, she decided to make a small detour towards the beech woods where she knew there was a spring with cool water. She preferred the thought of the spring to the idea of drinking from the water-skin in her basket which would have warmed in the heat.

Rounding a small, rocky outcrop, Lillia came to a sudden stop as something ahead caught her eye, making her stare in surprise. Out of the woods emerged two small, round, grey shapes. They tottered down towards the spring, play-fighting as they went. At first, she thought they must be badgers or stoats, but as they got closer she was surprised to see that they were wolf cubs. The princess giggled as they rolled through the long grass, jumping over each other with small barks of delight, but her joy very quickly turned to fear as she spotted a much bigger wolf coming up behind them.

Lillia guessed it must be the mother, and she realised that she would be in danger if the she-wolf spotted her there. Her father had told her many times that most wild animals ignored people if they did not feel threatened. However, a mother with young was always dangerous. The princess cautiously crept back behind the outcrop and crouched, only partially hidden, watching as the she-wolf took the cubs to the water.

The creature suddenly paused mid-stride and looked for signs of danger, sniffing the air with one foot lifted. Lillia immediately became conscious of the dried meat that she carried in her basket. She silently prayed that the distance would be enough to hide any smells.

I haven't even got anything I can use to protect myself, she cursed inwardly. *Not even a stick!* She quickly glanced around. *There are no sticks here. I can only hope it won't notice me.* She tried to calm herself as her gasps became more rapid and her heart began to race.

Wolves are usually in packs! She suddenly remembered and began looking around frantically to see if there were any more approaching. She scanned the tree-line beyond the spring but could see nothing moving or unusual. Satisfied that the she-wolf was alone, Lillia returned her gaze to the cubs.

When they reached the spring, the two cubs immediately jumped in with small excited yips as they continued to play, occasionally lapping up some of the water. The mother lowered her head down to the clear spring, ever attentive to her surroundings. When she had drunk her fill, the she-wolf jumped the small rivulet and slowly headed toward the outcrop where the princess continued to hide. Lillia fixed her sight on the adult, her fear rising.

The she-wolf sniffed the air again, stopping as it picked up Lillia's scent. It began to growl, looking directly at the outcrop. As it came closer Lillia froze in terror, clueless as to what she should do.

Then a thought came to the princess. *I am sure it can smell the meat. Maybe I can throw it at the wolf and make my escape while it's busy eating.*

Praying the plan would work, she quickly lifted the cloth that covered her basket and unpacked the pieces of dried meat. Standing up slowly she prepared to throw the meat, but before she could act, the she-wolf locked eyes with her and sprang forward with such speed that Lillia screamed and threw the meat up into the air. She turned to run and, looking back over her shoulder, saw the wolf bounding towards her. Then suddenly it was in the air, its teeth bared into a snarl as it filled Lillia's vision. She tripped and hit the ground screaming, her arms raised to protect herself.

Expecting to be savaged at any moment, she closed her eyes as terror overcame her – but the attack never came. Instead, she heard a loud noise like the crack of a whip, followed by a yelp, and then someone shouting, 'Get away. Get away.' The princess opened her eyes cautiously and saw that there was someone in between her and the ferocious beast. Moving her hands away from her face to see properly, she realised it was the handsome shepherd.

He turned to look at Lillia, determination in his strong face as he instructed her, 'Stay behind me, Princess. I won't let it anywhere near you, I promise – if it dare come back for another taste of my staff,' he added.

Lillia stayed silent, too shocked to do anything but nod her head quickly and take large gulps of air as the young man stood guard. She gently eased herself up and craned her neck to see above the rocks and plants, spotting the she-wolf on the other side of the spring, reunited with its cubs. The shepherd watched the wolves, and Lillia noticed how his defensive hold upon his long staff caused his arms to bulge.

'It's gone now,' her rescuer finally announced in a deep voice. 'It won't be back.'

Lillia heaved a sigh of relief and muttered a quick prayer of thanks to Zeus as she looked at the shepherd, who was now close enough to offer her a hand. She accepted the help and started to get up, but tripped again, falling into the shepherd's arms as she felt an ache in her lower back.

'Are you hurt?' asked the young man with a look of concern in his kind eyes.

'I am fine,' she replied with a half-smile as she steadied herself on his bare arm. 'I think I hit a stone or something when I fell. It is a little sore that is all.' Still holding his arm, she pulled herself up again. 'Thank you,' she said as she let go and tested her balance. 'You saved me. If you had not come…' *I would be dead now,* she thought, but she could not bring herself to say it aloud, and immediately burst into tears.

Unsure what to do for the distressed girl, the shepherd looked around as if hoping to spot someone who could help. He scratched behind his ear and took a tentative step forward, cautiously putting his large hand on Lillia's shoulder to try and comfort her. 'It's fine,' he whispered gently. 'It won't hurt you now.'

'I know, I'll be all right,' she spluttered in between sobs. *What must I look like,* she berated herself, avoiding his eyes. Then she found herself talking again, trying to explain. 'It's just… I was so scared, and I thought… I was going to die. Then you came… and I hurt my back, and now I'm going to be late for Sylvanna's…' She continued to sob for a few more moments before calming herself down. 'I am so rude. I do not even know your name,' she said between sniffles, and wiped her teary cheeks as she waited for his reply.

'I am Marcus, son of Colradus,' he answered, bowing his head to Lillia.

Lillia wiped away the remaining tears and brushed aside a lock of hair that was obscuring her eye, and she was rewarded with her first proper look at the shepherd's suntanned face. He had bright, inquisitive brown eyes beneath a strong brow with thick dark eyebrows. Although his face looked young, there was plenty of stubble around his square chin, giving the impression of someone older. 'Marcus,' she repeated, 'I am Lillia, and I must thank you again for helping me.'

Looking a little confused, Marcus scratched his curly hair. 'I thought you were Princess Rhea, I was sure you were.'

'I am Princess Rhea, Marcus. I am Lillia to my family and friends,' she finished shyly.

'Then you must forgive me, Your Highness, I didn't mean to doubt you,' he replied nervously.

'Oh no, you must not call me that, Marcus. You saved me and, for that reason, you will always be my friend. My friends call me Lillia,' she insisted.

Marcus laughed, 'I will call you Lillia then, if it pleases Your Highness.'

It was Lillia's turn to laugh. She noticed how his face lit up when he smiled. Feeling a little heat coming to her cheeks again she turned away slightly and stated, 'I will make sure you are properly rewarded for helping me, Marcus. My father will be happy to pay you for what you did.'

At the mention of her father, Marcus lost his smile. 'You do not need to do that, Your High... Lillia.' He looked around apprehensively.

'What is the matter?' she asked with genuine concern.

'It is nothing, really,' he answered quickly. 'It's just my father said I should stay away from the palace, lest your uncle force me into his army.'

It was Lillia's turn to be confused as she replied, 'I am not sure what you mean, Marcus.'

'The prince has been sending his men to the villages to recruit for his army, and... well, my parents are old and they need me to watch the flock, or else they would starve.'

'The war on Samnium,' remembered Lillia. 'We are going to stop them attacking our villages. Well, not everyone can go and fight, and we do need shepherds,' she said eagerly. 'I would not let Uncle Amulius take you, Marcus. My father would see to it,' she said defiantly.

Marcus' smile returned. 'Where are you going, Princess Lillia? Maybe I can walk with you – just to protect you from any wolves,' he added quickly.

'I'm on my way to Vilini, to see my friend,' she replied, looking nervously towards the spring. The wolves were no longer in sight, but she was eager not to be left alone and found herself nodding in agreement. 'That would be very kind of you, if you do not mind,' she said. 'Although, I could do with having a drink first.'

Giving her a glowing smile, Marcus gestured toward the spring. 'I don't mind at all, Princess. I will enjoy the company.'

* * *

On arriving at Vilini, Lillia stopped and waved to Marcus, who had accompanied her to the edge of the village. She then headed for the biggest of the houses that overlooked the lake. Her mind returned to the conversation she'd had with the shepherd as they walked together. He had made her laugh with his quick quips and stories of the people in his village. His friendly nature and his good looks had made a deep impression on the princess, and an image of his handsome face now shone inside her head, making her smile as she walked.

People wandered by, greeting the princess with a polite nod or smile. Lillia was well-known from her many visits to Vilini and she felt comfortable among the villagers, who enjoyed their connection to the royal family. This connection was exploited in particular by Sylvanna's father, Paridé. As the head of the village, he had gained further status as a result of his daughter's friendship with the princess, and he had gone on to become good friends with Prince Numitor.

Knocking softly on the door of her friend's house, Lillia waited patiently as she listened to the locking bar being lifted from behind. It was Sylvanna who opened the door and, upon seeing Lillia, she let out a happy shriek. 'Lillia, I wasn't expecting you today,' she said, with a concerned look now on her face. 'Have I forgotten an arrangement we had?'

Lillia laughed, 'No, you have not forgotten anything, Sylla. I was just getting weary of all the arrangements for the feast and I needed a distraction. Do you fancy a swim?'

'Well, all the morning's chores have been done, I suppose,' Sylvanna replied. 'I think a swim would be wonderful. I'll need to get a few things first, though.' Suddenly Sylvanna gasped. 'What must you think of me, Lillia? Please come in, you must be parched. Would you like some honey-water?'

'I am fine, thank you,' smiled Lillia. After entering the building and sitting herself down, the princess proceeded to tell her friend all about her terrifying encounter with the wolves.

'We must tell Papa,' said Sylvanna when the other girl had finished her tale. 'If there are wolves around, then the other shepherds must be warned.' Sylvanna giggled as she caught the flush on Lillia's face at the mention of shepherds. 'I'll admit he is a handsome one, that boy Marcus, but much too lowly for a princess.'

'I know he is,' acknowledged Lillia with regret, 'but if I could get father to bestow a title on him...' she said, smiling at her brave attempt to make light of the matter. 'Well, I am allowed to dream, aren't I?'

Sylvanna started to reply but was interrupted by the arrival of her father, Paridé. He was wiping his hands on a rag as his athletic figure entered the room. 'Princess Rhea,' he bellowed in surprise. 'A royal visit!'

The amused girls giggled.

'For what honour are you gracing us with your presence, Your Highness?' he jested with an elaborate bow. 'I have prepared nothing with which to feed you, and I have sent away all the nobles who were waiting here to offer you their hands in marriage. I felt none of them were good enough.'

Lillia laughed. 'Please do not call me that, Paridé. In private I am Lillia. I do not feel like a highness at the moment, and I certainly do not want to be married just yet.'

'Nevertheless,' he said, adopting a more serious tone, 'that time is not so far away, either for you or for my own daughter.' He turned to Sylvanna.

Uncomfortable with the direction that the conversation had taken, Sylvanna promptly changed the subject. 'Papa, Lillia saw some wolves on the way here this morning. One of them even attacked her!'

Paridé turned back to Lillia with a face full of concern. 'Are you hurt? Tell me what happened.' He beckoned her to sit at the table with him.

Lillia told the story of her encounter once again. Paridé listened quietly, asking questions only occasionally. When she had finished, he sat for a moment to let the information sink in. 'I will send some men to check that the wolves have gone. It will not be safe for you to return alone when you go home later, so I will send two of my men with you.'

'That is very kind of you, but not at all necessary,' replied Lillia. 'I will stick to the main path when I return. I shall be perfectly safe.'

'I must insist, Lillia – there will be no argument on this occasion. Your father would have me flayed if anything were to happen to you on your homeward journey.'

Lillia conceded. 'That is kind of you, Paridé, but first I had hoped to spend the afternoon by the lake with Sylla. Would that be all right?'

'Of course it is, Your Highness,' he said, returning to his mocking tone.

Lillia smiled. 'Well Sylla, we should be going before we lose the best of the day.'

* * *

Later that day, after spending a wonderful afternoon bathing and chatting, the two girls arrived back at Vilini to find a large gathering at the centre of the village. Making their way through the small crowd, they stopped when they came to Paridé. He stood with his back to them, and Lillia could see he was deep in conversation with three other men. 'What of the mother?' she heard him enquire.

'I couldn't get near her,' one of the men replied. 'These two were easy enough – got 'em with me bow – but the mother scarpered before I could get another shot off.'

As he spoke, the man stepped aside and there, laid out on a bench, were the bodies of the two wolf cubs Lillia had seen earlier. The princess let out a stifled cry upon seeing them and turned on the man. 'Why did they have to be killed? They were only cubs.'

Paridé answered on behalf of the shocked hunter. 'They would have been grown soon enough, Princess Rhea,' he said loudly. 'It is just a shame that we were not able to get the mother today as well, but we will have her shortly.'

On mention of the mother, Lillia welled up. 'What have I done?' she said quietly, looking at the dead cubs. 'They were only babies.' She fought back more tears.

Seeing Lillia's anguish, Sylvanna spoke softly to her friend. 'They would have grown, Lillia, and then they could have hurt someone. It is better this way.'

Nodding sadly in acceptance, Lillia allowed her friend to lead her away. Paridé had arranged for two men to escort the princess back to the villa, but she chose to follow the men along the path slowly with her head down. As they crossed the meadow, she caught sight of Marcus watching from a distance. She waved to him and smiled when he returned the gesture. The princess then daydreamed about him all the way back to the villa, all further thought of the two cubs quickly forgotten.

Chapter Fifteen

Prince Amulius arrived at the palace on the night of the feast as the sun was setting. He would have gladly missed the festivities had it not been for Numitor's insistence that he attend. The prince handed the reins of his horse to a groom, and as he did so, one of the waiting slaves quickly ran to the side of the black horse and dropped to a curl, offering the prince an easy step down. As he approached the courtyards and gardens, Amulius could hear the chaotic sounds of talk and laughter mingling with light music, and his nostrils detected the aroma of roasting meat. Stopping next to one of the guards, he studied the scene before him.

The terrace that overlooked the gardens was usually bare, furnished only with a few benches and statues, but now it had been transformed into the most luxurious of settings in which comfort had been given priority. Taking his time to descend the wide stone steps to the gardens, the prince saw that small tables were scattered around the mosaicked floors, each laden with silver dishes that were overflowing with a huge variety of foods. Piles of clams and mussels cooked in wine were presented alongside whole roast pigs and boiled lambs' heads. He could see that his brother had spared no expense, and the guests certainly seemed to be making the most of it. The majority of them were lounging on large, comfortable cushions that had been positioned around the area to create an entertainment space in its centre. *My foolish brother thinks he can win favour with food and music*, reflected the prince as he spotted the wide, raised platform at the other side of the large courtyard that hosted King Corros and his entourage.

The Etruscans were easily identified by their unusually colourful robes and the long golden chains that were draped around their necks and arms. Even the king's personal servants wore impressive garments embellished with intricate silver-threaded designs. The prince scoffed at the shameless display of opulence. *I should take all their gold and skin them alive for daring to set foot in my country,* he thought as he considered what he could do with the wealth of these foreigners. He could see that their riches were well protected by two muscular Etruscan guards that stood to attention at either side of the platform; their tall iron spears matched their pointed helmets, and they held large shields that covered most of their bodies. The king was dressed in green robes, his head balancing a thick golden crown inlaid with rubies and emeralds that glittered in the torchlight. Amulius stared at the Etruscan crown with envy, his own desire for power staying his gaze for several moments.

The prince finally lowered his eyes, his fists clenched at his sides, and he took a few calming breaths before deciding to delay his greetings to the royal visitors. Instead he headed through the noisy crowd, welcoming one or two other guests along the way. He noticed that large, thin drapes had been erected around the courtyard to create separate areas that would provide privacy for those who might require it. Amulius knew that much use would be made of these areas as the festivities wore on. He glanced at a group of semi-naked girls who were milling around one of the fountains. They had evidently been chosen for their desirability and their seductive powers, and each would have been instructed to encourage their admirers to talk – as a result of this arrangement, Amulius would eventually gain snippets of information that might prove to be of use at a later date.

With so many people present, it was a while before the prince spotted his brother. Numitor was standing next to a statue of Hercules that loomed over one of the small fishponds at the edge of the courtyard. Amulius smiled at what he saw as being an ironic contradiction between the statue and his brother: *while one was a great hero of legend, the other was a mere pretender to the throne!* Pleased with his improvised quip, he began to make his way over to the statue.

Amulius eased his way through the disorderly crowd, nodding politely to occasional dignitaries who insisted upon seizing the moment to offer greetings and invitations. The prince loathed these false pleasantries. These pathetic attempts to gain favour served only to make him despise the people he helped to rule. *But they will all have their uses, eventually,* he thought, imagining the day he would become king.

While returning yet another greeting, Amulius noticed the wife of a noble eyeing him with inviting promise. He shuddered inwardly as his treacherous mind compared her to the pig roasting on a spit next to her. The image brought an involuntary smile to his face, which unfortunately seemed to be taken by the woman as a sign of possible future acceptance. The prince quickly turned away, grabbing a goblet of wine from a passing servant, and continued to wind his way over to his brother.

As he drew nearer, he saw that Numitor was deep in conversation with General Agrillis. They both wore bright white togas edged in gold thread, and yet Agrillis seemed strangely out of place without his usual military tunic. His cropped white hair almost matched the brilliance of the toga, and the prince pondered on the age of the man. *He should have retired when father died*, thought Amulius, who had always felt that Agrillis was little more than his brother's keeper. When the general looked up and saw Amulius approaching, his discussion with Numitor came to an abrupt stop. Annoyed and curious as to the nature of their hastily concluded whispers, Amulius hid his irritation by raising his goblet to Numitor. 'My compliments on your efforts, Brother. It seems you have thrown a feast fit for a king.' The statement was loaded with deeper meaning. 'And the good general,' he said, turning to Agrillis with a mock salute. 'How smart you look, and all on a warrior's pay!'

The general ignored the jibe, promptly replying in his gruff voice, 'I thought it would be appropriate to make an effort on such an important occasion, Your Highness.' He eyed Amulius up and down to make his point.

Amulius had dressed completely in black, with a simple tunic over a tight shirt and leggings. His usual black leather boots completed the outfit. He returned Agrillis' look with a scowl as he scratched the back of his neck, but his retort was interrupted when Numitor cut in.

'Come, gentlemen,' Numitor said, 'let us not argue tonight. We are here to enjoy good food, good wine, and good company.' He turned to his brother. 'Have you eaten yet, Amulius? I had the cooks make up some of your favourite dishes. This feast is, after all, costing us both.' He fixed his brother with a hard stare and waited.

Amulius relaxed his shoulders in feigned acceptance of the situation and stroked his beard. 'Of course, you are right, Numitor.' Smiling, he said, 'Come, Brother, guide me through this fine spread so that I can begin to enjoy our hospitality. I am sure I noticed some stuffed sparrows on a table over there.' *I may as well get my money's worth*, he finished silently. Turning his back on Agrillis, he put his arm around Numitor's shoulders and, without a second thought for the general, led his brother away.

* * *

'I think it is high time you met King Corros, Brother,' Numitor announced.

Amulius swallowed a mouthful of roasted dormouse, washing it down with wine before replying. 'I have every intention of meeting him. I simply wish to attend to the needs of my empty stomach first.' There was humour in his voice.

'Well, all I ask is that you do not do anything to embarrass the country, Amulius – we need this alliance with the Etruscans, now more than ever. And it would certainly not be prudent to have yet another enemy at our borders.'

Amulius took a bite from a spear of asparagus. Chewing as he spoke, he said, 'I am with you on this one, Brother. Do not worry. I can see the sense of the trade-route agreement. It will generate much wealth for us. So many of our merchants are robbed and set upon at present. It will be a wise move to protect these routes and bring more trade to Latium.'

'So, are you going to apologise to King Corros, then?' asked Numitor as his brother took another sip of wine.

Nearly spitting the wine back into the goblet, Amulius glared at the older prince. 'Are you jesting, Brother?' His mood had changed in a moment.

'It would be a wise thing to do, Amulius. It would go a long way to gaining their trust,' Numitor spoke in serious tones.

'I will never apologise for my actions, Brother. You know this, so why must you push?'

Numitor shrugged. 'I had hoped that you might be willing to put the Kingdom first for a change, instead of focusing only upon your own pride.'

Amulius shook his head in defiant disagreement with his brother's request. He felt that he had been justified in his actions towards the Etruscans during their competition fifteen years previously. Admittedly, it had not won him the crown, but it had at least denied his brother the throne whilst also gaining Amulius the rule of half the kingdom – which was a lot more than he had started out with. Numitor was waiting patiently now, his hands folded in front of him, and Amulius' eye was drawn to his brother's ring. Unconsciously, he brought his own hand up to the scar on his cheek, and into his mind flashed a memory of how it had been acquired. Ignoring Numitor's glance, he finally offered his reply. 'I will speak to King Corros and make amends, Brother. But I will not apologise.'

Numitor had no choice but to concede with a nod, and it was at this point that Brascus walked up to the pair, also wearing a toga. The older prince felt a moment of discomfort at the man's approach, now that he had come to suspect his former mentor was possibly a member of the secret organisation he was trying to investigate. Numitor had decided that he would not confront Brascus with his beliefs until he had more information. So, with a warm smile he addressed the man in his friendliest tones. 'Brascus, I did not recognise you for a moment. I cannot remember ever having seen you in a toga.'

Brascus looked down sheepishly. 'Felicia insisted,' he shook his head in wonder. 'She feels that a noble representing the Julii family should dress appropriately. Wives!' he laughed.

'It takes more than a toga to make a noble,' sniped Amulius.

'Yes, the family name also helps,' smiled Brascus, not bothered in the least by Amulius' jibe.

The younger prince ignored the retort and an uneasy silence followed. After a few moments, Numitor turned to his old mentor. 'Brascus, you must excuse us. You have joined us just as we were about to go and sit with King Corros. I will come and talk with you a little later.' He gestured to his brother to lead the way.

As the older prince climbed the few steps onto the platform, King Corros looked up and smiled. 'Ah, Prince Numitor, I see you have brought someone to meet me.' He glanced at Amulius, who had the good grace to bow upon reaching the king.

'It is a pleasure, Your Highness,' stated Amulius before Numitor could begin the introductions. 'I welcome you to my country and hope you find our hospitality to be satisfactory. I am Prince Amulius,' he smiled at the Etruscan leader.

'Yes, Prince Amulius…' the king nodded his bald head in recognition of the name. 'Well, the hospitality certainly has improved since the last time I crossed your borders.' Corros laughed as he leant back into his cushions. Accepting a fresh goblet of wine from one of the servants, he exclaimed with apparent joy, 'I believe it was you who was responsible for that little welcome, if I am not mistaken.'

'You are not, Sire,' replied the prince, continuing to smile, 'but please do not take it personally – it could have happened to anyone. I was merely doing what I thought best to protect my interests at the time. Of course, with the benefit of hindsight, I now see that it was but a childish error of judgment. I sent in far too few men.'

Numitor gasped in horror. 'Amulius!' he growled.

King Corros let out a loud hearty laugh. 'It is fine, Numitor,' he said. 'I appreciate your brother's sense of humour. And he is quite right – he did send in far too few men to overcome my riders.'

His brother's rudeness had left Numitor fighting to control his rising anger, but seeing the king take it in good humour, he quietly let it all out with a deep breath.

'I promise I will not make the same mistake again, Your Highness, lest I dishonour your fine guards,' said Amulius, gesturing to the muscle-bound men nearby. 'They look very impressive.' Continuing to smile, the prince lowered himself onto a cushion next to King Corros and encouraged Numitor to do likewise. 'Let us talk about this trade agreement that my brother is so eager to implement. I do believe that there is much profit to be made by both sides.'

Relieved that Amulius was beginning to take the meeting seriously, Numitor took the opportunity to seize control of the conversation and commented, 'Yes, in fact, even more profit than we first realised, Brother.' Smiling at King Corros, he continued. 'It seems our two countries have much more in common than wine and slaves.'

The three men conversed for some time, Amulius surprising his brother by becoming the perfect diplomat as he discussed everything from bridge crossings to leather manufacture – something for which the Etruscans were famed. The prince's own boots were made from leather purchased in Corros' hometown of Veii. After a while, Amulius excused himself and left Numitor alone with the king. As the older prince watched his brother thread through the guests, he felt relief that the first encounter between the two men had gone so well.

'He is an interesting character, your brother,' remarked Corros as Numitor turned back to face him.

'Yes. I apologise if he offended you with his sharp tongue. Amulius does not communicate well.' The prince lowered his eyes and swirled his wine around the goblet before taking a sip.

'On the contrary, Numitor,' assured the king. 'He expresses himself very clearly. You should take great care with him. He is far more dangerous to you than he is to me.'

Numitor was surprised by this observation and did not know how best to reply, so he simply shook his head in resignation.

'By the way, did you find my gift to be of interest?' asked Corros, referring to the old chest.

'Yes,' replied Numitor, 'it was fascinating – from an historical point of view,' he added quickly, not wanting to give anything away about his suspicions.

The king laughed as he passed his empty goblet to a servant and accepted a full one in return. 'More than fascinating, I should say,' he commented, 'and perhaps not quite as historical as you assume.'

Intrigued by the remark, Numitor guessed that the king must have read the contents of the chest – at least the Latin texts. He doubted that Corros or any of his people would have the ability to read the ancient Trojan words. The prince had learnt much from the documents, leading him to begin research into other avenues. Alba Longa had a long tradition of keeping records, and these had begun to provide Numitor with clues to secrets that might relate to the mysterious man that had rescued him. Nevertheless, many of his investigations had led to dead ends, leaving him with unsolved riddles. 'Do you happen to know, Your Highness, where the chest originally came from?' he asked.

'I honestly do not, Numitor. But I read much of its contents, and it was more enlightening than you know.'

'I do not understand, Sire. How was it enlightening?'

The king looked Numitor in the eye. 'You really do need to be careful, Numitor. You are a good man. I thought that the first time we met, and I suspect you would make a fine king for Latium. However, I fear your destiny is not your own, and I have reason to suspect that you are being manipulated by people beyond your control.' Corros then pulled out a leather bundle from behind him and handed it to the speechless prince before continuing. 'In there are letters that were part of the chest's contents. I was divided in my opinion as to whether I should give them to you. They answer many questions that are posed by the various writings and accounts that were left inside the chest. Having met your brother and seen for myself the hatred in his eyes, I would want you to have every advantage you can.'

Numitor accepted the bundle and quickly hid it in a fold of his toga. He felt a kinship with Corros, and sensed that he had an ally in the man. 'I am most grateful for this, Sire. Any advantage I can get is appreciated, but may I ask, why are you doing this for me? You gave me the chest before you had even met Amulius.'

'I met Amulius fifteen years ago, not man to man, but through his actions. Today only confirmed my belief that he is a dangerous enemy to have and, I fear, an even more dangerous brother.' Corros craned his head to whisper in Numitor's ear. 'Some serpents are known to eat their siblings.'

Numitor laughed at the analogy, trying to cover his true feelings – the king's words had cut him deeply.

***

As the evening wore on, the guests took great pleasure in drinking and eating their fill. Adding to their enjoyment was the abundance of entertainers that Numitor had provided. Those who watched the performers found themselves joining in with claps and cheers. Meanwhile, other guests retreated into small groups and chatted amongst themselves, their actions animated by wine. An announcement informed the guests that there was about to be a special performance from the House of Vesta, and a buzz of excitement spread around the feast: this was a rare treat. Eventually, the guests quietened in readiness for the beginning of the evening's highlight.

Lillia watched from the edge of the courtyard, gazing in awe as a procession of graceful dancers glided and twirled into the performance area. She became mesmerised as the seven beautiful women began to trail their white shawls in concentric circles around their heads and bodies. To the deep, pounding beat of large drums, their movements became increasingly enticing and suggestive, punctuated with high, tiptoed kicks and leaps of almost acrobatic agility.

A collective gasp escaped from the crowd as one of the dancers deftly back-flipped over her companion to land at the feet of another. The ingenious choreography managed to give the impression of an attacking lioness in the throes of a kill. The dance grew in momentum, with the music of reed flutes and stringed citharas adding to the intensity. The crowd clapped along to the accelerating beat of the drums until finally, with a shriek, the dancers collapsed in a heap and the music abruptly stopped. Then, with anticipation hanging in the air, the women rose slowly from the floor, their movements gentle yet purposeful.

Lillia loved the exotic flavour of the dance, and for a moment she wished that she could move with the same grace and elegance as these pretty young dancers. When the performance ended, the guests roared with appreciation. Lillia clapped vigorously and turned to speak with Sylvanna, who had been watching beside her.

To the princess' annoyance, she found that her friend was busy talking with an unfamiliar boy. Lillia started to walk away, irritated that Sylvanna had missed the performance. The boy glanced up and nudged her friend, who turned and, upon seeing the princess, quickly grabbed her hand. 'Oh Lillia, please forgive my rudeness,' she spoke hurriedly. 'I must introduce you to Jason: he is from Lavinium – his father is a councillor there.'

Jason bowed, 'I am honoured to meet you, my Lady Princess,' he said.

'That is a silly way to address me,' Lillia scolded impatiently. 'I am either a lady or a princess. You should make up your mind! You may call me either Princess Rhea or Your Highness,' she continued in a serious tone, 'depending on how I feel.'

'And how will I know that?' he replied, starting to look a little uncomfortable.

'"And how will I know that, *Your Highness*!" demanded Lillia.

'S-s-sorry, Your Princess,' he shook his head in frustration. 'I mean, Your Highness,' he blurted, the colour rising in his cheeks.

'Lillia, please stop it,' laughed Sylvanna. Turning to Jason, she said, 'She is only teasing you,' and then back to the princess, with a pleading look she asked, 'aren't you, Lillia?'

As she met her friend's eyes, Lillia didn't honestly feel as if she had been teasing. She was very annoyed – they had waited all day to see the dancers, and then Sylvanna had ended up missing most of it. Still, she could see that the boy was not to blame for her anger, and she began to feel a little pity towards him. Turning back to him, she said, 'I am sorry, Jason. My friends call me Lillia. I would be happy for you to call me by that name.' The boy seemed a little confused by this sudden change. 'I hope you have been enjoying the entertainment,' added the princess, glancing at Sylvanna as she spoke.

Jason nodded enthusiastically. 'The Vestal dancers were beautiful,' he said, then paused before adding sheepishly, 'but not as pretty as you.'

Lillia sighed, 'You do not need to pay me compliments, Jason. I am not yet allowed to have people executed.' A cheeky smile appeared on her face as his eyes widened. Without a further glance at the boy, she grabbed her friend's hand. 'Come, Sylla, I must prepare for my part in tonight's entertainment.' She wished the dumbfounded boy a good evening over her shoulder and left, pulling Sylvanna along behind her.

As they made their way through the throng, Sylvanna giggled, 'He nearly wet himself, Lillia. You may have frightened him away for life,' she said. 'And that would be a shame, because he is very handsome.'

'I cannot say that I noticed,' lied Lillia, her thoughts now turning to Marcus, the shepherd. 'I'm far too busy for boys!'

***

Lucius hurried from guest to guest, attending to their various needs whilst gathering messages for Numitor, and he couldn't help but reflect on how much he hated these events. The shy man normally avoided crowds and preferred solitude to the boisterousness of those under the influence of grain and grape. Unfortunately, he had been given no choice as to his involvement with tonight's festivities. As Numitor's personal assistant, his position required him to be the prince's ears, and it seemed that every guest at the feast wanted to pass on a suggestion or an idea that would either "make great riches" or "benefit the populous" in some manner.

'I've become nothing more than an errand boy,' he muttered to himself as he organised a dish of *"those lovely crayfish"* for the fat wife of a dignitary. *Has my life really come to this?* Lucius felt that he had become a slave to too many masters. His obligations to Numitor provided more than enough work for one person, and yet he was also required to answer to the Dius, the King's council and, it seemed, anyone else who felt like giving him an order.

With yet another message to give to Numitor, the assistant stared across the gathering, his eyes searching frantically until they spotted the prince seated with a group of men in one of the cushioned areas. As Lucius approached, he saw that Numitor was engrossed in debate with Brascus, Arbitrator Fabii and Ugo Curiatii. None of them appeared to notice him as he stopped a few steps away from the cosy enclosure. Waiting for an appropriate moment to interrupt, the assistant listened as the men argued.

'Nothing can beat a Slavic Wide-hoof up a hill – those horses are built for power.' Ugo's high voice sounded a little slurred.

Brascus responded quickly, pointing at the horse dealer. 'Yet, they cost double that of an Illyrian.'

The other men agreed with Brascus and jeered at Ugo, who defended himself without hesitation.

'It takes twice as long to get the Slavics here from the Slav steeps, and, as you all know, it is a treacherous land – of course the horses are more costly.'

'Now we know you lie, Curiatii,' laughed the Arbitrator. 'You acquire those horses from the same breeders as you do the Illyrian stock and, I hear, at the same price.'

Growing impatient as he continued to be unnoticed by the group, Lucius cleared his throat, and instantly came to regret it as four pairs of eyes suddenly scrutinised him with varying degrees of sobriety.

'Well, spit it out then, man,' Numitor smiled.

'Yes, Your Highness, um, well, I have many messages, most of which I can deal with myself, Sire, but, well, Larissa Cloellii is insistent upon speaking with you, but she will not say what it concerns.' Lucius took a large breath, wrestling to control his frustration as it tried to surface.

'Ha ha, we know what it concerns,' laughed Brascus. 'I think the widow has eyes on our prince.'

To Lucius' annoyance, the others joined in with nods and winks. 'She is a mare that needs a good stud, that one,' Curiatii commented. 'No man is safe so long as she is near.'

'Why do you think she is a widow?' chuckled Brascus. 'Poor Silenius, she sucked the life out of him.'

'And I am sure that is not all she sucked,' roared Fabii, his observation only adding to the exuberance of the others. Numitor began to look uncomfortable with the direction of the conversation and returned his attention to his assistant.

'Anything else, Lucius? If not, you should try and enjoy the festivities a little. You can work tomorrow.'

'Thank you, Sire, but I will retire to my chambers shortly, if you do not mind. Just one final matter – you did ask me to tell you when Densara Potitii arrives. He is here now, Sire, presently speaking with His Highness, Prince Amulius. Would you like me to send him to you?'

'No, Lucius, I will track him down myself. Go and give Larissa my apologies and explain my need to be elsewhere.' Numitor rose from his cushions. 'I will see you later, gentlemen,' he said to his friends before leaving the group.

Lucius waited a moment, then nervously gave a cursory nod to the remaining men before setting off in search of the annoying Cloellii woman to deliver the prince's excuses.

* * *

Rounding one of the Grecian pillars that supported the terrace above the atrium, Numitor almost stumbled into Densara and Amulius. Both men instantly ceased their conversation, looking a little startled by the sudden intrusion of the older prince.

'Brother,' exclaimed Amulius, a little too quickly for Numitor's liking, 'we were just talking about you.'

'All good things, I hope,' Numitor replied, greeting Densara with a smile.

'Of course, Brother. It appears we have a mutual business arrangement with the good merchant here,' Amulius gestured. 'We were discussing some of the issues we face when transporting Samnite slaves back to Alba. Wolves, unforgiving terrain, the list is endless.'

Numitor saw through his brother's evasive veil and wondered what they had really been discussing. 'That is interesting, Amulius,' he smiled, 'but I was hoping to speak with Merchant Potitii myself about our joint venture. King Corros mentioned he was looking to buy slaves and I thought we might be able to help. There is a shortage of stock in all the Etruscan kingdoms.'

'As there is everywhere, Sire,' interjected Densara, fidgeting in his red and orange dress robes. 'Kushites buying them all up, you see.'

'Yes, I have heard about the situation in Egypt from Brascus,' replied Numitor, 'but the Kushites will have to wait. First, we have rebuilding of our own to do before we worry about them. Etruria is our neighbour and will become our ally if we can establish good trade. Your participation is essential, Densara. You have an important role to play if we are to ensure a successful outcome to this situation, and there would be a great deal for you to gain from it.'

'That is kind of you to say, Sire,' responded Densara, 'but I am surprised you choose to talk to me of slaves, and not Brascus.'

Feeling a little awkward, Numitor lowered his eyes as he answered, 'Again, Brascus... Kushites...'

Densara dipped his head in understanding. 'Say no more, Your Highness, and as it happens, I may be able to help King Corros, provided there are no objections.' He looked to Amulius for approval.

'No objections on my part.' Amulius shrugged his shoulders. 'So long as we gain a good profit, I see no harm in providing slaves to the Etruscans.'

Numitor had a feeling that his brother was merely humouring him, but he kept his thoughts to himself. 'I am glad we are agreed,' he said. 'Now you must excuse me, for I have entertainment to announce. I trust I will see you again shortly, Amulius, for King Corros is expecting us to join him. And bring Densara with you.'

Amulius did not look pleased at the prospect as Numitor turned away to bid Densara a good evening. The older prince then left the two men to their unfinished conversation.

* * *

A short while later, Lillia was sitting in the courtyard and watching as a troop of Greek actors played out the fable of Perseus and Medusa. Their colourful costumes and humorous antics brought bouts of laughter from the delighted audience. The actor portraying Medusa had a painted red face and wore a hideous wig of real snake-skins, giving him a fierce, otherworldly look. They finished the act with cheers from the audience and collected their props. Then Numitor made his way to the front of the guests and raised a hand to call for quiet.

'Honoured guests...'

The crowd silenced slowly as people finished their conversations.

'Honoured guests and visitors,' repeated the prince. 'I have a special gift for you all this evening...' He paused for effect. 'My beloved daughter has been instrumental in making this wonderful evening happen. I have had her running everywhere over the last few weeks in preparation for this feast.' His expression changed to one of seriousness. 'Of course, one would expect her to earn her keep.'

The visitors laughed at his joke, the odd comment of agreement coming from some of the older guests. Lillia shook her head at her father, who smiled as he walked over to put an affectionate arm around her shoulder. 'I am going to impose on her one last time,' he announced. 'After much persuasion, Princess Rhea has agreed to sing for us.'

The crowd dutifully clapped and a single cheer echoed around the courtyard. In the corner, a somewhat sheepish Jason took a step backwards in embarrassment. The other guests turned their heads in his direction and laughed at the lad.

Numitor was unsure whether to be annoyed with Jason or flattered for his daughter, and remarked to the guests, 'It seems the princess already has a following, and without her even having sung yet. Maybe I should keep a closer eye on her!'

Another chorus of laughter erupted from the crowd.

Lillia's cheeks burned as she quietly said, 'Father, please, you are embarrassing me.'

Numitor signalled again for quiet. 'Princess Rhea will now perform a lament to Aeneas and his last days in Troy. Accompanying her on the cithara will be my close friend, Paridé, who has also been good enough to provide the grain beer that you have all been drinking with such enthusiasm tonight.' This brought another round of cheers.

The servants extinguished all the lamps, leaving only two lit behind Lillia. The sudden darkness added to the anticipation of the now silent audience. The princess began to sing a quiet, sweet, melody that told of the desperation and agony suffered by Prince Aeneas as he watched his city burning under the attack of the Greeks. The cithara came in on the second verse, the stringed accompaniment adding its own sorrowful countermelody to the song. Lillia's voice, clear and sad, soon captured the hearts of the attentive guests. As the tale of the love between Helen and Paris was told in verse, there was real sorrow to be heard in the princess' tones, and many of the audience members were shedding tears by the time she sang of the lovers' death and the fall of the great city.

* * *

Standing alone, Prince Amulius watched as his niece captured her audience. She looked magnificent in her long white dress; the eagle motif on the front glittered as the mother-of-pearl feathers caught in the light. As impressive as the dress might look, it would also have been costly, judging by the gold wire that had been used to outline the bird's details. The guests watched in silence as they remained engrossed by the song. The prince felt a moment of pride at Lillia's talent, but quickly put it aside as his thoughts turned to his plans for her. He looked away from his niece, deciding it was time to conduct a little more business.

Scanning the courtyard, his eyes settled on one particular man who stood looking uncomfortable by a pillar. It didn't take long for Amulius to gain the man's attention and, with a nod, the prince directed him through the iron gates to a large patio at the side of the villa. Lillia still held everyone's gaze, allowing the prince to slip away unnoticed. He eventually found the man standing next to a pond where a bronze statue of Poseidon rose out of the water. Amulius gestured to a bench and they both sat down. Lillia's siren voice drifted from the courtyard. The prince ignored it.

'Servius, my friend,' said Amulius, focusing his thoughts. 'Thank you for meeting with me.' The soldier seemed a little uneasy in his brown toga. *Out of his comfort zone*, guessed the prince.

'It's me who should thank you, sir,' replied the man, seeming genuinely grateful, 'but I'm sorry to say the feast's not really my scene, sir, if you get m' meaning.'

Amulius laughed, 'Not enough spit and blood on the floor for a real soldier, eh?'

Smiling, Servius nodded, 'You know us well, sir.' Relaxing a little, he added, 'I remember you joining us a few times on the drink – even got into a few fights, if I recall rightly.'

'Yes, your memory serves you well,' chuckled the Prince. 'Best you forget some of those nights or I might get a reputation.'

'You already have a good'n with the lads, sir. I wouldn't worry.'

The prince smiled, 'I wasn't planning to worry, Servius. How long have we known each other now?' he asked.

'I'd say about ten years, sir.'

'Has it really been that long since you saved my life?' The prince shook his head in disbelief. He still had clear memories of the battle that had ensued when a Ligurian war party had trespassed too far into Latin territory. Many of the enemy had perished that day, but not before Servius had saved the prince from a Ligurian spear. The offending weapon nearly hit Amulius in the back, but Servius had blocked it, the spear managing to pierce his shield before burying itself into the soldier's arm.

'It was nothing, sir,' said Servius, unconsciously rubbing his scar. 'Just a lucky blow on m' shield, could've been anyone.'

'Lucky for me!' agreed Amulius. 'You deserve recognition, Servius. You are loyal and trustworthy, and as I promised before, you shall be rewarded.'

'There's no need for that, sir. I'm happy doing m' duty, and the captain's pay is a big help to the family.'

'You think too little of yourself, Servius. You are a great warrior. How long have you been enlisted now?'

'It's been fourteen years since I joined up, sir. Seen lots of good men come and go. I s'pose I'm one of the lucky ones.' He nodded his head a few times to emphasise the point.

Amulius returned the gesture in agreement, 'All of us that live to tell the tale are lucky, my friend.' Then, with an air of curiosity, he asked, 'What are the warriors like in your section?'

'Got a decent bunch of men, sir. Itching for a bit of glory and gold, they are. Not much good, mind you, when we have to put up with these "peaceful" times,' he added.

Amulius stroked his beard, tweaking the end. 'No, peaceful times are not much fun for warriors, I know, but that is all about to change. New recruits are they, or veterans?' he asked.

'A bit of both actually, sir, but they've all been bloodied – had a few skirmishes on Samnite duty. Those bastards keep raiding our villages in the east and we keep having to see them off.' He shook his head. 'It's about time we taught 'em a lesson, once and for all.'

'Don't you worry about that,' said Amulius, offhandedly, 'you will have your chance soon enough! And that brings me to the reason why I have asked you to talk with me tonight.' His tone had now become serious. 'I agree, those Samnites should have been properly dealt with years ago. In a few days' time, our entire force of warriors will be marching upon them. Before then, we need to ensure that our warriors are being led by the very best of our men. This is why we meet tonight, Servius. It is time to discuss your future.' The Prince stood up and faced the quiet man. 'You are to be promoted to the rank of commander, under General Agrillis. The general will be announcing all the promotions shortly, but I am choosing to tell you of yours in advance because I want you know that I am behind the decision.'

Servius nodded, a look of disbelief on his face. 'I am honoured you think so highly of me, sir. I wouldn't 'ave dreamed I could go any higher than section captain, not the likes of me, sir.'

'There you go, putting yourself down again,' exclaimed Amulius. 'I would not promote you if I doubted you. Now, what do you say?'

Servius stammered slightly. 'Sir, thank you, I- I don't know what to say. Of course, I accept the offer,' he added hurriedly.

'Good!' cheered Amulius, patting the man on the shoulder. 'Then it is settled. However, I must insist that you tell no one of this until Agrillis makes his announcements, is that clear?'

'Absolutely, sir,' replied the stunned soldier. 'I'll tell no one, as you command.'

Amulius reached into his tunic and pulled out a pouch of coins. 'There is a half year's pay here, in gold.' He shook the pouch to confirm its contents. 'Take this for your family, as a gesture of goodwill. When you take up your new rank, you will still collect your pay, so think of this pouch as an extra bonus. In addition, I will see to it that you get a similar bonus at the start of every winter, along with your share of plunder profits.' He passed the pouch to Servius who accepted it with a slight tremble in his hand.

'Thank you, sir. This is all so unexpected. It'll be a pleasure to serve you again.'

Amulius smiled, 'As it will be for me. There is just one final matter, Commander,' he said, using the man's new title for effect. 'I want you to choose the best and most trustworthy of your men. You will be taking them with you on special missions of particular importance to the crown.' He added, 'I know you have experience in this field, so I have every confidence that you will choose your men wisely. During these assignments, you will be reporting to me – and only to me! Do you understand?'

'Yes, sir, I do,' replied Servius. With a smile, he added, 'Anything is better than waiting for a fight, and it'll certainly make life a bit more interesting.'

'That is what I like to hear,' laughed Amulius. 'Now, go and enjoy the feast. Give my regards to your family and, remember, not a word to anyone – especially the general.'

Servius nodded, 'As you say, sir, not a word.'

Chapter Sixteen

The days that followed the feast were full of activity at both the villa and the palace as dignitaries began to make their departures for their respective homes and countries. Numitor found himself busier than ever as he met with delegates and nobles to finalise the arrangements for the commencement of trading with the Etruscans. One meeting in particular did not go as planned. The owner of the obsidian mines near the town of Velitrae, Amicus Maranii, had objected strongly to the idea of trading with the Etruscans, claiming that he would make far more gold by selling his stone to the Phoenicians, who were known to have a penchant for obsidian. Numitor had quickly reminded Amicus that the Phoenicians were an old enemy, and any trading with them was likely to be looked upon with prejudice. It had done little to lighten the noble's mood, but he had finally agreed to sell a portion of his stock to Etruria in exchange for a one-year reprieve on his trade levy, a tax that every merchant was obliged to pay to the treasury. This meeting had been an exception, though – the rest were far more productive, and the prince had been left feeling extremely confident that his trade ideas would finally work.

Three days after the feast, Numitor watched the awesome sight of his brother leading an army of thirty thousand Latin warriors toward the Samnium border. The long columns of spear-wielding men marched five abreast, the warriors proudly displaying on their leather tunics the new emblem of the Latin army: an eagle in flight, grasping the fiery swords of Mars. The trail that wound around the slopes of Mount Albanus was now invisible under the feet of so many warriors – to the prince, the procession had the look of a giant serpent as it slowly edged across the landscape. Mules pulled small catapults along the rough path, accompanied by donkeys that were laden with equipment and supplies. Riding proudly at the front of the column, to either side of Prince Amulius, were the Generals Agrillis and Tyco. They wore bronze armour and helmets adorned with large, white crests, and they shone in the glare of the morning sun. Occasional shards of yellow light bounced off the gleaming metal and caused the prince to squint. The commanders, including the recently appointed Servius, cantered alongside Vasco, Tyco's second-in-command.

Numitor watched with a heavy heart as the scores of foot soldiers marched off, followed by a further three thousand riders, the heavy tread of both men and horses echoing around the mountain as crowds of wives, children and parents cheered out to their departing champions. The prince felt rather dejected at having to stay behind and miss all the action, but at the same time, he was glad of the opportunity it would give him to focus on running the country. He would be able to see the trade agreement through without the interference of his brother. Above all, he would have a chance to continue his secret research. With so little time to spare of late, the prince had yet to study the letters he had received from King Corros. The leather pouch had remained hidden amongst his belongings ever since the feast.

As the last of the supply carts rounded the mountain and followed the warriors out of sight, Numitor found himself presented with the first spell of free time he'd had in weeks. He had barely seen Lillia over the past days. Nima had informed him that she had been spending the warm days out with Sylvanna. So, upon discovering that his daughter was absent once again, he decided to go to the villa and try to find out what had caused King Corros to take such an interest in the letters. Bidding farewell to Captain Miron, who had accompanied the prince since the army's departure, Numitor led his chestnut horse up the villa path.

The villa felt empty and quiet as the prince made his way through the large atrium and along the adjoining corridor that led to his private chambers. A few servants hurried to their chores, bowing to Numitor as he passed. He smiled his greetings briefly as he went.

As usual, his bedchamber was tidy. Sunlight streamed through the slatted window shutters onto the ornate carvings of the bedposts and the surrounding drapes. The prince began to search through his assorted robes for the letters he had hidden, and after a brief panic, he finally laid his hands on the bundle. Deciding that he would try to cross-reference the letters with the accounts written on the vellum sheets that he had examined previously, Numitor went to retrieve the sheets from the chest, but upon lifting its lid he immediately noticed that its contents had been disturbed. The tablets and scrolls no longer lay in the neat, straight rows which he had so painstakingly organised – they were now slightly out of line, as if someone had been prying without taking the trouble to cover their intrusion.

Quickly counting all the documents, the prince discovered that one of the vellum sheets was missing. He ransacked his memory to see if he could work out which one was absent, and managed to narrow it down to being one of the Trojan texts. *Who would want that?* he asked himself, and he began to feel a strong pang of anger at this invasion upon his privacy. His first impulse was to question the servants immediately, but he then decided he would deal with the matter later, after an examination of the additional letters.

Numitor opened the first letter and saw that it was written in Latin. At the top of the page was the same antler symbol that he had seen on other documents. He started to read the letter quietly to himself:

'The gathering has made its judgement. Pinarii...' the prince paused at seeing the familiar name, *'has mentioned the unmentionable. Give this to the Carpenter.'* Numitor sat down on the bed as he continued to read. *'The current Pinarii representative is now close to residing with Diana. He is no longer able to continue. When the general is silent, I will choose the new Dius to replace him. It must be done in time for the next gathering. Diana be with you. MV'*

Dropping the letter into his lap, Numitor stared into space as he tried to digest the implications of the information. Clearly, it would seem the Pinarii family were somehow involved with this secret cult that he had been chasing for so long. The prince remembered the death of General Pinarii as having been a tragic accident following a night of heavy celebrating. And yet the letter seemed to indicate that the death had been organised. A shiver went down Numitor's spine. 'And who is *MV*?' he asked himself in a mutter. Then, in a moment of sudden clarity, another thought came to him – *Lucius; he is a Pinarii!*

Then there was the letter's reference to a 'Dius', that mysterious word again. He wondered how Brascus fitted into this cult, and his mind turned back to the rescue. The prince found himself wondering if Brascus' connection to the cult had, in fact, saved his life. He had become certain that his old mentor had always been his secret protector – it was now just a matter of proving it.

Over the next few hours, Numitor read the pile of correspondence and then re-read it. The letters came from someone who appeared to act as a go-between for the cult. It began to emerge that this group of megalomaniacs were not merely watching and following the country's prominent citizens, they were also arranging the slaughter of those that did not please the cult.

The prince spent time cross-referencing the information in the letters with that of the chest's contents, and he began to see that many of the accounts and notes corresponded with what he had read in the letters. Feeling a little overwhelmed by so many pages of information, he decided he would take a walk and try to mull over all he had learned. As he went to shut the chest, he suddenly remembered that he had found evidence of its contents having been disturbed. With the information he had now acquired, he suspected that the intruder may have been Lucius. He felt there was more to the absent-minded young man than he had first thought. On reflection, Numitor decided not to question anyone about the chest for the moment. Instead, he would give himself some time to consider exactly what to do with his new knowledge.

***

Out beyond the villa walls near the beach woods, Lillia sat between Marcus and Sylvanna on an old dead tree. They watched the sturdy brown sheep and spring lambs grazing on the colourful slopes of the large meadow. Flowers dotted the landscape, the yellow snouts of daffodils competing in the tall grass with pink clover and spindly buttercups. At the edge of the neighbouring woods, the undergrowth of budding trees was penetrated by carpets of bluebells and small patches of snowdrops.

Since watching the warriors leave, Sylvanna had spent most of her time talking about her continuing infatuation with Jason. 'He has two servants,' she remarked excitedly, 'just for himself, you know.'

Lillia did know – Sylvanna had mentioned it twice before – but she was happy to let her friend talk for as long as it continued to give her an opportunity to be near Marcus. The way he looked at the princess when they spoke made her feel very special inside. They had been chatting intermittently, ignoring Sylvanna's endless talk of Jason.

'You must come to the cabin with us one day, Marcus,' said Lillia. 'We can swim in the lake and roast cheese over the fire afterwards.' She tipped her head as she waited for the young shepherd to respond.

His smile dimmed a little as he replied. 'The cheese sounds good, but I have to confess I'm not much of a swimmer. I'm sorry.' He lowered his eyes to the ground and picked a long stalk of grass as the colour rose in his cheeks, darkening his already sun-burnt face.

Seeing his discomfort, Lillia smiled. 'I can teach you. I am an excellent swimmer, although my father thinks I go out much too far when I am in the lake.' She touched his muscular arm and added, 'You have strong arms and shoulders, and I would wager that you will make a fine swimmer.'

Marcus smiled. 'My father has always said I have bones of lead – that's why I sank when I fell into the river when I was younger.' His voice showed no emotion as he spoke. 'He had to pull me out, otherwise I wouldn't be here now,' he added quickly. Wrinkling his nose, he went on, 'but not until I'd swallowed half the river. I've not been in water since.'

'You should definitely learn to swim, then, Marcus,' Lillia urged him. 'What if you were to fall out of a boat?'

Marcus laughed so loudly that Sylvanna almost fell off the log in surprise, her quiet daydreams of Jason suddenly shattered.

Not seeing the joke, Lillia asked, 'Why is that funny?'

'I'm a shepherd, Lillia,' he chuckled, 'and so long as I am one, then I won't have any need to be in a boat.'

'Is that all you want to be, though, just a shepherd?' interjected Sylvanna, twirling her black hair through her fingers.

'Sylla!' cried Lillia. 'That is rude – you shouldn't say such things.'

Marcus laughed again. 'It's fine, Lillia. It's a fair question, and I'm happy to give an answer. At the moment I'm a shepherd because I have no choice in the matter.' He stood up and glanced quickly over the meadow to check on the animals before looking down at the girls again. 'My father is too old to watch the flock, so it's my duty to help.'

'I understand, Marcus,' said Lillia in sympathy. 'It is the same for me – and Sylvanna,' she added with an edge of resentment in her voice. 'We also have no choice but to do what is best for our families.'

'Well, I don't care who my father wants me to marry,' announced Sylvanna abruptly, sucking the ends of her hair into a point. 'I'm going to marry Jason, I've decided.'

'And how does he feel about that?' asked Marcus, eliciting a small giggle from Lillia.

'Well... he is... he said... well, he didn't exactly say it...' Sylvanna struggled to think of a reply. 'A girl just knows,' she finally declared, standing up and patting down her dress in preparation to leave. 'Come, Lillia, we should go now. I'm getting hungry.'

Marcus raised his eyebrows at Sylvanna and smiled to Lillia. 'She's right. It's time to go. I have to get these over to the clover fields,' he pointed down the meadow. 'My father thinks it makes the meat taste better when they eat over there.'

'That's fine,' whispered Lillia, looking down at the ground in disappointment. 'Are you here tomorrow?' she asked hopefully. 'I can bring some dried meat and cheese, if you like.'

'I won't be coming here tomorrow,' warned Sylvanna. 'I promised my mother I would help her sew.'

Lillia scowled at her friend and was quick in her reply. 'Well, we do not need you to be here, anyway.'

Seeing the first flames of an argument ignite, Marcus quickly interrupted the seething girls. 'I'm afraid it will be another three days before I can be here again, Lillia, but I would be happy to meet you then. Or, if you prefer, I could meet you closer to the villa – it would be safer nearer your home if you were wanting to come alone.'

'You can't do that, Lillia,' hissed Sylvanna. 'It wouldn't be right for you to be alone with him.'

Lillia ignored her friend and smiled at Marcus. 'There is an old oak tree half way down the trail, between the meadow and the villa path – it's the one that has a big split up the trunk. I will meet you there at noon in three days' time. We can sit on the branch and eat while we talk.'

'Lillia, you will get into trouble if you are caught,' insisted Sylvanna, getting angrier by the moment.

'I don't want to get you into any trouble, Lillia,' said Marcus, starting to sound alarmed at the situation.

'Do not worry, Marcus. I will be perfectly fine.' The princess continued to glare at Sylvanna, who responded by turning her back and stomping away towards the trail. 'I'll see you in a few days,' whispered Lillia, and with a glowing smile she turned from the shepherd and hurried after her departing friend.

When Lillia caught up, Sylvanna insisted upon ignoring her for most of the way back. It wasn't until they reached the villa path that the princess decided she'd had enough and confronted the moody girl. 'I do not see why you object so much to my friendship with Marcus.'

'He is a shepherd, Lillia. You are a princess,' Sylvanna replied with venom. 'It doesn't matter what I think about the idiot. You're just wasting your time with him.'

Lillia felt her own temper rising. 'Do not call him that,' she ordered Sylvanna. 'And so what if he is a shepherd? I can still be friends with him. It is none of your concern.'

Sylvanna's face reddened. She clenched her fists by her sides as she shouted back, 'Friends? I have seen the way you look at him with those doe eyes, Lillia. You're just going to end up getting hurt over something you can't have.'

'I can be friends with whomever I choose, Sylla. I do not need your permission,' replied the princess, choking down her anger.

'No, but you will need your father's permission.' Sylvanna's tone took on a threatening note as she continued, 'And I'm sure your Uncle Amulius would be interested in knowing about a good strong shepherd who is too scared to fight for him.'

'You wouldn't!' Lillia was incensed that her friend could even suggest such betrayal.

'I will if you see him again, Lillia. You shouldn't be around a peasant like that, and I certainly don't want to be around one either.' Sylvanna narrowed her dark eyes into a mean scowl as she stared at the princess.

Lillia was dumbstruck, her mind whirling with a maelstrom of untethered emotions. *It has nothing to do with Sylvanna!* she seethed. The princess loved spending time with the handsome shepherd, and she could not contemplate the idea of ending their friendship. Still, she knew her father would be angry if he found out – he would confine her to the villa to stop her from seeing Marcus. As the first prick of tears began to itch at the corners of Lillia's eyes, she offered her bitter reply. 'You do whatever you want, Sylvanna, but if you ruin what I have with Marcus, then you and I will never be friends again.'

Sylvanna opened her mouth to answer, but nothing came out as she looked into the princess' angry eyes.

Lillia turned her back on Sylvanna as the tears spilled down her milky cheeks, and without another glance towards her friend, she rushed up the path back to the villa.

Chapter Seventeen

Six Months Later

Under the shade of a fig tree, Numitor sat in utter discomfort, dabbing the sweat from his brow with the sleeve of his tunic as the midday sun blazed onto the palace gardens. Beside him, Lucius poured them goblets of wine and water. The prince accepted one of the goblets with a cursory nod, hiding the worries he now felt about his nervous assistant. After much reflection, Numitor had decided to start keeping a close eye on Lucius, noting every oddity and absence, even following him late at night when the man returned to his quarters in the palace. Now, six months after the start of the Samnium invasion, the prince believed he had found the pattern he was looking for.

'I am sorry, Sire, but we have finally run out of ice, and I'm told there won't be any more for a couple of days,' said Lucius apologetically. 'We're still waiting for Densara's men to return from the mountains with the next load.'

Taking a sip of the warm wine, Numitor shook his head and reached over to put the drink on the table. 'He is making a fortune on those ice blocks. Trust him to find a way to turn a hot summer into profit. He is a clever one, that merchant. Maybe we should put a levy on ice – it may persuade him to be a little more generous when negotiating prices. Why should we have to drink warm wine in this terrible heat?'

'Maybe I could drop him a casual hint that we are considering a levy, Sire – it would not hurt.'

'No, Lucius,' smiled the prince, 'I do not want to upset my brother's fox, and besides, he does do a fine job of providing us with many other essential goods. Sometimes you just have to compromise.'

'You are wise in your judgement, Sire, but I still wonder if a hint of a levy could provide us with a little more ice. It would come in very useful at the meat stores – with all this hot weather, we are having problems in keeping our meat from spoiling.'

Numitor took another sip of wine, savouring the sharp flavour as he swallowed. He was quickly tiring of the conversation but kept up a pretence of interest, as he did so often these days to keep Lucius from knowing his true thoughts. 'Well maybe just a hint, then, dropped casually into conversation,' said the prince. 'If he objects too strongly, suggest we are thinking of sending our own men to the mountains – after all, the ice belongs to the whole kingdom, as do the mountains themselves. The potential loss of profit will sway him, I'm sure.' He paused to wipe his brow again. 'Three months we have suffered this weather, but I never expected that it would end up placing the lives of our people at such risk. The lakes are lower than I have ever seen, and at the rate we are currently using the water they will soon be empty! As for the crops, they have already suffered badly. An invasion from the Sabine would not have surprised me, but this...' he gestured with a slow wave of his hand, 'this I definitely would not have predicted.'

Lucius nodded, 'We have not had a summer like this since I was a child, Sire, but I have been assured by the Augur that there will be rain before the next full moon.'

Numitor laughed, 'What does that old fool know? If he has so much foresight then he would have seen this heatwave coming and my people could have prepared for it.' The prince had no time for the Augur who, like Densara, seemed to be rather too close to Amulius for Numitor's liking.

Lucius, by contrast, had always seemed a little frightened of the strange diviner. He was quick to respond to the prince. 'The Augur says this heat is Hades giving blessing to our invasion of Samnium, Sire. The heat is coming from the underworld as the gates are fully open to welcome the dead.'

'Lucius, if Hades were on our side, do you really think that he would act in such a way as to hurt the people of Latium?' asked Numitor, annoyed at the statement.

Lucius bowed his head. 'No, your Majesty – but it made sense at the time,' he added quickly.

Numitor glanced up at Lucius, raising his eyebrows. 'I think you should stop listening to the Augur. I am sure there are men of greater knowledge you can go to for advice.' The prince instantly regretted the statement as the assistant opened his mouth to protest. Lucius quickly snapped it shut again as Numitor hastily resumed. 'Anyway, as far as I can see, the heat is coming from up there,' he said, pointing to the blazing sun overhead. 'If what the Augur says is true, then the ground would burn with flame and the lakes would boil, as did the water in the bay at Neopolis when my great-grandfather was king.' He sipped from his wine again, recalling his visit to the place years earlier. 'I have seen the Phlegraean Plain near the green mountain. Spires of smoke rise from the earth, and it is rumoured that if you breathe from them, the ground will split, sending you directly to the underworld. That is not the case here.'

Lucius shrugged, 'I'm no expert, Sire, the augurs are often wrong.'

'I would think that the Augur might have surmised it is Mars who is causing this. We are at war with the Samnites, and we know that the god of war shows his presence with heat – is this not why we speak of "the heat of battle"?'

'Yes, Sire,' replied Lucius. 'I shall mention this to the Augur so he can meditate on it.'

More likely drink on it, thought Numitor, not airing his opinion aloud. He shifted in his seat to try and get a little more shade from the branches of the tree. 'So, what other business do we have today, Lucius?'

The assistant picked up a slate from the table and ran his finger down the list of hastily written reminders. 'I have an update on your brother's campaign in Samnium, Sire. Prince Amulius has set up camp near the Volturnus River, now that he has cleared all the villages in that area. He believes the Samnites have congregated at the city of Pietrabbondante, high in the mountains. He is preparing to march there in a few days' time. General Agrillis believes this will lead to a siege.'

Numitor nodded thoughtfully, rolling his eagle ring around his finger. 'Yes, I understand from the general that the Samnites took a heavy loss at the Volturnus and will undoubtedly refuse to meet us on open ground. What do we know of their new leader? I was informed that his father was killed in the first battle, dying under the point of Commander Tyco's own sword.'

'That is correct, Sire,' nodded Lucius, 'but unfortunately Lohran escaped into the hills with many of his followers. He has been rallying in the mountain villages and has managed to raise another army. We believe he now has around ten thousand men in the city.'

'Only ten thousand?' said Numitor, surprised. 'My brother commands three times that number – this should be an easy city to take.'

Lucius shook his head. 'The number of men is not an issue, Sire. If I understand correctly,' he said cautiously, 'the problem now is the city itself. It is situated high on a mountain crest, and apparently has very impressive defences. I was told that the approach is open and easily protected,' he continued. 'It is said that Prince Amulius disagrees with General Agrillis. The prince believes a siege would take too long, and is planning a frontal assault instead.'

'But that sounds like madness!' exclaimed Numitor, before drinking from his goblet. 'However, Amulius is a good tactician, so I can only assume he has some deeper plan. Perhaps he is wise to reject the idea of a siege – we certainly cannot profit from our own men going hungry whilst they wait for siege preparations to be completed.'

'That has been one of your brother's considerations,' replied Lucius. 'This is why he has made camp, Sire. The prince has ordered stronger catapults and larger onagers', he said. The onager was a fearsome one-armed war machine that could fling bigger rocks than a catapult, and over a longer distance. 'They are also making ladders to scale the walls,' he added.

Numitor cut in with a question. 'How long will all this take to prepare?'

'Ten days to build the equipment, Sire, and another five to transport it across.'

'Why so long?' enquired the prince. 'Can they not build the equipment closer to the city?'

'Unfortunately not, Sire – the area around the city has only small trees and bushes.'

'That is a problem,' Numitor sighed, 'but I'm sure my brother has it all under control. What of the spoils from the campaign so far?'

The assistant consulted his slate. 'The prince has sent back to us around three thousand goats and sheep, two hundred horses and more than a thousand slaves. Various treasures have also been found, including gold, silver and gems. It seems that the rumours of the Samnites' pirating are true. Our men have found items from all around the Tyrrhenian Sea, including statues of onyx and ivory. The war has been very profitable so far, Sire, with little loss on our part.'

'Well, we will now be putting a stop to the Samnites' raiding for good,' replied Numitor, remembering with sadness the torched village. He brought his mind back to the present and studied Lucius as the assistant waited for him to continue.

Numitor was almost certain that Lucius would be meeting with his contact this evening. From his recent study of Lucius' movements, the prince has observed that the man went missing, without explanation, once every ten days, during the later hours of the night. One evening, Numitor had secretly followed the young man down into the woods, only to then lose him in the trees. The following day the prince had gone back to the spot and, using the same skills that helped him to track deer, he had found a lightly trodden track that led to a small clearing. He guessed that this was where Lucius went during his mysterious absences. It would be where the assistant would go later – and this time the prince intended to witness the meeting for himself.

'I shall not keep you from your tasks any longer today, Lucius,' said Numitor, finally. 'I plan on visiting Paridé this evening. I haven't seen him in a while, not since our daughters fell out, and I am looking forward to trying his new grain beer.'

'Thank you, Sire,' Lucius said with a hint of relief. 'I do have many things to do today.' He got up and arranged his scribe-board in the crook of his arm before bowing and backing away quickly.

Numitor watched his assistant leave and felt a moment of pity for the man, who obviously felt uncomfortable with deception. Having spent much time interpreting the cache of documents, the prince had begun to realise that the obligations of those who served the mysterious cult were not only unavoidable, but undertaken under threat of painful death. Lucius was as much a victim of circumstance as was he. Numitor felt the loneliness of having no one with whom to share his burdens, and was at a loss to know whom to trust. He poured himself another drink and cursed Densara again for the lack of ice.

* * *

The night had taken on a chill as the mountain breeze swept through the woods. Prince Numitor was lying on the ground, concealed in a hideout. Not wanting to risk detection, the prince had waited until sunset before following the trail into the woods and finding his spot. He had chosen to hide his presence within a hollow bramble bush that had proved to be particularly thick and painful. The middle of the bush was mostly dead with dry, spiny branches that snapped on contact. He had spent a while pushing aside offending tendrils before climbing in and gently easing the live brambles around to cover the bush's opening. His position provided him with a good view of the clearing while being practically undetectable, so long as he was able to stay still.

Before long, birds quietened and creatures began to stir in the bushes as darkness covered the wood completely. Numitor waited quietly for any signs of approach and found himself glancing this way and that as the night was disturbed by rustling and small snapping sounds. It wasn't long before the prince began to feel the first threat of cramp, and he shifted his position gently to relieve the pressure on his thighs. He paused as he suddenly heard the sound of footfall coming up the trail. A dark figure then appeared in the clearing.

The man's face was obscured by the darkness. He had stopped within a few paces of Numitor's hiding place, and the prince was forced to hold his breath as the man had a quick look around before heading out of the clearing. To Numitor's surprise, the man then hauled himself up onto the branch of a tree and disappeared into its foliage. The concealed vantage-point would offer a good view of the meeting and the approaching trail. The prince could only guess that this stranger was a look-out for Lucius's other master.

Now having the company of another watcher concealed nearby, Numitor accepted that he would have to remain lying in the same position for a long while, but his wait was soon ended by fresh sounds of approach.

This time, two people made their way along the trail. Both wore hooded cloaks, and as far as Numitor could discern, the leading figure was female. As they came into the clearing, the prince had to stifle a surprised gasp as he glimpsed the face of Hades upon the larger figure at the rear. Numitor realised it was only a mask, but he couldn't suppress a shiver at the unnerving sight. Shifting his gaze to the cloaked woman, he noticed that she also wore a mask, but hers was white and depicted a female face. He then recognised the likeness; it was the goddess Vesta. *An acolyte from the House of Vesta*, surmised the prince. *So, they must also be involved in some way with this secret sect.*

The woman positioned herself before her taller associate and, a few moments later, Lucius hurried into the clearing. He stopped a few paces in front of the masked pair.

Numitor watched as the man behind lent forward and whispered something into the ear of the woman. To his surprise it was the female who spoke first, her voice betraying her young age. "What do you report, Lucius?"

The prince quickly realised that the young woman was speaking the words of the man behind her. He found it unsettling as he listened to Lucius' reply.

'Um, well, there is… very little to report… Dius. Prince Numitor is busy at the palace most days. There has been nothing unusual in his activities and he seems happy that the campaign against the Samnites is going well.' Lucius shuffled his feet as he waited for a reply.

Numitor instantly felt his anger rise at seeing his concerns over Lucius confirmed, but was more intrigued by the title the assistant had used: *Dius*. He wondered for a moment if the masked man was Brascus. He watched the man lean forward again and decided that the stature and height of this person did not match that of his former mentor. The prince concentrated on the scene before him as the girl spoke again.

"Has he had any visitors we should know of?"

Lucius thought for a moment, 'No, just merchants and traders coming to talk about his trade agreement.' He paused and then added, 'Tonight the prince is visiting Paridé, at Vilini, but I believe there is nothing more to their friendship than a shared fondness for hunting.'

"Yes, we know about him," responded the girl. She then produced a thin package from beneath her robe and handed it to Lucius. "This is the vellum sheet you took from the chest. You are to return it and get a different one for us to examine. We will need to see all the documents over time, without raising the prince's suspicions."

'I think the prince has been too busy to look at the chest's contents, Dius,' replied Lucius. 'I have kept an eye on it, and it does not seem to have been disturbed recently. I have been wondering if he is losing interest in it.'

"That may be so, but the Hounds of Diana cannot allow the contents of that chest to be further investigated, or it could lead to a larger problem for us." The girl received more information from the masked man before continuing. "We are concerned that its contents could have dangerous information regarding our private business, and if that is so, then we shall have to dispose of it."

Lucius was about to respond when he was halted by a snap of twigs that also drew the attention of the two masked figures. The Dius looked up to the tree where his look-out was hiding, but Numitor could see little else in the darkness. The sound of rustling, along with a little grunting, suggested an animal in bushes nearby. Numitor prayed that whatever sort of beast it might be, it would choose not to reveal him. The Dius leant forward to the girl and whispered.

"It is fine, you may continue," she said softly.

'Well, hmm, ah yes... I'm not sure I would be able to dispose of the chest alone without being seen. It is very big and quite heavy, especially with all those clay tablets inside.'

The Dius leant forward quickly, seemingly disturbed about something, but the girl continued to speak without a trace of emotion. "What is this about clay tablets? You only told me there were scrolls and sheets of vellum."

'Oh, did I? Sorry, I thought I'd told you. But it does not matter – the tablets are just old accounts or some such thing. I didn't really think they would be of importance to you.'

Numitor smiled to himself as he saw the Dius fidget, obviously annoyed at Lucius' typically absent-minded behaviour. He almost felt sympathy towards the masked man's frustration. The prince then listened quietly as the girl recanted the Dius' anger.

"It is not for you to judge what is important, Lucius. You must get me one of these tablets immediately. Leave it here tomorrow evening at sunset, and someone will collect it."

Lucius nodded, though his head hung in shame. 'Yes, Dius.'

The acolyte spoke again. "How are our plans going with regard to the girl?"

Numitor became more attentive at the mention of a girl. He listened carefully as the young woman continued, "Have you made the arrangements?"

'Everything has been organised as per your wishes, Dius. When you give me the order, I can get the horse moving, so to speak.'

"Good, then our business is concluded for this evening. Get me a clay tablet and I will return it the next time we meet. In the meantime, watch Numitor closely. There are dangerous times ahead."

'Yes, Dius,' was Lucius' only reply before he turned and scurried out of the clearing, clearly eager to be gone.

Numitor watched to see if the Dius would remove his mask, but neither the man nor the girl moved until the hoot of an owl came down from the watcher's hiding place. The Dius then whispered something to the girl before they both left the clearing and headed up the trail. A short while later the mysterious watcher appeared at the bottom of his tree and also departed along the path, leaving Numitor alone.

When he was quite sure that everybody had gone, the prince gently eased himself out of the bush and stretched his legs whilst pondering on what to do next. He had told Lucius he would be visiting his friend, but he now realised that the information had provided the assistant with an opportunity to collect one of the clay tablets. Numitor considered going up to the villa immediately to try and catch Lucius in the act of stealing, but instantly dismissed the idea, preferring to keep his knowledge of the situation secret for the time being.

Instead, Numitor decided that he might as well go to Vilini as planned. As he headed cautiously up the trail, his mind was a whir of thoughts and worries. Everything he had read regarding the secret organisation suggested that they were known as 'the Hounds of Diana', and this had been confirmed by the acolyte's mention of the name. He was also sure that the girl of whom they had spoken was his own daughter, and the prince was now desperate to find out more. He vowed to keep a tighter rein on Lillia for the present, until he knew exactly what Lucius and the Dius had been talking about. Numitor felt like he should make a priority of finding out the identity of the Dius, given that he was almost certain the man was not Brascus. He needed to devise a plan that would unmask the man whilst also allowing the prince to avoid the people that shadowed him. Numitor realised that he would have to learn how to become a shadow himself.

Chapter Eighteen

The dark paved streets of Alba Longa glistened after a rainstorm as Densara clutched his robes tighter, though they did little to protect him against the cold wind. Looking up, he saw clouds drifting over the semi-circle of the moon, and the darkness deepened. The merchant glanced around nervously as the shadows grew and he upped his pace. By the time he reached his destination he was sweating and in need of a rest.

On entering the taverna, Densara found the place to be busy with nearly every seat taken, and he felt a pang of annoyance. As he was removing his outer-robe, a young woman approached him with a smile. She wore a white wrap and as the merchant passed her his wet garment, he realised he recognised her from one of his previous visits. 'Good evening, Perla,' he said, remembering her name at the last moment.

'Good evening, sir. Can I get you some warm spiced wine?'

'That won't be necessary. I may take some later, but for now I wish to speak with the master. Is he here?'

'Of course, sir. I will just go and get him.' She departed through a door and returned within moments followed by Brascus.

'Densara, my friend, it is good to see you again. You have become quite a regular.' He picked up a jug and gestured to the stocky merchant, 'Can I offer you some wine?'

'Well, all right, if you insist,' smiled Densara. 'I have some interesting news for you. Amulius believes that we should soon have our first lot of slaves to sell at market, now that we have fulfilled our obligations to King Corros.'

Passing a goblet to Densara, Brascus pointed to an empty table, 'Come, and let us sit while we talk.' They took their seats and the taverna's owner sipped his wine before commenting. 'Yes, I hear we are to have only three-hundred slaves. I had been under the impression there was going to be quite a few more than that.'

'Oh?' replied Densara. He wondered how Brascus had come by this information but quickly hid his curiosity before continuing. 'I believe that many of the slaves were kept at the camp for some reason. I can only surmise that the prince needed the extra man-power for his preparations to take Pietrabbondante.'

'As long as he is not keeping them for his own personal profit, there should not be a problem. I do, however, wonder what Numitor thinks of this delay?'

Densara laughed, although he detected a veiled threat in Brascus' deep voice. Meeting the eyes of his business partner, he cradled his goblet and replied. 'I doubt Numitor has anything to worry about. In a few days his only concern will be in trying to decide what to do with all the gold that we'll have made for him.'

Brascus nodded in agreement, 'Yes, I am looking forward to it. Extra gold is always useful. With regards to my role in this endeavour, I am happy to report that I am ready. I have secured extra shackles and chain as required, and I have my men at the ready to collect the slaves from our meeting point at the Volturnus camp.' He swirled the remainder of his wine in the goblet before swallowing it in a single gulp. 'In a few days' time, we will dominate the slave market, and we will continue to do so for weeks to come. Old Gaganii will have a hard task dealing with the other slave traders,' he said, referring to the owner of Alba Longa's slave market. 'Our slaves will take priority at market or he risks the wrath of the younger prince. At least, that's what Gaganii told me when I saw him a few days ago. He did not look happy.'

'Ah, he never looks happy, yet he always takes his share gladly enough.' With his goblet now empty, Densara took the opportunity to change the subject, broaching the real reason for his visit. 'Well, it has been a long day,' he said, rubbing the sides of his bloated belly, 'and I have been looking forward to a massage from Louisa.'

'Yes, I understand she is very good at massage,' replied Brascus, smiling in understanding. 'Sadly, my wife has forbidden me from finding out for myself,' he laughed. 'She is a wise woman who understands men far too well.'

'She is correct to think that way,' nodded Densara, chuckling. 'You would lose a fortune if you kept Louisa for yourself. She would be a big distraction, I can assure you.' Densara was speaking from recent experience. The merchant had spent enough gold on Louisa to have bought himself a dozen whores, for she had taken a hold on him like no other woman before. *If only Brascus would sell her to me, I wouldn't have to expose my weakness like this,* he thought angrily. Brascus had rebuffed all his offers, making it clear that he would sell the girl for nothing less than her earning potential over the next few years. Judging by the amount of gold that the merchant had already handed over to the establishment, the girl was worth a fortune. He waited politely as Brascus summoned Perla, who arrived promptly.

'How may I be of service?' asked the skinny girl, flashing a big smile at Densara as she spoke.

'Get Louisa. Tell her she has a visitor,' ordered Brascus abruptly.

The girl gave Densara a sympathetic look. 'I'm afraid Louisa is unavailable this evening, sir, she is taken for the night. Maybe another girl would be to your liking? I'm sure we can find someone to your favour,' she added with a promising wink.

Densara's heart sunk and a little jealousy crept in. Not wanting to make a scene, he covered his feelings. 'No, that is fine,' he said, shaking his head dismissively. 'It was only a whim. I am tired anyway, so perhaps a good night's rest is what I most need.'

Brascus put a hand on Densara's shoulder. 'I am sorry that Louisa is busy tonight, my friend. There are other very nice girls here, or maybe you could try again tomorrow?'

'No, I'm busy tomorrow,' the merchant answered quickly. 'Possibly the day after?'

'Fine, but you should try to arrive earlier – at this time of the evening my best earners are at their busiest. So tell me, what will be keeping you so busy tomorrow?' asked Brascus, casually. 'We are hosting an evening of special entertainment,' he added, his wink offering enticing prospects. 'Unfortunately, I will not be able to be here myself, but I could reserve Louisa to keep you company.'

'Thank you, Brascus, but the day after tomorrow will be fine,' said Densara, wondering why the taverna owner would be absent from his own function. 'So, what keeps you away from such an exciting evening? Some interesting business, maybe?'

'Ha,' laughed the big man, 'always keeping your eye open for a little profit. You need not concern yourself, Densara, it is just a family matter,' he explained, scratching behind his ear. 'You know how women can be!'

The merchant noted the unconscious reflex and smiled. 'Well, that's what happens when you get a wife, my friend. Why do you think I am so happy?'

'It is not so bad,' Brascus shrugged. 'I have lovely daughters and, although my wife may appear to be tougher than an ox hide, underneath it all...' he smiled, 'she is like a rabid dog!'

About to respond automatically with his agreement, Densara hesitated a moment and realised what Brascus had just said, causing him to let out a roar of laughter that drew glances from a few patrons. Though amused by the quip, the merchant was also impressed by the ease with which Brascus had deflected his question, a move that had only served to inflame his curiosity. Still, there was nothing to be gained from lingering any longer at the taverna this evening. 'Thank you, Brascus, you have cheered me up a little, but I think I will get going now.'

'Fair enough, my friend, and thank you for coming this evening. I am eager for us to get busy and sell some slaves.'

Having collected his damp robes, Densara bid Brascus a good evening and made his departure. Barely noticing the blustery weather as he returned to the stables, the merchant turned over the conversation in his mind: Brascus was clearly hiding things – it was obvious that the man was skilled in deception. There was far more to the taverna owner than slaves and whores – Densara could feel it in his bones. He wondered if Prince Numitor still confided in his old mentor and, if so, how far would Brascus be willing to go to help his former pupil. If the merchant were to fulfil his plans, he realised he would have to find out more about the man. Instead of going home, Densara collected his horse and headed out of the city to arrange a meeting with someone who could get him the answers he required.

Chapter Nineteen

Prince Amulius watched the distant city walls of Pietrabbondante from his vantage point close to the camp. Beside him, the recently promoted Servius stood in silence, the reins of their horses held loosely in his hand. The city was built in part on a cliff. The prince tracked its walls from the cliff face in the east to the furthest point west. The long battlements gave the impression of a much greater city beyond. *The illusion is perfect*, thought Amulius. Having seen the plans that one of his spies had drawn, he knew places where the city was only a few streets deep. A sheer cliff to the north made an attack from that direction impossible. It would be difficult to conquer Pietrabbondante, but the prince could see that it would also be a difficult place from which to escape.

He tapped his foot impatiently and gestured towards the city. 'If those cowards would only come out and meet us,' he hissed through gritted teeth, 'we would not have to waste extra days waiting for our new equipment.' The thought of another cold night on the mountain did little to brighten his mood. *And I also have to feed all these men – this is costing me far more coin than I had anticipated,* he silently seethed. The prince returned his gaze to the city. 'I need to get in there soon, or all this will be for nothing.'

The main battlements were illuminated by the lights from hundreds of torches that seemed to taunt Amulius, as if daring him to attack. Even the silhouettes of the city's look-outs felt as though they were calling to him in defiance as they moved along the wall. Servius shuffled his feet and nodded as he met the prince's gaze; Amulius held it for a few moments before looking down the hill, back towards his camp.

A sea of tents interspersed with firelight was spread across the curves of the valley. The prince could see his warriors huddled in small clusters around cooking pots, warding off the cold. The summer days were extremely hot, but as soon as the sun sank, the thin mountain air was quick to suck the heat from the land.

Amulius pulled his bearskin tightly around his shoulders. 'Our men need to fight soon or their wits will dull. They will not see any action if we remain outside those gates,' he said, pointing towards the city's imposing entrance. 'At this rate, I fear the battle may be won or lost before we ever reach the wall.'

'They do have fine defences, sir,' agreed Servius. 'But they're fools if they think they can keep our lot out,' he said, raising his bristled chin in defiance.

'Exactly!' laughed Amulius, 'and they will never expect what we are about to unleash on them.' Looking up at the towering cliff face which formed part of the city's defending wall, the prince had to acknowledge that the Samnites had chosen an exceptional location in which to build – the defences were nearly faultless. There was nothing he could do now but secure his position and wait for the new catapults and onagers to arrive. He gestured to the commander. 'What of our other plans?'

Servius brought his plump figure to attention as he answered, 'I've ordered two sections to hide in the woods, at the bottom of them cliffs, Sir. When the fighting starts, half of them will slip away and make for the Etruscan border. We've already chosen a camp, sir. It's the perfect spot. The Etruscans will definitely see us there.'

'Just remember, we must not engage them,' warned the prince. 'Unless they cross the river, of course,' he added.

'No, sir, the men have strict instructions. They'll stay concealed until I send a rider, then they'll set up their camp, as planned.'

The prince nodded, 'It must go as planned. I have invested too much for it to fail.' He reached up and felt the scar on his cheek. *When this battle is over, I shall have everything I need to gain the throne and become king.*

Pointing to the illuminated city, he continued, 'Tell your men in those woods not to kill too many Samnites. They need to give them a chance to surrender. I want plenty of stock for my merchants. If the Samnites decide to run, we must capture as many as we can.'

Servius agreed. 'It'd be difficult to follow 'em into the hills, sir, but we won't 'ave to cos they're not getting past my lads.'

Servius shivered and Amulius realised the man had not brought a cloak. *I bet he is cursing me for bringing him up here*, he thought, a little amused. 'Let us get back to camp,' he said. 'I need some food and a hot jug of spiced wine. We can make a toast to Mars; may he look down on us with favour.'

Servius nodded, 'As you say, sir.' He handed the reins to the prince.

'How are the prisoners doing?' asked Amulius as he climbed on to his horse.

'They're in good health, sir,' replied the warrior. 'We're holding 'em a few leagues to the east. I left a section to watch over 'em.'

'Good,' commented the prince, glancing again at the Samnite city. 'I want them healthy enough to walk, but arrange for their tongues to be cut out. After all, they will not be needing them again.'

'Will do, sir,' Servius replied promptly.

'If General Tyco would just hurry up with that equipment, then we could get out of these infernal hills, but without the bigger catapults we cannot even smoke the bastards out.'

Servius shook his head. 'We weren't to know they'd hold up 'ere, sir. I'm told that the Samnites see death as some kind of honour. To them it's like a promotion – they become demigods or some such rubbish. But even their gods can't save 'em now.'

Amulius snorted. 'Lohran obviously has his own views on death and honour. He was very much alive when he turned tail.'

'He has nowhere else to run now, sir,' the commander laughed. 'We have 'im trapped. He don't stand a chance!'

The prince patted Servius affectionately on the back. 'This is exactly why I chose you, my good man – you're always such an optimist. In a few days' time, you can prove yourself correct when Lohran's head sits on one of the spikes of his own battlements.' Amulius then frowned as he remembered that his brother had requested that Lohran be judged by the King's Council. The younger prince knew he had little choice but to obey, otherwise he would only raise Numitor's suspicions. 'That is, if Lohran survives the battle...' he muttered to himself as he scratched at the scar on his cheek.

Climbing up onto his horse, Amulius addressed Servius again. 'In the morning I will be returning to Alba Longa for a few days. When I return, I shall want to launch our attack at dawn the following day. Make sure you are ready. Send a rider to the Volturnus camp to find out what is keeping Tyco. I must get into that city if my plan is to work.'

The prince had a last look at the long city walls before he and Servius headed down the trail to the waiting fires of the Latin camp.

* * *

Lillia waited by the statue of Poseidon in the villa gardens. The grounds were quiet and shrouded in darkness. The princess was sitting on a cold bench watching the clouds float across the sky as she waited patiently, listening carefully for the familiar sounds of rustling from the bushes that would signal Marcus' approach. They had begun to meet frequently late at night since Lillia's disagreement with Sylvanna – it was her only way of meeting the boy without causing suspicion. It did not help that her father had now become increasingly protective towards her and seemed to want to know every detail of how she spent her days. She had been careful to avoid any mention of Marcus, knowing that Numitor would forbid their friendship. *If only I could get Father to see how wonderful Marcus really is, then he would surely come to approve of him, I am certain of it.* She had contemplated many times upon the idea of trying to explain everything to the prince, but fear of losing her friendship with Marcus had kept her quiet.

Whilst she waited, Lillia thought back to their last meeting, a few nights earlier. The time had gone by too quickly, but she treasured every moment she had spent with him, and felt the ache of loneliness in her heart after he had left. The princess knew that she was expected to marry someone chosen for her, and the thought sent her into a silent panic every time it entered her head. She knew the time was drawing ever nearer, and by her next birthday she was certain to have been betrothed. She dreamed only of being with Marcus, of having his children and living with him in happiness for the rest of her life – but she had no idea how to make it happen.

A scraping sound from one of the villa's walls brought Lillia back to the present. She wanted to turn and see if Marcus had arrived, but she resisted the urge and made herself sit patiently as she listened for the familiar footsteps. Another noise, this time from the courtyard, made the princess stand up to see if anyone was there, but she saw no-one. Then suddenly from nowhere Marcus was beside her. Lillia gasped in surprise and instantly berated him. 'Oh Marcus, you made me jump! I thought there was someone in the courtyard.'

The shepherd boy grinned, his eyes sparkling with mischief. 'Don't worry, princess,' he said softly, 'I made sure nobody saw me.' Taking her hand in his, he continued to speak, a serious tone now entering his voice, 'Forgive me, but I hate having to meet you in secret all the time. I want to tell the whole world that I have fallen for the loveliest woman in Latium.'

Lillia giggled at the flattery. 'You could win my heart with such compliments,' she smiled. *Not that you haven't already*, she added silently.

'So, what else must I do to win it? Shall I kill a lion, maybe? Or perhaps sacrifice a lamb in your honour?'

'You do not need to do any of that,' she said shyly. 'You are perfect as you are. Well, almost,' she added with a sigh. *If only you were a prince, then things really would be perfect.*

Marcus took a step back. 'What do mean by that, Lillia?' he asked, his smile fading.

The princess was instantly sorry for her words. With her own smile now gone she replied, 'I am sorry Marcus, I did not mean anything by it, but it's… well, it's just that… you are the nicest person I have ever met.' She sighed deeply. 'And yet… well, the truth is, my father will never allow us to marry. We would not even get to see each other any more if he were to find out about us.' Unable to hold back her tears, she began to weep.

'Don't cry, Lillia,' Marcus whispered, putting an arm around her and pulling her close. 'There is always a way where love is concerned. My mother told me that.'

At Marcus' mention of his mother, Lillia felt the tug of loss at her own mother's absence. The princess often longed to turn to her for advice. *Maybe Mother can hear me in the afterlife*, she would tell herself, but it did little to help her sense of isolation. Now that she and Sylvanna were no longer talking, Lillia was left with no-one else to go to and she felt lonelier than she ever had before. Besides, she could guess what her mother would have said: *'As a princess of Latium, you have no choice but to do your duty.'* These were the last words that Lillia wanted to hear. Then an idea struck her. 'Maybe we can run away together,' she said, suddenly perking up.

'Where would we go?' asked Marcus, looking rather shocked. 'We would be found in Latium, and everywhere else is dangerous. I would have to leave my parents. It would be very hard on them.'

'I know, and my father would be furious.'

'And I would end up dead!' exclaimed the shepherd.

'Father wouldn't do that,' assured the princess, 'but I fear he would forbid me from seeing you.' *And that would be enough to make me die inside*, she realised, and her anguish deepened.

Marcus stayed silent and looked down in concern as he held Lillia in his strong embrace. When her sobs had finally subsided, he spoke gently to the princess. 'I have an uncle in Neopolis, in Magna Grecia. He has always said that if I didn't want to be a shepherd, he could give me work as a boatwright.'

Rubbing her eyes, Lillia giggled. 'At least you can do that without getting wet,' she teased, remembering his aversion to water. 'But what would I do with my time while you were out working?' she asked, starting to like the idea.

'Well, you would be busy looking after all the children,' he said. 'I want us to have at least two sons and a few daughters.'

'Five children… then I will definitely need a maid.'

'We could always ask Sylvanna,' he replied quickly, trying to hide his smile.

Lillia broke into more giggles. 'I am sure she would love that.'

'Well then, you had better make up with her. I'm sure she must be missing you.'

'I miss her too,' sighed Lillia, 'but she was so difficult about you, and if she forced me to choose between you… well, I would have lost a dear friend.' *Not that she has been much of a friend of late*, she thought bitterly.

'There's no need to tell her about us,' Marcus replied, removing his arm from Lillia's shoulder as he stood up. 'You could tell her that I never came back to see you again. You could let her think that you argued over nothing.'

Lillia gave the idea some thought. 'It may work, especially if you agree to carry on seeing me here only after it is dark. Sylvanna might never find out about us.'

Marcus took hold of the princess' hand as he spoke. 'I'm troubled that your friendship has suffered because of me. I never wanted to come between the two of you.'

'Well, I will send her a message tomorrow,' Lillia decided. 'I would go to Vilini to see her in person, but my father wants me to stay close to home for a while. I don't know why. He has seemed a little strange of late.'

'Fathers are always protective of their daughters, even more so when they start to become women. There's a girl in our village and when I tried to speak to her once, her father chased me away with a sickle.'

'Oh? And who is this girl?' asked Lillia with a hint of jealousy.

Marcus' cheeks reddened as he realised his error. 'She's no-one,' he quickly assured the princess, 'just someone I used to know. She doesn't even live at the village anymore.' He shrugged dismissively.

'Well, I will be chasing her with a sickle if she comes anywhere near you,' said the princess, not bothering to disguise her disbelief in the shepherd's words.

Marcus laughed and feigned a bow, 'As you wish, Your Highness.'

She slapped his arm playfully. 'Please do not address me that way, Marcus, and if you bow again I shall have to call the guards.' She smiled as he anxiously glanced towards the courtyard and the villa gates beyond.

'I had better be careful. You are obviously a woman of means while I'm nothing more than a shepherd boy,' he said, sounding somewhat hurt.

Marcus' expression was hidden by shadow and Lillia wondered if she had really injured his feelings. 'I am sorry, Marcus. I was only jesting,' she whispered. 'You are so much more than just a shepherd boy, and I would not want you to be any other way.' She stood up and stepped forward, coming face to face with him. She felt her pulse quicken as they stared silently into each other's eyes. He reached out and pulled her closer until she felt the warmth of his breath on her cheek. Then she felt his lips as his mouth brushed

140

against hers, pausing briefly as he waited for her response. Her first instinct was to pull away as shyness overtook her desire, but he pulled her close again, encircling her waist. She looked up into his eyes, conscious of her glowing face and the pounding of her heart.

Then she kissed him. His lips felt soft and moist as he returned the kiss, slowly at first, then increasing in intensity. When they finally stopped neither of them spoke – it was enough for them just to hold each other. The princess never wanted to let go.

They sat for a long while, chatting about nothing and everything. Finally, the chill got the better of Lillia, forcing her to bring an end to their meeting. She kissed the shepherd one last time and bid him a good night. Walking back up the path, she thought about the ideas they had discussed. The princess could not see a future for herself without Marcus in it. She would have to find a way of being with him, even if it did require her to run away from home. It was now only six months until her fourteenth birthday and by then there would be no doubt that her father would have chosen someone for her to marry. The seriousness of her predicament began to sink in. *If I want to be with Marcus, then I need to start planning right away,* she thought to herself, *otherwise it will too late and I'll be married off to an Etruscan prince.* The thought hadn't occurred to her until that moment, but as she considered it, she realised it was the most likely plan. Suddenly all the pieces came together in her mind: she remembered the Etruscans at the feast, how they had smiled and complimented her – *as if I were on show,* she thought. She could see that her marriage to one of these foreign princes would be a great aid to her father in his continuing quest to unite the two countries. Lillia's fears grew and tears began to pool in her eyes. In no time she had convinced herself that she was destined to live a life amongst strangers in Etruria. She had no choice but to take action and do something about the situation.

* * *

It was the following night. From behind the shuttered window of the damp room he currently occupied, the carpenter watched customers leave the Taverna Dionysus. The cramped box of a room was barely big enough for two people to sleep side by side. In this part of the city the rents were very cheap, catering to the needs of Alba Longa's less fortunate residents. The accommodation was basic: it was a luxury for the carpenter to have so much as a shuttered window.

The taverna's customers came and went during the course of the evening. The carpenter took in every detail. He noted the patrons' faces, when they arrived and left, and in particular, whether they were followed.

The Dius had instructed him to watch for one person in particular. Normally this would not have been a problem for the carpenter, if the observation was to last for no more than a day or two, but on this occasion he had been told it would continue "until notified to stop". The seat in his bare room was hard and, with no heat or candle, it had been an unpleasant night. He could not understand why the Dius had chosen him for such a tedious mission, but he assumed there must be wisdom in the order. The carpenter had already learnt much about the Taverna Dionysus. It attracted unusual clientele, although this was not entirely surprising given its dubious location within the city.

Feeling a little deflated from not having seen his target, he decided to end his observation for the evening. Grabbing his bag, he made his way through the wooden building, past the sound of snoring coming from one of the other rooms, and out into the cool night air.

As he walked briskly through the quiet streets, he turned his thoughts to the other task that the Dius had set him. It was proving to be no less frustrating than his watch of the Dionysus. Princess Rhea was a difficult person to follow. She was becoming ever more cautious when leaving the villa, and the carpenter guessed it had much to do with her new male friend. He had reported back to the Dius about Lillia's relationship with the young shepherd. His master had seemed pleased by this unexpected turn of events, and had suggested that the boy could become useful later on.

The carpenter couldn't help but wonder exactly what it was that the Dius had planned for the princess. She would produce Numitor's heirs and therefore she was of vital importance to the country. And yet, he could not begin to conceive of why his masters were choosing to use him, their most experienced assassin, to watch her. He could only guess that he was also protecting her from somebody. Perhaps at some point he would have to defend her, and his skills would finally be put to some use. He hoped that was to be the case.

Chapter Twenty

It was the night of the next meeting between Lucius and the mysterious Dius, and once again Numitor was hiding in the woods. Clad in black leggings and shirt beneath a tunic, on this occasion the prince had chosen a spot close to the pathway. He was too far from the meeting to witness anything, but from his new vantage point, he had a good view of the trail that led into the clearing.

The watcher had arrived first, silent and stealthy. Numitor had only spotted the man by chance as he had quietly walked by. Shortly after came the Dius, arriving with a young woman. The prince could not be sure if it was the same girl as before. They both carried cloth bags which Numitor guessed would contain their masks. He was unable to see their facial features in the darkness, but he watched quietly as the Dius pulled out a clay tablet from his bag and handed it to the girl, before they both disappeared down the trail. Shortly afterwards Lucius appeared, stumbling as he hurried past Numitor's hiding place. The assistant then stopped briefly at the top of the trail and panted before walking out of view.

When Numitor was sure the man had gone, he carefully slipped out from behind the bushes and crept over to the path. Having already established there were no other trails in the area, he made his way to the fork in the path. One route led to the villa, while the other went down to the city. The prince chose to settle in a spot that gave him a clear view down to the city gates. Concealing himself once again behind some bushes, he waited.

All too aware that the meeting was now taking place without his being there to witness it, Numitor wondered what Lucius would be saying to the masked man. Having kept himself busy over the last few days, Numitor doubted that the assistant's report would take long. The prince gazed over Alba Longa as he waited, pondering upon what he would do when he finally discovered the identity of the Dius. If this secret Diana sect were there to protect him, then he could inadvertently put himself in danger by exposing them. He had wrestled with the idea many times over recent weeks, but no matter how he tried, he could not come to terms with the fact that the rule of the country was being manipulated by other men. He was sure that Amulius would never stand for it. For a change, he felt a sense of comradeship with his brother, suspecting they were probably both being spied on. Then again, he had always assumed Amulius had spies of his own. *But what if his brother's spies were really working for the Hounds of Diana?* mused the prince.

Not knowing who to trust any more, Numitor had found himself beginning to suspect everyone of being a part of the secret sect. Even his closest friends had come under suspicion. He had discounted Paridé as he saw him so rarely and usually only spent time with him whilst hunting. Aside from Brascus and Lucius, the prince knew of no-one else's involvement but he felt certain that the King's Council was bound to have a spy amongst them. A few names had come to mind, but only as a result of his own personal prejudices towards those individuals. Underlying everything was Numitor's own sense of honour – he could not allow his rule to be undermined. How could he let a secret organisation like this run the country?

His reverie was broken by the slap of sandals on the stone surface of the path and the prince watched as Lucius unwittingly approached his hidden position. At the fork, the assistant headed up the path to the villa and Numitor thought he could guess the reason: Lucius believed that the prince was busy at the palace and would probably want to use the opportunity to return the clay tablet.

Expecting that he would see the approach of the masked man and the girl next, the prince was surprised when the young acolyte rounded the bend accompanied by the mysterious watcher. Numitor felt his spirits rise as he realised he would no longer have to face the problem of trying to trail the Dius with the watcher following. He waited nervously as the pair continued down the deserted path towards the city.

In a few moments, Numitor spied his quarry and remained still as the dark silhouette walked past him and down the path. The prince waited until the man had reached the next fork, and was relieved to see him take the trail that headed away from the city gates – Numitor would have easily lost the man in the city. Kissing his gold ascension ring for luck, he headed after the figure, keeping to the edge of the path so that he could dart quickly into the trees if the need arose. After a while the figure headed down to the plateau between the two lakes and disappeared from Numitor's view. Thinking he may have lost the man, the prince hurried along the path before coming to an abrupt stop as he once again spotted the hooded stranger. He crouched down and watched as the Dius suddenly darted into the trees.

Numitor waited a few moments before cautiously standing and surveying the scene around him. He craned his neck to see where the man had gone, but found himself ducking down again quickly as he heard the bray of a horse. In a moment he saw the animal come out of the trees. On its back, with his hood now down, sat the merchant Densara.

***

The following morning, in the throne room of the royal palace, Prince Numitor waited for the arrival of Brascus. Having spent most of the night contemplating the implications of his discovery, the prince realised he needed help. Knowing that to confide in Brascus would be a great risk, he had nevertheless come to the conclusion that it was a risk worth taking – the man had been willing to help him before, and, now it was not only the prince himself in danger but possibly his daughter too. Thus he had arranged for a messenger to be dispatched to the Taverna Dionysus at first light to summon his former mentor. Now, preoccupied and nervous, Numitor sat on his father's old throne, trying to rehearse what he would say to Brascus.

The prince had been surprised to discover that Densara was one of the Hounds of Diana, but after spending a little time musing over the matter, he realised it made a certain sense. The merchant was extremely rich and influential in his circles. Numitor had never felt inclined to trust him as he always came across as being overly jovial. He conceded that the man had been helpful in dealing with King Corros, and yet he had looked to Amulius for permission. This apparent connection between his brother and the merchant gave Numitor cause for concern. He worried that Densara might be using his position to aid Amulius in his schemes.

The large doors opened and Brascus walked in with a concerned expression. 'Your Highness,' he said, coming to a stop in front of the throne, 'is everything all right? Your message seemed urgent.'

Numitor didn't bother to reply but simply looked at his old mentor, who seemed confused at not receiving an answer. Standing up, the prince gestured for Brascus to sit with him at the dark table. When they had both taken their seats, he waited until the taverna owner met his eyes before speaking. 'I know about the Hounds of Diana,' he stated, dispassionately.

A hint of surprise passed over Brascus' dark features, but he was quick to respond. 'I'm not sure what you are talking about, Sire.'

Numitor laughed, 'I am sure you do, *Dius*.'

145

With a frown of annoyance, Brascus enquired, 'Why do you call me that?'

'Is that not your correct title, Brascus? It is what our rescuer called you, when we were taken by the Etruscans all those years ago.'

'As I said at the time, Sire, you must have misheard.'

'Enough!' shouted Numitor, slapping his hand down onto the table. 'No more lies, Brascus. I have neither the patience nor the mind for it. I need your help, but you will be of no use if you are not completely honest with me. Do you understand?'

Brascus stared at Numitor for a few moments before responding. 'Why don't you tell me what is going on, Sire? I can only help you if I have an understanding of the problem.' He put a placatory hand on Numitor's shoulder. 'Come, Sire, tell me from the beginning.'

Numitor shrugged and nodded in assent. He then proceeded to recount the tale of his investigations, and the revelations that had resulted. Brascus listened without interruption as the extent of the prince's delving became evident. He raised his eyebrows at mention of Lucius' part and wore a look of concern when the prince spoke about his fears for Lillia. Yet, Brascus was unable to disguise his interest when Numitor spoke of his most recent discovery the previous evening. When the prince had finished, Brascus spent a few moments in silent contemplation before he spoke.

'You have been a busy man, Your Highness, and I would imagine your investigations have been placing you at great risk. However, it seems to me that if you truly believe this organisation to exist then you must also understand that a member would never talk about it on fear of death.'

'If no-one else knows, then there can be no danger, Brascus. Regardless of whether you will admit to your involvement, I have to believe that you will help me nevertheless. I fear that my daughter may be in danger, for reasons that I have yet to unravel. She must be protected.'

'If the princess is in danger, Sire, then I would guess the reason would be to do with her importance to the country. She will bear the royal heirs. Therefore, she presents a problem for any person wanting the throne for themselves.'

'Then you do know something of the plot,' accused the prince.

'No, Sire, I know of no threats to your daughter, but if a plot does exist, I'm sure it is something that I will be able to uncover.'

'So, do you admit to being one of these Hounds of Diana, Brascus?

'No, Sire, as I said, if I were a part of this, it would be more than my life was worth to speak of it. You must forget this obsession, or you could put yourself and many others in danger.'

'How can I forget this?' demanded the prince with clenched fists. 'My kingdom is not my own, my daughter may be in danger, my assistant turns out to be a traitor and now even my former mentor appears to be one.'

'A traitor is someone who acts against the country's interests, Sire, and not someone who is seeking to protect it,' came the sharp response. 'You may be firing your arrow at the wrong side.'

'Then help me, Brascus, please. If you are what I believe you to be, then you can use your position to find out what Densara is up to. Or could it be that the two of you are already working together?'

'Of course we are working together, Sire, with the selling of the slaves. Otherwise, I have no dealings with the man, aside from having to cope with his obsession for one of my whores.'

'Well, maybe she can find out his plans?'

'My whores are very skilled at many things, but not at prising information from a man who is obviously adept in the art of deception. Leave Densara to me, Sire. In the meantime, I suggest we put a plan in place to protect the princess, in case she is really in danger.'

Numitor nodded. 'And what of Lucius and Densara?'

Brascus glanced at the prince with warning in his eyes. 'We should tread carefully there, Sire. If your beliefs about the merchant are correct, then he will be very well protected and dangerous. People who wish to remain anonymous will go to great lengths to ensure that they do so. For all our sakes, Sire, you must be silent about your beliefs. You could be placing yourself in great peril.'

'But this is my point, Brascus – I am joint ruler of Latium. I should not have to stay silent. I should be protecting my people.'

'You know this country's history, Sire. Is it not possible that our prosperity has been achieved through the assistance of others? Would it not be fair to say that some of our former rulers would have surely squandered our riches, and yet something prevented them from doing so?' Brascus shifted in his seat and pointed at the latest statue to be placed in the throne room. 'Not all our kings have been as wise as your father. Some may well have brought us to our knees had their paths not been guided by faithful citizens.'

'I understand what you are saying, Brascus, but I will not be guided in this way. I am given more than enough to contend with in my attempts to keep my brother in order. I do not need the additional worry of the Hounds of Diana in my life.'

'If your belief in the sect is correct, Sire, then do you not think that the Hounds of Diana could be the very reason you are still alive? It is, perhaps, something you should consider before you condemn them.'

'That is a fair point, though I say it with reluctance,' conceded Numitor.

'You must not mention this conversation to anyone else, Sire. If I am to help you further, then we cannot discuss any of this in public, and that would include our upcoming hunting trip. You never know who might be listening – your own investigations over the last few weeks should give you an idea of how easy it is to be overheard.'

Numitor held out his arm to Brascus in a gesture of agreement, 'You have my word. No-one will hear of this from me.'

Chapter Twenty-One

Under the cover of darkness, the Latin Army prepared for battle. The new onagers towered over the men who dragged them into position, placing them just outside the range of enemy archers. Behind them, hundreds of smaller catapults were being lined up. Warriors hurried around the camp, attending to the final preparations of their equipment; sharpening swords, checking arrows for weak shafts or re-tying feathers. Others rubbed animal fat into slings to soften them, and still more collected pebbles from nearby streams for use as projectiles when they'd exhausted their allocation of iron shot. When their chores were finally completed, many of the men settled around the campfires and ate a light meal before retiring for a few hours' rest.

For Amulius, sleep would not come. His mind was far too active as he went over his plans once again, looking for any flaws that might jeopardise his victory. He did this despite having already spent most of the afternoon discussing the battle strategy at length with the generals and commanders. Eventually, they had worked out all the details and by nightfall the plan had finally come together. And yet, the prince was now wakeful and restless.

Amulius decided that he might as well take a stroll around the huge camp – it did the men good to see their leader. Upon leaving his tent, two large guards immediately began to trail him as he walked through the camp. He was surprised to see how many men were still awake. They sat around in small groups, quietly chatting and sharing jugs of their favourite liquor to calm their nerves. The prince stopped by one of their fires and made small talk with the warriors, who seemed pleased to have him take an interest. They offered him a drink, and he obliged them with a toast to the coming battle. He knew that this would be a tale they would take home with them, the tale of how Prince Amulius had come to their fire and shared a drink with them on the eve of battle. He moved on and chatted with other groups of men. Finally he began to feel the effects of their wine and sundry other drinks that he'd been offered, many of which he could not even name. It was time that he retired to the command tent once again to shut his eyes. Sunrise was a few hours away and the most important battle of his life was about to begin.

**

The first light of dawn was penetrating the tent as Amulius woke to the new day. He sat up instantly, dragging his long hair away from his face and immediately came to regret the sudden movement as hammers in his head began to beat to the rhythm of too much drink. The busy camp was noisy, adding to the drone behind his temples. Recalling the reason for his headache, he got up gingerly and walked over to a basin of water on an otherwise bare table. Picking up the heavy clay bowl, he leant forward and then poured its contents over his head. The water was cold, instantly bringing him to his senses as he squeezed the excess liquid out of his hair before combing it back with his fingers. Without prompting, a servant came in and knelt behind the prince. Making no acknowledgement of the young man, Amulius reached for a tunic.

'Bring me my armour, and have the cook prepare some food,' he ordered.

The slave bowed his head and exited quickly, just as General Tyco was coming through the tent flap, nearly causing the warrior to stumble over him.

'Careful there boy!' shouted the general. 'I don't want to be felled before I've even met the enemy.' The boy cowered, his eyes wide with fear in anticipation of a beating, but Tyco ignored him and strode over to Amulius. He saluted the prince, 'The men are ready to form up, Sir. We await your orders.'

Amulius sat on a chair and reached for his boots. 'You must have ridden all night to get here, Tyco – you do not want to miss all the fun, eh?'

'Better than watching trees being felled,' huffed the general. 'Would you believe Agrillis actually thought he could order me to stay behind? He might need to lead his men, but so do I.'

'Do not worry about Agrillis. Today you will see our finest victory, Tyco. Instruct the good general to get everyone into position, as soon as he can.' The prince finished tying his boots and stood up, looking at the tall man. 'That should remind him who gives the orders around here! Do you know if the prisoners have been prepared?' he asked.

'Yes, sir. Our men took some pleasure in getting them ready – those Samnites have no idea what is about to happen,' he laughed.

'They will soon enough,' replied Amulius dryly.

Tyco chuckled. 'It should be interesting to see, sir.'

'Go and give my message to Agrillis. I will see you at the battle.'

Tyco noted the dismissal and saluted with a fist to his chest before leaving the command tent. Amulius followed a moment later and stopped outside to look over the camp. The area was alive, bustling with activity which then came to a gradual stop as the men noticed their leader watching.

Amulius smiled. Thrusting his fist into the air, he cheered, 'To victory!'

The camp roared, the returning cheers growing as more and more of the thirty-thousand warriors joined in. Lowering his arm, the prince shouted, 'Today will see our enemy vanquished.' Another round of cheering echoed through the encampment as Amulius re-entered his tent, overcome with pride. *And they say I have no skills with people,* he chuckled to himself.

***

No enemy had ever breached the city walls of Pietrabbondante, so it was with mild amusement that the Samnite lookouts on the battlements watched the Latin army form into their respective sections. Behind them, the city was busily preparing for the assault. Archers readied bundles of arrows, whilst catapults were checked for weaknesses, and vats of oil were heated on burning coals.

The Samnite leader, Lohran, walked along the defensive wall shouting the occasional command to his men. Dressed only in a sleeveless sheepskin tunic that hung down to his knees, the young chieftain wiped his dark brow as the sun rose in the pale blue sky. He glanced around as his men worked and reflected that, compared to the Latins, his own warriors looked nothing like an army, with most of them choosing to strip from the waste up when in battle. Many wore helmets that they had taken as trophies in past conflicts, some of which still bore the scars of the axes and swords that had separated them from their original owners. Even without armour, Lohran knew the terror his warriors could inflict: *if my men want more helmets, there will be plenty going spare by the end of this battle,* he mused. He looked down the valley to the growing number of Latin warriors as they organised their lines. Even though the enemy outnumbered his force by three to one, he was not concerned: Lohran knew he had the advantage.

The long city wall was an extension of a natural cliff face, presenting only a steep plunge to the valley below – nothing could breach it. The only way the Latins could attack would be by means of a head-on assault. Lohran anticipated a massacre as they came up the hill and approached his defences. The archers would cut them down in their hundreds and the chieftain would lead his men to the final slaughter. He'd been worried when first light had revealed the enemy's huge onagers, but reasoned that they wouldn't get close enough to use them, for his archer's arrows had more than enough range to prevent any of the Latin warriors from loading their machines. All Lohran had to do was wait for the enemy to begin the attack, and he would bring it to a swift finish.

He cast his mind back to the horrific occasion in his childhood when Amulius had orchestrated the slaughter of so many of his people. He could remember hearing the screams and shouts around him as he had buried his face in his mother's skirt. At the time it had merely been a frightening experience for the boy, but as he had grown older and begun to understand exactly what had occurred that day, he had vowed to get his revenge upon the Latin prince. Now, with the additional memory of his father's death still fresh in his mind, Lohran was more determined than ever to put an end to Amulius.

* * *

General Agrillis sat upon his restless horse and inspected his warriors as the army moved into position. Their eyes were now fixed on the hill before them, their red shields and long spears pointing menacingly at the city. A little envy intruded into the general's thoughts as he saw that the men were all wearing short summer tunics under their leather armour. He wore a woollen shirt beneath his own heavy breastplate and was already getting uncomfortably warm as the sun heated its bronze surface. Even so, it made the general proud to see his men so well turned out. A movement behind the ranks caught his attention as the lines of archers parted, allowing a group of slaves to pull one of the onagers forward.

Agrillis wiped away a bead of sweat that rolled down from beneath his helmet and looked to his commander. The prince gave him a curt nod before shouting to one of the captains, 'Bring them forward.' Long lines of prisoners had been dressed in Latin battle tunics and were now forced to march to the front. Their arms had been tied to their sides. Wooden swords dangled from the men, making it appear from a distance that they were carrying weapons. Agrillis was pleased with their appearance. Most of them looked terrified, but were unable to make much noise because their tongues had been removed – the general acknowledged grudgingly that Amulius had been correct to make that particular order. Agrillis signalled to Servius, who ordered the guards to line up the disguised Samnites into three rows. A hundred archers then marched into position behind them as the guards whipped the prisoners into compliance.

Amulius rode forward, his horse whinnying as he faced the frightened men. 'Today is your lucky day,' he bellowed. 'As a good-will gesture towards your brave leader – who currently hides in your city...' he paused as a murmur of laughter rippled through the Latin ranks, 'I have decided to let you all go free.'

The Samnites shifted uneasily as a thousand eyes looked up to the high city walls.

'On my command,' continued the prince, 'you will all march to your city gates. Behind you will be my archers,' he gestured to the marksmen, 'ready to direct you, should you decide to go astray,' he said, sarcastically. 'You are to get to your city as quickly as possible. Therefore, you will be given a count of ten, after which my archers will begin to use your backs for target practice.'

Suddenly, out of the ranks lunged one of the prisoners who then ran at Amulius. The movement caught the prince's horse by surprise. Rearing up, it kicked its hooves out and caught the prisoner in the face, felling him instantly. Amulius, who was a skilful rider, leant forward to keep his balance and patted the horse's neck to calm it. To Servius, he said, 'Cut the throat of the next man who dares to move a muscle.'

The commander nodded.

The prince then steered his mount towards Agrillis, 'Let us begin,' he ordered.

General Agrillis unsheathed his sword and held it up as he let out a roar, 'To victory.'

The thundering voices of the Latin warriors returned with cries of, 'Victory is ours.' The ear-splitting noise filled the air, echoing off the high city walls.

Servius signalled to the guards. Using their swords to harry the reluctant Samnites, the warriors began shouting at the men, as the Latin army broke out in another deafening war cry. The terrified prisoners began to press forward, fear pushing them ahead of the swords. The guards continued to poke and prod until the prisoners began to run towards the hill, leaving their captors behind. Stumbling their way forward, they headed up the slope, some losing balance and falling without the use of their hands. Agrillis' eye was caught by a surge of activity on the city wall, indicating that the Samnites were preparing to defend.

As the prisoners ascended the hill, they were soon within the range of the Samnite catapults. Large blocks of rock immediately rose up from behind the city walls, appearing to float briefly as they reached the end of their trajectory and started the journey down. Then the boulders hit the ground and bounced off at odd angles, taking two or three of the prisoners at a time. The victims were torn apart by the impact, forcing the survivors to dodge the flying debris of flesh and bone.

Now that he had range of the enemy's catapults, General Agrillis ordered Servius to deploy the onagers. As they were brought forward, he returned his gaze to the Samnite decoys and watched as they slipped on the remains of their comrades. Some began to disappear into bear-pits that had been prepared for the Latins. With all the noise around, the general could only imagine the muffled screams of those who were now impaled upon the sharpened stakes which presumably lined the pits. He noted, with grudging respect, the spring-loaded traps that had flown up from the ground, spiking men in their chests and stomachs. *Not good for the horses,* he mused, seeing the damage that these particular Samnite weapons were currently inflicting on the prisoners.

Looking up, Agrillis smiled as he began to realise that the plan was working. He watched as some of the prisoners suddenly stopped running and looked up to the city walls. A moment later their panic was evident as they started to scatter and fall under a dark cloud of Samnite arrows. Unable to shout or signal, the decoys could do little to protect themselves as they became the targets of their own unwitting comrades.

* * *

High on the city walls, the roaring war cries of the Latin army thundered up from the valley below, the noise stopping the Samnite defenders for a moment as nervous looks skimmed their faces, but they soon returned to their tasks as their commanders bellowed at them to keep going.

At Lohran's signal, the archers took their places, bows at the ready, and waited for the command to fire. Other warriors stood beside piles of rocks, poised to drop on to any unfortunate Latin who came too close to the walls. The Samnite leader had watched as the first three ranks of Amulius' men had begun to run towards the city gates. While they looked impressive in their uniforms, they also seemed somewhat undisciplined. The scene became all the more engrossing as the advancing warriors began to encounter the traps and bear-pits.

Turning to his guards, Lohran laughed. 'A bunch of idiots, this lot,' he said, tipping his head toward the Latins. 'Amulius must think his men are invincible, sending them in without artillery cover. He really is an arrogant bastard.' To the archers he shouted, 'Wait until they are beyond the traps and then finish them off. Maybe they will think twice before sending any more of their men to die.'

With all eyes on the approaching warriors, the Samnites failed to notice the Latin war machines that were being positioned at the bottom of the hill. Then, a shout from further along the wall drew Lohran's attention to the situation. He could just make out the enemy, busily turning the tension ropes and loading the onagers with what appeared to be balls of hay. He thought he could guess their plan and, so it seemed, did the men around him.

'Careful now, lads,' he shouted, trying to alleviate their fears, 'I think we are about to be pelted with grass.' He laughed, as did a few of his warriors, but many others continued to watch the Latins nervously. Lohran signalled to one of his captains, who ordered his archers to send up a volley of arrows. The battlements filled with the twang of hundreds of bowstrings, followed by near-silent swishes as the arrows rained down upon the men ascending the hill. Those that had made it through the traps were now skewered by deadly points. Behind them, the ground was littered by a trail of dead men and debris.

Lohran could see that many of the traps had now been exposed, but he guessed they would still succeed in slowing the Latin advance, making easier targets of the enemy. Looking down the hill, he estimated that half of the original warriors who had charged at the city were now dead. His archers were swiftly picking off the remainder as they came closer.

The chieftain then noticed some rather odd behaviour from the approaching men. He looked more closely and suddenly realised that none of them had a weapon in hand. Turning to the captain, he asked, 'Why are they not drawing their swords or returning fire with arrows? They seem intent on sacrificing themselves!'

A shout then came from one of his archers. 'They don't have arms.'

'How is that possible?' said Lohran in disbelief. He stepped closer to the edge of the battlements to have another look, and finally spotted the reason. The approaching men were now clearly visible. 'They've been tied – their arms have been tied,' he said in confusion.

Then, with sickening clarity, he understood the true nature of the deception. 'Those are our men,' he breathed, his voice a barely audible whisper. With panic rising, he shouted to his men, 'Stop firing, you fools. Stop the arrows, now!' Running along the wall until he reached the first of the archers, he then ripped the bow from the surprised man's hand. 'We're killing our own people!' he screamed.

Before the archer could react, there was a terrified shout from his right: 'Incoming!' One of Lohran's men was pointing upwards. The sky was suddenly full of huge boulders and burning balls of fire, heading straight for them. The chieftain threw himself down, ducking behind the battlements as the first wave of artillery whistled over his head before smashing into the city behind. Screams and crashes came from nearby as the lethal projectiles started to obliterate many of the surrounding buildings. Flames engulfed thatched roofs and dry wooden beams as the burning globes crashed into their targets.

Lohran started to rise from his position, but the captain, who had been crouching beside him, quickly dragged the Samnite leader back down as a second volley of artillery rose up from the Latins. This time the projectiles were better aimed. Lohran braced himself for the inevitable impact of rock on rock as he watched the missiles plunging down. Then the world around him exploded: battlements and men were smashed. Massive chunks of stone were hurled beyond the wall and went crashing into the city. The chieftain looked up and sent a quick prayer to his gods: all he got in return was another cloud of destruction as more Latin fire rained down on to the walls.

***

Agrillis watched with satisfaction as pillars of smoke rose from the stricken city. The war machines continued to smite the walls and, for the moment, there came little retaliation. With the way ahead clear, he ordered three units forward to be led by Tyco. As the men started to climb the hill, some dragging ladders between them, the general then ordered his archers and fire bearers to take their positions behind the advancing warriors. He waited as the men began to make progress. They were not meeting any resistance, so Agrillis held back the order to fire. *Better they have targets in their sights than waste the arrows blindly*, he decided.

Another group of Latin warriors were also following Tyco. Between them they carried a long, bronze-tipped battering ram. Above the city's entrance, dozens of Samnites busied themselves preparing large cauldrons of boiling oil and piles of rocks. Servius was directing the men operating the onagers. Agrillis called to him and pointed up to the gates. With a nod of understanding, the commander shouted a few orders and one of the war machines was slowly turned. Under Servius' watchful eye, teams of sweating men turned the winch, slowly lowering the onager's long oak arm into place. Others lifted a large boulder into the cup of the sling that was attached to the end of the huge lever. When all was ready, one of the warriors smashed the release pin with a heavy mallet, sending the arm of the onager flying forward, dragging the sling behind it. The boulder flew up in an arch over the heads of the advancing rammers and moments later had cleared the city wall. After the launch, the men briefly adjusted the tension ropes and the next rock was quickly loaded. This time, the aim was perfect – the projectile hit its mark, causing huge chunks of the city wall and dozens of enemy warriors to vanish from sight.

From the great cliffs which comprised the city's southern defences, Lohran's catapults sent their own rain of death down onto the Latin army. The initial barrages sent many of the warriors diving for cover. Moans and agonised screams came from wounded men as small rocks smashed into them. Servius immediately called for the onagers to be turned again, this time towards the Samnite artillery. Meanwhile, Agrillis called to the captain of the archers. 'Time for your boys to earn their gold – get rid of them!' he ordered, pointing to the top of the cliff.

The archers assembled five lines deep. The front row drew their strings while the torch-bearers ran up the line, setting fire to the prepared tips. The first volley flew up as the second row of arrows were being lit; row by row, the blazing points shot into the sky. Fire began to rain on to the Samnite catapults, making it almost impossible for the enemy to load the weapons. As the arrows found their targets, the wooden launchers began to blaze and the enemy lost valuable time trying to douse the flames.

Three Latin units had now reached the wall. General Agrillis instructed his men to aim the onagers away from their fellow fighters, towards other parts of the city. Meanwhile, the Latin warriors at the wall erected siege ladders against the crumbling defences and held them in place as their comrades began to climb.

The pause in the bombardment allowed the Samnites watching the gates enough time to recover their wits. They began to rain arrows and rocks on to the warriors below. Hoisting their shields over their heads in protection, the climbing Latins continued to advance upwards, determination etched on their battle-hardened faces. Many of their comrades fell to the ground screaming as rocks collided with them. From the foot of the wall, the Latin archers began to target their enemies at the top, gaining their comrades more time to ascend the ladders. Eventually, a few started to reach the top. With swords and axes in hand, they clambered onto the battlements and quickly met the resistance that awaited them. The Latins found themselves outnumbered, but the seasoned fighters slashed and hacked into the Samnites, slowly pushing them back as more Latins made it up the ladders. Soon the battlements were thick with blood as enemies met face to face.

Meanwhile, the Latin onagers and catapults continued their onslaught, smashing wood and stone. The resistance of the Samnites was lessening and more Latin warriors made their way up the ladders. Eventually, they were breaching all along the wall, meeting little opposition. The invaders were quickly overwhelming the enemy. With the battlements above the city's entrance now taken, the rammers began to work on the great gates, pounding them in a steady rhythm counted out by one of the captains. The walls shook with each impact of the ram. After half a dozen such poundings, one of the unattended cauldrons fell from the battlements above, sending a torrent of scorching oil directly onto the rammers. The air was pierced by screams from scalded men as the skin separated from their flesh, bubbling and burning to the bone. A few rolled on the ground, while others ran around in agony. Undaunted by the suffering of their comrades, some of the remaining warriors picked up the ram again, and the pounding quickly resumed.

With the perimeter of Pietrabbondante now fully engaged in combat, General Agrillis ordered all the Latin archers to send their fire over the walls and into the city itself. He dispatched two more battalions to wait at the gates, while keeping the remaining half of the Latin army in reserve. The advancing attackers steadily drove the enemy further into the city, and all the while more Latins were continuing to climb the ladders.

Agrillis spotted the large distinctive form of Tyco at the top of one of the ladders, sword drawn as he slashed at an attacking warrior whilst shouting out orders to his men. Agrillis smiled in wonder at the skill of a warrior able fight with one hand whilst also directing others without getting killed. With a hint of admiration, he decided that Tyco was almost certainly the most gifted fighter he had ever met.

The general's thoughts were interrupted by a loud cracking noise as the city's gates started to give way. With two more impacts from the ram, the great doors finally parted as one was torn from the gateway and left to hang at an angle. A roar went up from the Latin warriors as they stampeded through the gap without hesitation, disappearing into a throng of waiting Samnites.

Coming in from the flanks of the Latin forces, Prince Amulius led his riders up the hill, slowly at first, then picking up speed as the horses gained momentum. A war horn sounded nearby, giving the signal for five-hundred heavily armed men on horseback to charge at the now-flattened city gates.

Upon seeing the charge, Agrillis called to Servius. 'I'm going in,' he shouted. 'A warrior needs to get a little blood on his sword!' Servius nodded, although his disappointment at having to remain behind was clearly evident. Agrillis was forced to slow as he arrived at the gates, for a bottleneck of riders had already formed at the fallen entrance. Warriors and horses were pouring through, but the agitated animals moved slowly as they navigated their way through bodies and rubble.

In the city, the fighting continued throughout the streets. The general's ears filled with the sounds of swords clashing and men dying. He could see frightened women who were unable to escape, trying to shield their children as they avoided burning houses and sparring men. The Latin warriors were under strict instructions from the prince to allow civilians to remain unharmed unless they carried arms. Seeing how few civilians were amongst the dead, Agrillis noted that the men had followed their orders. The decision to spare the citizens was of a purely financial nature: in due course, they would be destined for the slave markets. The general smiled, knowing the prince could not help but count the costs.

Agrillis rode deeper into the city. The fighting continued fiercely around him. He swung his sword down at any unlucky Samnite that happened his way, but there was only so much that he needed to do – it seemed that the Latins were already overwhelming the enemy.

He spotted the prince a short distance ahead with three of his riders, engaged in a horseback battle with the Samnite leader and some of his followers. Kicking his heels into his mount's side, the general charged over and swiped at the nearest enemy, who raised his weapon to parry. Agrillis hammered his sword down and pushed back his opponent. The angry Samnite charged forward in an effort to slam his body into the general but received a dagger in his chest, having failed to notice that Agrillis had drawn the small weapon in readiness. The general removed the blade and looked for his next target. Prince Amulius was still engaged in battle with an axe-wielding Samnite – Agrillis watched as his commander blocked a blow whilst plunging a dagger into the man's thigh. Then, as the Samnite roared with pain, Amulius drove his sword through the warrior's mouth. The blade exited with a crunch through the top of his skull, silencing the man.

Agrillis blocked an attack from a horseman on his left while another rider came at him from the right. As the closer of the riders parried, the general stabbed at the horse's head, causing the animal to rear backwards and fall, crushing its rider. The second horseman charged at the general, who deflected the impact with his shield, unseating the stunned warrior. A third Samnite then wheeled his screaming horse around and slashed at Agrillis with a spear, missing him by a hair's width. Agrillis managed to grab the spear, pulling his enemy closer and smashing his fist into the man's face. Then, with a backhanded swipe, the general followed through with his sword, severing the warrior's windpipe. Wasting no time, Agrillis quickly turned to search for his next quarry.

He saw that only four horsemen remained fighting in the small battle. Lohran was exchanging blows with one of the Latin riders, while Amulius was defending himself against a large and very skilled Samnite. The prince could only parry as the strong warrior rained blow after blow upon his sword. Agrillis spurred his horse into a charge straight at the sparring pair, distracting the big warrior and giving Amulius the opportunity to make his kill. It would have been all too easy for the general to have killed the man himself, but this would have been disrespectful to the prince – regretfully, it was one of Agrillis' duties to allow Amulius to have his moments of glory.

Lohran dealt with his Latin opponent by cleaving the rider's head from his body, causing a fountain of blood to spray over the dying man's horse. The animal bolted, taking the decapitated body with it. With a look of hatred now on his bloodied face, Lohran then fixed his gaze on his remaining adversary and charged at Prince Amulius.

Reacting instantly, Agrillis turned his horse into the path of the enemy leader and managed to slam the butt of his sword into Lohran's face just as he was speeding past. The impact sent the chieftain tumbling backwards from his horse and he hit the ground unconscious. Amulius nodded a gesture of thanks to the general.

Agrillis paused to survey his surroundings: the scene was littered with the aftermath of battle. The streets around them were devoid of life – just a number of dying men, few of which were his own. From the diminishing sounds in the air, he could tell that the fight was all but over. Straining to see through the smoke that wafted above the burning buildings, the general noticed the sun had just passed its zenith. That would make this one of the quickest ends to a siege he had ever known. The plan to use the Samnite decoys had made all the difference.

Continuing to scan the area, he heard the prince's horse approaching him. As he waited for Amulius to dismount, Agrillis returned his gaze to the smouldering buildings and wondered just how many had perished in them. Suddenly a glint caught his eye and, turning to look, his mind registered a blur as a sword swept towards him. For a moment Agrillis was confused, seeing only the prince standing before him. He felt nothing as the weapon swept past him, but his next breath sprayed a mist of blood that covered the front of his armour as it came to rest. Clutching his throat, Agrillis gasped in disbelief, his face taking on a veil of shock. Time lost all meaning as the general watched the scarred prince draw his sword back once again. The last thing that General Agrillis saw before his head was severed from his neck was the dark smiling face of Prince Amulius.

'I will send your regards to my brother, Agrillis,' said Amulius dispassionately, looking down at the dead general. 'And now I shall gladly go forward and take my kingdom, without having to concern myself with your petty interference.' And with that, the prince calmly walked away from the general's decapitated body.

Chapter Twenty-Two

Patting down her cream robes and pushing a loose strand of hair back under the shawl that covered her head, Mother Vesta prepared to leave for the ceremony. As the head priestess of the Vestal Virgins, there were some obligations that she found less than appealing, and her least favourite of these were the gatherings of the Hounds. Fortunately, she needed to attend their meetings only occasionally, and for that she was grateful – the masked men had always made her feel nervous.

She had never sought the position of Mother Vesta. Instead, it had been bestowed upon her by her predecessor, through whom the goddess Vesta spoke. A high priestess was seen as the embodiment of the goddess of the hearth. Her word carried the authority of the gods, and yet amongst the Hounds of Diana, she felt powerless and vulnerable.

Climbing down the steep steps into the cellars beneath the House of Vesta, she waited for her acolyte to follow. 'Come, Rosaria, and close the door behind you.' Without waiting for the girl, Mother Vesta headed for another door at a distant corner of the cellars. When she opened it, a dark passageway was revealed beyond. The black tunnel led deep into the mountain, where it was joined by many other passages, some of which ended abruptly, while others led only to the lips of seemingly bottomless crevices. However, Mother Vesta had made the journey on many occasions and was now able to navigate the passages with ease, turning left at one fork and then right at another, until her route eventually took her into a much larger tunnel.

The acolyte soon caught up. Neither woman spoke as they followed the tunnel, and Mother Vesta's thoughts turned to her first days in the order. She had joined at the age of ten, and was committed to the House of Vesta for a period of thirty years, as was the case for all acolytes. With more candidates than there were available positions for the coveted title of priestess, only the girls that were deemed most worthy went on to become one. The most crucial role of the priestesses was to attend the Eternal Flame that would burn constantly in each temple of Vesta. For the last third of their service, the older women would train the young acolytes.

A multitude of temples had arisen in the cities and towns of Latium, creating a great demand for priestesses, but before the candidates could ascend to any such position, they first had to spend ten years in training at the House of Vesta. Those that did not ascend would serve Vesta in other ways, such as acting as the voices of the Hounds of Diana. Many died before they ever reached the end of their thirty-year commitment.

The present Mother Vesta had reached the chief position after twenty-one years with the order, when the previous one had died suddenly. Although she had been chosen by her predecessor to ascend, she had felt at the time that she was not fully prepared for the weight of responsibility. Nevertheless, the position ensured her a place at the House until she died, and she considered this to be preferable to the prospect of having to face a world that she did not understand.

Much had changed since she had left her naive younger self behind. Although she remained a stranger to the world outside, the responsibilities that came with being Mother Vesta had opened her eyes to many of its ways. Tonight's meeting with the Hounds would bring about yet another change – she could only hope that they would choose the right candidate, but even that decision was in the hands of the gods. Mother Vesta was the only person who knew the identity of each member of the Hounds. It had always been this way. The Hounds had always been so secretive about the identity of each Dius that it had been necessary from the outset for a discrete outsider to oversee the choosing of new members, and keep track of the changes in personnel. The most common reason for a change in membership was a death, as was the case on this occasion. Although the order had chosen to place their trust in the head priestesses, Mother Vesta often wished they had not.

She muttered to herself as she walked, reciting her list of tasks for the meeting. Turning to the acolyte who followed closely behind, she calmly asked, 'Did you put the bag in the compartment, Rosaria?'

'Yes, Mother Vesta, I did. It's the third time you've asked me,' came the girl's agitated response.

Ignoring the insolent remark, she turned again. 'And the stones, did you count them?'

'Yes, Mother Vesta – you checked them yourself before I put them away last night.' Impatiently, the girl added, 'And the antlers have been polished, and the old mask has been removed, and the torn robe has been replaced.'

'Good, good,' Mother Vesta said, not bothering to turn as she hid her smile. Rosaria had served her now for thirteen years, and she liked the young woman well enough but thought her to be a little careless at times.

Soon they had arrived at a small candlelit cave where they stopped. Mother Vesta then put on her mask before continuing through the next passage, leaving the acolyte behind. Ahead of her loomed the great cavern, into which she now entered alone.

***

Brascus waited patiently as the last of the Dius' arrived. He rubbed his legs to help circulate the blood as they were already becoming numb from sitting too long. The arrival process seemed to be taking longer than usual, and anticipation gnawed in his gut.

Eventually, all the Dius' had taken their places, accompanied by their corresponding Vestal Virgin acolytes. Collectively they looked to the archway from which the Prima would normally appear. Instead, without song or ceremony, out of the passage walked the head priestess of the Vestal Virgins. She was wearing a white mask carved in the image of Vesta.

Brascus had always thought the likeness was almost childlike, as if the carver had wanted to overstate the innocence of the goddess.

The woman carried a simple wooden box which she placed on the altar. Out of it she withdrew the golden antlers. A few small gasps came from the Hounds, as they immediately grasped the significance of the antlers' arrival. A hush quickly fell upon the cavern.

'The Prima is no more,' announced Mother Vesta. 'He now hunts with Diana.'

Behind his mask, Brascus felt his mouth open in surprise. He noticed some of the other members fidgeting in their seats as the tension amongst them became heightened.

'We ask Diana to welcome her Hound, and to choose a new Prima.' From behind the stone altar, Mother Vesta produced a long leather pouch and took it over to the closest Dius. 'Choose your fate,' she said, 'and may you be blessed by Diana.'

The masked man placed his hand deep into the bag and took out one of the pebbles it contained. The priestess spoke again: 'Clasp your pebble in front of you until all the stones have been chosen,' she instructed, 'but ensure that it remains hidden in your hand.'

She made her way around the circle of men, inviting each to take a stone until it was Brascus' turn. He placed his hand into the bag and rummaged a little to mix the remaining pebbles, before choosing one and removing it with his hand closed tightly around it. After each remaining Dius had taken a stone, Mother Vesta returned to the altar and retrieved the golden antlers.

'Diana has chosen,' she solemnly announced. 'Show her your hand.' The priestess made an elaborate motion of opening her own hand in front of herself.

The men around Brascus copied the action, and he could see one or two of the white stones they held. He felt his own hand shake slightly before he opened it to reveal the stone that he had chosen. It was black.

For a few moments he didn't move, but simply stared at the black pebble in his hand. *It is black... which means that... I... I am Prima!* Brascus felt a wave of dizziness as he tried to comprehend the situation. In an instant, he had become the most powerful individual in all of Latium.

The priestess approached and stood before him. 'In honour of our ancestors, I bestow upon you the title of Prima.' She held the golden antlers above his head. At their base were two spikes that fitted into a pair of holes at the top of his mask. She carefully lowered the heavy object into position. All the acolytes then turned to face Brascus and Mother Vesta motioned for him to stand. As he did so, they spoke in unison: 'You who are called to speak for Diana, we honour you with the keeping of her Hounds. We accept you as Prima of Diana.'

***

The last Dius had departed, and Brascus found himself alone in the cavern for the first time since becoming a Hound. Mother Vesta had handed him a set of scrolls bound with a silver ring before she had led the young acolytes away.

What great fortune, he mused, still trying to come to terms with the events of the evening's gathering. He could barely believe his luck in having gained the coveted position, and at such a time. With command of the Hounds of Diana now in his hands, his power was unrivalled in Latium, and the possibilities that presented themselves were endless. Eager to understand more about the position of Prima, he reached for the scrolls. Removing the ring, he unrolled the yellow parchment.

There were seven scrolls in total. The first few listed the names of all the previous Primas. Brascus recognised a few names on the extensive list and quickly scanned to the end, to find out whom he had replaced. He had a suspicion that the death of the Prima was associated with the recent death of Numitor's general, Agrillis, and he was keen to know if he was correct.

Reaching the bottom of the list, he smiled to see his hunch verified. The last name on the list was *Servilii Agrillis.*

Had it not been for the general's untimely death, Brascus imagined he would never have made the connection between the arrogant, boisterous soldier, and the calm, open-minded Prima whom he had grown to respect. *Of course, we all sound calm when the Vestas speak for us*, he thought, smiling at the irony. Looking back at the name on the list, he reflected on how Agrillis had managed to wield far more power than anyone had ever realised. Reading on through the scrolls, Brascus learnt of the sheer vastness of the Dormienti and the extent to which they infiltrated all levels of power. They were now all under his control. Other pages contained details of the sect's wealth and where it was located. The acquisitions listed included whole estates, houses in the city, gold, weapons, livestock... the entries seemed endless. He had assumed the organisation would have acquired wealth after five hundred years of being, and yet what he was reading was staggering, even by his standards. The only information missing from the scrolls were the names of the other Hounds. Brascus had always assumed that the Prima would know who they all were, and was surprised by the discovery that even the leader was blind to this dangerous information. He would need time to study the pages further to develop his understanding of how the network functioned. Like all the members, he had always had a principal role within the gatherings, but now this role would change. Another member of his extended family would take his place as a Dius, while his primary role would now be to guide the Hounds of Diana in their endeavours. He settled down in a chair and continued to read.

Chapter Twenty-Three

As the sun set over the city of Alba Longa, a cool breeze whipped over the crowd of mourners that had congregated outside the palace walls. Quiet sobs emanated from the throng of bereaved citizens as loved ones consoled each other. Occasionally the air was split by a wail from a heartbroken mother or wife.

Funeral pyres were being prepared around the hill. Groups of people stood next to them, waiting for the arrival of the procession that bore the body of General Agrillis and all the other fallen warriors. Numitor led the line of Royal Guards carrying the general's corpse, which lay on a stretcher covered in white cloth. The prince's head was bowed in grief for the loss of his friend. Ahead of him was the High Priest Cluillii, dressed in long white robes and with his wrinkled face painted ochre, chanting quietly to the gods. Beside Numitor walked Lillia and Amulius, whose head was also bowed as his hand rested on his brother's shoulder in a display of sympathy.

Amulius was reflecting on how easy it had been to explain Agrillis' death after the battle. He had concocted a tale that told of the general's bravery when cornered by six mounted Samnites, and how Agrillis had managed to kill three of them before being overwhelmed. The prince had also described in detail how he had barely escaped with his own life and would not be here had it not been for the general's timely arrival. Tyco had been first at the scene and had accepted the story with ease, the bodies of the fallen Samnites adding credence to the tale. Numitor had not been so easily convinced, and Amulius had been forced to use a few tricks he knew to persuade his brother to believe him. At one point he had even feigned anger, when Numitor had dared to suggest that Amulius was secretly glad to be rid of the general.

As the younger prince kept up with his brother's stride, he looked around at the mourners who lined the trail. They held long burning torches that stretched into the darkness and lit the way. He noticed how their eyes all seemed fixed on Numitor, as if he was their only ruler. *He won't be around for long,* Amulius told himself. *Without Agrillis' interference, I can now seize control of the entire Latin army.* The general had always made life difficult for Amulius, his loyalty having always been to King Proca and then to Numitor.

I did so enjoy the general's look of surprise when I took his head, Amulius smiled to himself.

Thinking back to the battle of Pietrabbondante, he congratulated himself on how well his plans had unfolded. It had always been his intention to kill Agrillis there, but the opportunity to do so had presented itself so conveniently that Amulius believed the gods had helped him.

The Augur has always said I am favoured by Mars, he reminded himself. He had often found solace in the diviner's words; the old man seemed convinced that Amulius was destined for greatness.

He glanced back at the two generals, Tyco and Servius, who walked beside Agrillis' sons as they held their grief-stricken mother between them. *She will be better off without him,* Amulius thought dispassionately and quickly looked away, his gaze falling on to Lillia, who was trailing after her father.

My next problem – my lovely niece. The prince grimaced inwardly. *Your time will also be coming soon, Princess Rhea. Then it will be my line that will rule Latium.*

Amulius had always known that any male offspring that came from Numitor's children would be the legitimate heirs to the crown. His dreams had come under further threat a few years previously when it had been announced that his brother's wife was expecting yet another child. *Thankfully, the black herbs took care of them,* he recalled, with a degree of relish. The poisonous plant that had caused the death of his sister-in-law and her child had worked better than Amulius had anticipated. The plant was commonly used by women to prevent conception, but when it was taken later in a pregnancy, it would cause a miscarriage. The prince had not intended to kill Numitor's wife, but had seen her death as a fortunate twist of fate. The fact that the child had been born a boy had felt like all the justification that Amulius had needed. Now, the only remaining problem was Lillia. *By the time I am finished with you, there will be absolutely no danger of you ever bearing children,* he thought smugly as he glared at the girl.

Lillia looked up and noticed her uncle staring; a brief frown creased her forehead and she looked away.

You won't be ignoring me for long, Amulius silently promised, returning his eyes to the trail. As they arrived at the general's pyre, the prince looked up at the moon, which had now climbed into the purple sky. Its new silver crescent hung over the highlands, thin and incomplete. *Soon we will both be whole*, he assured it.

Amulius drew his attention back to Tyco and Servius as they arranged the body on the pyre while all around them the sounds of mourning died down. Meanwhile, the High Priest poured scented oils onto the stack of neatly arranged logs that formed the pyre, all the while chanting to the gods.

With a torch in hand, Numitor stepped forward until he was next to the large wooden platform that held his friend's body. He lowered his head in respect before turning and addressing the mourners. 'May all the sons of Latium find peace in the afterlife,' he shouted. 'Let our ancestors welcome them to the great halls and let them feast with the gods in honour of their bravery on the battlefield.' He waited a few moments before continuing. 'General Servilii Agrillis served Latium for thirty-five years. He started from the lowest ranks, even though his family title would have promoted him sooner, and on his own merit became a great warrior. Later, he grew to be an even greater commander, winning many battles for Latium. He brought us glory.'

Numitor paused to let his words sink in. The slopes were silent except for the odd cough or a cry from a bored child. The mourners held hundreds of torches between them which cast small shadows around the crowd, illuminating tearstained faces and heads bowed in grief.

With renewed vigour in his voice, Prince Numitor returned to his speech. 'Agrillis was a man who knew exactly when to fight and when not to. His wisdom and skill in knowing his enemy protected our country and kept our people safe. His loyalty to Latium was surpassed only by his loyalty to his family and friends, among whom I considered myself fortunate to have been included.'

A few murmurs of agreement came from the surrounding darkness. Numitor waited for quiet to return. 'The underworld is about to welcome a true Latin hero,' he concluded. 'May the gods welcome him with honour.'

With heavy heart, the prince then placed his torch into the pyre and watched as the flames started to spread along its base, climbing upwards as the oil vaporised, creating a carpet of fire that soon engulfed the wrapped body. Within moments flames from the other pyres began to light the crowded hill.

The fires roared, the sounds of burning mixing with wails that drifted with the smoke; the smell of charred flesh and wood soon permeated the area. Gentle singing could be heard within the din, the mourning song slowly spreading over the crowd and growing in intensity as more joined in.

The words of the song told of the journey that the fallen warriors would take to the underworld. The singing hit a crescendo and fell to a murmur as the song came to its end. With silence descending, the mourners looked to Numitor who turned once more to Agrillis' pyre and bowed his head as he sank to one knee. The thousands of Latin men and women followed his example and the crowds gradually became still.

Later, in the warmth of the dying flames, Lillia stood with her father. Most of the mourners had returned to the city to attend various feasts that were being held in honour of the dead. The princess had chosen to remain behind with a few guards, who stood to attention at a respectful distance. Her father was talking to her about the life of his childhood friend. As she listened, Lillia pulled her shawl tighter around her shoulders, shivering as the cold seeped through. She wanted to get back to the villa, but she was not prepared to leave her father alone with his grief. He was obviously very upset about the death of Agrillis, and although he didn't show it, she knew her presence was providing him with some comfort. She felt his arm pulling her closer to him, giving her a little warmth. She hugged him back, her motive for doing so not entirely selfless as her shivers began to lessen.

'He will be greatly missed,' whispered Numitor. 'I have never known a warrior who was as respected as was he: Agrillis shall never be replaced.'

Lillia nodded without answering, knowing it was giving her father some release just to be able to speak freely. She had known the general all her life – he had been like an uncle to her, more so than Amulius. The news of Agrillis' death had come as a shock to her and she had already shed many tears. Her father, however, had kept a brave face in front of his people but, as she looked at him now, she could see the tears rolling steadily down his cheeks. With all the people now gone, Numitor had let his grief take over, his shoulders convulsing a little as he quietly wept. Lillia felt her father's pain and wiped away a single tear of her own.

After a short while, Numitor composed himself. Taking a final look at the burning pyre, he then turned to Lillia. 'Will you be joining us for the feast, my dear?'

'Yes, Father,' she said, as they started to walk back down to the city, 'at least, for a while. I'm meeting with Sylla,' she lied. 'She is going to stay with me tonight.'

'Have the two of you made up, then?'

'Yes, Father. I went to see her home and we spoke about our disagreement, and now everything is back to normal with us,' she explained promptly.

Numitor stopped walking to face his daughter. 'Well I am very glad you did – good friends do not come by every day. So tell me, what are you two doing tonight?'

Feeling ashamed at having to deceive her father, Lillia wanted nothing more than to finish the conversation. She quickly replied, 'Oh, we don't have anything planned for tonight. Tomorrow, Sylla and I will be going down to the cabin, to spend the day by the lake, so we thought it would be a good idea if she stayed over tonight instead of having to come all the way in the morning.' She paused to breathe, then added, 'We would lose half the day.'

Numitor accepted his daughter's explanation with a shrug and a nod as they resumed walking. 'So what are you going to do this evening?' he asked again.

'We'll be going to the piazza for the main wake. Some of the families are roasting a boar and there are going to be musicians and dancers.' The last part of this was true, but she did not intend to stay for the music.

'Are you going to sing tonight?' asked the prince, hopefully. 'I may come down and have a listen, if that is the case.'

'No, Father, I'm not,' replied Lillia, a little harshly. Realising her abruptness, she quickly added, 'I didn't mean to snap, Father, I'm just not in the mood for singing at the moment.'

Numitor laughed. 'Do not worry, my dear, I will not embarrass you this evening. Just be careful and remember: if you are out late, I shall—'

'Send the guards to find me?'

Numitor laughed again. 'You have learnt well, my girl. Just take care, and then there will be no need for me to send any guards.'

Lillia smiled, but sighed inwardly with relief as her father made no further enquiry into her plans.

Numitor walked back to the city, arm in arm with his daughter as two guards followed closely behind. The prince quietly reflected on how mature Lillia had become. Six months previously she had still been the playful child that he was accustomed to, but now she was suddenly blossoming into a woman. Although he saw the princess most days, at first he had not noticed the changes in her, but the slim child that he pictured in his mind had now suddenly developed curves and grown taller. He had lost his little girl, and in her place was this charming and beautiful young lady.

Numitor's mind began to drift as his daughter chatted away beside him. He took in the deeper tone of her voice and compared it to his memories of her squeals of delight and childish laughter of past years. The person beside him seemed a far cry from that little girl. He tried to put aside thoughts of her future betrothal – having already lost his wife and new-born son, he did not want to contemplate the loss of Lillia as well. He still thought about his departed wife and child every day, but the pain had lessened over time as his duty to his surviving daughter and his country had occupied his attention and helped to fill the void.

He realised that choosing a suitable husband for the princess was going to be harder than he had first anticipated. The idea of Lillia moving away from Alba Longa filled Numitor with dread. He much preferred the idea of her marrying someone closer to home, if only he could find a man worthy of the honour. *Maybe I am being too harsh in my judgements*, he wondered. *I want her to be happy... and yet none of the young men I hear about seem good enough for her.*

'Father?'

Numitor was jolted from his thoughts, having not noticed that he and Lillia had stopped walking. His daughter was now looking at him expectantly.

'So, can I tell her to get some, Father?'

Not sure what Lillia was talking about, Numitor asked, 'Tell whom?'

Lillia frowned, 'Nima, of course. Have you not been listening?'

Shaking his head, he replied, 'I apologise, Lillia, my mind wandered. Tell me again.'

The princess tilted her head and searched her father's eyes. 'I am sorry, it was not important, Father. I just want some dresses made for the winter, and I was hoping to send Nima down to the city to pick up the cloth.'

Numitor smiled at his daughter and nodded. 'Of course you can, Lillia, and there is no need to ask.'

'Thank you,' said Lillia as she continued to study him, a look of uncertainty starting to appear on her cheerful face. 'Is there something else troubling you, Father? You seem more distracted than usual.'

Little gets past you, thought Numitor. *There is so much that I could unburden, but I will not share my troubles with one who should be free of such concerns.* Aloud he replied, 'No, Lillia, I am fine. I have too many duties these days to allow me to dwell on troubles.'

Accepting the prince's words, Lillia turned to resume their journey back to the palace, grabbing Numitor's hand as she did so. 'Come, Father,' she said cheerfully, 'I need to get ready for tonight.'

They walked in silence for a while. Numitor found himself thinking once more of the death of Agrillis, and of the man who would be his replacement, Commander Servius. *No, it is General Servius now,* the prince corrected himself. He considered the old warrior to be competent, if a little quiet for someone so highly ranked. However, Numitor had a suspicion that the man's loyalty might lie with Amulius. There was no denying that Servius had been wounded while saving his brother from attack all those years before – everyone knew the story – and it had been Agrillis who had gone on to nurture the commander, but nevertheless, Numitor had never felt any connection to the man. The prince's mind was also occupied with worries over his suspicion that his brother had played a part in Agrillis' death. Tyco had confirmed that the scene had been as Amulius had described, and yet he had shown little grief over the death of his old general.

Time will tell, decided Numitor, *but with the loss of Agrillis, I am running out of allies. Maybe I should place more faith in old friends.* Brascus came to mind. Despite the misgivings that the prince held towards the secret sect with which Brascus was involved, Numitor felt a seed of hope that he and his daughter would ultimately be protected from the treachery of his brother.

***

The city's main square was crowded and noisy when Lillia arrived. Boars and lambs were roasting slowly on fires that had been built around a large statue of Zeus. The aroma of cooking meat was enticing the crowds to eat and drink in honour of their dead. Most of the men were chatting animatedly as their drinks took effect, and their sadness was put aside to be replaced by fond memories of those who had passed. Lillia found a seat and listened to the sounds of chatter and music as she looked around the square, waiting for Marcus to arrive. Losing herself in thought, her mind drifted back through the day, and she realised how glad she felt that it was nearly over. Much as the princess wanted to support her father, it was hard to comfort him when there were always so many people around. *Father must never get a moment to himself,* she mused.

When she had left the palace a short while earlier, her father had been engrossed in a lively debate with Amulius, and it had seemed to her that his mood was showing the first signs of brightening since the funeral. Lillia suppressed a shiver as she suddenly recalled the cold look that her uncle had given her during the procession, but she quickly put the thought aside and chose to focus instead on how pleasing it had been to see her father smiling again before she had departed from the palace; it helped to alleviate her feelings of guilt regarding her secret plans.

For some time now, Lillia had been spending every available moment with Marcus, either in the pastures or during his late night visits to the villa, and she had come to realise that she loved the shepherd with all her heart. It was only in his company that she was truly happy. *And it is obvious that he feels the same*, she thought, recalling the way he looked at her with his eyes full of love and desire. Their future had been their most debated subject, with both of them wanting the same thing, but finding themselves unable to see a clear way of achieving their dreams. Lillia knew her father would never let her marry a shepherd, and she did not dare risk asking him to raise Marcus' status to that of a noble – she was scared of what Numitor might do if he did not agree to the request. On top of this, she still carried the worry of her father arranging for her to be married off to an Etruscan. After much thought, Lillia had come to realise that she had very few options. She loved her father dearly, but her feelings for Marcus pulled at her heart in a way that almost overpowered her senses.

Looking around the piazza, she saw that most people seemed to be in good spirits. Having now attended to their dead, their attention would quickly return to the living, with the night of waking being the traditional start of the process. Lillia, however, was not there to join in. She tapped her foot impatiently as she scanned the crowds until a touch on her arm caused her to jump. She looked up to see Marcus standing beside her, a huge smile on his face.

'I wasn't sure you would come with so many people around,' he said quietly, ignoring a few curious looks that were cast his way by some of the mourners in the square.

Lillia glanced around and agreed that less company would be preferable. 'Maybe we should go elsewhere,' she suggested. 'I imagine it would be a lot quieter at the stables.'

Marcus thought for a moment. 'That's a good idea,' he said, before adding a little nervously, 'but I'll go first.'

The look in his eyes told Lillia that he was genuinely concerned about the danger of being spotted with her. Once again, she felt the constriction of the barriers that were created by their differences. She watched him walk away and disappear into the crowd, and she felt the weight of the situation bearing down on her heart. Lillia hated being separated from Marcus, but she could still see no way of being with him whilst in Alba Longa. The princess had been plagued by the thought of what her father would do if he found out about her involvement with the shepherd, and the more she had considered her options, the more she knew that only one choice was available if she wanted to be with him permanently.

Arriving at the stables, Lillia found Marcus looking glum as he sat on a fence behind the long wooden building. She sat beside him and, after a few moments, broke the silence. 'It is so difficult to meet in the city, Marcus. Too many people know my face.'

'I know,' he replied softly. 'It is better when we are in the pastures. Maybe we would get away with it if I didn't look so much like a shepherd.'

'Or, if I looked like a shepherdess,' joked Lillia.

'You will always look like a princess, Lillia. Shepherd's clothes cannot hide that.'

Lillia felt her heart swell at his words, but she held a serious look in her blue eyes as she replied. 'Well, if our plan is going to work, then I need to look com- I mean, less like a princess.' She blushed as she realised how close she had been to insulting him.

Marcus chuckled. 'It is fine to say common, Lillia… just not in front of common people,' he winked, bringing a smile to the princess' face.

'Well, I shall have the chance to learn how to be common very soon,' she smiled. 'In a few days' time, Father is going off hunting with his friends, so we will be able to stay at the lake cabin overnight, and then we can begin our journey to Neopolis at first light.'

'So soon!' exclaimed Marcus. 'Then I must speak to my cousin to make sure the flock is watched. Just until we are settled, then my parents can sell the animals and come to Neopolis to live with us.'

Hearing Marcus talk about their grand plan sent shivers of excitement through Lillia. She imagined the great journey they would undertake together, and the blissful life that awaited her as Marcus' common wife. Somewhere in the back of her mind, the princess' conscience was pricked by the calls of duty and destiny, and the thought of her father's reaction threatened to break her heart. Yet, the feelings that Lillia felt for the shepherd were more than enough to drown all her concerns, leaving room for only one focus in her mind: to be with Marcus, whatever the consequences.

Chapter Twenty-Four

One Week Later

The stag made its way through the low-lying bushes and tall trees, picking off the sweeter green shoots as he grazed, all the while on the lookout, attentive to every movement and sound. The beast's large antlers snagged small branches as he wandered, raining broken leaves down onto his glossy, dark-red coat.

The rest of the herd browsed cautiously, never straying too far, appearing to take comfort from the stag's proximity. Stopping at a patch of grass, he paused before dipping his head for a taste of the new growth. A few mouthfuls and he moved on, chewing as he went, keeping his harem ahead of him. Once or twice he stopped as the forest was disturbed by the crack of a twig or the sudden noisy squawk of a crow. Then, on hearing a slight rustle from the trees, the stag tensed, ready to balk at the slightest movement, muscles tight and ears erect.

From the cover of low bushes, Prince Numitor trained his eye along the shaft of his readied arrow, and admired the elegant beauty of the beast as it grazed. Concentrating on his target, he noticed how proudly the animal stood, with its wide antlers spreading over its large head, as if it were wearing them like a crown of honour. Although the prince knew how badly his food stores were in need of fresh stocks of venison, he felt a fleeting hint of regret at the prospect of killing such a fine creature. Casting aside his sentimentality, Numitor took his aim, and on seeing that the stag was about to balk, he fired the arrow.

It found its target, causing the stag to screech a warning and leap for cover. The does dispersed quickly into the trees, frightened by their leader's call. The stag was lifted into the air as another arrow hit him, and his legs betrayed him when he tumbled back to the ground.

Numitor cautiously approached. The stag bellowed its anguish as it failed in its attempts to rise and run. As the beast lay dying, the prince sent a silent prayer of thanks to Diana, goddess of the hunt, but became unsettled by the gesture as it brought to his mind the Hounds of Diana.

'That is a fine stag,' said Paridé, wiping away drops of sweat that had collected over his thick eyebrows, 'but he was wily. I was beginning to think we would never get a clear shot at him.'

Numitor put aside his private thoughts and offered his friend a slight nod of agreement. The prince then stooped to examine the large antlers attached to the kill. 'Yes, he certainly gave us a good hunt until he was finally downed by your arrow,' he said, pointing to the red feathered shaft that protruded from the animal's chest. 'A great shot, I think, considering he was in mid-air when you hit him.'

Paridé smiled. 'He certainly gave us a run around, but I can't take all the credit for the kill – it was your arrow that found him first.'

'Paridé, we have known each other far too long for you to be so gracious,' laughed Numitor. 'We both know that mine was but an injuring hit at best. Without your arrow, we would have lost him.'

'Well, then let us agree on a joint effort!'

'Of course it was, my friend.' The prince retrieved the remains of his arrow which had snapped when the stag had fallen. 'That was unfortunate,' he said, holding the broken pieces. 'I was only able to shoot one arrow all day, and this is what became of it!'

'Better a broken arrow with a good meal than a full quiver and an empty stomach,' remarked Paridé.

Numitor laughed, 'So, you have become a philosopher now! Where did that saying come from?'

Patting his belly, Paridé smiled. 'That is merely my hunger talking, Sire.'

'Well, I shall have to use that with my brother sometime,' replied the prince with a grin, 'although I am sure he won't appreciate it,' he laughed.

* * *

After returning to the hunting lodge at the edge of the forest, Numitor found himself watching the sun crown the distant hills. He was sharing an amphora of wine with Brascus and Paridé, along with a handful of guards and servants that had accompanied them. It was rare that Numitor indulged his servants in such a manner, but in recent years it had become a tradition to celebrate a successful hunt in this way. The gesture was always well received, and the prince believed it helped to create loyalty in his staff.

The shaded clearing offered a good view of the meadow beyond, while a collection of large, felled trees made practical, if not comfortable, seating. The tired men were enjoying the mild evening and discussing the hunt as the smell of roasting meat wafted over from the leg of venison that was cooking over a fire at the centre of the clearing. While keeping an eye on the fire, Brascus was brooding over his own disastrous hunt. He had been unlucky in his pursuit of a large boar. He had spent most of the day tracking it, without ever having the opportunity for a clear shot. He hated coming back empty-handed and had sulked ever since his return.

With a mischievous grin, Paridé addressed no-one in particular: 'I was really looking forward to some roast boar this evening. It is a shame that they are so good at hiding in these infernal woods!'

With a half-smile, Brascus offered a retort. 'When one goes after such a large target, it is hard to miss.'

Numitor smiled sheepishly and nodded in sympathy, 'Do not be so glum, Brascus. Boars make a difficult target.' Turning to his hunting partner, he said, 'Of course, deer can also be difficult to hit. Paridé should think himself lucky that he had the company of such a good marksman to help him make that kill.'

Paridé rarely let anyone have the last say and was about to protest, when both Brascus and the prince burst into laughter, stopping him before he could speak. Accepting that the joke had been turned against him, he chuckled and conceded with a shrug.

For a few moments they all fell silent, content to sit and enjoy the vista, until Brascus suddenly noticed a man on horseback approaching the cabin at speed from across the meadow. He stood up quickly and grabbed his bow, placing himself between Numitor and the rider. The others followed, swiftly drawing swords, ready to defend the prince.

As the visitor came closer, it became evident that he wore the uniform of the palace's Royal Guard. When he reached the party, the man dismounted quickly. 'I apologise for disturbing you, Sire,' he said, hurrying to the prince. 'Lucius has asked that you return to the palace at your earliest convenience. Princess Rhea is missing.' The guard stopped and waited for a response.

Numitor blanched as he looked at the man in disbelief. 'When?'

'Her Highness has not been seen since yesterday morning, Sire,' said the guard, looking at the ground.

'And I am only hearing about it now?' growled Numitor. 'Why has it taken this long to get a message to me?'

'I am not sure, Sire. I came as soon as I was ordered to.'

The guard shuffled nervously but Numitor ignored him while he fought the churning in his stomach as the implication set in. With an anxious look he caught the eye of Brascus and motioned him to come near. 'This may be what we have feared,' he said.

178

Brascus paused and thought for a moment before replying. 'You return to the palace, Sire. I will try to find out what I can before I come and report to you there. In the meantime, Paridé should talk to his daughter to see if she knows anything.' He glanced at Sylvanna's father, who was sheathing his weapon.

'I will go and see her now, Sire,' agreed Paridé.

'Good,' said Numitor. 'Come to the palace when you are done. Brascus, you take the guards with you and use them as you see fit. I want her found quickly and taken to safety as we discussed.' Without waiting for a reply, the prince mounted his horse, kicked his heels, and galloped back towards Alba Longa.

Chapter Twenty-Five

Numitor burst into the throne room to find Lucius sitting alone at the obsidian table with a worried look on his pale face. Without hesitating, the prince stormed across the large expanse of floor and grabbed the young assistant by his throat, lifting him off his chair before the man could react. 'You will tell me where my daughter has been taken,' growled Numitor.

In a choked whisper Lucius replied, 'I... I don't know what you are talking about, Sire.'

The prince released his hold only to then punch Lucius in the midriff, sending him sprawling to the floor.

'Sire, please, no,' begged the assistant as he gasped for air, but Numitor descended again, this time grabbing him by the scruff and hauling the whimpering man up to face him.

'Lucius, I know about your Dius. And I know you had a plan that involved Lillia.' The prince pulled the trembling man closer to his face. 'Tell me all you know this instant, or you will come to regret it.'

'Oh no, Sire, no!' cried Lucius. 'Forgive me, but you are supposed to know nothing of the Dius. It would be far too dangerous for us both. I would be boiled alive if I were to speak of him, Sire.'

'And if you do not, I will see to it that you are burned slowly,' threatened the prince. 'Lillia is missing and I believe you have knowledge of where she is.'

'No, Sire,' whined the assistant, 'I truly do not. I sent for you because the princess has not been seen since yesterday morning. I have been so worried about her.' At this, Lucius began to weep.

Numitor felt only disgust at the sight of the blubbering man and let him fall to the ground in a heap. 'Speak now, man, and quickly.'

Gazing up at the prince, the assistant sniffed and wiped his face. Then, with his shoulders slumped in defeat, he answered. 'I am supposed to help protect you and the princess, Sire. The Dius warned me that this might happen, but he didn't tell me when it would be.'

'What are you talking about, man?' demanded Numitor. 'You are making no sense.'

Lucius took a deep breath before speaking again, 'We had a plan in place, Sire, to protect the princess if they came for her. But it's too early. The Dius told me not to initiate the plan until they had made a move.'

'Too early for what, Lucius? Stop mumbling and tell me what this plan is.'

Lucius sat up and tried to calm himself. 'The Dius told me that your enemies would be coming for the princess, Sire. He said that, as soon as I was given the signal, I was to take her immediately to the Temple of Apollo, from where she would then be escorted to a place of safety. I was told to wait until he sent me word, Sire, but I haven't heard from him. No black stones have appeared in my bedrolls – I have been checking carefully.'

'Black stones?' interrupted Numitor.

'To summon me, Sire.'

'And what enemies are these that you talk of? Who are these unseen people that would dare to take my daughter?'

Lucius dipped his eyes and quietly uttered, 'Your brother, Sire.'

'Ah, yes, my brother.' Numitor sighed. 'Yes, sadly, I had already come to suspect that Amulius was working with your Dius.'

'But that is not possible, Sire,' Lucius declared. 'You are mistaken – the Dius only wishes to protect you and the princess. He would never hurt either of you.'

'Could it not be possible that he is merely using you to do his bidding, you fool?'

Shaking his head vigorously, Lucius then stared at Numitor with his mouth half open, unable to formulate a response. The prince had further questions to ask, but was interrupted when Paridé rushed into the throne room.

'We need to talk, Sire. Sylvanna tells me that she has not had contact with the princess since they argued six months ago.' Paridé stopped abruptly when he noticed Lucius on the floor. Looking up at the prince in confusion, he asked, 'Is everything all right, Sire?'

'Do not worry about him, Paridé. Tell me, did you learn anything at all about my daughter's whereabouts?'

As it turned out, Paridé had much to report. Numitor listened with mounting surprise. He was shocked to learn of his own daughter's involvement with a shepherd boy, and it hurt him to discover that she had chosen to keep the relationship a secret for all this time. When Paridé had finished his tale, the prince sat down and took a few moments to try and absorb the information, absently rolling his eagle ring around his finger. He then turned to address his cowering assistant, 'I will deal with you later, Lucius. Go to your quarters and remain there until I send for you. Do you understand?'

Lucius acknowledged the prince's commands with the barest of nods, lowering his eyes as he departed, leaving Numitor alone with Paridé. Waiting until the large oak doors had been shut by the guards, the prince turned to his friend.

'I am going to need your help once again, Paridé. There are only a few people I can trust now, and I fear that my daughter's life is in danger.'

As darkness descended upon Alba Longa, Numitor waited anxiously for the return of Brascus. After his conversation with Paridé, the prince had sent members of the Royal Guard to scour the city for information on the whereabouts of Densara. Believing that the merchant was involved with Lillia's disappearance, he had questioned Lucius further. However, it had become apparent that, not only was the assistant ignorant of the identity of his Dius, but also that he genuinely had no knowledge of Lillia's disappearance. With so little to go on, Numitor had sent guards to the home of the shepherd boy to question his parents, as well as arranging for Densara's villa to be watched. The merchant was to be detained the moment he appeared.

With regard to his brother, Numitor was confused. Nothing suspicious or out of the ordinary had been reported in relation to Amulius' recent activities. The younger prince had returned to Pietrabbondante to be with the Latin army, and was due to return again to Alba Longa at some point over the next few days. Numitor had heard nothing unusual from his sources, other than that Amulius had captured many thousands of slaves.

Sipping from a black cup, Numitor cradled his wine as he watched the first stars appearing in the night sky. Wanting to be ready to spring into action the moment Brascus arrived, he had taken a seat in the courtyard from which he could see the palace gates. As the evening wore on, however, no news was forthcoming, only a steady throng of guards with nothing of consequence to report, their visits bringing only disappointment. The prince's feelings were a muddle of worry and anger, so he stood up and began to pace around the courtyard as he tried to consider his options. Numitor's thoughts were interrupted when Lucius suddenly ran out of the atrium, craning his neck as he searched for his master.

'Sire, Sire,' he called. Catching sight of the prince, he rushed over to him. 'They are thought to be heading for Neopolis, Sire,' he said hurriedly.

'Where did you hear this?' demanded Numitor.

'The shepherd's parents, Sire. They said it was the only place they could think of. They have relatives there.'

'Why would my daughter go to Neopolis?' roared the prince as his temper broke.

'I... I do not know, Sire,' came the assistant's shaky reply. 'It could be that they are just going for a visit, Sire.'

'Then why did she not mention it to me? No, there is more to this, I am certain, and I intend to find out the whole story.' Numitor allowed his voice to become calmer as he asked, 'Neopolis you say?'

'Yes, yes, Sire. They said Neopolis... the parents.'

'Then they should be easy to track. They will have to take the trail along the Corra Pass and then make their way through the great forests further south,' he surmised. 'Are they on foot?'

'I do not know, Sire, but I will check to see if any of our horses are missing.'

'I am sure they cannot have travelled too far as yet,' said Numitor, optimistically. 'Right, the time has come for me to take action. Lucius, I want six guards to be ready to depart at my order. I am going after Lillia myself. While I head for the Corra Pass, I want you to send out parties of guards along all the other routes south. Instruct them to search every village and question anyone they meet travelling along those routes. I want my daughter found.'

Numitor was about to leave the courtyard when he remembered that Brascus had not yet arrived, so he turned to Lucius again. 'If Brascus returns tonight, let him know that I am heading for Corra.'

'Um... That was something else I meant to say, Sire. The shepherd's parents spoke to Brascus earlier today. They told him all that I have just reported to you. My guess would be that Brascus has already gone after the princess himself. I imagine this is the reason why he has not yet returned.'

'Then I am at a loss. Brascus was instructed to bring news to me here. Why would he have gone after Lillia on his own?'

Lucius thought for a moment. 'I... I'm not sure, Sire. He did have two guards with him. Perhaps he thought he had a good chance of catching up with the princess and did not want to waste time.'

Numitor conceded the point. 'Well, I am still going after her myself. I cannot just sit here and wait.'

The assistant nodded in understanding, and the two men left the courtyard in silence.

Chapter Twenty-Six

The Carpenter watched from the cover of trees as the young couple made their way along the lush valley floor. They led their only horse beside a small stream that meandered through the green surroundings. Slowly he trailed them, as he had the previous two days, and he watched their loving antics with disinterest. His instruction from the Dius had been clear: "Do not let them out of your sight." So far, this had resulted in the Carpenter having to spend two nights out in the cold without a fire, watching whilst the princess and the shepherd huddled under a sheepskin to ward off the highland chill.

Princess Rhea was travelling in peasant clothing – a simple fabric dress with sheepskin boots and a blanket around her shoulders. She looked like she belonged with the boy who walked beside her. The Carpenter had worried about the risk of losing the couple in a town or village, so it had come as a relief to observe that the two runaways had thus far avoided busy places, choosing instead to keep to the goat trails and high passes.

Leading his horse through the trees above the valley, the Carpenter spotted a hare bounding across the steep slopes below him, and his stomach rumbled. He reached into his pocket and pulled out a chunk of salted meat, tearing off a little with his teeth. As he slowly chewed the morsel, a breeze rolled around the hills causing him to suppress a shiver.

The first night he had spent trailing the princess had not been so bad. The forest was always a little warmer than the open ground and his cloak had proved to be adequate, but as they had started to climb into the highlands south of Alba Longa, he began to regret not having brought warmer clothes. Thankfully, the end of this particular task was now within sight. By nightfall, he knew, the Dius would have made his move, and the Carpenter would then be free to pursue other targets.

With a light mist covering the sides of the valley, he continued cautiously to trail the couple, sometimes losing sight of them briefly as they rounded bends or disappeared behind rocky outcrops. On one occasion he almost stumbled into them when they had stopped to eat, but fortunately an agitated crow had squawked its warning in time for him to avoid being detected. After the event, the Carpenter had kept a greater distance between himself and his targets. Ahead of them, he knew, was a large forest – it would be there that the Dius would make his move.

***

The clear mountain air filled Lillia's senses as the sweet smell of flowers mingled with the musty aromas of wild sheep. She loved the sense of freedom that the open valleys and high peaks gave her, far away from the world of titles and duty that had been her life in Alba Longa. The journey had proved harder than she had expected and the nights were cold, but nothing could remove the smile from her face whenever she looked over at Marcus. He had kept her cheerful and distracted from their hardship, pointing out things of interest along the route and making her laugh with his stories.

'That one over there,' he said, pointing to a light green plant that clung to a rock, 'that is sheep's bane. When the sheep eat it, they become sick and their eyes go yellow. I always have to be careful to keep them away from it.'

Lillia had little interest in plants, but was nevertheless impressed by the knowledge that Marcus seemed to have about many different topics. He knew what was safe for them to eat, and along the way he had collected mushrooms, nuts and beets. They had hardly touched the food that Lillia had taken from the villa stores, and yet they had eaten well at every meal.

As they began to climb higher into the mountains, the princess found herself mesmerised by the views across the deep valleys, and for the first time she started to understand the beauty of the Latin countryside. Tall thin waterfalls fell from dizzying heights down into deep pools that fed the small streams where they drank and occasionally frolicked in fits of laughter as they washed away the inevitable dust and grime that came with sleeping outdoors.

With nothing to do but concentrate on her steps, Lillia cast her mind back to the night before they had begun their journey. She recalled Marcus' touch and the way it had made her feel, and unconsciously brought her hand to her mouth. The evening had been perfect. Marcus had met her as planned at the shepherd's well, and hand in hand they had strolled to the lakeside cabin, talking about their hopes and dreams, blissfully content in each other's company.

Beside the lake, they had watched the sun go down and talked about everything from Marcus' family in Neopolis, to what they would call their

186

children. Later they had gone swimming, and afterwards sat beside the fire in the cabin. Once they were dry, Marcus had poured them cups of wine from the supplies that Lillia had taken from the palace store, and slowly she had drunk herself into his arms.

She remembered the way that Marcus had been reluctant at first to take advantage of her somewhat inebriated encouragement but she'd been more than a little persuasive – not because of the wine, she had told him, but because she loved him. Marcus had been gentle and careful with her. Lillia felt her skin tingle as she recalled how he had kissed her mouth, before moving on to her face and neck. His hands had explored and caressed her as she had nervously surrendered to his lead. The memory caused a small shiver to travel down her spine as she relived the pleasure.

The princess felt herself blush as her concentration was suddenly broken by Marcus, who had stopped to help her over a boulder in their path. When they had resumed their walk, her mind returned to the intense feelings and the pain that she had experienced when the shepherd had first entered her, and how quickly the pain had then been overcome by the most exquisite pleasure. An overwhelming feeling of love had then taken over, and she had begun to move with his rhythms and urgency, until all too soon it was over. Afterwards, they had rested in each other's arms and Lillia knew that she could have stayed in that moment for ever.

Reaching the top of their climb, Lillia and Marcus could see a large expanse of trees in the distance. 'That's the forest I was telling you about,' said Marcus as he pointed. 'We should get there by nightfall. And our nights will be warmer in there. We can collect firewood as we go,' he smiled.

'But won't it be dangerous?' asked Lillia with an edge of worry in her tone. 'There are wolves in the forest,' she added, remembering her close encounter with the she-wolf.

'Don't worry, Lillia, we will have a fire. Wolves won't come near us,' the shepherd assured her.

'And what about bears and boars?' she asked. 'Are they also frightened of fires?'

'All animals are frightened of fire,' he chuckled, then added in a more serious tone, 'but it's not just the animals we need to be wary of. Sometimes there are thieves or runaway slaves hiding, so we'll have to be cautious all the same.'

An anxious look flitted across Lillia's eyes as she turned her gaze towards the massive forest in the distance. Marcus noticed her concern and tried to offer further assurance. 'I have my sling and my dagger. I won't let anyone or anything hurt you. I promise.'

The princess believed him and felt her spirits rise as he took her into his arms and held her in his firm embrace. Lillia enjoyed the sensation for a few moments before gently releasing herself. She took his hand. 'We had better carry on then, or we will never get to Neopolis.'

**

As he watched the two runaways lead their mount across the barren moor that edged the great forest, the Carpenter mounted his own horse, ready to pursue the couple and trap them at the forest edge where his Dius would be waiting. He bided his time, judging the perfect moment to begin the chase, knowing that if he showed himself too early, they would have a chance to avoid capture in the forest, and if that were to happen there would then be the risk of them running into the Dius without his support.

Not for the first time, the Carpenter's Dius would be attending this secret meeting without his mask. The masks had always irritated the Carpenter – he preferred to deal with people face to face and see the eyes of those that addressed him – but in this situation it would be necessary for the princess to see a familiar face if their plan were to succeed. The Carpenter was all too aware that failure here would have devastating consequences upon the entire kingdom. The princess, whether she knew it or not, was a crucial piece in a complicated game, and so much depended on the outcome of his next move.

When he judged that the perfect moment had arrived, the Carpenter coaxed his horse forward and set off after the couple. With the setting sun hovering over the horizon, he had to squint as he concentrated on the silhouettes of the two travellers and their horse. He cantered towards them and had covered half the distance before they spotted him, upon which the princess and the shepherd boy quickly mounted their dappled horse and galloped towards the trees.

Chapter Twenty-Seven

Lillia held Marcus tightly as he urged the horse to go faster. After spotting the dark rider trailing them, she had begun to worry that it might be someone from the palace, but as the horseman drew nearer it had become clear from his dark hooded cloak that he was not one of the Royal Guard. 'He is gaining on us, Marcus,' shouted the princess into the shepherd's ear. 'We need to go faster!' The sound of the rushing wind all but drowned her words.

Leaning back in the saddle, Marcus turned to answer. 'We have another problem. Look.'

Ahead of them the trail was blocked by a figure on a white horse. Lillia could see that the man wore simple travelling clothes and was short and stocky, contrasting greatly with the slender dark rider to their rear. For an instant she wondered if she recognised this new arrival, but her attention was quickly diverted as Marcus steered their horse away from the trail.

'We have to find another way into the forest,' he shouted over his shoulder.

Lillia glanced back and saw that the dark rider had anticipated their move, and had already begun to race across the moor to intercept them. 'Quick Marcus, go the other way,' she screamed. 'He is trying to cut us off!'

The stocky rider at the forest edge also began to gallop forward, making straight for their position. Marcus was forced to change tact and headed directly for the white horse. 'I'll try and get round him,' he shouted to the princess. 'Hang on.' With a shake of the reins, he began to charge.

The stocky horseman shouted to the pair as they made their rapid approach. 'Princess Rhea, it is I, Densara Potitii. Please stop, it is most important.'

Hearing the familiar name, Lillia tugged at the shepherd's side. 'Marcus, slow down please. I know this man.'

'No, it could be a trick,' answered Marcus in a worried tone. 'Stay on the horse. I won't let him near you.'

'Well, if it is a trick, then we shall try to get past him and into the forest. But first, I want to make sure that my father is all right,' she said, knowing that she would never forgive herself if Densara's reason for being there was to bring her important news of Numitor. As their horse slowed she looked behind and saw that the dark rider had brought his animal to a stop a good distance away from them.

'Your Highness, you must come with me immediately,' said Densara as he hurriedly dismounted. 'If you do not, your life may be in danger.'

Marcus jumped off their horse and placed himself between Lillia and the advancing merchant. 'Do not come any closer,' he shouted to the man. 'You can talk from there.'

The princess felt a moment of pride at seeing Marcus defending her once again. She turned to address Densara. 'I am in no danger. Marcus is looking after me.'

'It is not him that I am worried about, Princess,' replied the merchant in a serious tone. 'There are others who move against your father and wish you harm. I need to take you to safety.'

A moment of alarm was quickly replaced by doubt as Lillia considered his words. 'If I am in danger, then why would my father send you?'

'He did not send me,' came the abrupt reply. 'Look, I cannot explain now, Princess. We have no time to waste. We must go.' There was a hint of irritation in his voice.

'She is not going anywhere with you,' growled Marcus, taking a step closer.

'Do not be a fool, boy,' replied Densara. 'Don't you think you have already caused enough trouble?' he said as he began to approach.

Frightened for the shepherd, Lillia screamed, 'Marcus, quick, let's go,' but as Densara continued to draw nearer, Marcus suddenly threw himself at the stocky man.

With speed that defied his build, Densara deflected Marcus with ease, turning quickly as they made contact and sending the young man sprawling to the ground with a thud.

'Go, Lillia,' grunted the shepherd as he gasped for air.

'Leave him alone,' screamed the princess as Densara bore down on her lover. Her anger then quickly turned to fear as she heard a noise behind her. Looking back she could see that the dark rider was now starting to approach. Without hesitation, the princess slapped her hand down onto the rump of her horse. With a squeal of displeasure, the animal reared up, causing the merchant to scuttle out of the way of its flailing limbs. The distraction was enough for Marcus to have the time to jump up and out of Densara's reach.

Then the dark rider charged forward, aiming his horse at Marcus. Seeing the move, Lillia panicked. 'Run, Marcus, run!' she screamed, before her attention was drawn back to Densara, who was now advancing towards her. She tugged on her reins and forced her mount to turn just before the merchant had reached her. Densara's hand brushed her leg, causing her to scream again as he collided with the horse's rear, leaving Lillia only the barest of moments to ride out of his reach.

As the merchant staggered back, Marcus threw himself at the man, and it was at this point that the dark rider reached the affray. At the arrival of the menacing man, Marcus shouted to the princess, 'Go, Lillia! I will keep them busy here.'

Torn between helping Marcus and escaping from the two men, Lillia hesitated a moment and looked back. She saw Densara struggling as Marcus held on to him with his arms wrapped around the merchant's neck. It was clear that the shepherd would be overwhelmed as soon as the dark rider chose to intervene, so the princess sought to lead the man away, kicking her heals into her horse's side and starting to race back across the moor.

'Get after her!' shouted Densara, his voice choked by Marcus' grip.

As the dark rider wheeled his mount around and set off after the princess, Densara reached over his shoulder and grabbed Marcus by the scruff. The agile merchant then bent to his knee, the move unbalancing Marcus and causing him to tumble forward. The shepherd hit the ground hard but immediately jumped back up and started to sprint after Lillia and the dark rider.

The princess felt her heart thumping as she pushed her horse to gallop with all its might, but she quickly realised that her mount was no match for the large stallion of her pursuer, and all too soon the dark rider was abreast and reaching out for her. In desperation, Lillia wheeled from left to right, trying to dodge his grasp, but he kept close, grabbing at her every time he neared.

Ahead lay a copse of stunted trees and bushes, and the princess angled her horse towards them, hoping to fool her pursuer as she rounded them. Keeping low as the wind blew her hair into her eyes, she quickly glanced behind only to discover that the dark rider had suddenly disappeared. She felt fear rising as she wondered where he had gone. Hoping to confuse the man, Lillia then took her mount on a zigzagging route through the bushes, on the look-out for an opening that would allow her to head back and help Marcus.

Spying a suitable gap in the trees, the princess quickly turned her horse towards it. As the mount tore through the thin branches that obstructed the opening, Lillia suddenly found herself face to face with the dark rider.

Bringing her horse to an abrupt stop, she stared in shock at the unnerving sight of his small piercing eyes that peered at her over the top of a black cloth that covered the rest of his face. She noted that the skin around his eyes seemed old, like her grandfather's had been, but her thoughts were cast aside as he lunged forward and grabbed her shoulder tightly in his thin fingers. With his free hand, he tried to grab Lillia's reins while she could only scream and struggle against his grip. She tried as hard as she could to prise his hand away, but the man simply leant over and latched onto her arm, whereupon he started trying to drag her from her horse with a strength that defied his slim build.

Suddenly, another cloaked figure appeared behind her attacker, and Lillia glimpsed the flash of a sword as it swung towards the dark rider. The blade hit his arm, cutting through his clothing to leave a bloodied gash. Without uttering the slightest sound of pain, the dark rider let the princess go before ducking another swipe of the sword and pulling away out of its reach.

It was then that Lillia realised her rescuer was Brascus. She watched in relief as the dark rider galloped away, closely followed by two similarly cloaked men. Guessing that they must be with Brascus, the princess turned to thank the big man but was distracted by the sight of Densara, who was riding towards the forest with two Royal Guards in pursuit. Unable to see any sign of the shepherd, she turned back to Brascus. 'Where is Marcus?' she asked before returning her anxious gaze to the moor. Determined to find him, she kicked her horse forward before Brascus could reply and rode past him, out into the open.

Lillia quickly spotted the prone figure of Marcus on the bare ground close to where she had left him. Realising that he wasn't moving, she felt her heart breaking as she raced towards him. She dismounted early and ran the last few strides before throwing herself down beside him. His eyes were closed, but with an enormous sense of relief she saw that his chest still rose and fell with his breaths. She shook him gently. 'Marcus,' she whispered, 'Marcus, please, wake up.'

With a low grown he began to stir. His hand moved up to his head.

'Marcus, talk to me,' urged the princess as she gently stroked his cheek.

He finally opened his eyes and took a moment to focus before a weak smile started to tug at his mouth. 'I'm fine,' he whispered.

Lillia began to cry with relief. 'I thought he hurt you,' she blurted through her tears. 'Are you hurt?' she asked, checking him over with a frantic glance.

'Just sore,' he replied weakly. 'He hit me with something hard… Would have finished me too, I reckon, if it hadn't been for those two guards.' Marcus grimaced as he tried to get up.

Lillia helped him into a sitting position and then kissed his cheek. 'You are safe now, my love,' she whispered as she gently embraced him. 'My father's friend, Brascus, is here. He and his men saved us both, but I don't understand why those other men wanted to take me.'

'Maybe he can tell you,' Marcus replied, gesturing to the large man that had now appeared behind the princess.

As Brascus dismounted, Lillia turned to him and asked, 'Why was that man chasing us? He said I was in danger and then he tried to take me.'

'You are indeed in danger, Your Highness. Your father sent me to escort you to safety, and to judge from what I have just seen, we must go quickly.'

'Where is father? How did he know to find me here?' She looked down at the ground in shame and added, 'Does he know about Marcus?'

Brascus smiled. 'Do not worry, Princess. Your father is concerned only with your safety.'

Lillia felt a moment of immense relief before remembering why she had run away in the first place. With a sinking heart, she realised there was no way that she and Marcus would be able to continue with their journey now. With men set on taking her away, and her father's friend now escorting them, she knew it would be almost impossible to escape with the shepherd. Her thoughts were then interrupted as Brascus spoke again.

'Give the horse to the boy, Your Highness, so that he can make his way back to his home. You must come with me. Your father would never forgive me if something were to happen to you now.' He paused for a moment and then asked, 'Did you see the face of your other attacker?'

'Yes, it was Densara Potitii, the merchant who sells slaves for Uncle Amulius.'

Brascus nodded but made no further comment on the subject. 'We must get going, Your Highness.' He then turned at the sound of approaching riders. The two Royal Guards cantered into view and Brascus immediately went over to them, leaving Lillia alone with Marcus once more.

The princess felt as though her world was falling apart. She was torn between duty and love, but ultimately she knew what she had to do, even though it would break her heart. 'I have to go with him, Marcus,' she said as the tears rolled down her cheeks.

'Yes, you do have to go with him,' answered Marcus solemnly. 'That man was ready to kill me before taking you. There was nothing I could do to protect you.' He lowered his head in shame, avoiding Lillia's eyes.

'You were extremely brave, Marcus. I could not ask for more,' she assured him with a smile. 'You are my hero and my love. I promise I will get word to you as soon as I am safe.'

Marcus forced a smile in return and grabbed Lillia for a final embrace, 'Be safe, my princess,' he whispered. 'I will wait for you in the meadows as always. Try not to be gone too long, my love.'

Lillia choked back her tears and remained in the sanctuary of his arms until Brascus returned, bringing horses with him.

'I will send the two guards back with your… your friend, here,' said the big man, pointing at Marcus. 'You are to ride with me, Princess.'

With her head hanging in sorrow, Lillia stood up and allowed Brascus to help her up onto his horse. With a last look of longing at Marcus, she managed a smiled and mouthed the words 'I love you,' before the horse turned and left the young shepherd sitting alone in the dirt, battered and bruised.

Chapter Twenty-Eight

Numitor led six of his best guards on horseback along the narrow mountain ledge. He worried about his daughter as he thought of the treacherous journey that she had embarked upon. Feeling a mixture of anger and anxiety, he tried to fathom what Lillia had thought she would achieve by going off with the shepherd boy. The prince felt somewhat responsible for the situation and blamed himself for not being there when his daughter had most needed him. The fact that she had kept her new friendship a secret bothered him greatly, as Lillia had always been so open and honest in the past. It was completely out of character for her to deceive her father in this manner, and Numitor found himself wondering if the shepherd boy had manipulated her in some way.

With a mind full of questions that could only be answered when he caught up with his daughter, the prince pressed onward, keeping a careful eye on the trail ahead. After rounding a narrow bend under a high cliff face, the path opened onto a gravel slope which descended into a wide valley far below. Seeing the outline of a meandering stream in its depths, Numitor heaved a sigh of relief. Looking back to his guards, he called to their leader, Captain Miron. 'We will stop and water the horses down there,' he said, pointing to the valley floor.

The captain acknowledged the command and turned to his men. 'Go ahead of us and check the terrain down there,' he said. 'I do not want to encounter any surprises.'

The men departed down the slope, carefully guiding their horses through the thick gravel that seemed to suck the animals' hooves down, sending up small clouds of dust as they descended. Numitor followed cautiously, slowing his mount when the ground became slippery and urging it on as it nickered its fear. At the bottom of the slope they found a firm green carpet of lush grass that led to the edge of what turned out to be a small river. The guards that had gone on ahead were examining the remains of a fire when the prince caught up with them.

'Someone has been here in the last day, Sire,' remarked one of the men. 'The embers still have a little heat in them.'

Dismounting quickly, Numitor checked the fire himself. He glanced around and then walked down towards the river. 'Look there,' he shouted, pointing at some footprints at the water's muddy edge. 'Those could belong to my daughter.'

Captain Miron jumped from his mount, and grabbing the reins, led his horse down to where Numitor was standing. Kneeling down beside the prints, the captain studied them for a while. 'Definitely two people,' he said, 'and there are also some fresh hoof marks there. Look, Your Highness.'

Numitor saw them and frowned. 'Get the horses watered and let us get going,' he announced. 'I want to find my daughter before it gets dark.'

Looking up into the midday sky, Captain Miron hid any doubt that he felt towards Numitor's optimism. 'We will have to push the horses a little harder then, Sire,' he replied. 'Aside from that, all we can do is hope that they won't have reached the great forest before we get to them. There are so many trails through those woods that only the Huntress would be able to find her in there.'

Numitor narrowed his eyes at the mention of the goddess Diana. Even though Miron had only used the common name for her, it instantly put the prince on alert. The captain didn't seem to notice as he continued to speak. 'Let me send two of the men ahead, Sire. They can locate the princess and then wait for us to arrive.'

Experiencing a moment of acute paranoia, the prince shook his head. 'No, we do not want to frighten her. It is best that we stay together and she sees me first.'

Accepting the answer, Miron ordered his men to stand down and then set off for the river to fill his water-skin. After a quick bite of day-old bread and hard cheese, the party re-mounted and were about to leave when Numitor spotted two men on horseback, racing towards them on the trail ahead. As the riders neared, the prince recognised them as being the two guards that he had sent off with Brascus. They were returning without him.

Numitor listened carefully to everything that the guards had to report, but was left with more questions than they could answer. He wasn't surprised to learn that Densara had tried to take his daughter, and he felt great relief at hearing that she was now safe with Brascus. However, he was still unclear as to where they were now, so he continued to question the guards. 'If what you say is correct, then why have I not passed Brascus and my daughter?' he demanded. 'And how did you manage to lose the boy?'

Exchanging a nervous glance, the guards shook their heads in regret before one of them found the courage to speak. 'We passed through a rocky area, Sire, and he just vanished. We had a good look around, but the whole area was thick with boulders and outcrops.'

'Well, that still does not explain why I have not seen Brascus. Am I to assume that he is taking my daughter home by a different route?'

'I honestly don't know, Sire, but he had a good start on us. I expect he will get back to Alba before we do.'

'He had better,' whispered Numitor to himself. He sighed as he absently gazed back up the slope they had recently descended. 'We should get going. I am very keen to talk to my daughter, and then deal with that traitor, Densara.'

They set off back the way they had come, riding through the evening and into the night; stopping only once to rest the horses. Eventually they rode through the city gates of Alba Longa. Normally the streets would have been quiet at this late hour, but Numitor immediately saw that the place was busy with people rushing around everywhere, while sections of guards patrolled the surrounding area. With his mind running wild with theories, the prince called out to one of the patrols. 'Tell me what is going on,' he demanded. 'Why all this commotion?'

The section leader ignored Numitor's question, having failed to recognise the prince, who was still dressed in his hunting clothes. The man was about to offer a brusque retort when Numitor chose to urge his horse forward into the glow of a lamp outside the building where they had stopped.

'Your Highness!' gasped the surprised guard. 'I am sorry, I did not realise it was you.' He bowed several times.

'Yes, all right,' snapped Numitor. 'Now tell me what is going on?'

'Etruscans, Sire. Thousands of them… at the river border.'

Confused by the explanation, Numitor shook his head. 'What are you talking about? Are you sure they are Etruscans?'

'I have not seen them with my own eyes, Sire, but I'm told that King Corros is with them.'

The prince's mind became clouded by a mixture of surprise and shock as he tried to absorb the information. Thanking the section leader, he then raced to the palace. Leaving his horse at the gate, he rushed to the throne room and found a small crowd of men waiting outside. He scanned the area, desperately hoping to spot either Brascus or Lillia, but saw only councillors and advisors, all of whom were waiting to speak with him. They started advancing towards the prince and began to voice their various questions and queries. It was necessary for Numitor to shout over their din in order to be heard. 'Where is Lucius?' he demanded.

'Sire, I am here,' came the high voice of his assistant. Lucius then appeared amongst the harassing group of councillors.

'In here,' ordered Numitor, gesturing towards the throne room. He glanced at the guards, spurring them into opening the doors. The prince marched in and waited for Lucius to catch up. 'Tell me what has happened,' he demanded as soon as they were alone.

'Oh, Sire,' cried Lucius, 'it was just after you left to find the princess. A returning patrol reported that they had seen thousands of warriors on the Etruscan side of the River Tiber. They have set up a massive camp there, and more keep arriving.'

'But why?' growled Numitor, mostly to himself. 'I thought I had an understanding with Corros. This is not right.'

'I... I do not know why the Etruscans are assembling, Sire, but they are putting the whole city on edge. People are getting nervous, and all those councillors keep asking me questions that I cannot answer,'

'Well, I cannot answer them either,' said Numitor in frustration. 'Where is my brother? Has he been informed?'

'Oh yes, Sire,' Lucius replied promptly. 'I sent a messenger to him the moment I heard... but I wasn't sure where you were, Sire, so I couldn't—'

'Yes, yes, I understand,' interrupted the prince impatiently. 'Where are Brascus and my daughter?'

Lucius looked up with a surprised expression, 'Are they not with you, Sire?'

'Obviously not, Lucius, or I would not be asking.'

Lowering his eyes, the assistant shook his head. 'I am sorry, Sire, but I have not seen them; they have not returned since you left. At least, I have not heard any news of their return,' he added trying to sound hopeful.

Numitor frowned in annoyance. 'They should be here by now,' he said quietly, and then louder he announced, 'I must go to the border and deal with this Etruscan mess – if my brother gets there first, he'll only start another war. Lucius, you are to send me a message the moment my daughter is back. She is in the custody of Brascus, but all the same, I need to know when she is safely back at home. And then, she will be answering to me,' he said angrily.

* * *

A short while later, with the sky turning pink in the east, Numitor found himself back in the saddle, deprived of rest, and with larger burdens than ever now bearing down upon him. In the company of a few hundred riders – mostly Royal Guard, along with a few sections of warriors that protected the city – the prince headed north to face the Etruscans.

Chapter Twenty-Nine

It was shortly after Prince Numitor had left for the Etruscan border, and the King's Council was buzzing with anticipation as the members took their seats around the table. They had been anticipating a summons ever since the news of the Etruscan force had begun to spread around the city like a plague, bringing fear and uncertainty into all its quarters.

Lucius, aware of Numitor's absence, paced the corridor outside the council chamber, wondering what was happening. Everyone he had spoken to had given him the same reply; they had all been summoned at dawn. The assistant had not received any such invitation, but after having seen various councillors arriving at the palace, he had soon realised that something was going on. Glancing through the open council chamber door, he saw that a few of the seats were still empty. Notable absentees included both of the princes, the generals, and a few of the representatives from the other cities, as well as the merchant Densara.

As Numitor's assistant, Lucius was normally permitted to attend meetings of the King's Council in order to take notes, but on this occasion, without his master present, he felt unsure as to what he should do. *The Dius will certainly want to know what is happening,* he thought. He could imagine that failure to provide information would earn him a severe reprimand from the masked girl, while the terrifying face of Hades would be looming over her shoulder. *And I will also have to report to the prince on the events of the meeting when he returns. Why was I not sent a summons? And for that matter, who is responsible for calling this meeting?* Wrestling with the dilemma, Lucius soon realised that he had too many unanswered questions, and his underlying fear of the Dius meant that he would have no choice but to attend the meeting. The assistant summoned his courage and reluctantly entered the large cold chamber, taking a seat at the back of the room. Having tried to make himself as inconspicuous as possible, he was pleased that nobody seemed to have noticed his arrival.

Whispered conversations mingled as they echoed around the chamber, but they soon died down as the sound of marching footsteps approached. Moments later, Prince Amulius came striding through the door, followed by Generals Tyco and Servius. The prince approached the head of the table and remained standing as the generals took their seats.

'Thank you, gentlemen, for coming so promptly,' said Amulius as the last of the whispers died away. 'I am sorry to say that the situation we now face requires an urgent resolution. Therefore, today we will have to proceed without the presence of some of our esteemed colleagues,' he said, referring to the six empty seats at the table.

'Your Highness, a meeting may not commence unless all members of the council are present. I wish to know why we are here,' demanded Arbitrator Fabii, sounding outraged.

'We are at war, Arbitrator. Circumstances such as these demand that we proceed regardless of absentees,' replied the prince casually.

'A state of war has not yet been confirmed, Your Highness,' interjected the High Priest Cluillii. The rich voice of the old man echoed around the chamber.

'Actually, that is my reason for calling this meeting,' said Amulius, smiling at the two councillors. 'General Servius has brought news. I think you should listen to what he has to report.' The prince turned to Servius, 'If you wouldn't mind, General...'

The stocky commander rose from his seat and assumed a stiff posture, almost as if he were standing to attention. He cleared his throat before commencing. 'Well, it's just like I said, sir. Took the lads out on patrol along the river border, and there they were! Etruscans, sir, and a lot of them.'

'What exactly do you mean by "a lot", General, if you do not mind?' interrupted Fabii.

'I'd say about ten thousand, sir, judging from the number of tents I saw on their side of the river.' Servius scratched the back of his cropped head. 'And they had hundreds of barges at the ready to take them across.'

'And who was leading these Etruscans, General?' asked the Arbitrator.

'Well, sir, we hid and watched them for a while, cos we were still trying to work out who they were and what they were up to, but I spotted their leader in the end, sir. It was King Corros – they had all come from Veii.'

Murmurs of worry spread throughout the chamber as Servius sat down. Ugo Curiatii was next to stand. 'These would be the same Etruscans that Prince Numitor wants us to trade with,' shouted the horse dealer. 'He has even asked me to sell them horses – horses which they would have then used against us.' His voice echoed around the stone walls.

'I realise this is difficult for you, Ugo,' said Amulius, sympathetically. 'If I am not mistaken, I believe that your grandfather and two of his brothers died at the hands of the Etruscans.'

'Yes, Sire, that is correct,' replied Curiatii as he lowered his head. 'Some wounds cannot be forgotten. And yet, your brother wants us to befriend this menace.'

Arbitrator Fabii stood up to address the council. 'My understanding is that Prince Numitor wishes only to make trade deals that will benefit Latium, bringing us peace and prosperity.'

'That is not true!' came the objection of a smartly dressed man. He rose from his chair and straightened his black tunic. 'Prince Numitor is helping the Etruscans to arm themselves. He has forced my father to supply obsidian to these people. Our stone is being used to tip their arrows and spears, and now they plan to launch them against the very people who mined it. Our town of Gabii will surely be the first place they attack as it so close to their border.'

'He actually ordered you to supply the obsidian, did he, Gaetano?' interrupted Amulius, acting shocked by the news. 'That must be putting the Maranii family in a very difficult position.'

'It was more of a threat than an order, Sire,' admitted the councillor. 'He suggested that our levies would rise if we did not supply the Etruscans for the next two years.'

Lucius had been listening quietly at the back of the chamber, but on hearing Gaetano Maranii's claim, which the assistant knew to be false, he felt obliged to interrupt. He stood up nervously and cleared his throat. 'Forgive me, Sire, but that man is not speaking the truth,' he blurted.

Every head in the large room turned to Lucius and he instantly regretted his outburst. Amulius' eyes were now boring into him.

'What are you doing here, boy?' demanded the prince. 'You were not summoned to this meeting.'

'I… I am taking notes for Prince Numitor in his absence,' replied the assistant with a little righteousness in his voice. 'It is quite normal for me to do so,' he continued.

'Let him speak,' ordered the High Priest Cluillii, 'while the prince is not here to defend himself against these vile accusations.' The final words were spoken with disgust.

Amulius gestured to Lucius, his annoyance clearly evident. 'Well, speak then.'

'Um… well, Prince Numitor actually offered a reprieve on the usual levy if the Maranii family agreed to trade with the Etruscans. There was no threat at all.'

'So he tried to coerce them?' Amulius sounded shocked. 'Has my brother become so twisted in his obsession to befriend our enemies that he would make such a grave error?' The prince shook his head and sighed. 'Our father would never have let this happen.'

Lucius was about to reply but before he could speak, Arbitrator Fabii rose again.

'None of this is important right now,' said Fabii. 'We should not be condemning Prince Numitor when he is not here to defend himself. We should be thinking about how to protect ourselves against an Etruscan invasion.'

Feeling relief at not having to remain standing any longer, Lucius quickly dropped to his seat as the muscular figure of General Tyco stood to address the prince.

'I can summon twenty thousand warriors to be at the river in two days, Sire,' he said, his deep voice resonating around the room, 'but I fear the Etruscans could reach our city before then, especially if they chose to cross now.'

'Thank you, General, but it will not be necessary to summon your warriors,' answered Amulius. 'I am not prepared to lead our army into a war against an enemy with whom my brother continues to play his games of friendship.'

'I do not think that is your decision to make, Your Highness,' interrupted High Priest Cluillii. 'The army does as the council wishes, I believe?'

'Actually, that is not true, Your Grace,' replied Tyco, who was still standing. 'We take our orders from our rulers, and Prince Amulius is the only ruler here. For all we know, Prince Numitor has already been captured by King Corros, which would make the good prince here our leader.'

The small hunched figure of the Augur stood up, his head barely reaching over the top of the table. 'There was a red sunrise this morning. It can only mean blood. Yet the morning star was bright over Alba Longa. It is a clear sign that Amulius will protect us.'

'Ridiculous!' hissed the High Priest. 'Your speculations have never amounted to anything.'

Before the Augur could respond, Amulius interrupted. 'Please, gentlemen, let us not argue while there are issues of far greater importance at hand. If we are to face this threat, then we must do it properly. First, however, we have to be united in our purpose. My father misjudged my brother's abilities, and as a result we are now on the verge of war. Let us put this right.'

Amulius paused for a moment and looked around the table at the faces of the council members. His gaze moved from person to person, but he was met only with passive glances or cursory nods.

Lucius had stopped taking notes, but was continuing to follow the proceedings with growing fear for his master. He could see that Amulius had a lot of support on the council. He held his breath as the younger prince began to speak again.

'Tyco, Servius, tell me – can I count on the support of the army?'

The generals answered simultaneously, 'Yes, sir.'

Amulius began to walk around the table. 'It is very good to hear that I have your backing, Generals, but I also need to know that the council is behind me. I want assurance that my brother will not be allowed to counter my orders. The only certain way to ensure that my orders are followed would be if this council was to declare me King.'

Several intakes of breath could be heard around the table as Arbitrator Fabii quickly rose again from his seat. 'This cannot happen, Sire. The King's Council was created in order to prevent this exact situation from happening. Furthermore, with you as King, we would be condemning ourselves. You would have no further use for the council.'

'On the contrary, Arbitrator,' responded Amulius. 'I will always have use for those upon whose support I can depend, but enough of this talk. I suggest we put the matter to a vote.'

'The council cannot vote, Sire,' said High Priest Cluillii. 'There are six people missing from this meeting.'

'We don't 'ave the time to waste, waiting for the others, Your Grace,' Servius replied to the priest. 'The Etruscans could be 'ere, anytime. We got to move quickly.'

'I agree with the good general,' interjected Amulius. 'We will have to do without the others on this occasion. So, without further ado, all those in favour of making me King, raise your hand.'

Lucius watched with baited breath as both generals raised their hands, along with Gaetano Maranii, Ugo Curiatii, the Augur and the councillor from the town of Cora, Ciro Manilii.

Amulius counted off the hands. 'Six, and then my own vote, which makes it seven. I need just one more vote.'

'The council has spoken, Sire,' smirked Fabii. 'You have lost.'

'Oh, I am not finished yet, Arbitrator. I only require one of you to change your vote. I am sure I can persuade you do this for me, Fabii.'

'I will do no such thing, Sire. Why would I support you?'

Amulius smiled, 'Yes, a good point – why would you support me? Could it be that you might feel more motivated if I were to promise you something in return?'

'You have nothing that I want,' came the quick retort, but the Arbitrator had begun to fidget nervously in his seat.

'How about your life, Arbitrator? I believe the penalty for corruption is death, is it not?'

With a look of shocked indignation, Fabii replied, 'I do not know what you are talking about, Sire.'

Amulius smiled again, 'Then I suggest you consider the nature of your recent negotiations in a land dispute with the widow Cloellii. Or, perhaps you should remind yourself of how you condemned a man to death so as to purchase his land from his wife. Then again, you could take this opportunity to inform the councillors here of which one of their wives it is that you visit regularly.'

Lucius watched the exchange with fascination. Fabii's bloated, pink face was becoming a deep crimson red as he stared at the prince, who simply smiled in return. The rest of the councillors kept their eyes fixed on the Arbitrator, and Lucius could not help wondering which one of them had the adulteress wife.

'Of course, if these claims were found to be false,' added Amulius, 'I would see to it that my informants were flogged for telling such terrible lies about one of my most valued supporters.'

The Arbitrator remained silent. High Priest Cluillii rose again. 'I must object, Sire. This is extortion,' cried the priest. 'You cannot gain votes in this manner.'

'It is fine, Your Grace,' replied the Arbitrator, hushing the priest. In a voice now humbled by defeat, Fabii continued. 'It seems I have been foolish and allowed my personal feelings to interfere with my duty.' With great reluctance in his tone, he added, 'I wish to change my vote and support His Highness in becoming King.'

Lucius could barely believe what he was hearing from the Arbitrator. Fabii had previously been unfailing in his support for Prince Numitor. *It seems that there must be some truth in Amulius' claims,* thought the assistant, and it was only then that the significance of this additional vote began to sink in.

'So with eight votes, I do believe I am now King,' said Amulius in tones of quiet satisfaction. He looked around the room expectantly.

General Servius stood immediately. 'Hail Amulius, king of Latium.'

The others began to rise from their seats and repeat the statement. Lucius stood and reluctantly copied the gesture, quietly muttering the words without conviction.

'My first action as king,' announced Amulius, 'is to decree the dissolution of this council.' He clapped his hands twice. An instant later, the doors to the council chamber burst open and two lines of Latin warriors marched in, quickly encircling the large table.

'Those of you who chose to vote in my favour without need of extra persuasion may leave at once.'

The councillors loyal to Amulius stood and left the cold room promptly, along with the two generals. Lucius quietly rose and began to make his way towards the door.

'Not you, Lucius,' said Amulius, spotting the young man as tried to leave the room. 'I think you should stay until we are finished here.'

Unsure what to do, Lucius hesitated a moment before returning to his seat.

'What is this, Your Highness?' demanded Fabii.

'Oh Arbitrator, did you really think I would allow your open hostility towards me to go unpunished? Your corruption brings disgrace to the good name of your profession. We cannot have thieves standing in judgement over our hard-working citizens.'

'But you said that if I supported you—'

'I know what I said, Fabii, but you and your colleague here,' he pointed to Cluillii, 'have been nothing but a bane to my plans ever since this council commenced. Now you must make amends.'

'Oh, anything, Sire,' begged the high priest as he stood up. 'I will make a sacrifice to Zeus in your name.'

'I like the sound of that, Your Grace,' said Amulius, slyly. 'That is a fine idea. I think we should make sacrifices to all the gods.' He turned toward the waiting warriors. 'Sacrifice all of them,' he ordered casually, and then started to proceed towards the doorway.

The remaining councillors began to scramble out of their seats but the warriors surged forward quickly and held the frightened men in place. Ignoring the pleas coming from the condemned men, Amulius continued to stride towards the doors but halted as he caught sight of the cowering assistant again. 'Ah yes. Lucius,' he said menacingly.

Lucius recoiled as Amulius pointed at him. 'I believe your services are no longer required.' Addressing the warriors, he said, 'Sacrifice that man last of all,' and without a second glance he marched out of the council chamber, not bothering to close the door behind him.

Chapter Thirty

As they approached the river valley, Numitor guided the riders around the eastern fringes of the large marshes that surrounded the hills of the Seven Sisters. He remembered the last time he had been in the area, many years earlier, when he had first invited the Etruscans to talk. Searching the horizon, the prince spotted smoke rising further up the river. Spurring his horse onward, he led the procession towards it along the river bank.

Sore from having spent too much time on the saddle, Numitor could anticipate what he would soon be facing. He was at a loss to understand why the Etruscans were behaving in this way. While many possibilities had crossed his mind, he had been unable to single out a definitive reason that could explain their sudden aggression. The prince cantered beside the flowing water and scanned the land ahead. The opposite bank of the river was hidden behind a wall of overhanging trees and bushes. The riders continued to follow the course of the river and eventually, as the bank began to climb, their view opened up, suddenly revealing a mass of tents and defences set up in a huge meadow on the Etruscan side of the River Tiber.

At the water's edge the prince could see dozens of rafts, all manned with young men carrying long poles with which to push the floating platforms. As yet, it seemed that none of the Etruscans had made the crossing. A commotion began to ensue along the opposite bank as Numitor and his riders were spotted. Numitor carefully descended the muddy bank with Captain Miron beside him. Stopping at the water's edge, the prince shouted across in Etruscan. 'I wish to talk with your king.'

Numitor waited for a reply, certain that his voice had been loud and clear enough for the men opposite to have understood him. He watched as one of the distant men ran up the bank and disappeared. Miron and the prince dismounted as they continued to watch. Moments later, on the horizon appeared the heavy-set figure of King Corros, riding a large white horse. The king spoke briefly to one of his men, who then ran to the river bank, whereupon one of the rafts was guided towards the Latin side of the river. When the floating platform had reached the bank, the young pole-man looked up and addressed Numitor.

'Only you. King Corros says you must come alone.'

'But he cannot do that,' objected Captain Miron, incensed by the suggestion.

The prince held up his arm to stay the captain, and nodded his assent. 'It is fine, Miron, I am willing to go alone. He will not harm me.'

'That is not a good idea, Sire, if anything should—'

Numitor interrupted and held the captain's gaze. 'Wait here,' he ordered, leaving no doubt that this was his final word on the matter.

With a slight tilt of his head, Captain Miron conceded and stepped back.

By the time that the raft had returned to the Etruscan bank, a table had been brought to the riverside and King Corros was seated on one side of it. Numitor, who was feeling the effects of nearly two days without sleep, was both amused and disappointed to see that there seemed to be no seat for him. He stepped off the raft and landed in the soft mud while holding up his hands to show that he was unarmed, having left his sword with Miron.

'Prince Numitor, have you come to ask for my surrender?' laughed Corros, his men quickly joining in.

The prince ignored the laughter and replied in stern tones. 'Your Highness, what is the meaning this?' He gestured towards the warriors that flanked the king. 'Why do you seem to be preparing for war?'

'Me?' bellowed the king. 'You accuse me of preparing for war, when it was your warriors that first lined the other bank in their thousands? There was no doubt as to their intentions until this very morning.'

Numitor looked across the river, his small retinue dwarfed in comparison to the Etruscan force. 'I do not understand. Most of the Latin army is in Pietrabbondante. What you are telling me does not make sense. Where are all these warriors that you speak of?'

'As I said, they were here until this morning, when they suddenly departed. Now I find myself facing only a few riders, with no sign of the promised battle in which I was due to engage today.' The king's voice carried confidence and threat.

'Your Highness,' protested Numitor, 'I cannot explain what has occurred here, but I can assure you that no threat has been intended by Latium. My brother has been waging war with the Samnites, and as far as I am aware he is still there. There has been a mistake here. Latium has no desire for war with Etruria. I thought we had an understanding.'

'We did,' replied the king abruptly, 'but then I was informed that a massive Latin force was assembling at our border, and I reacted accordingly. What would you expect me to do?'

Shaking his head in utter confusion, Numitor was silent for a moment as a wave of fatigue washed over him. He waited for the feeling to pass before addressing the king again. 'Let me find out what has been happening, Your Highness. I have been away for a couple of days, and I am currently unable to offer you an explanation as to what you claim has happened here.'

Corros considered the prince's words and nodded his head in agreement. 'It seems that, once again, there is discord in your kingdom, Numitor.' Leaning forward, the king continued, 'You must deal with this problem once and for all. If not, then the next time this happens, we will find ourselves at war.'

The prince bowed his head respectfully, and feeling himself burning with shame, turned back to the waiting raft.

* * *

The return journey to Alba Longa was a drag upon Numitor's patience as his desire to get answers grew stronger. As they rode into the highlands, the prince and his procession were met by another man on horseback. He galloped towards Numitor and called out to claim that he bore important news. Miron rode forward to meet the rider and after a few words, led him to the prince. Numitor looked at the young man and could instantly see a family resemblance to his friend, Paridé. The new arrival shared the same strong brow and thick eyebrows of the village leader. Even his hair was similarly curly, if not thicker than Paridé's. The prince waited until the captain had returned to his men before nodding to the rider to speak.

'Paridé sent me, Sire. He has captured the merchant.'

Some good news, at last, thought Numitor, pleased to hear that his friend had not failed him. 'Where is he being held?' he asked the young messenger.

'At the merchant's own villa, Sire,' replied the man. 'We surprised him as he arrived. Paridé and a few of the lads are making sure he stays put. He's not going anywhere.'

'Was he alone?' asked Numitor.

'Yes, Sire, but he didn't seem to be in good shape. It looked like he'd been in a tumble. His cloak was torn and muddy.'

The prince was not surprised, having already heard about Densara's struggle with Lillia's friend. Eager to conclude matters with the treacherous merchant, he called to Miron. 'Take the men back to the palace. I will meet

209

you there in due course.' Turning to the messenger, he said, 'You will now accompany me to the merchant's villa.'

Numitor's first impression of Densara's villa was that it was modest, showing little sign of the merchant's rumoured wealth. The prince then made his way through a bare vestibule and into a large open room dominated by a floor that was inlaid with an intricate mosaic depicting the god Zeus throwing a lightning bolt from the top of Mount Olympus. Numitor could tell that the mosaic would have cost Densara a fortune in gold. There was little else in the room other than a table that stood near an archway into a small atrium. There was also a distinct lack of evidence to suggest that anyone else lived there. The prince wondered if the villa was the merchant's main residence.

Spotting Paridé in the atrium, Numitor hurried through the archway, followed by the messenger, whom he now knew to be Paride's younger cousin, Falco. The young man remained at the atrium's entrance as Numitor greeted his friend.

'You have done well, Paridé. Where is he?'

Paridé pointed to the far side of a square pond from which the water had been drained. The merchant Densara was tied to a statue of three entwined sirens. Had there been water in the pond, he would have found himself submerged. The possibility was not lost on Numitor as he approached the pond's edge and stared down at the merchant.

'Sire,' pleaded Densara in a hoarse voice as he looked up at the prince, 'why have I been detained like this? I have done nothing wrong.'

Numitor narrowed his eyes. 'Are you jesting with me? I know all about your attempt to abduct my daughter.'

'Ah, then she is safe,' replied the merchant with apparent relief. 'You have her?'

The question came as such a surprise that the prince was completely thrown from his train of thought. 'Well, no,' he said, 'I have not actually seen her yet, but she has been taken to safety.' Numitor silently cursed himself for allowing the merchant to distract him. He then leant forward, bringing himself close to the infuriatingly calm man and bellowed in his face. 'I demand to know why you were trying to take the princess, and you are to tell me the name of the man who was accompanying you.'

'I was not trying to abduct the princess, Sire,' replied Densara, his voice remaining serene. 'I was seeking to protect her, and you. Regrettably, I was then chased off by the guards of the very people I was helping.'

Numitor felt his anger rise at hearing the merchant speak such obvious lies. There was an air of smugness in the man's unruffled tone, and, it was more than the prince could tolerate. Mustering his strength, he drew back his arm and then smashed his fist down into the side of the merchant's face. A streak of bloodied saliva splashed onto the pond's tiled floor. Densara's head hung to one side for a moment as a patch of redness appeared on his brow. Then the merchant slowly looked up at the prince with dark angry eyes that showed no sign whatsoever of having been weakened by the blow.

'Why would you injure the man who tries to help you?' he asked in a voice that remained just as placid as before.

The prince gestured for Paridé to leave the atrium and waited until he was alone with the merchant before addressing him. 'I know all about you, *Dius*. I know you to be a member of the Hounds of Diana. I know about the masked girls, and I am aware of the involvement of my assistant, Lucius. I suggest you do not lie to me anymore. What did you intend to do with my daughter?'

Densara betrayed no surprise when he answered. 'I have no idea what you are talking about, Sire. As I said, I was protecting the princess and nothing more.'

'So, you still deny being a Dius, do you, Densara? I have seen you with my own eyes, seen your red and black mask, your assassin in the tree, and I have witnessed your meetings with Lucius, in which you use a Vestal Virgin acolyte to speak on your behalf. I say it again – do not waste my time with lies!'

The merchant's face could not hide his shock as the prince recounted his observations, but when Densara finally offered an answer, his voice remained as calm as ever. 'If you knew anything of value, Your Highness, then you would be aware that both I and Lucius have a duty to protect you and the princess. Guarding your well-being is our greatest responsibility.'

Numitor had firm doubts about the merchant's claims. 'If your duty is to protect me, then why do you work for my brother?' he demanded.

'Well, Sire, would it not be true to say that one of the best ways to watch someone without detection is to work for them?' Densara remarked casually, not sounding in the least like a man tied to a statue. 'I protect you from your enemy by becoming the friend of your enemy. It is very simple, but most effective.'

The premise made sense to the prince, but then again, how could the merchant back up his claims? 'If it were true that either I or my daughter were in danger, then there would be proof. Tell me, where is your proof?' demanded Numitor.

'Sire, there is a plot to undermine your rule. Your brother acts as we speak. He bribes and cajoles those he wishes to use, he manipulates and nurtures them. He has always coveted the throne, and you have always been in his way.'

'And where does he get all the gold to fund these bribes, Densara? I see our treasury fill with the gold that my brother earns for the country.'

'May I ask you something, Sire?' Without waiting for a response, the merchant continued. 'How many slaves do you believe Amulius has taken over the last few months?'

The prince frowned. 'I do not see the relevance of your question, but I'm sufficiently intrigued to humour you: Amulius has captured around five thousand slaves.'

'Ha,' laughed the merchant. 'You do humour me, Sire. That is almost amusing.' He chuckled sarcastically as he looked up at the prince.

'What is amusing about that?' demanded Numitor, becoming increasingly furious at Densara's attitude.

'The figure you should have said, Sire, was fifteen thousand. Brascus and I have handled fifteen thousand slaves for your brother in the last two months alone.'

'But that is not true!' Numitor was shocked. 'Brascus told me... He handled everything... Fifteen thousand, you say?'

Densara nodded his head. 'Amulius has been using the extra gold to gain favour. I also know that he has been sending warriors to the Etruscan border. I realised something was wrong when I learned that half the Latin army were camped at the River Tiber. I then understood that your brother was about to make his move, whatever that was.' The merchant scratched his wiry hair. 'But I could do nothing – my priority at that point was to protect your daughter.'

'What has any of this to do with Princess Rhea? She is barely out of childhood.'

'That may be, but she is now of an age where she is almost ready to bear you an heir to the kingdom. She stands between Amulius and his dream of becoming king of Latium. With you removed from the scene, only the princess can ruin your brother's plans.'

'But I have not been removed from the scene, nor will I be!' The prince shook his head in anger and confusion. He was still unsure as to whether he even believed a word the merchant said. Sitting down at the edge of the dry pond, Numitor gave further consideration to Densara's claims. Most disturbing was the implication that Brascus was involved in this conspiracy. *Brascus – he has my daughter!* An overwhelming need to find Lillia came over Numitor. He remained unconvinced of the merchant's sincerity, but he was not prepared to allow his doubts to expose his daughter to potential danger. He was now desperate to leave the villa and do whatever was necessary to rescue the princess, but it occurred to him that the merchant might still have more to report. Densara interrupted the prince's thoughts as he spoke again.

'You say you have not seen your daughter, Sire. Can you tell me who was it that accompanied your guards? As I tried to rescue the princess, I saw men on horseback that were not wearing your guards' uniforms.'

Numitor recalled that Brascus' two guards had mentioned that other men had appeared at the scene. These unknown riders had chased off the unidentified man that had been helping Densara, but the prince had not had a chance to give the matter any further thought. 'The horsemen were with Brascus,' he replied quietly, realising as he spoke that he was merely making an assumption.

'Brascus?' said the merchant, surprised by the revelation. 'Brascus!' he repeated. After a moment of thought, he nodded slowly. 'Yes, yes of course, it is him,' he whispered. 'Brascus is the other Dius.'

'And I thank the gods that I have Brascus on my side,' said Numitor angrily, 'otherwise my daughter would be lost by now.' The prince did not even bother to acknowledge the inaccuracy of the merchant's latest claim.

Shaking his head with a defeated sigh, Densara then looked at the prince. 'She is lost already, Sire. Brascus is the Dius that watches over Amulius, so your daughter is now lost to you.'

'Whatever do you mean?' demanded the alarmed prince.

'I have long suspected that your brother has been receiving help from someone well connected. I had my ideas about possible suspects, but, in our circle it is difficult to be sure… if you follow my meaning.'

Numitor nodded, beginning to feel a little sick as his mind dealt with the information.

'Secrecy and such like,' added Densara. The merchant was finally starting to show the strain of being tied to the statue. He gyrated his shoulder, trying to ease his discomfort. 'To be honest, I had wondered if Amulius' helper might be your friend, Paridé, who has so graciously detained me today, but then I realised that if that were the case then one of us would be dead by now.'

'I see Paridé only rarely, and as for Brascus, he would not do such a thing – he is my friend.' Numitor's words were said defensively, and yet they lacked the weight of certainty.

'A friend that has concealed the profits from the sale of ten thousand slaves. A friend who supposedly has your daughter safe, and yet you have not seen her since her "rescue" yesterday.'

'But I have had things to do—' protested Numitor, but stopped mid-sentence as his thoughts suddenly became clear. 'It cannot be possible,' he growled. 'I will kill him myself if he truly has betrayed me.' His mind raced as he thought of all he had learnt over the past months, and he shuddered as he recalled the times he had confided in Brascus, bearing his darkest worries and suspicions. A growing sense of panic began to shroud him as he tried to work out what to do next. He needed to know that Lillia was safe, and he needed to confront both Brascus and Amulius. 'You will stay here with Paridé until I send word,' declared the prince, finally reaching a decision. 'I am going to the palace to get to the bottom of this.'

'Then be careful, Sire. Your brother is cunning,' cautioned Densara.

'Do not worry,' replied Numitor. 'I know all about my brother. However, if I find that you have been misleading me,' he warned, 'not even your Hounds of Diana will be able to save you.'

Chapter Thirty-One

Numitor knew that something was wrong as soon as he entered the palace compound. Instead of the usual Royal Guards standing to attention, Latin warriors now manned the entrance. Looking up, the prince could see that they also patrolled the walls and watchtowers. He handed the reins of his horse to a waiting stable hand as he dismounted, and with a quick glance around, headed up the steps into the palace. Marching through the long corridors, Numitor could feel his anger boiling as he battled with worry over Lillia, wrestled with the thought of Brascus' possible betrayal, and tried to bear the burden of his brother's actions which threatened to bring war.

The vestibule leading to the throne room was silent and empty as the prince headed for the open doors. Warriors guarded the entrance but he ignored them and entered the room, closing the doors behind him. Amulius was sitting in their father's old throne.

'Fits well, don't you think, brother?' The younger prince's voice echoed around the large room as he gestured to his new seat. 'I think I shall keep it – what do you reckon?'

'I think you have gone too far, Amulius!' Numitor spat the words in fury. Pulling out his sword, he advanced on his brother.

The scarred prince laughed and sprang out of the marble throne, his own blade ready as he prepared to defend himself. Numitor rushed forward. 'Where is Lillia?' he demanded, swinging his long blade down towards his brother's head. The strike was parried by the grinning prince – but Numitor was not finished, and slammed his fist into his brother's face. As Amulius staggered backwards, Numitor followed up with a kick to his brother's midriff. The younger prince fell to the ground, his sword slipping from his hand and out of reach.

Stunned and dazed, Amulius tried to retrieve his fallen blade but Numitor kicked it further away and stood over him. He attempted to rise but was halted as the tip of Numitor's sword found his throat.

'Where is she?' demanded the older prince again, pushing harder on the blade, forcing Amulius to draw back to avoid being pierced.

'She is safe, Brother,' came the strained reply. 'Truly, she is fine.'

'Where is she?' repeated Numitor. 'I will not ask again.'

Amulius was about to reply when he was interrupted by the sounds of approaching footsteps. The doors flew open and Captain Miron marched into the throne room, followed by six men from the Royal Guard. Seeing the familiar uniforms, Numitor felt a sense of relief as he addressed the captain. 'Miron, arrest my brother,' he commanded, stepping back and sheathing his sword.

Two guards immediately stepped forward, but instead of going to Amulius, they flanked Numitor, each grabbing an arm. The older prince, shocked by the move, looked to Miron questioningly.

The captain shook his head and, dropping his gaze, said, 'I am sorry, Sire, but I cannot do that.'

'You will do as I say, captain, or you will find yourself in irons.'

Miron refused to meet Numitor's gaze and looked to Amulius instead.

'This is treason,' snapped Numitor, his anger growing again.

'No, it is not, Brother,' said Amulius as he started to get up. 'He is simply obeying his king.'

'I am sure the council will have something to say about that.' Numitor shrugged away the guards' hold, but continued to stand his ground while his brother resumed his position on the white throne.

'The council has spoken, voted, and now no longer exists,' Amulius replied with casual smugness. 'Both generals have pledged me their support, thus giving me full control over our forces. There is no one left alive to oppose me,' he added, his tone becoming darker. 'And if you want to continue living, Brother, then I suggest you calm down and accept that you have lost.'

'What reason is there in all this?' demanded Numitor loudly. 'You are bringing our country to its knees in war and treachery.'

Amulius slapped his hand down onto the marble armrest, his own anger growing, and shouted back. 'The reason for all of this lies in the fact that I am the only one of us fit to rule, Numitor. I was always underestimated because of you. Our father could see only you when we were children, as if I were merely an afterthought. It was because of this that I was compelled to ruin your little battle against the Phoenicians all those years ago.'

Numitor cocked his head. 'What do you mean? You arranged my rescue on that occasion, Amulius.'

'No Brother, it was I who arranged your entrapment that day. Foolishly, you took the word of a few paid lookouts, and then committed our army to an almost certain defeat. If I had not ridden in as your rescuing hero, Father would never have listened to me, and I would not have had this opportunity to take your kingdom from you. Maybe I should have left you to your fate that day,' he said thoughtfully, 'but then again, I would have missed out on all fun I have been having recently.'

'You are sick in the head, Amulius,' growled Numitor as he took a step forward, but the guards reacted promptly and grabbed his arms again.

'On the contrary, Brother', replied Amulius. 'I have always been very clear in my thinking. I have always anticipated your next move. Remember your first attempts to befriend the Etruscans all those years ago? It was I who chose your meeting point – it was the perfect location for the ambush I had planned.'

Numitor stared at his brother in disgust. He had always harboured a suspicion that Amulius had arranged the kidnapping attempt in which he and Brascus had subsequently been rescued by the dark rider, but it sent a wave of sadness through him to hear confirmation of the betrayal. 'You have no family loyalty, Amulius. I am ashamed to call you kin. Nonetheless, you now have what you want, *Your Highness*,' said the prince with a scowl. 'So be it. Now let me see my daughter.'

A brief frown crossed Amulius's forehead. 'All in good time, Brother,' he replied. Looking Numitor up and down, he added, 'I suggest you get some rest – you look a mess.'

'You…' Numitor lunged forward with his fists clenched, but the two guards restrained him in an instant as two more approached, ready to back up their colleagues.

Looking to Captain Miron, Amulius pointed at his brother. 'See that he is escorted to the royal villa. He will be a guest there for the foreseeable future.'

'You will not get away with this, Amulius! There are people in this Kingdom who will never allow you to take the throne,' shouted the prince. Although his brother had never made reference to The Hounds of Diana, Numitor was sure Amulius would be aware of them through Brascus, and was therefore surprised by his brother's next words.

'And what people would these be? Anyone of any influence has already pledged their alliances to me. Those few that refused are now dead. As I have already informed you, there is no-one left to help you.'

Puzzled by the reply, Numitor restrained his anger and decided to probe a little further, curious to see if his brother would reveal any knowledge of the Hounds. 'And Brascus,' he challenged, 'how does he fit into your plans?'

'Brascus has been helpful,' said Amulius thoughtfully, scratching his beard. 'How do you think he became so wealthy? A few whores? No, it was me – I look after my friends.'

'But why would he do this to me?' demanded the prince. 'I have never harmed him.'

'No, but you have never really helped him either, have you?' replied Amulius. 'I showed him the value of my friendship.'

'You merely bought his loyalty,' said Numitor, disgusted by the idea.

Amulius wagged his finger at his older brother. 'It is a shame that you did not recognise the value of having Brascus as an ally. His uncanny ability to see what others do not has made him extremely useful to me. He was even able to gain information about your plan to smuggle Lillia to safety. What wonders he must hear in his taverna?' Smiling at Numitor he added, 'I also hear from Brascus that you are friendlier with Densara than I was ever led to believe. I understand the merchant even tried to put your little plan into action. He was too late, of course, as I was a few steps ahead of you as usual, Brother, but even so, Densara will pay for his betrayal.'

Numitor began to realise that Amulius was unaware of Brascus' true position, appearing to know nothing of his involvement with the secret sect. The revelation came as a surprise to the prince, but given what he had learnt about The Hounds of Diana, it made a certain sense. The thought gave him some hope that Amulius' treachery could potentially be undone. It seemed that Densara had been truthful after all, and Numitor instantly began to regret at not freeing the merchant. The one man who could have been his greatest ally was now tied to a statue under the guard of Paridé. Surrounded by guards himself, the prince realised the full extent of his failure. He had been blind to the treachery around him, failing to protect his daughter and now, he realised, turning himself into the easiest of targets.

Numitor struggled against the guards' hold as they began to drag him away. 'Where is Lillia, you bastard? I demand to see her!' he shouted. 'Where is she, Amulius? What have you done with my daughter?'

With a click of Amulius' fingers, the guards stopped dragging Numitor and held him still. 'Princess Rhea is in a place of safety, Brother. That is all you need to know for now. If you behave, then she will come to no harm.' Amulius spoke with a calmness that sent a chill through his brother. 'She has been taken to a place where she will not be able to cause me any further problems.'

It was then that Amulius noticed Numitor's gold eagle ring. He felt his cheek ache from where his brother had recently punched him, and purposely stopped himself from reaching up to his scar. 'Hold him,' he ordered the guards.

The guards tightened their grip on Numitor as Amulius walked over and reached for his brother's hand, quickly pulling off the ring. 'This was meant for the future king, I believe. Our foolish father gave it to the wrong son,' he growled.

'That is mine!' roared Numitor. 'I was first born. Father gave it to me.'

'A mere error in judgement,' replied the new king. 'It is time it went to its rightful owner.' Amulius slipped the ring onto his own finger. 'Ah, it fits perfectly,' he said joyfully, as the guards began once again to drag his defeated brother away.

Chapter Thirty-Two

Lillia allowed Brascus to help her down from the horse, thankful that the journey had ended. They had stopped at a busy Latin encampment and the princess wondered if this was where they would spend the night. Their previous night's shelter had been an abandoned hut, close to a small stream, and although very basic, its stone oven had soon warmed the place, allowing them to get some sleep before daybreak. She had not slept well, her thoughts of Marcus keeping her awake. Lillia yearned for his company and was desperate to be with him again.

As Brascus led her through the camp's assortment of hide shelters, the princess saw that the warriors were busy loading carts, carrying supplies and cleaning weapons. The sight came as a surprise to Lillia, who had only ever seen them marching out of Alba Longa in colourful and cheerful parades. It gave her a new insight into the reality of their lives to see the men engaged in menial chores. Many of them were young. Once or twice Lillia's heart skipped a beat when she saw someone resembling Marcus, but on closer inspection she would see that they were not as tall, or less handsome. The close proximity of the warriors made her more aware of Marcus' absence than ever. The princess wondered how long she would be at the camp – Brascus had told her nothing of where he was taking her, other than that it would be a place of safety. When she had asked what it was that she needed to be safe from, his only reply had been, "people like Densara". Lillia found it appalling to know that there were people out there who wished her harm. Even with Brascus and the warriors around to protect her, she still felt vulnerable. Her only hope was that her final destination would be Alba Longa and the safety of the palace, and then she could be with Marcus again. Being in the warriors' camp only added to her hopes that she would soon be home.

Coming to a stop outside a large tent, Brascus turned to face the princess. 'You will be staying here tonight, Your Highness. Someone will come to collect you in the morning.'

Glancing around the camp, Lillia's eyes widened as she realised that Brascus meant to leave her there alone. 'Are you not staying?' she asked, the words sticking in her throat.

'You will be safe here, Princess,' he assured her. 'Everyone knows who you are. However, I do have to be somewhere this evening, so I am not able to accompany you any longer today.'

Somewhat worried by the news, Lillia nonetheless nodded her acceptance. She looked down at her dirty sandals and muddy knees, realising that she had not washed since the previous day. 'I must clean myself and change,' she said quietly.

'Everything you need is in there, Your Highness,' replied Brascus, pointing to the tent. With a friendly smile, he added, 'It is like a palace inside. There is even food laid out for you.'

Lillia heard her stomach rumble at the mention of food and she found herself eager to get to it. She returned the smile and said, 'Thank you, Brascus, for rescuing me from that horrible man. If you see Father, please tell him I love him and that I am sorry I went away without telling him.'

'I... I will,' he answered, avoiding her eyes.

The mood seemed to change, making Lillia feel a little awkward. 'Well then, I had better get in there and have a wash,' she said quickly to hide her discomfort. 'This is no way for a princess to look.'

With a slight bow, Brascus then turned and walked away. Lillia felt a moment of deep sadness for no reason that she could discern, yet it remained heavy on her as she pulled back the flap of hide and entered the tent.

When her eyes had adjusted to the sudden gloom, Lillia saw that the tent's interior seemed much larger than she had anticipated. At one end was a raised sleeping platform laden with furs and blankets. On the table beside it was a large white bowl and an amphora, which the princess assumed would contain water. Feeling her hunger stirring again, she looked around for the food and spotted it on another table to her left.

Eat first, and then wash, she decided, grabbing a loaf of floured bread and tearing off a chunk before stuffing it into her mouth. Lillia savoured the flavour – she had not eaten since being separated from Marcus. *I do hope he is all right. I wonder if he is home yet. I miss him so much.*

Tears threatened again and her throat became dry just as she tried to swallow the large morsel of bread. It stuck in her throat. Close to panic, Lillia reached for the amphora of water and drank from it, forcing the dry bread down. Having gone too long without air, she inhaled deeply, only for the action to then make her cough. Throwing up her arms in despair she sank to the rugs on the floor of the tent and began to cry.

'I'm so stupid,' she mumbled, trying to blame her tears on the choking, but deep down within herself she could feel a turmoil of anxiety and uncertainty. Her mind wondered and she found herself worrying about her father's reaction to her leaving. *He may never let me out again, and then I won't ever be able to see Marcus.* Then another thought struck her: *What will Father do to him? And what will Sylvanna have to say about me going away with Marcus?* Thinking of Sylvanna only made her feel worse – she deeply regretted not having spoken to her for so long and realised that she had treated her friend badly. Lillia resolved to see Sylvanna at her first opportunity as soon as she returned to Alba Longa.

The next morning, the princess awoke with the rising sun after a fitful sleep. She got up quickly and set about preparing breakfast, choosing some hard goat's cheese to eat with her bread. She was reminded of the meals that she had shared with Marcus in the meadows. Although she continued to miss him greatly, Lillia consoled herself with the thought that she would not have to wait long before seeing him again. As she ate she noticed shards of sunlight poking through gaps in the tent, and she felt a need to escape from the dim interior. Pulling back one of the flaps, she peered outside and saw that the camp was in the process of being dismantled.

Are they leaving? wondered the princess, watching the bare-chested men sweating as they rolled up hides and loaded them on to carts. The voices of the bantering warriors collided with the sound of mules braying with anticipation. Lillia stepped out into the open, but felt a little uncomfortable as she fell under the scrutiny of many pairs of eyes.

Maybe I should find out who is in charge and then ask him what is going on, she decided. The princess began to walk away from her tent. Two guards had been stationed nearby – they immediately rose and started to follow Lillia. *I could ask them, I suppose,* she thought, but then found herself feeling nervous about the idea of speaking to them. It occurred to her that they were probably under orders to keep her in sight, and Lillia suddenly started to feel more like a prisoner than a guest.

Ignoring the trailing men, she began to make her way across the camp, dodging the carts and busy warriors as she went. Many of the men stared as she walked by, some offering shy smiles while others bowed their heads. She returned the gestures with smiles of her own. She even had to suppress a giggle at one point when one of the men nudged his comrade with his elbow, giving the man such a start that he bashed his head against a cart.

The princess then spotted an older warrior who was overseeing some of the younger men. Plucking up courage, she approached him with her enquiry.

'Excuse me, sir, but where are you all going?' *Should I have called him "sir"?* she wondered, having had no experience in talking to warriors.

Looking a little startled, the veteran cleared his throat before replying. 'Orders to march to Alba Longa, Your Highness. We leave at midday.'

The news brought great pleasure to Lillia. She thanked the man with a shy smile and continued on her walk. With a spring now in her step, she thought of her home and all that she missed there. Her stroll eventually brought her back to the large tent in which she had spent the night, and she found that horses were now waiting outside. Eager to get going, she quickly entered the tent, but stopped in surprise as her eyes adjusted to the gloom.

Her Uncle Amulius was sitting at the table on which her food had previously been laid out. Standing to his right was an older woman in robes, accompanied by four fat bald men. The fat men were bare from the waist up and looked as if they were developing breasts. Lillia stared for a moment in disbelief and then glanced at her uncle.

Amulius smiled, 'Do not worry about them, Princess. They are eunuchs – they cannot hurt you.'

'Oh!' was all she could manage to say. *Why are they here?*

'You are probably wondering why you have been brought to this camp,' said Amulius, casually. 'I do not have much time now, but I want you to be under no false impressions, so I will explain matters to you clearly.'

'Fine,' she replied with a nod, but a growing sense of suspicion made her add, 'Where is Father?' Everything about this sudden development was making her feel nervous.

Amulius stood up and walked around the table. 'As of yesterday, I am now the king of Latium.'

Lillia blanched. 'You cannot do that, Uncle! Father would never allow it.'

'It is done, Rhea. I have now gained all the control that I was needing. Your father will soon come to see the sense of it.'

Tears began to well in the princess' eyes as she quickly abandoned any hope that her uncle might only be playing a cruel joke. It was hard to take in such shocking news: *poor Father, how must he be feeling?* Lillia found herself desperately worried for his safety, and yet, oddly, it did not occur to her to feel frightened for herself – she was too focussed upon the fury that now burned in her towards Amulius. He rage quickly overcame her and, without thinking, she marched over to her uncle and slapped him hard across the face.

'I hate you!' she screamed. 'How can you do this? He is your brother – he loves you.' Lillia raised her hand for another blow, but Amulius quickly grabbed her arm and pushed her to the ground. The princess could only look up at her uncle in shock, the tears now pouring down her cheeks.

'If you are sensible, then your father will live,' stated her uncle, flatly. 'It is up to you.' He bent down to his niece, who refused to meet his gaze. 'You are to do as I say.'

'You're a monster,' cried Lillia. 'I will never take orders from you.'

'If that is the way you feel, then both you and your father will have to die. It is not what I would have wanted for you, Princess, but you are leaving me no choice.'

Lillia tried to calm herself and looked up at her uncle, tears still running freely down her cheek. 'Please, Uncle Amulius, do not hurt my father. He does not deserve that. He has never hurt you.'

'The situation is simple. Do as I say and you will both be spared. Do you understand?' He looked into her eyes and waited for a response.

Lillia glanced down at her uncle's scar before meeting his stare. Fighting back her tears, she nodded in reply, but silently continued her scorn: *You are an evil man. I hate you. Father will never let you get away with this.*

Amulius rose and gestured towards the robed woman. 'This is Mother Vesta,' he said. 'She will be escorting you to the House of Vesta, where you are to take your place amongst the acolytes. If you behave, then you may even become one of the priestesses and a flame keeper. I am giving you an opportunity to make us all proud,' he pronounced.

Lillia's eyes widened in shock as she listened. 'Vesta? You are sending me away to be a Vestal Virgin?'

'No, Lillia, you are to be an acolyte. It takes years to become a priestess, and not all are chosen. Your first concern ought to be for your father's safely – if you wish him to remain unharmed then you must do your duty and cause no trouble,' he replied. 'To become an acolyte of Vesta is a great honour, but to defy the order is punishable by death. Do you understand?' he asked gruffly.

'How long will I have to stay there?'

'It is a commitment of thirty years,' he answered casually, 'and then you will be free.'

'Thirty years!' Panic resonated in Lillia's voice. *Marcus! I'll never see him again – he won't wait for thirty years, and Sylvanna... and Nima. And Father.* As the reality of her uncle's plans hit her, a hole started to open up inside the princess, and she felt all her hopes and dreams escaping through it.

'Please, Uncle,' she begged, 'there must be another way. I will not make any trouble, I swear to Zeus, I promise.' She grabbed his hand in desperation. 'Please do not send me there. *Please.*'

'It is done,' growled Amulius, pulling his hand away from the pleading girl. Turning to the priestess, he ordered, 'Take her now.' Without waiting for a response, he then strutted out of the tent.

Chapter Thirty-Three

Paridé was woken from his slumber by the sound of heavy knocking. He sat up instantly, trying to clear his mind of the haze of sleep. He looked toward the wooden shutters and saw that it was still dark. Stumbling out of bed, he began to work his way through the large house. The knocking came again, this time louder. 'Yes, yes, I'm coming,' he grumbled.

At the door was Paridé's cousin, Falco. His sister's son was almost a copy of Paridé's younger self, with thick curly hair and dark skin. Having had no father around, Paridé had mentored the boy and guided him in his youth. Now there was no-one whom Paridé trusted more. It was Falco who had been guarding Densara – the merchant had now been transferred to a house outside of the city. After hearing about Numitor's incarceration, it had been difficult for Paridé to decide what to do with the captive. News had reached him that the new king, Amulius, was searching for Densara. The merchant had overheard the rumour and then tried to convince his captors to set him free, promising that he could be of help to Numitor. However, Paridé had been unwilling to make any such rash decisions and had come home instead to get some rest.

'He's gone, Cuz!' exclaimed Falco, looking very worried.

Although shocked by this sudden turn of events, Paridé also felt a sense of relief as he realised that the decision of what to do with Densara was now out of his hands. He quickly questioned his cousin. 'How did he manage to escape?'

'I'm not sure,' replied the young man, raising his thick eyebrows, 'but he had help – I can tell you that much for certain. Someone cut his ropes while I was preparing food. One moment he was there, and then, pah – he'd gone.'

Annoyed by the vague explanation, Paridé narrowed his eyes. 'You make it sound like augury. How could the man just disappear?' he demanded, his hands gesticulating wildly in agitation.

'Cuz, you know me, I'm not stupid. I wasn't gone for more than a few moments,' Falco replied with animation, 'but when I returned there was no trace of him or anyone else. It was eerie, I can tell you, so yes, maybe augury was involved. Who knows what magic Densara might know?'

Shaking his head at his young cousin, Paridé tried to consider the situation. 'I very much doubt it was augury, Cousin, but still, there is nothing more we can do now. Let us hope that Densara really can help Numitor as he claims, because the gods seem content to leave our prince to rot in his villa.'

'I can get some men to search for him in the morning, Cuz,' said Falco with enthusiasm. 'We will get him.'

Paridé smiled, 'I wouldn't bother. I believe your efforts would be in vain. As you say, Densara must have had help. I would imagine that if the merchant does not wish to be found now, then we will not find him.' With a heavy heart he bid his cousin a good night and closed the door. Taking a seat in the atrium, Paridé then sipped some wine and wondered what the merchant's next move might be.

***

Lost in anguish and feelings of betrayal, Lillia barely noticed the ride to her new home. She was flanked by four eunuchs while Mother Vesta rode a little behind, but the princess ignored them all. Lillia could only battle with the turmoil of her emotions. She felt faint with grief, the foreknowledge of her impending incarceration weighing heavily upon her heart.

Marcus will come for me, she attempted to assure herself. *He loves me, and he said he would love me forever! He has to come.* Marcus was never far from her thoughts. She tried to imagine how she would get to see him once she was locked away in the House of Vesta. The princess was also missing her father and had begun to regret running away. She felt as though she had managed to desert him in his time of greatest need. Now, more than ever, she and her father needed to be together. Her tears had flowed continuously along the journey so far. Eventually, Lillia was overtaken by sheer exhaustion, and she fell into a troubled sleep on the horse.

The princess woke as they arrived at the House of Vesta, and for a moment she was unsure of where she was. High cliffs towered over her, feeling oppressive and overbearing as she thought of the thirty-year commitment her uncle had told her she now faced with the holy order. After dismounting, Lillia obediently followed Mother Vesta along a worn path through a dark maze of gardens, until eventually they came to an iron gate set in a high wall.

Lillia had never previously seen the House of Vesta and, despite her trepidation, she was curious. They waited at the gate as a gangly young woman dressed in a grey wrap approached.

'Mother Vesta, you have returned,' said the girl, cheerfully.

'Come, Daniela, save the greetings for later and open the gate, will you?'

Daniela's eyes widened as she noticed Lillia. 'We have a new arrival!' she shrieked.

'Enough,' said the priestess impatiently. 'Remember where you are, Daniela. Grace and divinity!'

The thin girl bowed her head. 'Yes, Mother Vesta: "Grace given by Vesta. Divine is the gift",' she said, obviously not for the first time.

Lillia looked on, a little amused by the ticking-off, but then remembered that this was to become her life. Suddenly she felt an overwhelming need to get away. Taking a step backwards, she began to shake her head. 'No, I do not want to go in,' she said quietly.

Both Mother Vesta and Daniela stared at Lillia, the latter with a confused look on her face. 'But it is an honour!' exclaimed the young acolyte.

'Please do not make me,' the princess pleaded to Mother Vesta. 'I want to go home.' She began to cry.

'Come girl, we cannot stand here,' replied the head priestess impatiently as she headed through the gate.

Lillia stood still, unwilling to go forward, frightened that she would never see the outside world again. Her curiosity had vanished – she hardly even noticed the numerous flower-laden balconies that decorated the high wall. Then she felt hands on her back, pushing her forward. Glancing behind, she saw that the four large eunuchs had encircled her and were now trying to ease her through the gate. Feeling intimidated by the bald men, Lillia allowed herself to edge onward, following Mother Vesta through the gate and into a large courtyard beyond.

She barely glanced at her surroundings as they made their way towards a set of ornate archways that stood in the middle of the dark stone building's facade. Passing through the tallest of the arches, they entered an atrium, at the centre of which was a large pool overlooked by a statue of the goddess Vesta. The painted marble statue had been sculpted to resemble a naked young woman that looked away from the observer with an expression of innocence captured in life-like tones. Lillia was momentarily mesmerised by the beauty of the effigy, and watched as the priestess and Daniela bowed to it before turning to her, urging her to copy the gesture. Reluctantly she obeyed, finding it strange, having never bowed to anyone other than King Corros, on that occasion long ago when he had visited for the feast that her father had arranged. The thought of her father brought a fresh lump to her throat.

'What is your name?' asked Daniela as they continued into the torch-lit building.

Before Lillia could answer, Mother Vesta interrupted. 'Her name is Rhea.'

'My friends and family call me Lillia,' interjected the princess to the skinny girl.

Mother Vesta stopped walking and turned to face Lillia, her soft features becoming stern. 'You must now forget everything from your old life, girl. You are to become an acolyte of the Vestal Virgins. This means that you will soon be divine.' She placed a hand on Lillia's shoulder and a look of sympathy crept into her eyes. 'From now on, no man can ever touch you, on pain of death. You will be revered and entrusted with the secrets of the Vesta. You will live a pure and privileged life, serving our order.' She smiled warmly at the princess and added, 'From now on, you will be known as Rhea Silva, daughter of the House of Vesta.'

Lillia nodded slowly and felt an emptiness in the pit of her stomach, knowing that her life was about to change forever.

* * *

Brascus stood in the atrium of the royal villa, hands clasped in front of him as he waited for one of the guards to fetch Numitor. He took a few deep breaths, pondering the events of the past few days. Brascus had found it all a trial, especially his role in leading Lillia to what she thought was safety while knowing that she faced only a life-sentence at the House of Vesta. He felt a lot less guilt about the role he had played in helping Amulius to become king. He firmly believed that the younger prince was the best choice to lead Latium to greatness. Meanwhile, in the light of recent events, he was growing increasingly apprehensive about his new position as Prima of the Hounds. He worried about the possible consequences of knowing the identity of another member.

Densara's membership of the cult made life difficult for Brascus. The merchant had always spent much time in the company of Amulius, and although the new king did not appear to be aware of the Hounds of Diana, Brascus was concerned that Densara might speak about the organisation if he was arrested.

He decided that he would have to make sure that he found the missing merchant before the king tracked him down, otherwise the Hounds of Diana would be at risk. Much as Amulius would have appreciated the discovery that a secret organisation had helped him to become king, he would not have accepted their challenge to his authority. Brascus imagined that Numitor might have an idea of where Densara was to be found, and it was this that had brought him to the villa. He would also use the opportunity to assure the prince of his daughter's safety.

In a short while, Numitor was escorted into the atrium. Brascus was immediately conscious of how tired and dishevelled the prince looked. His usual vibrancy was replaced by an impression of a gaunt and broken man. When Numitor saw Brascus, his face took on a look of disgust which quickly turned to anger.

'Why?' he shouted. 'Why did you do this to me?' The prince marched towards Brascus with his fists balled, but quickly stopped when the two guards flanked him.

Expecting fury from his former pupil, Brascus had a reply ready. 'I did what needed to be done to stop our country from declining into civil war. Your brother would never have rested until he became king. Had I not saved you, you would be dead by now.'

'Do not try to justify your actions with meaningless words. You cannot hide your true nature – you are a traitor. You are just like all my brother's allies – your greed allowed him to buy your loyalty.' raged the prince. 'Now leave me alone.' He turned to leave the atrium.

'Please, one moment, Sire,' called Brascus.

'I have nothing more to say to you, traitor,' came the gruff reply.

'I know you are angry, Numitor, but as I said, I did it for our country.'

Numitor stopped in his tracks and turned before stomping back towards Brascus with his face contorted in anger. 'Do you honestly think you have done a service to our country? You have ruined all that my ancestors have built; my brother will destroy any good that remains in Latium.' The prince then moved as if he were about to descend on his former mentor. The two guards rushed forward to intervene, but Numitor brushed them off. 'Do not worry,' he said. 'I would not dirty my hands on this… this traitor.'

The words stung Brascus a little and he looked away, shamed by the hurt in Numitor's eyes. 'I am sorry you feel this way, Sire. However, I have not come here to discuss this with you – it is done and there is little that can change it.'

'And what of my daughter – where is she?' demanded the prince. 'I understand you also betrayed her.'

'I saved her from your brother, Sire,' replied Brascus defensively. 'He would have seen her dead were it not for my suggestions.'

'So, it was your idea to abduct her, was it? It was you who chose to take her away from her friends and family, hiding her in some dire location known only to yourself.'

'I saved the princess from her own reckless actions, Numitor. When I found her she was about to be abducted by Densara. What was I supposed to do?' he asked, his voice now raised.

'You were supposed to bring her back here to me. Were it not for people like you, then she would never have been in danger.'

'Well, no one can hurt her now,' replied Brascus. 'She is safely behind the walls of the House of Vesta.'

'Vesta?' The prince looked confused. 'But only Vestal Virgins... She is to become a Vestal Virgin? No!' Numitor lowered himself on to a bench as he tried to deal with the shocking revelation.

'No-one can touch her now, Numitor – not even your brother. One day you may even thank me.'

'That day will never come,' snapped the prince.

'That may be so, but nonetheless, I did my best for the princess. Now, enough of this. I need you to tell me where I will find Densara.'

'I have no idea where he is,' lied the prince. 'He is my brother's spy, so I suggest you ask him.'

Brascus dismissed the guards so that he and Numitor could talk in privacy. He then sat himself on the bench beside the prince. 'I already know that you were holding the merchant in custody at his own villa, Sire, but it seems he has now been moved. It is vital that I get to him before your brother. Whatever else is happening in the kingdom, I have a life oath to protect Densara and others like him.'

A look of disbelief appeared on Numitor's face. 'You seek to protect him even after he goes against the kingdom?'

Shaking his head, Brascus tried to explain himself. 'There are matters in this kingdom that you cannot hope to understand, Sire. You know what I am, and what I represent. We have been protecting this kingdom now for five hundred years, and our methods have always been successful. Admittedly, the secrecy of our organisation brings its own problems and I confess there are times when one hand does not know what the other is doing. This is why I need to find the merchant. So tell me, where was Densara taken after leaving the villa?'

The barest of smiles tugged at the corners of Numitor's mouth. *So, Paridé had the sense to move Densara*, he mused. *Thank the gods.* Although reassured, the prince wondered what his friend would have done with the merchant. He suspected that Paridé's only option would have been to let

Densara go. Remembering how the merchant had claimed that he wanted to help the prince, Numitor hoped that he would now keep his word. Speaking with complete honesty, he offered Brascus a reply. 'I left Densara at his villa under guard. Whatever has happened since is not known to me. As you can see, I have been somewhat detained of late.' His tone was filled with frustration.

Brascus sighed. 'Well, in that case, I can only pray to Diana that your brother does not get to him before I do, or else the merchant will die.'

Numitor could not deny the truth in the words of his former mentor. It occurred to the prince that Densara might now prove to be his only remaining ally, in which case it would be a grave mistake not to help Brascus find the merchant. He wrestled with the dilemma in silence for a few moments before making his reply. 'Speak to Paridé – he may be able to help you.' Without a further glance at Brascus, Numitor rose from the bench and began to walk out of the atrium.

'Before you go, Sire, just one more question.' When Numitor failed to stop, Brascus raised his voice. 'Please, Sire.'

The prince turned, his face betraying his impatience.

'Does Densara know what I am?' The seriousness of Brascus' question was reflected in his eyes.

Without looking at his former mentor, Numitor nodded his head. 'Yes,' he replied. 'He guessed.'

Brascus remained seated and watched with a heavy heart as the prince exited the atrium. He had always liked Numitor – the man was pleasant and loyal, but Brascus believed he lacked the heart of a true leader. While Amulius would never allow his sentiment to interfere with a decision, Numitor always looked for the best in people, which Brascus believed was a dangerous trait for any leader.

Now, with the unsought mantle of Prima to consider, Brascus mused that he would have to be very careful in his dealings with Densara. It was now his responsibility to provide protection to every member of the Hounds of Diana – the fact that his own views were not in accordance with those of the merchant was irrelevant. Now that he knew that Densara was aware of his own involvement with the Hounds, he realised it would be extremely dangerous for both of them if anyone were to discover that they knew each other's secret identities. He needed to find Densara quickly.

***

The thunder clouds rolled over the choppy waters of Lake Albano, threatening to break at any moment over the small boat that rocked unsteadily beneath them. A flash of lightning lit up the hills and silhouetted the two men in the boat, as the waters splashed against the sides of their vessel. Bracing themselves for the thunder, they waited a few moments, but when it came, the sound was distant and muffled – a mere echo of the lightning that had preceded it.

The Carpenter held on to the oars and waited for the larger figure behind him to resume speaking.

'With regard to your new target,' said the Dius, leaning forward so as to be heard over the stormy waters, 'it is important that he is eliminated quickly in order to protect us, so you must not fail.'

'How and when, Dius?' replied the assassin.

'As soon as it can be arranged, and nothing elaborate. Just a quick kill and an audience to witness it.'

'As you command, Dius,' answered the Carpenter. 'I will not fail. He puts us all in danger.'

The Dius nodded. 'Good, and be careful – he may be protected by a Dormienti watcher. It could prove dangerous for you.'

'And, if he does have a watcher?'

'Avoid him,' replied the Dius with warning in his voice. 'Dormienti only ever follow our orders. We cannot punish one for doing as he has been commanded.'

'And if he interferes?'

'Do your job well, and he will not know about it until it is done. After that, I will take care of matters.'

The Dius said no more on the subject as the Carpenter rowed the boat back to the shore. Looking up into the thundery sky, the assassin mused that much had changed in Latium. The gods did not seem to be happy, demonstrating their wrath in cloud-breaking claps of thunder and ferocious forks of lightning that struck the mountains in blinding flashes. It was clear to him that the gods needed appeasing.

Chapter Thirty-Four

Densara kept to the shadows as he made his way through the dirty streets of the fishing district. His nerves were on edge as he glanced this way and that, noticing every movement, every shadow. Once or twice he darted into an alleyway when he thought his pursuers were close, barely managing to keep himself hidden from his new enemies as he moved from street to street. Eventually he came to a stop opposite the taverna, peering out from under his hood as he watched the evening's clientele depart. He soon spotted Brascus seeing the last of his customers out. Densara waited until the drunk patron had stumbled across the street. He quickly glanced left and right before darting over to the taverna and slipping in through the unlocked door.

Brascus was busy counting coins at one of the tables, but otherwise the place seemed deserted. The taverna owner glanced up and saw the hooded man before him. He instantly sprang from his seat and produced a knife. 'Who are you?' he demanded with a growl.

Densara calmly raised his empty hands and pulled back his hood. 'Can we speak,' he asked in serious tones, 'or do we need to summon a couple of acolytes?'

Brascus' mouth dropped open in surprise. For a few moments he simply stared at the merchant in disbelief.

The shocked look on Brascus' face spurred the merchant into continuing. 'I gather from your expression, Dius, that there will be no need for the Vestal Virgins on this occasion.' Densara smiled and gestured to the table. 'Shall we sit?'

Recovering from the initial shock, Brascus nodded. 'Yes, we must do that, but first we should go into my private room if we do not want to be disturbed by one of my workers.' He pointed up. 'Some of them live above,' he explained.

As Brascus began to lead the way, Densara glanced around quickly to assure himself that this was not a trap, and nodded his agreement. Once in the privacy of Brascus' room, the taverna owner took his time in pouring two goblets of wine, one of which he handed to the merchant.

'So you know my secret,' said Brascus after taking a large gulp of the wine. 'I suppose it was Numitor that mentioned it to you.' There was a hint of sadness in his voice.

Surprised by Brascus' tone, Densara sipped his own drink before replying. 'Yes, I know your secret, just as you know mine, but you are mistaken in thinking that Numitor gave you away. I always knew I was working against another Dius in my dealings with the princes. It would not have taken much probing to discover it was you.'

Brascus shrugged his shoulders. 'I found myself in a difficult situation. Amulius chose not to heed the advice I gave to him. I showed him how he could rule Latium alongside his brother while still retaining all the power for himself. Regrettably, it was not enough for him, and I was forced to make contingencies.'

'And imprisoning Princess Rhea within the House of Vesta – was that one of these contingencies?' asked Densara in a calm voice. He glared at the taverna owner. 'It seems convenient how your contingencies played right into the hands of her enemies.'

'I had no choice,' Brascus replied angrily. 'Amulius would have had her executed to prevent her from bearing heirs. This was the only way to save her.' He glowered at the merchant and added, 'You did no better.'

Densara raised his eyebrows. 'I believe it was you who spoilt that plan, was it not?' He still felt bitter about his own failed attempt to save the princess.

For a few moments neither man spoke as they stared at each other. Brascus eventually looked away and commented, 'I am sure that situations like this must happen from time to time. We obey the rules as best we can, each with our own primary obligation. You know mine, and now, I know yours. I believe we are caught in a dilemma that has no clear resolution.'

Densara considered the statement. *Yes, this affects us both, and yet I am the only one who is being hunted,* he thought. 'The resolution to our situation is simple. Either we both boil in the sulphur pools as traitors, or we agree to live in denial and forget all about this little problem.' Brascus nodded in agreement, encouraging Densara to continue. 'I believe our obligations have been met. Both Amulius and Numitor are alive and well, although I gather the older prince is now a permanent resident of his villa.'

Brascus lowered his eyes as a hint of shame passed over him. He swirled his wine absentmindedly as the merchant continued.

'And the princess is safe, even if it is not in the manner that I would have preferred.' Densara looked Brascus in the eye. 'Therefore, if we agree to forget what we know of each other, I believe we are free to carry on with our lives. I certainly have no wish to die.'

'Nor I,' agreed Brascus, meeting the merchant's gaze. 'However, you have a bigger problem to address. This is why I have been looking for you.'

'Yes, I did notice,' huffed Densara. 'There have been many people searching for me. I have had a difficult time avoiding them.'

'You are obviously a skilled man, Densara. The king has an army looking for you and yet, here you are.' There was more than a hint of respect in Brascus' voice.

'That's as may be,' replied the merchant, 'yet it still does not solve the problem of my being hunted.'

'Yes, I know, but it is not only your problem,' stated Brascus. 'Our new king must not gain knowledge of the Hounds of Diana. He would destroy us. Even with your skills, you would not survive an interrogation by Amulius.'

'And what of Numitor? How can we be sure that he will not speak of us to his brother at some point in the future?' asked Densara.

Brascus considered the question before responding. 'It is up to us to ensure that the prince remains silent. He already knows that we are dangerous, but we must now convince him that we can also be helpful. It will take time, but I believe you are up to the job.'

'Well, I certainly won't be if I am dead,' Densara reminded the man.

For the first time that night Brascus looked confident. 'I do have an idea of how I could convince Amulius that you are innocent of any wrong-doing. You would be free of your pursuers, and we could get on with the task of steering our bloodthirsty king on his journey.'

'Do you really think you can clear my name?' asked Densara.

Nodding, Brascus smiled. 'I will provide evidence that Amulius cannot doubt. A body will convince him.'

Densara laughed. 'As long as it is not my body, I will be happy. I will need to know the details, however, so that I am prepared for when I come to see Amulius myself. I will not be unhappy to put this mess behind me,' he laughed. 'I have enough enemies already, as I'm sure you are aware.'

'As do we all,' agreed Brascus.

Densara smiled but his tone became more serious. 'We must both be careful, my fellow Dius, but perhaps it might just be possible that together we can keep our secret hidden. Let us hope that we remain free to use our power to keep the new king out of trouble.'

'I will drink to that,' said Brascus, tipping his goblet towards the merchant in a toast before downing the rest of his wine.

* * *

It was a few days later and night was starting to fall over Alba Longa. Marcus was hiding in the boughs of a conifer, watching the royal villa intently. He shivered a little and regretted not having brought anything warmer to wear. His loose-fitting shirt and leggings were doing little to protect him from the cool breeze.

He was waiting for the servants to finish the last of their evening chores and retire to their sleeping quarters. He tried to make himself more comfortable, although over the last few days he had grown quite accustomed to crouching and hiding in awkward spaces.

Brushing away the dry needles that fell from the branches above him, Marcus let his thoughts turn to the morning when Lillia and Brascus had departed, leaving him alone with the guards. He remembered his feeling of immense sadness as she disappeared into the distance, and how quickly his grief had then subsided when the guards became aggressive towards him in their attitude. He had been ordered to mount the horse, and they had watched him closely as he did so, quickly flanking him before they set off.

They had journeyed back across the moors, giving Marcus time to consider all that had occurred. The first two men who had tried to take Lillia were obviously dangerous, and yet the timely arrival of Brascus had struck the shepherd as seeming less than coincidental. It was at that point that he had begun to worry for Lillia's safety. Something about the circumstances had not felt right at all.

While riding between the two guards, he had kept his head down and waited in the hope of an opportunity to escape. His chance came when the trio had begun urging their horses up a steep ravine, lined with thick bushes and littered with gravel. The two guards had skilfully guided their horses around fallen rocks and loose stones, soon pushing ahead of the shepherd. As the guards concentrated on the trail, Marcus had quietly slipped off the back of his mount. The moment his feet touched the ground, he had darted behind a bush. Making use of skills he had learnt as a shepherd, he had then been able to steal silently away.

He had heard the guards calling to him a few moments later. 'You wait till we get hold of you,' one of them had shouted while the shepherd was busy jumping nimbly over rocks and rounding bushes. He knew they would lose time in trying to find him, so he had taken the opportunity to muster all his speed and run for his life.

He had been scurrying downhill, making for the woods that hemmed the mountain, when he had realised that he could no longer hear the guards' pursuit. From there it had been easy for Marcus to lose them and begin his search for Lillia, although he had no idea of where Brascus had taken her. He had presumed it would probably be either the palace, or the royal villa, so without further delay he had set off.

Without a horse, the shepherd's journey back to Mount Albanus had taken two days. He had reached the city walls tired and hungry, by which time the news that Amulius had become king was common knowledge. After visiting his aged parents, he had felt a twinge of guilt as he recalled seeing them full of worry and frightened for his safety, but they had informed him of all that had happened since his departure with Lillia, including Numitor's incarceration at the villa. He had guessed that Lillia would also be there.

A cramp in his leg disturbed Marcus from his reverie, and he returned his attention to the villa, noting that there were more guards on duty than he had anticipated. Occasionally two of them would walk around the perimeter of the villa grounds, coming close to his hiding place. He guessed that Lillia's home must have become nothing more than a comfortable cage in which to hold the princess and her father.

Waiting until there were no guards nearby, Marcus quietly climbed down from the tree and clambered over the villa's rough wall, landing without a sound on the other side. Keeping to the shadows, he made his way through the gardens until he was close to the building. Having never been inside Lillia's home, he had no idea where the sleeping quarters were to be found. Studying the villa, the shepherd saw an open archway that led to an atrium, and was about to move when he heard voices coming from the side of the building. The two patrolling guards appeared to his left, deep in conversation. Marcus held his breath as they passed within grabbing distance. They were clearly oblivious to his presence. He felt a moment of relief and quietly exhaled as they disappeared around another corner. His prior scrutiny of the villa had convinced him that there were no guards inside, and he was now eager to get in. Quietly, he headed for the atrium, keeping low and alert to any sounds.

Once inside, the shepherd made his way around a rectangular pool that dominated the large atrium. He passed through another arch on the opposite side and entered a wide corridor. At its end he was faced with the choice of going either left or right. He listened for a few moments but heard only the pounding of his own heart. Forcing himself to calm down, Marcus waited quietly and focused his hearing. Soon, the faint sound of snoring filtered through from his right. He turned into a small vestibule and saw that it opened onto a darkened room. Slipping in, he saw a curtain hanging in the middle of the otherwise plain chamber. Gently pulling it aside, he found himself beside a bed occupied by the sleeping form of Prince Numitor.

Marcus looked at the prince and scratched his head, having given no thought as to what he planned to do. The idea of waking the sleeping man made him uneasy, but what other choice did he have? He cautiously reached forward, and gently grasped the prince's shoulder, giving it a timid shake.

'Hmm, wha...' the prince muttered as he brushed off the hand.

'Your Highness,' whispered Marcus, 'please wake up.' He shook him again.

This time Numitor opened his eyes, and, upon seeing a dark figure leaning over him, leapt out of the bed. Realising that the prince was about to yell, Marcus hurriedly gestured to Numitor to remain quiet. 'Please don't shout, Your Highness,' he whispered. 'I'm here to rescue you, and the princess.'

Numitor stared at the young man. 'Do I know you?'

Marcus shook his head. 'No, Your Highness.' He returned the prince's gaze and saw that the man looked very little like the regal figure he had seen on public occasions and in parades. With sagging shoulders and a face that was drawn and deeply lined, the majestic prince from his memory had now been replaced by this tired and defeated husk of a man.

'Then you are Dormienti?' asked the prince.

Confused by the unfamiliar term, Marcus shook his head again. 'What is that? No, Your Highness, I am just a shepherd.'

It was Numitor's turn to look confused, prompting Marcus to elaborate. 'And a friend of Princess Lillia... sorry, I mean Rhea, Your Highness.'

'Ah, *that* shepherd,' said Numitor, his expression changing to one of distaste. 'You are the reason that I could not keep her safe. How dare you show your face?' He rounded the bed and advanced on Marcus.

The shepherd stood his ground and made no attempt to defend himself from Numitor. 'I meant no harm,' he said sadly, his head bowed. 'I love her and would protect her with my life.'

Numitor stopped in his tracks and studied the rough-looking boy afresh, seeing the genuine misery in his face. Something in the lad's gaze resonated with the prince, and his anger quickly evaporated. In a calm voice, he said, 'My daughter obviously saw something in you.' With a sigh, the prince sat down on the edge of the bed. 'But, sadly, you are too late. You cannot help Lillia now.'

'What do you mean?' asked Marcus, his voice rising with anxiety.

'She is out of reach, somewhere where not even I can see her.'

'Then she *is* alive,' said the shepherd, feeling greatly relieved. 'We must go and rescue her, Your Highness, wherever she is. I will help you.'

Numitor shook his head. 'You must forget her, boy. As much as you may think you love her, you must put her out of your mind. No-one but I need suffer from her absence.'

'I don't understand, Your Highness. I cannot forget Lillia. Why can't we rescue her?'

'She cannot be rescued from an oath,' insisted Numitor. 'She has become an acolyte of the Vestal Virgins.'

It took a moment for Marcus to comprehend what he was hearing, but when the news began to sink in, it felt like a blow to his gut. He looked up at the prince with tears in his eyes. 'The forbidden women,' he whispered. 'She has become one of those? But, why?'

'In serving the Vesta, she serves us all, boy. She has given her life to the holy order so as to keep herself safe from harm and, in so doing, she offers me protection. My brother believes he knows how to get to her, and because of this he also knows that I will not dare to rise against him. Therefore, he has no need to kill me.'

Marcus' legs began to shake as he grappled with the information. Numitor empathised with him, and tried to speak in the mildest of tones. 'You had better go. I cannot leave here, nor would I choose to leave. However, I must warn you, the time will come when my brother will start searching for you. If he should find you, he will hurt you. For your own safety, you should go far away from here. If you are able, you should leave Latium altogether – only then will you be beyond the reach of my brother's spies.'

The prince's advice alarmed Marcus greatly. His first thoughts were for his parents. It was only now that he could see that his actions had also placed them in danger. Numitor's suggestion was probably his best course of action, but would he be able to take his elderly parents with him? Meanwhile, the thought of leaving Lillia behind sickened him, and yet he knew in his heart that there was nothing to be done for her now. Everybody knew that to defy the goddess Vesta was punishable by death – once a girl was devoted to the goddess, her life was no longer her own. Feeling his heart breaking, Marcus let his tears fall freely as he tried to come to terms with a terrible fact: Lillia was now lost to him forever.

Chapter Thirty-Five

Eight Months Later: 771 BCE

The late winter snow lined the top of the rim around Lake Nemi. It encircled the lake's deep bowl like the white walls of Lillia's new home. She sighed as she held onto a cold stone pillar, dizziness threatening to unbalance her. It was quiet on the balcony – a few moans and snores drifted in from the dormitory behind her, but otherwise the dark night was silent.

Lillia was feeling sick again and hoped that the fresh air would soon help a little. Shivering as a breeze whipped around the building, she wanted to fetch the cover from her bed but she did not trust her balance, so she remained standing on the balcony in her nightgown and accepted the cold.

It will not matter if I freeze. At least I would be free. The princess had already prayed for the gods to take her, but her pleas had been ignored. She had wished herself dead many times since her induction into the Vestal Virgins, her dark thoughts fuelled by her separation from everyone she loved. Often she fantasised about Marcus rescuing her, willing him to come up with a daring plan.

The first month at the House of Vesta had been the worst of Lillia's life. The agony she felt for her father, along with her horror at her uncle's betrayal took the princess to the limits of her endurance. For days she had not even known whether or not Numitor was alive. News of his incarceration had finally come via gossip, which tended to spread within the House of Vesta like fire. While having to obey the strict rules of segregation, the young women would gorge on any rumours or revelations they could obtain, and Lillia often heard gossip from Alba Longa, but it almost always proved to be trivial.

The princess' worries had slowly turned to despair as she had begun to realise that she was not going to be rescued – life in the House of Vesta was all she had to look forward to. The following weeks had passed in a haze for the broken girl. She had become sullen and quiet, barely speaking, lost in deep grief. Nothing could drown the despair that haunted her.

She found that only eating seemed to help fill her emptiness.

One morning, Mother Vesta had taken her aside to talk with her, but Lillia had just looked down at the floor, barely aware of her surroundings. The older woman had tried to get her to speak, the pity in her voice evident as she did her best to coax the heartbroken girl.

'I hear your father is fit and well, Rhea,' said Mother Vesta.

Lillia hated hearing her formal name – it felt impersonal and reminded her of her isolation. She had continued to stare at the floor, staying silent.

'The girls here like you. You should try to make some friends.'

I want my old friends, Lillia thought as she had battled the heavy feeling in her heart.

'Talk to me, girl. I cannot help you otherwise. You must talk to me.'

More silence.

Mother Vesta had sat beside her and held the girl's hand. 'I know how hard it must be for you, Rhea,' she said. 'You miss your family and friends – that is natural – but you have to understand that you have a new family now. We care about you. We want to help you.'

No-one can help me. The thought had triggered something within Lillia, and suddenly she'd had no choice but to let go of her pent-up emotions. Clutching her hands to her chest, she had then released a wail of grief and fallen to the floor in a heap. Her cries continued, eventually turning to gasps as her anxiety had reached its peak, breaking through her wall of sorrow. Mother Vesta had held her gently, waiting patiently until Lillia had spent her tears.

After that day, Lillia had followed her routines sombrely. Prayers took up the mornings, and in the afternoons she would take part in singing or dancing rehearsals. The songs, which were mostly hymns to the goddess Vesta, would often bring tears to her eyes as the dulcet melodies pulled at her emotions. Although Lillia had always tried to honour the gods whenever possible, she was struggling with the idea of giving herself to just one of them. The princess never lost sight of the fact that she was there through no choice of her own, and this made her feel as though she was Vesta's prisoner rather than her devotee. Perhaps the biggest of the adjustments she was having to make was the challenge of being treated as an equal to the other girls. Lillia had always taken for granted the reverence and obedience offered to her as a princess, and yet now, she was suddenly considered no better than any other girl at the house. She was finding that some of the women were taking great pleasure in ordering her to do menial tasks. Lillia would obey without acknowledgement, her features remaining sombre and uninterested.

The young acolytes spent most of their time learning the rituals and practises of the Vesta. They did not leave the House of Vesta during the first part of their training, moving on to other temples only when they finally became priestesses.

The senior girls would host the entertainment of nobles and dignitaries, as was the custom at the House of Vesta. Until Lillia received The Blessing of Vesta – a symbolic achievement, gained after ten years of service – she would not be joining these events.

The Vestal Virgins spent some of their free time in the hot baths. Without the stern gaze of the older women to subdue the young acolytes' childish tendencies, the girls would relax and enjoy a brief respite from the strict rules of conduct normally imposed on them.

In her depressed state, Lillia had continued to turn to food for comfort, and was spending less and less time at the baths as she became aware of her increasing girth. The other girls had taken very little interest in her at first, but as Lillia gained weight, they began to whisper cruel comments. She often heard her name in the same sentences as "mortadella" or "porcella" – they were calling her a piglet. Much of the time she was able to ignore it, usually choosing to eat extra servings at dinner just to spite them. Otherwise, she tried to get on with life as best she could, but the pain of loss was never far away.

The long days gave way to lonely nights. During the day, Lillia always had distractions but, in the darkness of the dormitory, she had only the sounds of sleeping for company. Most nights, she would wake up in a sweat from bad dreams – Amulius had been laughing as he buried her alive or locked her in a cage. Whenever these dreams woke her, she would end up wandering off to the culina, taking dried meats or cheeses from the store, and gorging herself until she could eat no more.

The cooks had noticed the missing food and were complaining about it whenever anyone walked within earshot. One morning Lillia overheard a cook saying, "She's the culprit, you just have to look at her to see it!" The conversation abruptly ended on her arrival, leaving Lillia in no doubt that they had been speaking about her.

Tonight, however, she did not want to eat, feeling much too sick to think about food. An ache in her belly made her wonder if she needed to use her night bowl, but suddenly the aches turned into sharp pains that tore into her abdomen and brought her to her knees. She cried out for help and, within moments, one of her roommates was beside her.

'What is wrong?' gasped the young woman as she knelt next to Lillia.

Lillia found herself unable to talk. She recognised the girl as Rosaria and grabbed her hand tightly as more pain burned inside. This time it was followed by a warm, wet sensation between her legs. Rosaria jumped back with a gasp, her eyes wide as she stared at the growing patch of darkness on Lillia's nightgown. A few hurried whispers came from the crowd of girls that had gathered as they all gazed at the soiled gown. Lillia made herself look down. At the sight of the blood, she began to scream.

Mother Vesta pushed her way through the girls. 'Let me through, let me see.' said the panicking woman. 'Oh, Vesta, give me strength.' she muttered when she saw Lillia. 'Quick, get me a sheet,' she ordered one of the young women, 'and you,' pointing to another, 'get Emulinda at once.'

Lillia felt another stab of pain and cried out again as she started to shiver uncontrollably. *It hurts so much. What is happening to me?* she thought in desperation between moments of agony. *Am I dying?*

'You're as cold as winter!' cried Mother Vesta. She pointed to one of the gawping girls. 'Get a blanket for her.' She put her arm around the shaking princess. 'Do not worry, Rhea, help is coming.'

More pain burned in Lillia's abdomen, but this time it did not stop. Instead it simply grew in intensity until, finally, the princess lost consciousness.

Time lost all meaning for Lillia as she continued to battle with the agony that still managed to penetrate the dark corners of her unconscious mind. Visions of terrifying monsters filled her head, snapping and clawing at her stomach. When she could take no more, she pushed her thoughts away from the pain. Then the dream changed.

Marcus was there. He appeared as Mars, the God of War. He was at the lake cabin, facing Amulius. Mars' sword of fire bore down on Amulius' head, but suddenly Amulius was behind Mars, swinging an axe at the god. 'He's behind you, look, look!' Lillia screamed to Mars, but the screams were silent, her voice caught in her throat. She felt a distant pain in her groin but refused to look, knowing what she would see. Instead, she fixed her eyes on Marcus, who was once again just her lover on the beach at Lake Albano. He reached out to her; she leant towards him to take his hand, but then Amulius was there again, pulling her away.

The pain came back, this time closer. She screamed out for Marcus, who had again become Mars. He held two wolf cubs and offered them protection as Amulius tried to club them to death. 'These two are mine,' Mars shouted at the king. 'You cannot have them.'

The god floated out over the lake and the cubs began to grow in his hands, their eyes glowing like sunshine and their tails becoming swords of fire. Lillia felt a jolt as Mars ordered the cubs to go to her. They jumped at the princess and disappeared through the wall of her bloated belly. Lillia tried to run to Mars but, although it was only a short distance, the more she ran, the further away he became. She panicked and called to him. The god turned and floated towards her until she could feel his breath. She reached up to kiss him but suddenly his face froze in agony as two flaming swords appeared out of his chest.

Amulius laughed. 'You can never have her!'

Lillia called out to Mars again but the flames of the swords had caught the god and he now burned like a star. Then the pain returned once more, but this time it was different. The princess was burning inside – something was pushing down on her bladder and it felt as if her belly was splitting in two. Then Lillia saw a woman in a white wrap who had no face, but she bore the voice of her mother. The woman was singing to Numitor. The prince cried as he sat beside his dying wife. Then Amulius appeared again and pointed, a manic grin upon his face. Lillia looked to where he gestured and saw that her mother was now on a funeral pyre. She watched in astonishment as the woman then rose from amongst the flames and shouted to her daughter. 'Do not lose them, my love. They must live. They are the future – they must live…'

Lillia felt herself falling. She was flying to her freedom, leaving behind all her worries and grief on a dark cliff face where men had battled and died. She could see the black mirror of the lake growing bigger by the moment, its dark depths offering solace and peace. The princess welcomed its embrace.

***

Eventually, the dreams came to an end and Lillia awoke, dizzy and confused, only vaguely aware of being in the dorm with some of the older women.

Where are all the girls? she wondered. She began to notice a feeling of pressure in her abdomen, and then saw that her knees had been hoisted up. Mother Vesta was standing at the foot of the bed with another woman. Lillia recognised her as the herbalist, Emulinda.

Mother Vesta glanced at the princess and heaved a sigh as she came around the bed to stand beside her. 'Drink this.' She held a cup to Lillia's lips.

Lillia drank the bitter liquid and then tried to get up, but a sudden stab of pain stayed her and left her gasping for air. 'What is happening to me?' she cried. 'It hurts so much.'

The herbalist looked up. 'You're having a baby, my child. It probably won't live.' The heavyset woman spoke without a trace of sympathy. 'You have lost a lot of blood.'

'A baby?' Lillia managed to splutter before being wracked by another violent spasm of pain.

The night turned to dawn as the princess drifted in and out of consciousness. Battling with pain and delirium, she began to dream again. Eventually the pressure grew in her abdomen until it became unbearable. It felt to Lillia as if something was ripping her apart from the inside. From somewhere far away she could hear a voice telling her to push. She obeyed. There was a moment of relief, then the air was pierced by the shrill cry of a new-born baby. Lillia had only an instant to register the sound before the pain came back again. She thought she heard one of the women say something about 'a second one' before the darkness returned.

Sometime later Lillia awoke. She became aware of Mother Vesta dozing quietly beside her. Feeling thirsty, the princess gently nudged the woman, causing her to wake with a start.

'Sorry,' croaked Lillia. She lacked the energy to say more.

'It is fine, Rhea,' Mother Vesta softly replied. Reaching down, she produced a cup of water and put it gently to the girl's lips.

Lillia drank a few small mouthfuls and nodded her thanks. She wanted to ask why she was there, and it was then that she remembered what had happened.

The baby! I had a baby! The princess was instantly alert. She had a burning desire to be with her as-yet unseen offspring, a protective instinct screaming out within her. 'Where is my baby?' she demanded, beginning to panic.

'Calm yourself, Rhea – your babies are fine,' assured Mother Vesta. 'We have brought in a wet nurse to feed them. You are much too weak. You very nearly died. You will need a lot of rest if you are to make a full recovery.'

'"Them?"' she asked, confused.

'Yes, Rhea, you had twin boys.'

Lillia stared as she tried to comprehend what Mother Vesta had just told her. *Twins?* She suppressed a shiver, recalling the two wolf cubs of her dream. 'I want to see them,' she said. She began to sit up, intending to get out of the bed.

Mother Vesta quickly rose and clasped Lillia by the shoulders, gently pushing her back down until she was lying again. 'I'll have none of that,' said the priestess sternly. 'You must rest or you may start to bleed again. I will bring your sons to you in a while. They are sleeping now. You need to understand that they are also weak. I think they were born early. Tell me when they were conceived.'

Lillia guessed there could only have been that one time with Marcus, but she did not want to confess anything to Mother Vesta. Nevertheless, she could not understand how she had come to give birth. *I was not pregnant,* she thought. *I would have known. How can this be?* The princess frowned in confusion but then became aware of the disappointment in the priestess' eyes. 'I was not pregnant!' she exclaimed. 'I was not pregnant until last night.'

'It was actually three nights ago that you gave birth, Rhea, and do not talk such nonsense. You must have been pregnant beforehand. Did you not notice anything different all these months?' she inquired.

Three nights – has it been that long? The news shook Lillia. There was so much to take in. *Pregnant... giving birth to twin boys... how was all this possible?* Yes, she had gained some weight, but she still bled at every new moon. 'I bled as I should have,' said the princess, unconsciously putting her hand down to her sore belly.

A look of surprise grew on Mother Vesta's face. 'Yes, now I come to think of it, I remember the first time you bled here,' she remarked. 'I provided you with rags.'

Lillia nodded, embarrassed by the memory.

The priestess grew serious, 'Yet here we have two babies, and they definitely came from you. I helped to deliver them. How can you say that you were not pregnant? All the same, I cannot think of one moment when you could have had the chance.' She shook her head and her voice grew sterner. 'Whoever violated you will answer with his life. There will be consequences for you as well, unless, of course, you were forced. In such a situation we have a cleansing ritual that we would use to purify you. Either way, I believe it will not end well.'

Lillia shook her head. A stab of fear pierced her heart. Were they going to take her babies away? It certainly felt as if it was a possibility, and a tear ran down her cheek. She had no idea of what she might do if that were to happen. 'I did not do anything, I swear,' cried the princess, her panic rising.

'Hush now, Rhea,' said Mother Vesta as she started to fuss with the bed covers. 'Nothing is decided. Nobody outside of the House knows about your babies. The wet nurse has been sworn to secrecy – she will not tell. For the moment, the situation is contained, but news is bound to spread in the end. If I am to help you, then you must tell me everything.'

Lillia nodded, for the moment relieved.

'So, come on, Rhea, who is the father? He must answer for this. Making you pregnant was foolish in the extreme.'

'I was not pregnant when I came here,' pleaded the princess. 'You must believe me.'

'Well, you have certainly been pregnant since being here,' said the woman, frowning. 'Make this easy on yourself, Rhea. Tell me, who is the father? Was it the boy you ran away with, before you came here? Has he been visiting you? If he has, then it will be the end of you both. You will be put to death.'

Lillia fell silent as she considered Mother Vesta's grim words. *I have not even seen a man since I arrived here,* she thought, *aside from the eunuchs. I wish Marcus had visited me. I no longer want to die,* she realised, *not now that I have babies to look after.*

Another thought came to her, causing her to shudder afresh. *If Uncle finds out about the twins, he is bound to take them away from me. Not even the gods will be able to keep him from doing so.*

Something about the gods nagged at Lillia. There had been no man in her life since Marcus. She had had neither the will nor the opportunity to look for new romance. Marcus could well be the father, and yet the princess remained certain that she had not been pregnant until the night she had collapsed. She thought about her dreams again. *They must have something to do with what has happened to me,* she decided.

'It's the god, Mars,' Lillia blurted before she could stop herself. 'He is the father.'

'Do not be so silly!' was Mother Vesta's first reaction. Then something changed in the priestess' expression and she turned to Lillia. 'However, you were calling out to Mars during your labour,' said the woman, now looking bemused. 'Over and over you called to him.' She shook her head. 'No, it cannot be Mars – the gods do not act like that. It is not possible!'

The gods do act like that, thought Lillia. *I just need to convince you.* 'It is possible,' she said. 'He has been coming to me night after night. He wanted me to go with him but I couldn't reach him,' she explained.

Lillia did her best to recount the dreams to Mother Vesta. The older woman listened attentively to the tale and, by the time it was finished, the expression on the priestess' face gave Lillia a little hope, although a degree of doubt still remained in her eyes.

'If anyone else had told me such a tale, I would not have believed them.' The woman looked closely at Lillia and nodded her head, acknowledging a thought. 'Some of the things you say are possible – if unlikely – but I did hear you calling to Mars. The very fact that you are alive is a miracle. The

248

amount of blood you lost would have killed most people. I have heard of occasions when the gods have induced dreams, and I confess that it does sound as if this may have been the case for you.' She paused for a moment of further consideration. 'It is true – the gods are known to come to mortal men and women.'

Lillia was no stranger to all the legends herself and took the opportunity to strengthen her argument. 'The gods have often interfered with mortals. Hercules, Helen of Troy, and Perseus – they were all children of the gods.' The princess held Mother Vesta's gaze, desperately hoping that her words would convince the older woman. She could not bear to think of what would happen if Mother Vesta chose not to believe her. 'I really want to be with my babies now,' said the princess, her maternal needs pushing to the fore once again.

'All right,' agreed Mother Vesta. 'I will bring them to you when they next wake, but only for a short while – you must rest.'

* * *

The strength of feeling that Lillia experienced as Mother Vesta placed the two babies in her arms was overwhelming. She immediately started crying, the tears of joy rolling down her cheeks as she gazed down at her sons. Smiling, she began speaking to them quietly. They both had dark tufts of hair and blue eyes that looked up at her in innocence. They were the most beautiful creatures she had ever seen. As they rested in her arms, the princess instantly felt the depth of her love for them. She knew that she was ready to fight to protect them – she would even kill for them if necessary. Nothing would come before her twins.

To Lillia's surprise, both babies started to reach for her breasts. She pulled up her gown and helped them to find their way. Not sure if she even had any milk to offer, the princess watched in fascinated silence as they began suckling. It was only a few moments before she could see the tell-tale creamy lines appearing around the boys' mouths. Mother Vesta smiled and offered a reassuring nod to Lillia as the babies immersed themselves in their first feed from their mother. The proud parent felt the warmth of her babies' soft skin against her own as they nestled into her, occasionally kicking out and making tiny noises of pleasure. She relaxed into a cocoon of peace, all her troubles temporarily forgotten as she let the cloak of motherhood wrap itself around the new family. In those few moments, a solid bond was formed, and Lillia imagined that she could hear her boys silently speak to her, expressing their need for her protection. She felt them both filling her heart, infusing her with joy, embracing her with their love.

Chapter Thirty-Six

Amulius waited in the command tent for the barber to arrive. He had let his goatee grow to a full beard since the end of the last summer, and the constant itching around his jowls had started to annoy him.

Preferring to spend his time away from the heavy snow of the highlands, the king had accompanied his army down to the new river camp for training: he believed that winter was a good time for the army to sharpen its skills along with its swords, and in the Tiber Valley they could do so with the benefit of milder weather.

Much of the new king's time had been taken up with the planning of his next campaign. Several Samnite tribes still remained in the south that had yet to be brought under control. Rumours had come to Amulius that some of these tribes had forged alliances with Apulian raiders. In itself, this did not present a problem. He was confident that dealing with any resistance would be easy, but he was also aware that situations of this kind had a habit of growing out of control if left unchecked. The king's thoughts were disturbed as the stocky barber entered the tent, his usual leather wrap – containing his blades, in hand.

'Good morning, Sire,' smiled the cheerful, heavy-set man as he laid the wrap on a table.

Amulius could not help but return the smile. It amazed him how this veteran could always invoke the same response. *Must be a trick of the trade,* he mused. 'How are you today, Fabius? Are the men keeping you busy?'

'Busy as always, Sire,' replied the barber. 'Plenty of hair to cut.' He unrolled the wrap and removed a thin fabric sheet which he then spread out over the rugs that lined the floor. Positioning a chair in the middle of the sheet, he invited the king to sit. 'What will it be today, Sire – the usual?'

'This beard has to go,' said Amulius, scratching again as he sat down. 'Maybe a little trim as well – it has been a while.' There was a hint of embarrassment in the king's voice.

'I can see,' answered Fabius, jovially, 'but, of course, you are a busy man, Sire. Must be hard work to run a country. Small matters such as haircuts just have to wait.' He placed a cloth over the king's chest. 'I'll cut first and then do the shave, if that's all right, Sire.'

Amulius nodded and took the opportunity to engage in a little small talk. 'So, tell me, how long have you been with the army now, Fabius?'

'Did ten years under Agrillis, Sire, and then another ten as cropper. I enjoyed the fighting, don't get me wrong, but this is my proper position.' He started to comb through Amulius' tangled hair. 'It's going to tug a little here, Sire – there's a bit of a knot, I'm afraid.'

The king ignored the barber's tugging. He enjoyed chatting to the balding man. It was impossible not to like the cropper, and he was excellent as his job – Amulius had never received so much as a nick from him in five years. Fabius' blades were always sharp and his relaxed chatter invariably helped the king to set his worries aside, if only for a short while. Fabius was the last in a long line of croppers to serve Amulius – all his predecessors had ended up suffering the man's wrath after a particularly painful shave. After receiving his first shave from Fabius, Amulius had never allowed another barber near him. He was about to ask after the man's family, when the tent's flap opened and Captain Miron walked in, glancing at Fabius before he addressed the king.

'Sire, sorry to disturb you. I have news. It's the cook from the House of Vesta, Sabia.'

'Well, what are you waiting for?' growled the king, annoyed by the interruption.

Miron looked at Fabius again.

'Do not worry about him,' Amulius barked. 'You can trust him not to gossip – is that not correct, Fabius?'

With a little colour rising to his cheeks, the cropper hesitated briefly before replying. 'Deaf as a post, Sire.'

The captain looked unconvinced but turned back to the tent's entrance and called out, 'Bring her in.'

A short, plump woman ducked through the flap. She was sobbing. When she saw the king, she quickly fell to her knees before him. 'Your Highness, I'm so sorry,' she cried. 'They kept it a secret – I didn't know until last night. I came as quick as I could. I'm so sorry.'

Amulius looked at the woman and gestured to Fabius to stop his work for a moment. Leaning forward, the king gave her all his attention. 'Calm yourself woman, and report.'

Sabia nodded and took a few quick breaths. 'It's your niece, Sire – she's... she's...' The woman looked terrified. 'Oh, please don't be angry, Sire, but she's gone and given birth to twins.'

'She's done what?' Amulius thought he must have misheard the cook.

'Twins, Sire,' she replied meekly. 'She's given birth to twins.'

'No!' roared the king. He sprang out of the chair, tearing away the barber's cloth, the sudden outburst causing both Sabia and Fabius to jump back. The cook let out a shriek. 'How can this have happened?' shouted Amulius. 'Twins?' He glowered at the cook. 'When were they born? Why was I not told that Rhea was pregnant?'

'Sire, they kept it a secret,' cried Sabia again. 'It happened about a month ago. I only found out yesterday. I heard it from Filomena, who heard it from Lidianna. They've got your niece and her two boys hidden in Mother Vesta's room, so as no-one would see 'em, Sire.' Once again the cook lapsed into sobbing.

'Silence, woman,' hissed Amulius as he sat back down. 'Boys, you say?'

Sabia nodded, wiping her runny nose with the back of her hand. 'They say it was a miracle, Sire. She wasn't even pregnant. Then one night, the god Mars tried to take her away and she collapsed. They say he struck her with his sword of fire, and then she had the babies.'

The king narrowed his eyes in fury, fixing his stare on the cowering cook. 'Are you not well in the head, woman? Whatever are you talking about?'

Sabia edged back a little before nervously repeating her story. She paused, and then added, 'At least, that's what Lidianna told Filomena. Things have been a bit odd lately, Sire. I couldn't put my finger on it until last night. Now it all makes sense,' she sighed.

Amulius shook his finger at the frightened woman. 'If this turns out to be a lie, I will have you burning hotter than Mars' swords,' he threatened. 'Do you understand?'

'It's the truth, Sire, I swear.'

The king made a non-committal grunt and dismissed Sabia, who left the tent at speed. He leaned back in his chair to try and gather his thoughts. He did not know what to think. *Rhea must have been pregnant before she entered the House of Vesta,* he reasoned. *She could not have had contact with other men – it is not possible for an acolyte to do so. Otherwise, the only remaining explanation would be as the woman claimed – that the twins were fathered by a god.* He did a quick calculation and soon deduced that it was possible that his niece could have gone into the House of Vesta already pregnant.

Amulius was confounded by the situation. *Surely someone would have noticed if she was pregnant. And why has the priestess not told me of the births? She knows what the consequences will be for her defiance. Maybe she has grown too fond of the girl and is now trying to protect her.* He needed more information. Looking up, the king met the eyes of Miron, who had been waiting all the while by the tent's entrance.

'You know what I need you to do, Captain.'

Miron nodded. 'And, if it is true, Sire?'

Amulius thought for a moment before answering the captain. 'Bring them here. Just the babies though – leave the girl where she is.'

'What do you intend, Sire? If the gods are involved...' Miron shuffled uneasily.

'I will need to speak to the Mother Vesta first,' replied the king. 'This could all be nothing more than idle talk. We will know shortly.' He rubbed his shoulder, the uncertainty of the situation having already caused him to become tense. He stood up and faced Miron. 'Ride hard and bring me news. Escort the head priestess here with the babies. The augur and I will be waiting for you.'

Miron nodded. 'It will be around sunset I should think, Sire, when I return. If the woman objects, do you wish me to use force?' There was hesitation in his voice.

'Whatever it takes,' snapped Amulius. 'If I find that the priestess was trying to deceive me, she is going to regret it. However, I fear she may have other motives for keeping me in ignorance. After all, she does convene with Vesta – she is closer to the gods than most.' The king frowned in thought before his attention returned to Miron. 'Go now and bring me news.'

Amulius watched the captain leave and then turned to sit back down, but received a jolt of surprise upon seeing Fabius, still hovering by the tools of his trade. 'Ah, Fabius, forgive me. I forgot that you were here,' he apologised. 'Can we leave this until tomorrow morning? I have much to deal with now.'

'As you wish, Sire,' the cropper replied brightly. 'I know you are a busy man. I'll get out of your way at once.' He collected his belongings and started wrapping them.

'You will tell no-one of what you heard today,' warned Amulius. With a smile, he added, 'I do not want rampant rumours around camp – you know what the men are like.'

'As I said, Sire, deaf as a post, me.'

'Good,' said the king, placing a hand on Fabius' shoulder and gently ushering him out. 'I am glad to hear it. I will see you at sunrise.' He held the flap open.

'Good day, Sire,' said Fabius, and ambled out of the tent.

Amulius took a moment to compose himself. *If Rhea has really given birth, then I have a serious problem,* he mused. Any sons of Lillia would automatically be heirs to the kingdom. In the future, they would be certain to contest his position on the throne of Latium. The king was particularly unsettled by the idea that the gods might be involved – he had always thought the gods were on his side, believing that they had helped him gain the throne. *If the twins are truly the sons of Mars, then my options are extremely limited,* he realised. *It would be madness to threaten the offspring of a deity.* Amulius cast his mind back to when Lillia had been taken to the House of Vesta. On reflection, he decided that his first thought on the matter was the only convincing explanation – Rhea must have been pregnant before entering the House. *The twins are most likely nothing more than the sons of a shepherd,* he assured himself, remembering his niece's attempt to run away with Marcus before becoming an acolyte. However, Amulius continued to feel uneasy, and a sense of foreboding began to settle upon his thoughts.

* * *

Lillia sat in a reed chair, enjoying the view of the House of Vesta's extensive gardens. She was nursing her babies. She had quickly mastered the skill of feeding them together, preferring to sit upright while balancing the hungry boys on her thighs. The peaceful setting of Lake Nemi added to her contentment. She looked to the distant water, daydreaming about the people and places she loved.

One of the boys stopped feeding. His large eyes squinted and his small chubby face began to redden. Milk dribbled from the side of his mouth. Seeing her baby's discomfort, Lillia lifted him over her shoulder and gently tapped his back until she heard the small sound of his wind escaping, closely followed by more dribbling. She lowered the contented baby back down and wiped away the mess with a cloth.

When she had repeated the process with her other son, the princess settled back and studied the twins closely. She listened to their squeals and gurgles, looking for signs of any contrast between them. No difference was apparent in their features.

The boys had yet to be named, but in the interim Lillia had started to refer to them as First-born and Second-born. When she had spoken to Mother

Vesta about the naming of her babies, the priestess had explained that it was traditional for the father to choose the names of his sons, but in the case of Lillia's boys, she felt it that would be appropriate for Prince Numitor to give the babies their names. This made sense to Lillia, and yet she was forbidden to have contact with anyone on the outside, and her father probably had no knowledge of his grandsons' birth. In addition to this, the princess had to deal with her fear of Uncle Amulius finding out about the twins. She gave an involuntary shudder, not wanting to think about what the king would do to her babies.

Mother Vesta had promised that nothing would be said about the babies – at least, for a while. The priestess needed time to consult the gods. However, as each day passed, Lillia's love for her babies grew ever stronger, and with it grew her fear of losing them.

Her attention returned to her search for differences between the boys. She gently stroked the soft wisps of dark hair that lightly covered the tops of their heads. Whispering noises of encouragement, she noticed Second-born peer up at her, his blue eyes only half open. The only differences she had been able to see in the boys were to be found in their behaviour. Lillia had quickly learnt that Second-born seemed to be happier if held, while First-born was more dominant and independent. In the basket, she had observed that it was always Second-born who would cling to his brother, and never the other way around.

After a while, the princess gently placed her babies in the large basket that Mother Vesta had provided. It was not ideally suited to being put to such a use, but as the priestess had reminded her on more than one occasion, *"We do not usually have mothers here."*

Lillia reflected sadly on how few people she saw these days. Other than the babies, Mother Vesta was the only person who visited her regularly. Sometimes the herbalist would appear with a potion or salve, usually for the wellbeing of the babies. As she sat back down in the chair, the princess felt a deep longing to introduce her father to his grandsons.

He would be so proud, she thought wistfully. She wondered what he would have named them and imagined him holding her boys, smiling down at them. Slowly, Lillia drifted into sleep.

* * *

A loud noise woke the princess with a start. She immediately glanced down at the babies and saw they were both stirring. As she got up to tend to them, the door to the room opened and Mother Vesta appeared from the dark corridor beyond.

'Mother Vesta, the babies have just woken,' Lillia said with a smile.

The woman did not return the smile as she approached. Instead she wore a sorrowful look in her eyes. It was then that Lillia spotted Captain Miron standing behind the priestess with another uniformed man beside him. She gasped with surprise and quickly looked to Mother Vesta questioningly, her heart beginning to pound with fear.

Shaking her head, Mother Vesta stepped forward. 'I am so sorry, child,' she said tenderly, 'but your uncle has learnt of the twins.'

Lillia stared in disbelief. *They have come here to take my babies*, she realised. *My uncle will surely kill them!*

Suddenly, Lillia's fear was overthrown by the ferocity of her motherly instincts. 'No!' she yelled at the two men as they started to come through the doorway. Moving quickly, she placed herself between her sons and the advancing men. 'Get away from them,' she shouted, standing defensively in front of the basket.

Mother Vesta came closer and gestured for the men to stay back. 'Do not make this any more difficult for yourself, child', she said softly. 'The king has ordered this – there is nothing you or I can do about it.'

'No, he cannot have them! They are my sons. They are all I have.' The princess' voice shook with her rising panic.

Suddenly one of the babies began to cry, his screeching causing Lillia to look back down at the basket. The other twin joined his brother with a piercing wail. Torn between defending her boys and soothing them, Lillia glanced wildly around. Mother Vesta was edging forward, as were the two men, no longer obeying the woman's gesture to stay back.

Turning back to the cries of her children, Lillia threw herself down to the basket, wrapping her arms around the small boys and protecting them with her body. She glared at the three adults, her face wild and angry. 'Leave us alone!' she screamed at Mother Vesta. 'You promised you would not tell him. This is your fault. Amulius will kill them. How could you let this happen?' Tears began to stream down her cheeks.

The high-pitched wail of the babies' crying seemed to spur Captain Miron into action. 'I have had enough of this,' he said angrily to Mother Vesta. Coming forward, he stood behind Lillia. 'Come on girl, you have to let them go.' Reaching down, he wrapped his arms around her waist and began to lift her away.

'Get off me!' screamed Lillia. 'Get off! You cannot have them!' She fought to loosen herself from the captain's grasp, but his hold only tightened. She grabbed at the basket, bringing the babies closer to her.

Mother Vesta crouched down in front of the agonised girl. 'Come, Rhea, you must let them go,' she said gently as she began to prise Lillia's arms away from the babies.

Ignoring Miron's tight hold, Lillia tried to lunge forward. 'No! Get off!' she growled, pushing Mother Vesta away. In doing so, the princess momentarily released the basket. Captain Miron seized the opportunity to lift her out of its reach.

Furious at being separated from her babies, Lillia struggled violently against the burly man. 'Let me go!' she screamed in panic. Squirming and kicking, she watched helplessly as Mother Vesta picked up the basket and tried to sooth the screaming babies with gentle whispers.

Realising that she would never be able to release herself from the captain's powerful grip, Lillia tried a different tact. 'Miron, I order you to release me,' she commanded. 'You will obey. I am a princess of Latium. Let me go this instant!'

The captain ignored Lillia and continued to hold her in place. The priestess began to move away with the basket. 'Please, Mother Vesta, don't take my babies,' Lillia pleaded to her. 'The king will kill them. I am begging you,' she cried, 'please don't take them away. Don't let them be killed!' Lillia began to tremble uncontrollably. Her legs gave way beneath her as her heartache robbed the strength from her. Miron let her slip to the hard floor.

Mother Vesta turned away with the twins, causing the princess to scream afresh as she felt her heart being torn apart. 'No, not my babies! *Please* don't take my babies, Mother Vesta,' she pleaded again. 'I cannot live without them. They are all I have,' she stuttered through her tears.

The priestess was now being escorted by the guard that had arrived with Miron. She shook her head. 'I am so sorry, Rhea. There is nothing more I can do.'

A piercing scream escaped Lillia's mouth as she made a last, desperate attempt to get to her children, but as the princess lunged, Miron quickly grabbed her again, holding her back as Mother Vesta walked towards the door. Lillia began to wail uncontrollably as she watched the priestess leave the room with the two babies. Her grief only seemed to escalate until she let out a wail of anguish that continued long after Captain Miron had released her and made his own departure.

As he escorted Mother Vesta and the twin boys through the large building, Miron could still hear Lillia's sobs resonating through the walls of the House of Vesta. It was a sound that would haunt him forever.

Chapter Thirty-Seven

The Dormienti assassin crouched as he waited patiently in the shadows, the time passing slowly as he listened to the noises coming from the busy taverna. Having spent the last seven days watching and planning, he had almost completed his work. Shortly it would be over. All he needed was for his target to follow his normal routine. In the meantime, the assassin tried to ignore the soft moans and hog-like grunts that came from the rooms occupied by the working whores. The noisy footfalls of eager customers testified to the popularity of the girls.

The assassin had never used whores – he had never felt a need for them. His line of work made it too difficult and dangerous for him to consider having a wife, but he seldom felt lonely. As a single man he had opportunities for casual encounters when he needed them, but he rarely felt the desire. He did not trust women – they were expert liars. *They use their charm and their tits to take the silver from your pouch*, he mused. The possibility of slaying a woman tonight was high – he avoided killing them whenever possible but, sometimes, if a woman got in the way at the crucial moment, it would be necessary for him to kill her in the line of duty. Normally, the shock or the speed of his attack would stun a woman into submission, but a scream of warning always had the potential to cause problems. Whatever the case, at least one person would be dying before the night ended – of that, the assassin was sure.

* * *

Densara entered the taverna and saw that Brascus was busy talking with Louisa. As he approached the pair, he noticed that Louisa had been crying. The merchant felt a little concern for the girl. Turning his attention to the taverna owner, he summoned a smile and asked, 'How are you this evening, Brascus?'

The large man narrowed his eyes. 'I am fine, thank you, Densara. Louisa, on the other hand, needs a lesson in obedience.'

'Oh, that is unfortunate,' replied the merchant sympathetically. He turned to the puffy-eyed girl. 'What seems to be the problem?' he asked, a little concern in his voice.

Brascus was about to answer but was cut off by Louisa. 'I don't do it. I don't like man do that to me, not for all gold.' Her accent sounded thicker through her anger. More than a few customers looked towards the raised voice, but upon seeing the owner of the taverna, they quickly turned away. Brascus looked sternly at the girl, causing her to cower. She took a step closer to Densara.

'But what is it that you don't…' the merchant started to ask before being struck by a moment of clarity. He nodded, 'I understand.' He turned back to Brascus. 'She really doesn't like that, you know.'

'That is not the point,' said the taverna owner, glaring at the girl. 'We are an establishment that prides itself on catering for special guests with individual needs. Short of violence – which damages my property – anything goes. The customers pay very well for the privilege.'

'If I do this for all guests,' interjected Louisa, 'all time in pain, is no good. I get blood, and is hurt.' She started to cry.

Brascus shook his head. 'Not this again,' he pleaded. 'I do not think I can take any more tears.'

Ignoring Brascus, Densara slipped his arm around Louisa's shoulders. 'That's enough now,' he said gently. 'Crying won't solve the problem. Give me a minute with the master – I will be with you shortly.'

She nodded and walked away, sniffling as she went. Brascus quickly turned on the merchant. 'You cannot sway my mind, Densara. I will not have anyone dictating to me on how I should be running my whores.'

'I am not concerned with that in the least, Brascus,' said the merchant with disinterest. 'What you do with your whores is your business. I only wanted a moment with you to discuss our next auction.' Densara truly could not have cared less about the way that Brascus worked his whores, and yet he was angered by the thought of Louisa being treated badly. His obsession with the blonde prostitute had grown over the months, but he tried to put thoughts of her out of his mind as he sat down with Brascus to talk about the auction.

* * *

261

The angry whore's exotic accent filtered through to the ears of the waiting assassin. Amused by the nature of her complaints, he had listened carefully. He caught the taverna owner's remarks clearly enough, but the merchant spoke quietly, his words lost in the general noise of the taverna.

While he had been hiding, the assassin had been glad to hear the taverna becoming much busier. It had been easy enough to present himself as a customer – he had done it before. He drank none of the wine that was offered to him, and explained to the first whore who approached that he was only staying for one drink – his unforgiving wife was cooking. The girl very quickly lost interest.

The opportunity to disappear came when a small group of drunken fishermen entered the taverna. The noisy men could not help but draw attention to themselves, allowing the assassin to make for the doorway that led to the taverna's back rooms. Slipping through the door, he quickly made his way along a corridor. He had visited the previous day and had already chosen the spot where he would now conceal himself.

The assassin tensed as he heard the sounds of muttering and approaching footsteps, and someone passed his hiding place. He recognised the voice of the foreign whore, still clearly upset. A door then opened and shut, and the girl's voice was cut off. Although the minor delay caused by the whore was unexpected, events had subsequently gone as planned and it was now almost time. All that mattered was to ensure that the situation remained contained. A little while longer and his prey would arrive.

* * *

With his business concluded, Densara sat at a table and watched as Brascus sauntered off to speak with other customers. The lounge was filled with the sounds of quiet conversation and flirtatious giggles as customers relaxed with friends and bartered with the working girls. Jugs of grain beer were shared. Serving girls brought out plates stacked with salted meats, cheese and bread. The merchant drank a mouthful of wine and winced at its sour taste. *It seems I warrant only the cheap piss these days – obviously, Brascus no longer values me quite the way he used to,* thought Densara, watching the taverna owner as he continued to mingle with his patrons.

The merchant had begun to take a disliking to Brascus. He found that the man's ambition was motivated more by greed than honour. Brascus' thirst for riches was almost as severe as that of King Amulius. The taverna was making its owner wealthier by the day and, as for his profits from the sale of slaves, he was doing very well indeed. Yet, it never seemed to be enough for

Brascus. Densara remembered a phrase he had heard one of the councillors using: "Greed is always hungry" – the words seemed a fitting summery of the taverna owner's weakness.

Brascus passed by the table and put a hand on Densara's shoulder. 'I will bid you a good evening, my friend. I have some counting to do in my room.' He shook his head glumly. 'Tomorrow I have to go to the wine merchants to re-stock. More gold, always more gold.'

'That is business I'm afraid, Brascus. You need to sow a few seeds before you can reap the harvest – accept the situation, and be happy.'

A frown flitted across Brascus' forehead. He removed his hand and nodded at the merchant. 'You are right, of course. I just get a little irritated with it all at times. I think I may have undertaken too many endeavours for one life-time,' he laughed. 'Ah well, you enjoy yourself with Louisa. I will see you shortly.' He smiled and turned away. Densara finished his drink and headed eagerly for Louisa's room.

* * *

The assassin drew his knife carefully – the blade was very sharp. Success demanded that he take particular care of his tools. His target was heading to the final place that he would ever see. The assassin felt the anticipation and prepared to leave his hiding place.

The corridor was dark. He closed his eyes for a moment and let his other senses take over. Ignoring the sounds coming from the taverna's lounge, he concentrated on his surroundings. An array of scents hit his nostrils – the sharp aromas of spilled wine and grain beer mingled with the acrid odour of sweat against a background of roasting meat. Already aware of occupants in the nearby rooms, the assassin listened intently for the voice of his quarry.

His heartbeat slowed and calm descended as it always did when he was hunting. His mind and body were acting purely on instinct. Opening his eyes, he let his focus fall upon the doorway beyond which his target unknowingly waited.

From inside the room came the sounds that he had expected, and the assassin gently pushed the door open silently, knowing already that its hinges would not betray him. The flickering of candlelight spilled out, causing his shadow to dance on the wall behind him. He paused and listened. Nothing had changed – the opening of the door had not been noticed. He readied his knife and peered into the room. Keeping to the shadows, the assassin then slid through the doorway.

***

A scream brought the taverna to silence. Everyone stopped and looked towards the doorway from which the sound had come. No-one moved. A door banged and then footsteps could be heard. There was another piercing scream, filled with fear.

Then one of the taverna's whores walked slowly into the lounge, shock on her blood-drained face. She pointed back through the doorway. 'He's dead,' she said quietly. The tears began to spill over her cheeks. Her lips trembled. 'He's dead!'

Chapter Thirty-Eight

King Amulius was agitated as he paced the lightly furnished command tent. The aged augur stood out of the way, anxious not to anger him. Occasionally Amulius glanced outside. He watched as the darkness descended and waited for the return of Captain Miron. Finally, he heard the approach of hooves, accompanied by the high-pitched wailing of babies. Moments later, Mother Vesta entered the tent carrying a large basket, with Miron close on her heels. She glanced at Amulius and placed the basket on the table. 'Rhea was hysterical when I left,' she said angrily. 'Why did you order this now?'

Amulius ignored the woman, his gaze fixed on the basket. He approached it and tentatively peered in, seeing only a few tufts of hair poking out from beneath a blanket. He toyed with the material for a moment, then hesitated, unsure if he even wanted to see their faces. The capricious sounds coming from the basket told him enough. 'Two boys?'

'Yes.'

'How old?'

'Twenty-five days, or thereabouts.'

'And why did you not mention this to me before?' demanded Amulius. 'Am I not the king? Did you honestly think you could keep this from me?' he shouted.

Mother Vesta was unmoved by the king's outburst and stood her ground, confident in the authority bestowed upon her by the goddess Vesta. Amulius was waiting for her to reply, but the babies had resumed their crying and the priestess quickly made to calm them. 'It was not as simple as that,' she whispered sharply to the king. Gently shaking the basket, she continued. 'The circumstances of their birth... well, I needed time to reflect. To do anything rash could have dire consequences. It is not our place to tamper with the work of gods.'

Amulius sighed heavily. 'Yes, I have heard the rumours.' His forehead creased into a frown. 'You are to tell me everything – every detail. The augur will judge what you have to say.'

After listening to the full story of the twins' birth and consulting with the old augur, Amulius was worried. Both Mother Vesta and the diviner spoke of Mars' intervention. Lillia's descriptions of her dreams, her continual monthly bleeding and the apparent lack of a pregnancy were all being held as strong evidence of the god's involvement. Few choices were available to the king, and he was struggling to decide what would be the best course of action.

Amulius had initially wanted to kill the babies, but the augur had cautioned him that such an action would be likely to doom the king to the fire-pits of the underworld. The dishevelled old man had said he would consult the gods for guidance and would return in the morning.

Now alone with Mother Vesta, Amulius looked at her in the candlelight. He noticed, for the first time that she was a striking woman, with strong features and wise eyes. But, of course, she was untouchable, even to a king. Clearing his mind of such thoughts, he addressed the woman.

'I need you to explain to me why the head of the Vesta would behave as you have. Whatever possessed you to keep a matter of such importance from me?'

'I was trying to protect all of us, Your Highness. When one is entrusted with the keeping of Vesta's eternal flame, one must answer first to her, before mortal men. It is the way of the gods. A king should understand this.'

He understood all too well. Amulius clenched his fist, feeling his anger rising, but remained still. 'Your devotion to Vesta is admirable, but it does not explain why it took nearly a month for me to hear about the twins.'

'I needed to talk to the girl, question her. She trusted me – until tonight, that is. Now I fear she may be lost to me forever. The poor girl fought your brute of a man like a wild animal. Has she not suffered enough?'

'Yes, Rhea has spirit, but she is a danger to me. Now I will have to punish her for flouting the laws of Vesta.' A slight grin appeared.

'She has done nothing wrong, Your Highness.' Mother Vesta glared at the king. 'We cannot have her put to death if she was raped by a god – that much is certain. And if she was already pregnant before joining us, then she has not broken any law of ours.'

'Either way, the princess is not a virgin.' Amulius looked over to the basket.

'Who is to say?' The retort came quickly. 'The girl claimed that the babies were thrown into her belly by Mars himself. It is perfectly possible that she still could be a virgin.'

'I must also deal with the shepherd boy with whom she ran away. He will die for abducting a princess of Latium, when I find him,' promised the king.

'How brave you are, Your Highness, to kill a boy,' Mother Vesta chided sarcastically.

Amulius gritted his teeth at the woman's insolence. 'One way or another, the problem presented by these babies will be solved tomorrow.' He glanced at the basket again. 'We can decide the girl's fate later. She has caused me too many problems.'

'You cannot kill Rhea, Your Highness. You could lose everything if you were to harm her. You know how dangerous it is to anger the gods. She is protected by Vesta, and now it seems, Mars as well. As for the babies, you must tread very carefully. Mars is unforgiving.' She looked Amulius in the eye. 'Neither warriors nor gold can sway the wrath of a god,' she warned.

The king held her gaze for a moment before looking back to the basket. The crying had stopped and was now replaced by the smooth rhythms of sleep. For the first time in his life, Amulius found that he had no idea what to do. With a shrug of his shoulders, he was forced to conclude that the fate of the twins was now in the hands of the augur.

* * *

The following morning, Fabius trudged along the muddy track while the warriors busied themselves with their chores around the camp. He had been up for a while and had already trimmed one head – the cropper liked to get an early start. The late winter sun that peeped over the horizon filled him with cheer as he made his way to the command tent. Warriors were still stumbling from their tents, squinting as they emerged from the dark interiors. Fabius nodded to one or two while others called out to him.

'Hey, Fabius, be seeing you later, I hope,' shouted one of his regulars.

'You bloody need it,' laughed the stocky cropper. 'Look at that head – you look like Medusa!'

These exchanges were common, as much a part of his day as waking every morning. His years as an army cropper had boosted his popularity among the men, and they treated him as an honoured guest – most of the time.

As Fabius approached the command tent, two guards that had been stationed outside quickly straightened, looks of guilt appearing on their faces. They had obviously been trying to listen to what was going on inside. The sounds coming from the tent reminded Fabius of when his daughters had been infants. Piercing wails were competing against the voices of adults, and the wails were winning. Fabius heard the king shout, 'Can you not shut them up, woman?' He sounded angry.

'They're hungry – they need feeding,' replied a woman whose voice he did not recognise. To the cropper, it sounded as if she was scolding the king.

Fabius looked at the guards and shrugged. 'Do I go in?'

The guards quickly shook their heads. The closer one whispered, 'I wouldn't. He's in a foul mood.'

Suddenly, the tent's flap opened, bringing the guards to attention as King Amulius appeared. Upon seeing Fabius, he gestured to the interior, 'Come on in, man.'

The guard had not been exaggerating – the king was agitated. The dark bags under his eyes betrayed a lack of sleep. 'Right away, Sire,' smiled Fabius as Amulius stepped aside to let him in.

Before shutting the flap, the king addressed his guards. 'You two, go and stand over there,' he pointed. 'You are now both to be on latrine duty for a month. When you have finished your shift here, you will go and report there without delay. That should give you both plenty of time to develop foul moods of your own.'

As Fabius' eyes adjusted to the dark interior, he saw the woman whose voice he had heard. She was dressed in a long white gown and stood cooing over a basket. The cropper thought she might be a priestess. Seeing her unkempt hair, he wondered if she had just woken up. *Has she spent the night here*? He glanced again at the basket. He could guess its contents, remembering the events of the previous day.

To one side of the tent stood Captain Miron with the augur. Fabius shivered at the sight of the unsavoury old man. The augur's long, matted hair crawled with lice – that alone was enough to repulse the cropper. *As for his supposed gifts of divination* – he mused – *reading innards and all that strange stuff. It is just a waste of good food.*

The tiny old man cleared his throat. 'As I was saying Sire, the portents are clear. If you kill the sons of Mars yourself, you will die within seven sunsets. Even if you order them to be killed on your behalf, the punishment remains the same.'

'Then how am I supposed to rid myself of this menace?' growled Amulius in frustration.

Fabius felt awkward at having to witness the conversation. He really did not want to be hearing any of this, and could not understand why the king had brought him in. *Surely he doesn't want a shave whilst planning... whatever it is he is planning. This can't be good.*

'I think there is a way, Sire.' The augur took a step closer.

Amulius looked hopeful. 'Tell me. What is it?'

'A child born from a god and a mortal is considered a gift. Under certain circumstances, a person may choose to refuse the gift.' The aged man paused briefly. 'If, for instance, the gift's intention is to bring mischief, you thus have a reason to return it.' The augur squinted at the king. 'If you return these two gifts to the gods unharmed and make a suitable offering of gratitude, you may be spared their wrath.'

'And how exactly am I to do that?' asked the king, impatiently.

'Give them back through Almo.'

Fabius had never heard of Almo. He listened, intrigued.

'I take it, you are meaning the god of rivers?' Amulius enquired.

'One of them,' the augur corrected. He pushed away a stray hair. 'Almo is the best choice, as he looks over the Tiber. As long as the babies are alive when they enter the river, the gods will consider them unharmed. Whatever happens after that is not within your control.'

The king considered the old man's words. The woman with the basket looked horrified. 'You cannot be considering this, Your Highness! There must be another way,' she cried.

'There is only the will of the gods,' snapped the augur before the king could reply.

'What choice do I have?' shrieked Amulius. 'Why do the gods do this to me?' He slammed his fist on to the table, bringing fresh cries from the basket.

'Now look what you have done,' hissed the woman as she tried to placate the babies.

'What does it matter anyway?' he shouted over the din. 'Take them outside. I cannot think with all this racket around me.'

The tent lit up as the woman pulled back the flap and departed with the babies. Fabius felt the rush of cool morning air and gratefully breathed in a lungful. It cleared his head a little, but the disturbing scene was not helping his stomach, which had been feeling delicate since he had walked in. He watched the tired king slump into his chair and look at the augur. 'Are you sure about this?' he demanded. 'If you are wrong, I will leave instructions for you to be flayed alive.'

The augur took a step back at the threat. Nodding furiously, he said, 'I can see no other way, Sire. If you were to return them directly to Mars, they would have to return through fire. The flames would harm the babies before

He could take them. In the river, they will be in the care of Almo – if they should drown before arriving back to Mars, it will be Almo's doing.'

'It sounds very much like a gamble to me. Surely, if I have them thrown into the river, they will drown right away, and I will have killed them just the same.'

'No, Sire. If they are truly demigods, they should live. Hercules killed serpents with his bare hands whilst still in the crib,' the little augur pointed out. 'If they are demigods they will be strong. Almo will take the babies to Neptune who in turn will send them to Mars. If they should drown during their journey, then our problems will be over. Whatever happens, it is the only way.'

Fabius followed the logic, but he thought the babies would be certain to drown. He watched Amulius reflect silently on the augur's words, his expression contorted. *Like a man possessed by Hades,* thought the cropper.

Fabius had never seen Amulius in such a state and it made him very nervous. He felt a familiar urge deep in his bowels – *same time every morning*, he thought as he tensed to stay the feeling. *The king should be shaved by now, and I could be heading for the latrines – along with those two guards*, he thought, briefly seeing the funny side of his dilemma.

'Fine!' said Amulius, suddenly standing. 'Fabius, I want you to take those…' he hesitated. 'Take the basket. Take it far down river and throw it in.'

Fabius stared at the king in disbelief. *Why me?* He opened his mouth to protest but instantly shut it as he fell under Amulius' cold gaze. The cropper knew he would lose too much if he were to go against the king's wishes, however strongly he might object to the orders. He tried taking a different approach. 'How about I just shave you, Sire, whilst the good captain here,' he gestured to Miron, 'rides to the river on his horse? It would be a lot quicker. I'm not as agile as I used to be.'

'No – you are to do this for me, Fabius. When it is done, you will never need to crop hair again.'

I like cropping hair. I don't want to do this. Fabius stayed silent, looking down to avoid the king's eyes.

'I need someone I can trust, someone who will get the job done and not talk about it.' Amulius walked over to the cropper and grabbed his shoulder. 'A man who is as deaf as a post, and loyal with it.'

The pit of his stomach burned as Fabius realised he had baited his own trap. His own words of the previous day came hurtling back to him like rocks from a catapult. Without raising his eyes, the cropper nodded his assent.

Shortly after Fabius had left, Amulius walked out of the command tent with Miron. Once they were away from earshot, the king turned to his captain. 'The girl has to go.'

'Your niece?' came the shocked reply.

'Of course – who else would I be talking about?' snapped Amulius. 'She has been, and always will be, a threat to my rule. You will see to it that she is no more – but you must wait for seven or eight days. I do not want to be around when it happens. I will be leaving for the coast in a few days.'

'But she is your brother's daughter, Sire – it will destroy him.'

'He will get over it.' The king showed no remorse.

'I very much doubt that he will.' Miron looked unhappy. 'How do you want her killed?'

'I do not know,' answered Amulius impatiently. 'Something quick – there is no need for her to suffer. Beheading is the quickest way, is it not?'

Miron frowned, disgusted by the suggestion. 'There has to be a better way,' he said, shaking his head.

'No, there is not,' barked the king. 'We have already tried the Vestal Virgins, and look what happened. Just get it done – do I make myself clear, captain?'

'Yes, Sire, very clear, Sire.' Miron saluted the king and remained standing to attention until Amulius had returned to the tent.

* * *

Later that morning, Fabius was carrying the basket containing the two small babies along the bank of the River Tiber as it wound its way through the open countryside. The area was deserted, with only a few rotting shacks and overgrown plots to suggest recent habitation. Even the river itself, this close to the Etruscan boarder, was devoid of people and boats.

People are still nervous after the incident with King Corros, thought the cropper, glancing around. Keeping close to the bank, he continued to follow the river, looking for a spot from which to throw the basket. He could not quite believe that he was doing this. He tried to postpone the act, searching for any reason to delay, all the while heading further downstream. He stopped once or twice to rest, but no peace would come to him. His mind could not be distracted from the grim task ahead.

He peeked under the blanket at the two boys, the smell of urine hardly bothering him. He remembered the babyhood of his three girls.

Why did the king choose me to do this? I can't kill two babies! Maybe I could take them to my wife to raise. No – the king would find out and I would have put my family in danger. Perhaps they are already in danger. What lengths will Amulius go to in order to keep this secret? Fabius shuddered at the thought. He tried to dream up alternative methods which would allow him to complete the king's order without harming the twins. No ideas came to him that would not ultimately lead to his death. He had to consider his duty to his girls and his wife in addition to his duty to the king. He needed to be fit and working, putting bread on the table and clothes on his family's backs. It was a simple choice to make, but an unbearable deed.

By midday, Fabius was tired and footsore from his long trek along the river's rocky banks. The watercourse had begun to get wider and its banks steeper, making it harder for the cropper to walk along. He decided to stop for a while to get some rest and placed the basket by his feet. He looked at the babies – not once had they cried during the journey, which seemed incredible, considering the fuss that the priestess had made when he collected them.

Are they really the sons of Mars? If they are, will I incur his wrath? He looked at the river. If the twins were demigods, then they would be safe – the augur had said so. *Am I willing to throw them in to find out?* Tears started flowing down Fabius' cheeks, confusion and sorrow getting the better of him. He had not cried since the death of his father. Feeling foolish, he wiped away the wet trails. *Crying will not help me.*

He recalled the king's command and considered Amulius' choice of words: "Take the basket and throw it in." He turned the matter over in his mind – *take the basket, and throw it in. Amulius did not actually instruct me to throw the babies in the river. Maybe I could obey his order and still give the boys a chance.*

Fabius was struck by a sudden idea. He looked closely at the basket – it had a tight weave. He was sure that he had seen similar ones in the market. Traders used them to carry fresh meat – the weave was tight enough to prevent blood from dripping out.

Maybe it would work! He brought the basket to the water's edge and, with a firm hold, lowered it carefully onto the water. He sent a silent prayer to the gods and let it go – the basket floated. Relief flooded through the cropper as he quickly grabbed the basket before it floated away. He placed it back on the bank with care. *Now I just need to think this through.*

Fabius sat for a while and watched the twin boys doze as he tried to contemplate every possibility. He would tell the king that he had thrown the basket into the river. *I just won't tell him that it was a very small throw. Maybe some peasants will save the babies,* he consoled himself, *or, if the augur is correct, the river might deliver them to the gods. Either way, I won't have to live with the memory of drowning them.*

Having made up his mind, Fabius removed the twins from their basket and gently laid them on the bank, causing them both to start wailing. Ignoring the piercing sounds, the cropper picked up the basket and dropped it onto the water, quickly reaching for it before it floated away. He placed the babies back in it and covered them as best he could with the blanket. With great reluctance, he then gently pushed the basket out into the river's flow.

The cropper watched in silence as the basket slowly began to spin and float downstream. The boys' crying became distant as their makeshift boat drifted into the middle of the river, bobbing a little but staying afloat. After a while it disappeared around a bend. *May the gods protect you both,* thought Fabius with a heavy heart. As he climbed back up the river bank, tears streaming down his face.

Chapter Thirty-Nine

Paridé marched down the rocky path that led to the House of Vesta. The bitterness of the late afternoon penetrated the uniform he wore. *Amulius' warriors must like the cold,* he thought as he looked back at the six similarly dressed men that followed him. The armless tunics they all wore offered little protection against the chill of the cloudy day. Paridé's two cousins, Falco and Guido, seemed relaxed as he glanced their way. He gave them a nod of assurance. They returned the gesture, as did the other four men. They were from the village and had all served with him as Latin warriors in their younger days.

The path wound its way through trees that lined the basin of Lake Nemi. Paridé went over the rescue plan in his mind as they negotiated the path, which was occasionally broken by rough steps cut into the cliff face. He had realised that the time had come to put the plan into action after being visited by Captain Miron, who was deeply disturbed by the latest orders he had received from Amulius. *"Now is the best time to act"*, Miron had said, going on to explain that the king would be away for a few days.

Paridé had felt disgust at the cowardice of a king who was not even brave enough to look his niece in the eye before having her slaughtered – the girl deserved better. Miron had been in anguish over the part he had played in Numitor's downfall and now wanted to do what he could to help the princess. The captain had helped them devise the plan, and he had provided their military tunics and weapons.

When everything was in place, Paridé had sent one of his men to the House of Vesta. The man, who had been dressed as a palace runner, was to inform the House that Amulius' warriors would be arriving later that day to collect the princess. Paridé prayed that the ploy had worked. He knew he would be put to death if caught. Paridé had never liked Amulius, but had been Numitor's friend for years and, he found it surprising that the new king had not chosen to detain him. The treacherous new leader had clearly underestimated the strength of Paridé's loyalty to Numitor, not to mention Captain Miron's sense of justice.

Rumours of Lillia becoming the mother of twin boys had reached Paridé's village several days earlier, so it had been shocking to learn that Amulius had subsequently given orders for the babies to be drowned. It had been shortly after receiving this grim news that Miron had then informed Paridé of the king's plans for Lillia.

How could the man stoop so low? He could not begin to imagine how Lillia must be feeling. Her father was a prisoner, while she was separated from her all her friends and family. On top of such terrible pain, the princess was now having to face the loss of her children while being under threat of death herself. How much could the young woman take? Paridé thought of his own daughter, Sylvanna. She was a fighter and had proven herself to be strong-minded over the years, but even she could not have endured such torment.

The path became level as they approached the House of Vesta's gate. Shortly after Paridé had pulled the bell cord, a servant came out carrying a broom. He guessed she must have been working close to the entrance.

'Who is it?' asked the servant.

The voice was surprisingly deep for that of a woman, but on closer inspection Paridé realised that the servant was actually a eunuch. The strange man had definite signs of breasts – this was said to be a common feature amongst their kind. 'We're here on the king's orders to collect his niece,' said Paridé. 'You should be expecting us.'

'Yes, we received the message. In fact, we received the same message twice today from the palace. However, the runners failed to mention when exactly you would be arriving,' the eunuch replied, haughtily.

Twice? thought Paridé. *Has a real runner been sent with the same message?* Either Amulius had brought forward his plans for Lillia, or else Miron had betrayed Paridé. The only other possibility could be that Amulius had not trusted Miron to obey his order, and had taken matters into his own hands. Thinking quickly, Paridé scowled and answered the eunuch. 'Of course you were not given an exact time, you idiot! Do you really think the king would tell runners his business? Now, hurry up and fetch me the girl so that I can stop looking at your ugly face.' Paridé glowered at the eunuch, whose shocked expression made him wonder if he had pushed the servant too far.

The eunuch turned and ran into the house, but not before the servant's sobs had reached the ears of the disguised men. 'Just like a bloody woman!' Guido whispered from behind.

Paridé would normally have smiled, but present circumstances kept him serious. 'Quiet, Guido!' he warned, as he considered that if Amulius was planning to send guards to the House that evening, then there was a good chance that they would encounter them. The steep path down the cliff face that encircled Lake Nemi was very long with few places to hide. They would have to be cautious.

After waiting for a long while, three silhouettes eventually emerged from the House. As they reached the gate, Paridé saw that two of them were older women and between them they guided the girl.

Can't she walk properly? he wondered. *That would certainly give us a problem!* Paridé was shocked when he could finally see Lillia clearly. She was barely recognisable. Even robed and ready to travel, he could see her gaunt face and hollow cheeks. He had been concerned that she might recognise him too soon, but he could see that he need not have worried – *she is like a walking corpse,* he thought.

The two women ushered the princess through the open gate, after which one of them then turned to Paridé. 'She has neither said a word nor eaten a mouthful since the babies were taken. Rhea does nothing more than stare.' The woman shook her head in sadness as tears fell. 'She is passive – she will walk wherever you guide her, so be gentle.' The women then closed the gate and hurried back to the House.

Paridé stood still for a moment, not quite believing how easy it had been to rescue the princess. Lillia just stared at the ground. He carefully led her back through his comrades, ordering them to get behind. They set off along the path. As they reached its end, Paridé lifted Lillia and placed her over his shoulders, before starting the long walk back up the steep cliff-side pathway.

'Let us get away from here,' he said, turning to the men. 'It appears we may not be the only ones coming for Lillia today. We must move quickly and keep alert.'

Suddenly, the men were startled by a noise from further up the pathway. Paridé gave them a look of warning before pointing to the bushes. They promptly hid themselves in the thickets, leaving him standing alone with Lillia. He carried her into the foliage, finding a large thorn bush for them to hide behind. He then held the girl close and waited. Although Miron had assured him that Lillia's execution was not due to take place until the following day, Paridé was all too aware of the king's unpredictable nature and prepared himself for the worst.

After a few moments, the source of the disturbance marched into view. Paridé was relieved to see that it was merely a group of priests, probably from the Temple of Diana that was located near the House of Vesta. The priests walked in silence and soon disappeared down the hill.

When Paridé was sure the path was clear, they resumed their journey, doubling their speed, alert to any other potential encounters. The last few hundred yards of the path were the toughest climb they had endured so far. Finally reaching the top, they stopped to rest, shielding their eyes from the early evening sunlight that had appeared through a break in the clouds.

Paridé was last to arrive, puffing as he carefully put Lillia down against the rock face, away from the cliff edge. Looking over the precipice, he could see the temple in the distance, nestled amongst trees. Happy that the hardest part of the trek was now over, he joked with the men. 'All downhill from here, lads.'

'I'm glad I wasn't carrying the princess,' said one of the older men, pointing to Lillia. 'Couldn't have been easy, that climb.'

About to answer, Paridé paused as the sound of running reached his ears. With nowhere obvious to hide, he quickly pulled out his sword and headed to the front of the group as the rest of the men drew their own weapons. He sidled up to the rock face, signalling for his comrades to do the same. The sound became louder and a party of ten armed men jogged around the corner into view. They wore the same uniform as Lillia's rescuers – Paridé quickly realised that these newcomers had been sent by Amulius.

Paridé and his men were outnumbered. He knew that he had to act quickly if he was to have the benefit of surprise. One of the unsuspecting soldiers came close to Paridé's position and he grabbed the moment to charge forward, knocking the man to the ground. He then quickly swung his sword low at the legs of the next man before facing the rest. Paridé wheeled his sword around and swiped at the closest soldier, cutting open the man's tunic and leaving a gash across his chest.

Paridé's comrades had not expected him to act so swiftly, but they were quick to engage the warriors, letting out war cries and swinging their iron against leather and flesh. Paridé kicked his next challenger in the chest, forcing the warrior backwards. The winded man lost his footing and stumbled over a small rock. Unable to stop his fall, the soldier quickly grabbed at one of his own comrades, pulling them both over the cliff edge. The screams then came to an abrupt end as they hit the jagged rocks below.

The odds now seemed a little better as Paridé looked around, but soon found himself facing two more warriors. He parried the first sword that came towards him, grabbing his attacker's arm and pulling him into the arc of his comrade's strike. The man's severed arm fell to the ground as Paridé drove a dagger into the second warrior. Glancing around, he saw his cousin Falco struggling to fend off blows from a much larger man. Paridé retrieved his dagger and threw it at Falco's attacker, hitting the big warrior in the groin and felling him. Falco finished off the howling soldier with a quick slash of his own blade and gave Paridé a nod of thanks before returning to the affray.

Realising he now had no-one left to fight, Paridé glanced over to Lillia. She was sitting at the edge of the path, her eyes downcast, not even aware of the commotion around her. He saw one of Amulius' men edging toward her, a knife at the ready. Paridé instinctively reached for his own blade and cursed himself as he realised that he had just hurled it at Falco's assailant.

Without hesitating, he charged towards Lillia, screaming his anger, causing the warrior to look up. Paridé reached him a moment too late – the man had quickly grabbed Lillia and put his knife to her neck. She neither screamed nor struggled. 'Get your men to drop their swords, or the girl dies!' shouted the warrior.

The fighting ceased. Amulius' warriors were now outnumbered and they rapidly gathered around their comrade. With seven against four, Paridé had the advantage but was helpless as Amulius' soldier continued to hold his knife to the princess' throat.

'If you so much as break a hair on her head,' threatened Paridé, 'I will kill you and every one of your men very slowly.' He meant every word. 'You have nowhere to run, so just give the girl to me and I will let you all live.'

'You must be crazier than she is,' laughed the confident warrior, 'if you think we are going to give her up now. You will let us pass or the princess will die – the king won't mind either way.'

Out of the corner of his eye, Paridé could see one of his men, Mimo, slowly reaching behind to loosen a bow tied to his back. Mimo had been an archer during his service and Paridé understood immediately what the man intended.

Acting instantly, Paridé took a step forward, drawing the attention of the four nervous warriors. The man holding Lillia pulled her head back by the hair, exposing her throat. 'I will do it,' he shouted, 'I will kill her, don't…'

The sound of the arrow surprised everyone. They all looked to Mimo, who stood there smiling with an empty bow. The man who had been threatening Lillia was still in position, but now his head had rolled back and an arrow protruded from his eye socket.

Paridé ran to Lillia's side, knocking one of the surprised warriors to the ground. Mimo's second arrow found another target. The last of Amulius' soldiers dropped his sword, and turned to run down the path. He made it a few paces before he also fell. Mimo rarely missed.

Paridé saw that the princess seemed to be unscathed. She just stood and stared as if unaware of the confrontation that had just taken place. Paridé heaved a sigh of relief before turning to his men. 'We need to get the bodies over the cliff. Hopefully, they will not be discovered too soon.'

'What about him?' asked Guido. He pointed at the surviving warrior that Paridé had knocked down.

Paridé thought for a moment and shook his head. 'He could be a threat to you. Throw him off the cliff.'

The man started to shout for mercy. 'I won't say anything, I swear to the gods! Let me go!'

Ignoring his pleas, Guido and Mimo grabbed an arm each. The man started to struggle violently, screaming in terror. Paridé's other men then set about him, one slitting his throat as they pulled him closer to the cliff edge. With blood draining from his wound, there was little sound from the man as they lifted him by his arms and legs and swung him over the ledge.

* * *

Throughout the confrontation, Lillia had barely been aware of the commotion around her. Even when the man had grabbed her, his words had not registered with her. Nor had she noticed the fact that a few moments later, he had no longer been there. Staring out over the bowl of Lake Nemi far below, her only thoughts were of her sons. The look in Mother Vesta's eyes when she had returned to the House told Lillia that the decision had been made, and she would never see her boys again.

From that moment on, the princess had existed in a haze of despair and emptiness. Every morning when she woke, a deep longing would shroud her mind and the void in her heart would fill with pain and sorrow. Her life had become a dark, empty pit.

Looking down on to the round black lake, Lillia imagined losing herself in its depths, the water taking her pain and washing it away. Lifeless images of her babies entered her mind, the faces of those she had lost mingling with snippets of dreams in which she walked through meadows, happy and content, only to then be faced by the dark threat of men on horses. Somewhere in the distance she could hear her name being called, but to her it was the voice of Marcus floating up from the empty void. The whistling wind that accompanied the voice carried the cries of her babies.

Lillia took a step towards the cliff edge, her eyes fixed on the dark lake below. She longed to end the feelings of pain and sorrow. Another step closer, and again she heard her name being called. This time she turned.

Paridé was shouting to her – his mouth opened as he spoke but she heard only the small voices of her sons calling to her from below.

Paridé was coming towards her now, his hands held out, his silent pleas nothing more than unheard words. The princess looked at him and smiled as his eyes widened in panic. Turning away, her mind filled with the faces of her twin boys. 'I will see you soon,' she whispered to them. Lillia then stepped off the edge of the cliff and fell into the void.

Epilogue

The Hounds of Diana waited patiently for the arrival of the Prima. For the first time in their history, there were many empty seats – the result of the newly appointed king's paranoia.

Rumours of Amulius' treachery had reached all corners of the kingdom, his ruthlessness directly affecting the secret cult. Although the king did not know it, he had dealt the organisation a heavy blow whilst securing his position.

Most of the remaining Hounds were now looking for answers. Their objective had always been to keep the country safe and, in so doing, offer protection to their kings. They had protected the rightful heirs to the Latium throne for over five hundred years, until now. None of them could understand how Amulius had managed to overthrow the first-born heir without their knowledge. The Hounds had become very nervous, most suspecting that they had a traitor amongst them. They all shared the hope that someone within the gathering would explain what had happened.

For the second time in as many months, Mother Vesta entered the large dark cavern carrying the box that held the golden antlers. As ever, she was followed by her acolytes. 'The Prima is no more,' she announced. 'He has betrayed the Kingdom of Latium and handed our country into the hands of a tyrant. He will be eternally hunted by Diana.' The priestess ignored the sounds of disbelief coming from the masked men and quickly produced the bag of pebbles. 'Diana will now choose a new Prima. By the time of the next meeting, the new Dius' will also have been chosen, and the gathering will once again be complete. Then you may begin the task of protecting Latium from our new king.' The latter statement was delivered with cold authority.

It occurred to several of the remaining members that the priestess was not happy with the new king. They all knew of Princess Rhea's suicide and the drowning of her two sons. Two generations of the rightful bloodline to

281

the throne had been lost. All who had tried to protect the country had felt the sorrow of it.

The merchant Densara was the final person to be offered the bag of pebbles. He had reported the death of Brascus to Mother Vesta himself, as was the custom when one Dius had knowledge of another's betrayal. She had listened to his story patiently but had passed no comment. That had been a few days ago. Now he was once again before the masked priestess as she offered him the bag.

He put his hand into the long pouch and could find nothing in it at first. As he scrabbled around in the bottom of the bag, he felt Mother Vesta's fingers moving through the soft leather. Suddenly her hand opened a little, releasing a corner of the pouch from which she pushed a pebble into Densara's fingers. He drew out the stone and held it tightly in his closed fist. He was immediately suspicious of the reasons that might lie behind Mother Vesta's deception, but was given no time to dwell on the matter as the order came to reveal the pebbles. One by one the Hounds of Diana opened their hands. Each held a white pebble. By the time Densara came to open his, he had guessed what he would see.

'Diana has chosen,' announced Mother Vesta. She walked towards the merchant and placed the golden antlers onto his mask. 'May you protect us all and take vengeance on those who have wronged us.' She turned to the circle of men and acolytes.

Densara was surprised by the last statement. He was sure it was not part of the ceremony. He was both exhilarated and confused by this unexpected turn of events. He had just been handed the mantle of Prima by Mother Vesta, and yet he feared her reasons for manipulating the outcome of the choosing. He was also aware that she had probably saved his life by doing so. Densara understood Amulius well enough to know that the king would eventually try to kill him. Amulius was not one to forgive or forget any hint of transgression. Now, as Prima, the merchant would be able to protect himself with an army of Dormienti spies and assassins at his disposal. He wondered what Mother Vesta would want in return. Densara's thoughts were disturbed as the voices of the young acolytes called out in unison:

'You who are called to speak for Diana, we honour you with the keeping of her Hounds. We accept you as Prima of Diana.' The masked girls then repeated Mother Vesta's last statement. 'May you protect us all and take vengeance on those who have wronged us.

***

282

The River Tiber glided gently around a small, overgrown island as it meandered past the hills known as the Seven Sisters which overlooked the marshes and wetlands that flanked it. On the shore of the island, snagged by the roots of a leaning fig tree, the basket containing Lillia's sons swayed to the ebb of the river.

The tree's broad leaves intermingled with hard unripe fruits, offering the twins shade from the bright sunlight while hiding their basket from view. Under a thin damp blanket, the two babies clung to each other weakly as they shivered and suffered pangs of hunger. Having cried for most of their journey through the night, the boys were now exhausted, the lack of milk and the bumpy ride on the river having taken their toll.

The noise of a woodpecker hammering out its search for food disturbed the morning, whilst Kingfishers and herons patrolled the river banks. Suddenly, the whistles and bird calls stopped as a lone she-wolf appeared near the water's edge. Her belly sagged with the weight of milk as she lowered her head for a drink. She momentarily looked back the way she had come, as if expecting her dead cub to be following. With nothing there to see, she turned and lapped a few mouthfuls of the flowing water.

A strong acrid scent reached the wolf's nostrils, catching her attention. Her eyes settled on the small island in the middle of the river. She whined as she sniffed the air, her eyes now finding the basket, its contents intriguing and enticing her. The she-wolf began to pace the river bank, each step narrowly avoiding the water as she looked for a way to cross over to the island.

The End

To be continued in:

LUPA

The Romulus and Remus Trilogy – Part Two